GOD OF WAR

GOD OF WAR

MATTHEW STOVER
AND
ROBERT E. VARDEMAN

BALLANTINE BOOKS

NEW YORK

A Del Rey Trade Paperback Original

God of War is a registered trademark of Sony Computer Entertainment America
LLC. Copyright © 2005–2010 by Sony Computer Entertainment America LLC.
"PlayStation" and the "PS" Family Logo are registered trademarks of
Sony Computer Entertainment Inc.

Published in the United States by Del Rey, an imprint
of The Random House Publishing Group, a division
of Random House, Inc., New York.

DEL REY is a registered trademark and the Del Rey colophon
is a trademark of Random House, Inc.

ISBN 978-0-345-50867-6

Printed in the United States of America

www.delreybooks.com

2 4 6 8 9 7 5 3 1

First Edition

Book design by Christopher M. Zucker

FOR SCOTT AND JEN
—ROBERT E. VARDEMAN

ACKNOWLEDGMENTS

Many people worked long and hard on this book. William Weissbaum at Sony provided precisely the right solution to sticky plot problems as well as astute guidance throughout. Marianne Krawczyk's sharp eye and knowledge of the game are truly appreciated. Tricia Pasternak was the best editor—ever. "Raven Van Helsing" assisted in ways he never intended via YouTube. Finally, thanks to my agent, Howard Morhaim, and my stalwart co-author, Matthew Stover, for giving me the chance to help out on such a great project.

—ROBERT E. VARDEMAN

GOD OF WAR

PROLOGUE

AT THE BRINK OF NAMELESS CLIFFS he stands: a statue in travertine, pale as the clouds above. He can see no colors of life, not the scarlet slashes of his own tattoos, not the putrefying shreds of his wrists where chains were ripped from his flesh. His eyes are as black as the storm-churned Aegean below, set in a face whiter than the foam that boils among the jagged rocks.

Ashes, only ashes, despair, and the lash of winter rain: These are his wages for ten years' service to the gods. Ashes and rot and decay, a cold and lonely death.

His only dream now is of oblivion.

He has been called the Ghost of Sparta. He has been called the Fist of Ares and the Champion of Athena. He has been called a warrior. A murderer. A monster.

He is all of these things. And none of them.

His name is Kratos, and he knows who the real monsters are.

His arms hang, their vast cords of knotted muscle limp and useless now. His hands bear the hardened callus not only of sword and Spartan javelin but of the Blades of Chaos, the Trident of Poseidon, and even the legendary Thunderbolt of Zeus.

These hands have taken more lives than Kratos has taken breaths, but they have no weapon now to hold. These hands will not even flex and curl into fists. All they can feel is the slow trickle of blood and pus that drips from his torn wrists.

His wrists and forearms are the true symbol of his service to the gods. The ragged strips of flesh flutter in the cruel wind, blackening with rot; even the bone itself bears the scars of the chains that once were fused there: the chains of the Blades of Chaos. Those chains are gone now, ripped from him by the very god who inflicted them upon him. Those chains not only joined him to the blades and the blades to him; those chains were the bonds shackling him to the service of the gods.

But that service is done. The chains are gone and the blades with them.

Now he has nothing. Is nothing. Whatever has not abandoned him, he has thrown away.

No friends—he is feared and hated throughout the known world, and no living creature looks upon him with love or even a hint of affection. No enemies—he has none left to kill. No family—

And that, even now, is a place in his heart where he dare not look.

And, finally, the last refuge of the lost and alone, the gods . . .

The gods have made a mockery of his life. They took him, molded him, transformed him into a man he can no longer bear to be. Now, at the end, he can no longer even rage.

"The gods of Olympus have abandoned me."

He steps to the final inches of the cliff, his sandals scraping gravel over the crumbling brink. A thousand feet below, dirty rags of cloud twist and braid a net of mist between him and the jagged rocks where the Aegean crashes upon them. A net? He shakes his head.

A net? Rather, a shroud.

He has done more than any mortal could. He has accomplished feats the gods themselves could not match. But nothing has erased his pain. The past he cannot flee brings him the agony and madness that are his only companions.

"Now there is no hope."

No hope in this world—but in the next, within the bounds of the mighty Styx that marks the borders of Hades, runs the river Lethe. A draft of that dark water, it is said, erases the memory of the existence a shade has left behind, leaving the spirit to wander forever, without name, without home . . .

Without past.

This dream drives him forward in one final, fatal step, which topples him into clouds that shred around him as he falls. The sea-chewed rocks below materialize, gaining solidity along with size, racing upward to crush his life.

The impact swallows all he is, all he was, all he has done, and all that's been done to him, in one shattering burst of night.

THE GODDESS ATHENA STOOD in full armor before her mirror of burnished bronze, nocked an arrow in her bow, and drew back the string slowly. She watched her every move in the mirror for proper form. Athena raised her right elbow slightly. Any deviation in the proper angle would cause the arrow to go awry. She sought perfection in all things, as befitted the warrior goddess. She held the string back taut, feeling the muscles in her arms and shoulders begin to strain. The sensation buoyed her, made her aware of not only herself but also of everything around her. A half turn, witnessed in the mirror, a small correction to her form, and she aimed the arrow across her chambers at a huge tapestry showing the Fall of Troy. The arrow slipped from her fingers and flew straight and true to sink into the threaded figure that was Paris.

What a flawed hero, she mused. She had not made such a poor choice. She had risked much because the fate of Olympus hung in the balance when her brother Ares had flown out of control. Did Kratos experience such a moment of hesitation, just before the arrow flew from his bow? Doubt? Sureness? Un-characteristically, she felt a stab of panic. Had all her machina-tions been for naught, gaining his services from Ares in an all-too-clever ploy?

A small puff of air sent her spinning about, another arrow fit-ted to bowstring, then drawn back until the golden bow moaned with the strain. She considered her actions, then slowly eased her pull on the string, the arrow unflown.

Lounging half naked on her couch of wine-red cloud, with-out the slightest bit of shame, lay a stunningly beautiful youth. His wickedly charming smile was not at all dented by having the arrow of Athena pointed at his forehead. "Lovely to see you," he said. "Celebrating your victory, are you? You know what would make this occasion *really* special? Shed that perpetual virginity of yours. Don't look so solemn. Don't *be* so solemn. Let's ex-plore untrammeled territory. I am quite a good explorer and can show you the way down unfamiliar paths."

"Hermes," she said through her teeth. "Have I not warned you about spying on me in my chambers?"

"I'm certain you have," the Messenger of the Gods said indo-lently. He rubbed his bare back along the couch, wiggling sinu-ously with pleasure. "Ah, wonderful. I had such an itch. In fact, dear sister, there is another itch I have—one that you can help me with, which is only fair, since you're its inspiration."

"Am I?" Athena's face might have been carved of marble. "Shall I scratch your itch with my sword?" The bow in her grip vanished, replaced by a wicked razor-edged sword.

Hermes let himself sink back in the couch. He laced his fin-gers behind his head and spoke soulfully to the skies about Olympus. "Forever gazing upon what I cannot touch." He sighed. "Such cruel fates should be reserved for mortals."

Athena had learned from centuries of experience that Her-mes was so intoxicated with his own charms that, when he started flirting, the only way to deflect him was to change the subject. She used her sword to point at his sandals. "You're wear-ing your wings. Is this an official message?"

"Official? Oh, no, no, Zeus is off doing . . . something." He smiled wickedly. "Very likely some*one*. Another mortal girl, I'm sure. The Fates alone know. Really, I can't guess what he sees in mortal women, when any *normal* god would sacrifice an immortal private body part or two just for a chance to slip one past Hera's girdle—"

"The *message*," Athena said. "Your excuse for invading my chambers?"

"Oh, there *is* a message." He produced his caduceus and waved it at her. "Really. See? I have the wand."

"Your beauty lends you the impression of charm. Your behavior dispels it."

"Oh, I suppose that was wit. It was, wasn't it? I ask, beloved virgin of war, because otherwise there'd be no way to tell."

"Then let me reply with a question of my own. Is the message you bring of such import that I shouldn't have you killed for aggravating me?"

"Oh, please. The word of our father forbids any god to slay another . . ." His voice trailed off as he found something entirely uncomfortable in her chilly gray stare. "Athena, my dear sister, you know, I'm perfectly harmless, really."

"That's what I keep telling myself. So far."

"I was only trying to have a little fun. Just the tiniest amount. A bit of banter with my favorite sister. Cheer you up, yes? Take your mind off . . . well, you know."

"I do know. And you shouldn't forget it either." She glanced past Hermes to a dressing table, where lay a circlet of gold studded with precious gems. Yet another trinket made for a sacrificial offering to her by some ambitious craftsman in the city that bore her name. It was quite fine, for the work of a mortal. She supposed that she should probably answer his prayer—and she would have, if she had bothered to remember his name. Her preoccupation with Ares had taken her thoughts away from those mortals who so relied on her even as they died. That must change soon, to repair more than sundered buildings.

"And, I, uh, I *do* apologize for the spying. Of all the Olympian goddesses, you are truly the most beautiful. Your form was elegant—nay, perfect with the bow curved back and the string taut. It was a sight to behold. Any foe would quake, just as an ally would rally to your cause." Hermes rose from the couch, stretching his muscles in a fashion calculated to emphasize his lithe, youthful physique. "But you must admit, of the gods, I myself am the most handsome."

"If you were half as handsome as you think you are, you would indeed outshine the sun."

"You see? None can compare with me—"

"I'd like to hear you say so in front of Apollo."

Hermes tossed his head haughtily. "Oh, certainly he's pretty enough—but he's such a bore!"

"The next words from your lips had best concern your message." She leaned toward him and poked him lightly on the chest with the point of her sword. "You have lately seen, I believe, the consequences of making me angry."

The Messenger of the Gods looked down at the blade against his ribs, then back up at the war goddess's unwavering gray eyes. He drew himself up, adjusted his chlamys with exaggerated dignity, and said in a clarion voice, "It's your pet mortal."

"Kratos?" She frowned. Zeus had said he himself would be looking after Kratos until after the memorial. "What of him?"

"Well, I thought you might like to know, in view of all the aid he has given you and the concern you occasionally feel for him—"

"Hermes."

He flinched, just a bit. "Yes, yes. Here: Witness."

He lifted the caduceus and pointed. In the air between them, an image built of a mountain, tall beyond imagining, and a cliff, impossibly sheer, impossibly far above the Aegean's watery surge. On the edge of that cliff, Kratos paused and seemed to speak, though no one was there to hear.

"Your pet has chosen a perilous path to tread. This one will take him to Hades."

Athena felt herself go pale. "He takes his own life?"

"So it appears."

"He can't!" The disobedient mortal! And where was Zeus? Not looking after Kratos, obviously—or had he, she now wondered, said he would be looking *upon* the Spartan? Which would be an entirely different thing.

As her mind raced, sorting through all the possibilities and improbabilities, the Kratos in the image leaned forward and lifted a foot as though to step from the cliff into empty air . . . then he fell. Simply fell.

No struggle. No scream. No cry for help. He plunged head-first toward his death on the rocks below, and on his face was only calm.

"You didn't see this coming?" Hermes smirked. "Aren't you supposed to be the Goddess of Foresight?"

When she turned her level stare upon him, he smothered that smirk with a cough. "When next we meet," she said, low and deadly, "I will share what I foresee for *you*."

"I, uh . . . was only *teasing*." He swallowed hard. "Only teasing . . ."

"And that is why I haven't found it necessary to hurt you. Yet." Her sword cut the air in front of Hermes's nose. To his credit he did not flinch. Much.

She gathered herself, and with a twitch of will she burst from the chamber, leaving Hermes gaping owlishly behind her. At the speed of thought, Athena descended from Mount Olympus to the rain-lashed cliffs. She arrived as Kratos hurtled into the ragged clouds below.

The messenger had had the right of it. She'd had no inkling that suicide would be the end of Kratos's story. How could she have been so blind? How could Zeus have let this happen?

More important: How could Kratos be so disobedient?

The Grave of Ships, she thought. That's where Kratos's fall had really begun. It had to be. *The Grave of Ships in the Aegean Sea* . . .

ONE

THE ENTIRE SHIP GROANED and shuddered, lurching upward into the fierce winter squall as though it had struck unexpected shoals here in the Aegean's deepest reach. Kratos threw his arms around the statue of Athena at the prow of his battered ship, lips peeling from his teeth in an animal snarl. Above, on the mainmast, the last of the ship's square sails boomed and cracked in the gale like the detonation of a nearby thunderbolt. A huge flock of filthy, emaciated creatures like hideous women with the wings of bats swooped and wheeled above the mast, screaming rage and lust for the blood of men.

"Harpies," Kratos growled. He hated harpies.

A pair of the winged monsters shrieked above the wind's howl as they dove to slash at the sail with their blood-crusted talons. The sail boomed once more, then it finally shredded, whipping over the deck and slapping the harpies from the air. One vanished into the spray of the storm; the other managed to right herself by tangling viciously sharp talons into the hair of an oarsman. She dragged the unfortunate sailor screaming and flailing into the sky, twisting to sink her fangs into his neck and feast upon his blood, which spewed downward in a gory shower.

The harpy saw Kratos watching and screamed her eternal rage. She ripped away the sailor's head and hurled it at Kratos; when he slapped this grisly missile away with a contemptuous backhand, she flung the sailor's body with enough force to kill an ordinary man.

Her target, however, was nothing resembling ordinary.

Kratos slipped aside and snatched the decapitated sailor's rope belt as the corpse plummeted. A savage yank snapped the rope and sent the corpse over the rail into the churning sea. Kratos measured the dive of the harpy as she swooped on him like a falcon, knifelike talons extended to rip out his eyes.

Kratos reached back over his shoulders instinctively, his hands seeking the twin enormous, wickedly curved, and preternaturally sharp chopping swords that nestled against his back: His signature weapons, the Blades of Chaos, had been forged by the smith god Hephaestus in the furnaces of Hades itself. Chains from their hafts looped about his wrists and burned through his flesh until they fused with his very bones—but at the last instant he left the twin weapons where they were.

A harpy wasn't worth drawing on.

He cracked the slain sailor's belt like a whip. It spun out to meet the harpy's dive and looped around her neck. He leaped from the statue to the deck below, his sudden weight wrenching the creature from the sky. He pinned her to the deck with one sandal while he hauled upward on the rope with a fraction of his full strength. That fraction was enough: The harpy's head tore free of her body and flipped into the air.

He snatched the head with his free hand, shook it at the wheeling, screeching flock above, and roared, "Come down here again! See what you get!"

He punctuated his challenge by hurling the severed head at the nearest of the harpies with deadly accuracy and incredible force. It struck her full in the face, cutting off her screech like the blow of an ax. She flipped ass over fangs as she tumbled from the sky to crash into the storm churn, three spans off the port sweeps.

Kratos only glowered. Killing those vile creatures wasn't even fun.

No challenge.

Kratos's glower deepened as the storm gave him a glimpse of the merchantman he'd been pursuing. The big ship still had two sails up and was pulling away, running before the wind. Another instant showed him why his ship was falling behind. His oarsmen were cowering in fear of the harpies, pressing themselves into whatever space they might find below their benches or shielded by the thicket of oars. With a wordless snarl, Kratos seized a panicked oarsman by the scruff of his neck and, one-handed, lifted the man up over his head.

"The only monster *you* should fear is *me!*" A quick, effortless snap of his wrist cast the coward into the waves. "Now *row!*"

The surviving crew applied themselves to their oars with frantic energy. The only thing Kratos hated more than harpies was a coward. "And *you!*" He shook a massive fist at the steersman. "If I have to come back there to steer, I'll feed you to the harpies!

"Do you have the ship in sight?" His bull-throated roar caused the steersman to cringe. "*Do* you?"

"A quarter league off the starboard bow," the steersman called. "But he still has sail! We'll never catch him!"

"We'll catch him."

Kratos had pursued the merchant ship for days. The other captain was a shrewd and able sailor. He'd tried every trick Kratos knew, and even a few new ones, but with every passing day, Kratos's sleek galley had herded the merchantman ineluctably toward the one hazard no vessel could survive: the Grave of Ships.

Kratos knew his quarry had to come about. To enter that cursed strait was the last mistake any captain would ever make.

Ahead, looming like jagged rocks amid the narrow strait, lay shattered hulks of ships beyond number that had, through misfortune or miscalculation, found their way into the grave. No one knew how many there might be—hundreds, perhaps, or thousands, listing in the tides and the treacherous crosscurrents, grinding their hulls against one another until finally they either broke apart into splintered flotsam or took on enough water to sink. But even that was not the end of their hazard. So many wrecks rested on the seabed below that they had built themselves nearly back up to the Aegean's surface in artificial reefs, waiting to rip out the hull of any unlucky ship above. These reefs could never be mapped, for no ship that entered the grave ever left it. So many sailors had perished here that the sea itself had taken on a foul reek of rotting meat.

Kratos nodded to himself as the merchantman dropped its sails and unshipped its oars for the turn. Escape was close—or would have been, in any other region of the sea. But the ship was too near already to the Grave of Ships. Even as the merchantman began to reverse course, a colossal head rose from the depths and crashed down on the ship's deck; then its sinewy neck curled about and tried to break the mast.

Whenever the wind quieted for a moment, Kratos heard plainly the screams and battle cries of the merchantman's crew as they frantically hacked at the Hydra's neck with short swords and fire axes. More heads curled upward from the depths below. Kratos signaled the steersman to make straight for them. No point in waiting for them to get free; they were too busy fighting the Hydra to notice that they were being pulled into the grave.

All around floated the deserted, destroyed husks of ships either lacking the protection of the gods or bearing the fate of their condemnation. The closest vessel they passed had clearly arrived not long before Kratos and his quarry. A dozen or so sailors were pinned to the mast—impaled by a single immense spear. Harpies had picked at the bodies. Most of the sailors were mere shreds of flesh hanging on bloody skeletons—but the one closest to the mast was still alive. The sailor caught sight of Kratos and began to kick feebly, stretching out his hands in a silent plea for mercy.

Kratos was more interested in that immense spear—its presence hinted that a Cyclops might be nearby. He stepped to block the steersman's view of the death ship. "Pay heed to your course."

"Lord Ares *opposes* us," the sailor said in a choked voice. "The harpies—the Hydra—these are now his own creatures! All of them. Would you defy the God of War?"

Kratos cuffed the steersman hard enough to knock him to the deck. "That merchantman has fresh water. We have to take her before she sinks, or we'll all die swilling the sea. Forget Ares. Worry about Poseidon." He hauled the man back to his feet and set him at the tiller. "And if Poseidon doesn't worry you, there is always me."

For two days they had been without water. His mouth was drier than the Desert of Lost Souls, and his tongue had swollen. Kratos would gladly have traded for the water, but before the deal could be made, the captain of the merchantman had caught a glimpse of him and had decided a wiser course was to flee as though all the hounds of Hades bayed at his heels. Kratos would teach this captain the consequences of such wisdom.

He tugged at his short, pointed beard, combing from it thick clots of blood—harpy or human, he neither knew nor cared. He checked himself for wounds; in the heat of battle, one can be mortally injured without even noticing. Finding none, his fingers unconsciously traced the red tattoo that swept up across his face and shaved head before descending along his back. The red contrasted sharply with the bone white of his skin.

Blood and death. Those were Kratos's stock in trade. No one who'd ever seen him in battle, no one who'd even heard the tales of his legendary exploits, could mistake him for any other man.

Another impact knocked Kratos into his steersman. The ship shuddered and squealed, and the grinding shriek went on and on. The sailor fell to the deck, and Kratos grabbed the tiller— but it swung freely in his hands.

"The rudder!" the steersman gasped. "The rudder's sheared away!"

Kratos released the useless tiller and peered over the stern. One of the derelict hulks of the ship reefs had speared his galley like a fish—a spar as thick as his body had been driven up through the hull and had sliced away the entire rudder as it had penetrated the stern from inside and below.

"Starboard sweeps! Backwater! Now!" Kratos roared. "Port sweeps! Pull for your useless lives!"

With a tooth-grinding shriek, the galley ripped clear of the spar. As its bow swung toward the struggling merchantman, Kratos ordered the starboard sweeps to full ahead. He twisted and snarled at the steersman. "Beat the cadence. Make it fast!"

"But—but we're *sinking!*"

"Do it!" Kratos turned back to the oarsmen. "The first craven worm to take his hands off his sweep will die where he sits!"

The crew stared at him as if he had been driven mad by the gods.

"Now! *Pull!*"

Even as the stern sank lower and lower into the water, the galley surged ahead. The merchantman was only a couple of hundred paces away, then a hundred fifty, then—

An enormous swell driven by the Grave of Ships' treacherous crosscurrents heeled the galley half over—and instead of righting itself, it crashed down upon a rotting hulk and stuck fast. His ship had nowhere left to go except down.

"If you can, follow," Kratos told his crew.

If they couldn't, they weren't worth saving.

He vaulted the rail and landed cat-footed on a sea-slimed plank. He skidded along it, wheeling his arms for balance. The sea foamed among the jagged drifting planks, and every swell set derelict hulls grinding against one another like wooden millstones. To fall into these waters would be certain death.

Fifty feet ahead bobbed another ship. Its mast had been lopped off, and from the look of the encrusted barnacles and rot-blackened seaweed that festooned the hull, the ship had been a prisoner in the Grave of Ships for many years. Anything that still floated was better than his own galley, which was surrendering to the sea with a vast sucking sound and a chorus of screams from sailors too slow to leap away.

A moment later, the only sounds were the crash of waves and

the thin whistle of the slackening gale. Walking quickly across the broken remnants of perished ships, Kratos reached the abandoned hulk. The high curve of slimy hull looked impossible to climb, even for him.

He paused and glanced back to see if any of his crew had followed. Only a handful had avoided being sucked under with the galley—a Hydra's head rose up from the depths and snapped savagely, taking more of the crew by cutting them into bloody halves. In silence, Kratos watched them die.

He was used to being alone.

The spar on which he balanced rolled unexpectedly beneath him. Without hesitation he leaped, fingers scrabbling for the hulk's encrusted anchor chain. Barnacles slashed his fingers, but he only snarled and gripped so much the harder. His feet met the curve of the hull, and he carefully walked his way up, pulling himself along the chain. He swung himself up onto the deck.

This ship had been abandoned for years. The mast had broken off and left jagged splinters, now dulled by storm and wave. He turned and looked back to where his ship had been. He found naught but steel-gray chop and foam nearly as white as his ash-stained skin.

The stench of black decay was his first warning. His second was the sudden red-hot sear from the chains fused to the bones of his wrists. Ares had been a cruel master; Kratos hated even the thought of him, save for one single act. Ares had joined to his arms the Blades of Chaos.

The embedded chains burned now as though they hung in a bonfire. Flame dripped from the blades on his back, but again he didn't bother to draw. He turned and dropped into a fighting stance, hands wide to grapple and rip. The stench gained putrid strength as its source climbed into view.

That source was three of Ares's soldiers—rotting corpses of undead legionnaires. These were the only soldiers the God of War could now command. Their eyes burned with a cold green fire. Decomposing flesh hung in rags from their bones. Without a sound, they rushed him.

Undead though they might be, they moved with uncanny speed. One thrust a spear at his head, thinking to force him to dodge, as another swung a length of chain at his legs.

He snatched the spear haft with both hands, driving it down to tangle the whipping chains—then Kratos released the spear and drove his hand into the slimy guts of the nearest legionnaire, his fingers ripping through the decayed flesh to seize its hipbone from the inside. Kratos squeezed with inhuman force; the legionnaire's hip joint shattered, and the creature fell. Kratos moved on without looking back.

When the legionnaire with the chain swung it again, Kratos let it whip around his arms. He wasn't worried; he had chains of his own.

As the undead leaped for him, Kratos slipped a loop of the blade chain around its neck. A twitch of his massive arms tore the legionnaire's head from its shoulders. The third he dispatched with a simple blow of his fist, crushing its skull.

He looked for more creatures to destroy but saw nothing. He knew better than to believe all the monsters had disappeared.

Kratos wisely used the time he had bought himself to hunt for a pathway between the wrecked ships that might take him the last fifty-odd paces to the merchantman.

A wooden statue bobbing some distance away caught his eye.

"Athena!" He had placed her statue aboard his ship, at the prow, as tribute to the labors he had performed for the gods for the last ten years. He was unsure if the unending quests had been aided by the very gods sending him on them or if simple luck had been involved. Bad luck. Good luck. Nothing mattered. He had the blades.

That statue was hardly more than a hunk of ineptly wrought wood, no more significant than any of the flotsam throughout the Grave of Ships. Or so he had thought. Now the wooden Athena bobbed up and down on the waves, then rose three-quarters of the way from the water and leaned in the direction of a tangle of floating beams.

A wetly splintering crash behind warned Kratos that more than Athena's statue had broken free from the watery grave. He jumped, barely managing to seize a floating beam. He clawed his way onto it—and something cold and slick slid along his leg. He snarled and pulled harder, scraping his belly raw over the rough wood. He got his feet under him just as an undead hand tightened on his ankle and yanked hard.

He slammed down onto the beam and used the undead's grip on his leg for leverage as he hauled himself around to straddle the beam, then he plunged his hands into the sea. The red-hot chains blasted water into steam and seared the legionnaire so that it jerked about wildly and withdrew without pulling him down to his death.

Kratos got his feet back under him again. Not ten yards away, the statue of Athena still bobbed on the waves. The wooden statue lifted almost free of the water and turned with unmistakable urgency, leaning like a lodestone drawn by the merchant ship.

He didn't need another hint. He leaped and bounded, balanced and slipped and skidded across the tangle of floating beams toward a foundered ship that seemed to be relatively intact. Some of the merchantman's crew must have sought refuge there, fleeing the Hydra's assault; boarding planks, anchored at the merchantman's rail, spanned the small gap between the ships. If he could only reach the foundered one, he could board the merchant ship with ease—but before he could reach the rail, the sea exploded before him.

Up from the invisible depths rose a vast reptilian head with eyes like shields of flame and gleaming swords for teeth. Its jaws could bite chunks from the mightiest ship on the Aegean; its spiny ears swung wider than a galley's sails; from its nostrils poured a choking frigid smoke. It ignored the ships behind it, staring instead down at Kratos. Its immense neck arched, and its eyes blazed, and it roared down upon the Ghost of Sparta with a sound too vast to be called noise. The stark shattering thunder drove Kratos to his knees. Briefly.

Kratos rose. At last: something worth killing.

Harpies had died by his hand this day. The Hydra would be next. With grim satisfaction, he reached back and drew the Blades of Chaos.

TWO

"ZEUS, MY LORD . . ." Athena raised her eyes to the great Skyfather seated on his alabaster throne. The King of the Gods lounged upon his vast seat of authority, regal and at ease with the power he commanded from this high throne. "Zeus, my beloved *father*," she amended. She chose to remind him in this subtle way that she was his favorite. "It matters little what Ares thinks of me. But deliberately assaulting my pet human—you personally banned that sort of behavior at Troy."

"And Ares didn't take that edict very seriously even then. As I recall, neither did you."

Athena could not be so easily diverted. "Will you allow the God of Slaughter to defy your expressed will?"

"*My* will?" Zeus's laugh echoed throughout the audience chamber and across Mount Olympus. "I think you have developed a personal fondness for this mortal of yours. What's his name? Oh, yes. Kratos. Can it be you are . . . developing sympathy for him? A mortal?"

Athena was not so easily baited. "I listen to the supplications of my worshippers. Kratos is no different."

"But you do care more for him than others. I see it in your eyes."

"He is . . . entertaining. Nothing more."

"I've enjoyed his exploits myself. Especially while he was still Ares's tool—conquering all of Greece? His exploits were the stuff of legends. Then he had to go and ruin it all with that business in your little village temple. . . ."

"We don't have to dwell on *that* particular crime, do we, Father?"

Zeus stroked his long beard of braided clouds. "I considered stopping Kratos myself more than once, but I . . ." His rumbling voice died as he gazed into some invisible distance, lost in contemplation. "It never quite seemed the right time."

"He's not the one who needs stopping, Father. And you know it." As Zeus's favorite daughter, Athena dared speak with irreverence that might have earned any other god exile from Olympus and a fiery tumble to the earth to dodge thunderbolts for a century or two. But even for his favorite, the Skyfather's tolerance was limited.

A hint of frown darkened his brow and brought a gray-purple tinge to the clouds of his beard and hair. Distant thunder crackled over Olympus. "Don't presume to lecture your betters, child."

Athena took this without so much as a flicker in her level gaze. "Would you crush a puppet because its dance offends?"

"That depends on the puppet." A hint of fond smile touched the Skyfather's mouth, and Athena knew the danger had passed. "And, to be sure, on the puppeteer."

"Has Kratos not provided a consistently pleasurable diversion under my hand?" Athena was now on more certain ground. Boredom was an affliction more feared by the gods than the plague was feared by mortals below. "Do his struggles no longer entertain you?"

"No, he's wonderful, child. Really."

"Then why, Father, do you allow my brother Ares to torment him so? Ares *is* trying to kill him, you know."

"Yes, yes," Zeus replied. "But he hasn't had much success, has he? Kratos has proven . . . enjoyably durable."

"The Blades of Chaos grant him power above even his considerable natural gifts. But still, do you find it seemly for your own son to undertake the destruction of your favorite mortal?"

"My favorite?" Zeus again stroked his storm-cloud beard, musing. "Why, I suppose he is. In truth, Kratos can be of use to me. In my name, send him on a mission to Crete to take care of that unpleasantness. He is the perfect one to put right what is going awry. Yes, Kratos can be of service to me right away. Rest easy, Athena. I will speak with the Lord of Battles when next he presents himself before my throne and direct him to cease this persecution. Will that satisfy my most beloved daughter?"

Athena lowered her head demurely, the better to conceal the beginnings of her slim smile. "It is all I can ask, my lord father. I am certain Ares will not risk your displeasure."

"Are you, now?" Zeus sat straighter on the throne, bringing both hands to his knees as he leaned toward her. "There is something you're not telling me, my wily little goddess. Some design of yours progresses to your satisfaction. I've seen that look before—as when you made me consent to the destruction of Troy if they failed to protect your statue . . . then you pulled that dirty trick with Odysseus and Diomedes."

The King of the Gods gave forth a sigh tinged with melancholy. "I *loved* Troy. Several of my sons—your own half-mortal brothers—perished trying to save that city. I will not be deceived again, child."

"Deceive you, my lord? How could I hope to?" *And why would I need to?* she thought. *Truth suffices.* "Am I not Goddess of Justice as well as Wisdom? And it is justice that I seek here before your throne, beloved father. Kratos has suffered much at my brother's hands."

"Justice," Zeus murmured. "Justice is a chain invented by the weak—"

"—to shackle the strong," Athena finished with him. "I've

heard you say so before." A *thousand times*, she thought, but kept that disrespectful comment to herself. "It is not Kratos who asks. He has not called upon the gods for aid since that day he begged Ares to save him in the face of the barbarian horde. *I* ask, Father. Any instant may be his last," Athena said. She opened her hand toward the golden fountain that burbled beside the throne of Zeus. "Behold."

The fountain's spray resolved into an image of the storm-tossed Aegean, littered with the wreckage of countless ships. At the heart of the image, flame and lightning blasted from flashing steel as Kratos used the Blades of Chaos like grapnels to chop into the vast reptilian neck that he climbed relentlessly, pulling himself up to where he could get in some cuts at the head.

"Is that the Hydra?" Zeus said with a faint frown of puzzle-ment. "Didn't Hercules strangle that beast years ago? And was it always so huge?"

"This is a new Hydra, freshly born, my lord father. This Hydra is the spawn of Typhon and Echidna—the vast Titans you yourself defeated and imprisoned in the earth far deeper than the reach of even Tartarus. They are the ancestors of every disgusting perversion of nature that my brother inflicts upon Kratos."

Zeus's frown of puzzlement darkened toward a scowl of dis-taste. "Setting that creature on Kratos without my permission smacks of willfulness on the part of your brother, but there is lit-tle I can do to help Kratos. The sea is the kingdom of my brother Poseidon. To even so much as strike the creature dead with my thunderbolt would be an insult to his sovereignty—and Posei-don is sensitive about his dignity, as I'm sure you recall."

"I do, Father. Believe me, I do. But it's not aid in this particu-lar crisis that I seek. Kratos can handle this creature without your help."

Zeus's brow lifted. "Considerable faith you place in his abili-ties."

"My lord father, I believe he is nearly indestructible. But I have plans of my own for him, plans that he cannot fulfill if he must constantly fight off my brother's monstrous legions. I ask only that you forbid Ares any future assaults."

Zeus sat up straight on the throne, gathering about himself the radiant mantle of kingship. He turned toward the fountain. "Where is Ares now?"

Rainbows in the mist swirled about to show Ares striding across a desert land like a volcano come to life. His hair and beard roiled with ever-burning flame, and the black of his armor darkened the sun. His every step crushed numberless men beneath his blood-soaked sandals as a mortal might tread upon ants.

"Where is he?" Zeus said. "What is he doing in that desolate Egyptian desert?"

"Spreading terror and destruction."

"No doubt," Zeus said with an appreciative chuckle. "It is a pity to interrupt his fun."

The King of Olympus raised his mighty fist and drew in a breath so deep it altered storm patterns throughout the Mediterranean, then unleashed a single word:

"*Ares.*"

The image of the God of War twitched visibly and then threw a dark look back over one shoulder without replying. He deliberately returned to crushing humans.

"How dare he ignore me?" Zeus drew another breath, this one causing frost to form all around and clouds to pelt the earth with sleet.

"*My son, your presence is required upon Olympus.*"

Again the God of War twitched but only lowered his head sullenly as though he could not hear.

"You must cease your Hydra's attack immediately. I have use of the mortal Kratos. Ares? *Ares! I will not be ignored when I command you.*"

Zeus's brows drew together, and the clouds of his beard and flowing mane shaded dark as a winter storm. Athena stepped to one side. She had anticipated this moment as surely as an oracle scrying the future hidden to her godly powers, and she didn't want to get in the way.

Zeus lifted his hand, palm upward, and a small spear of scintillant energy formed. With a flick of his hand, as if he did nothing more than shoo away a fly, he loosed the thunderbolt. It seared past Athena and flashed away into the sky. An instant later, lightning struck the desert in the image, so close to Ares that the god recoiled from the explosion of molten rock and fused sand.

The God of War lifted his face to the sky, his features twisted with bitter resentment; Athena could feel the god's anger all the way from that twisted, devastated land. *"Why does my father disturb me as I go about my work?"*

"It is not your place to ask," thundered the King of the Gods. *"Your place is to obey. Come to Olympus and kneel before the throne to beg forgiveness."*

"I will not, so long as that treacherous, lying, frigid bitch-sow you name my sister is anywhere near the place. The stench of her corruption repels all honest gods."

Zeus rose to his feet. Lightning played about his brow. *"You dare to defy me?"*

"Your thunderbolt caught me unawares. I will not again be so easily startled." Ares set his mighty fists upon his hips. Every move caused his weapons to clash with the sound of battle. *"You are welcome to leave that padded throne in your honey-scented palace and come out into the world to get me."*

"Beware, Ares. My thunderbolt can strike even you."

Ares tossed his fiery locks scornfully. *"You think to frighten me with lights and noise? Me? The God of War? Am I a cold gray cowardly virgin, supplicating before your throne, speaking lies and treachery? I am Ares. If you think to bring war against me, Father, recall that war is my kingdom!"*

"You see?" Athena said softly. "He is as I have told you. His madness burgeons with every passing day. If he dares defy your command, what will he *not* dare? Father, it may become necessary—"

"No," Zeus said grimly. "No, Ares is not so foolish as to challenge me." Athena saw that the Skyfather spoke one thing and thought another. Getting Zeus to place Kratos under his protection, even for a short while, had given her a great opportunity.

"Is not death the penalty for defiance?"

"I have decreed that the gods will not make war upon one another. No god may slay a god. This law is *absolute* and binds even me. My brothers and I destroyed the Titans because they fought constantly among themselves; their bitterness over old, never-forgotten feuds divided them until too late. The Olympians will not suffer the Titans' fate. If Ares must be . . . destroyed, it will not be by my hand. Nor yours, Athena."

She lowered her head, again to conceal the birth of a smile. "As my father commands. I have no thirst for my brother's blood."

"I don't believe he would say the same about you."

She opened her hands helplessly. "He cannot accept that Kratos and all the armies of humanity are now mine to command, while among his legions are numbered only the undead and the dark spawn of Typhon and Echidna. But he has not been tricked, nor even treated unfairly. You were there, Father. You saw the contest, and you witnessed Ares's free agreement to my bargain."

"Yes. And I saw at the time the very gleam you have in your eye right now. He did not consider what your bargain might mean—and you knew well that he would come to regret this deal."

"My brother is impulsive and headstrong. Am I to blame that his lust for bloodshed overpowers his reason? Even had I offered him the gift of my foresight, do you think he would have accepted it?"

Zeus shook his head, smiling fondly despite the dire subject of their conversation. "Not even the King of Olympus can win an argument against the goddess of stratagems. What do you propose?"

"If he cannot be slain," Athena said carefully, "he can still be humiliated."

"A lesson in humility may well be warranted, since he cannot be allowed to ignore my commands in this arrogant fashion," Zeus murmured thoughtfully. "How do you intend to teach it?"

"I am not the teacher Ares needs," Athena said, still speaking nothing less than pure truth. "If my lord father would only speak with his brother Poseidon and ask that the King of the Ocean receive me and listen to my word, the lesson will teach itself."

"Indeed?" The flicker of lightning returned to Zeus's brow, and his eyes narrowed in suspicion. "This, too, you have planned, haven't you? It seems an overly intricate stratagem for such small reward."

"To embarrass my brother was never my goal," Athena said.

And this, too, was truth, absolute and unmistakable. Athena's plan had never been to shame her brother. Ever since the Kratos incident in her village temple, she had understood another truth, one that the rest of the Olympians had only begun to glimpse: Ares was more than headstrong and disobedient, far more than brutally ambitious and bloodthirsty.

The God of War was insane.

DOWN FROM OLYMPUS came the Goddess of Wisdom and War. Each step caused the singing of birds. Soon the birds' sweet tunes became the rush of water crashing against rocky shores. Salt spray misted her face and beaded in her hair, constellations of diamond stars. Her bronze armor shone in brilliant tropic sun.

When finally she stopped, she stood at a shoreline that stretched to either side farther than even a god could see. The endless sea before her rose to the far horizon.

"O mighty Lord of the Deep, the Goddess of War would speak with you," she said. "Heed my father's request, and hear my word."

Athena waited. Was this a deliberate insult? Was Poseidon still sulking about the destruction of Troy? Or was this the fruit of an earlier grudge? She had never been on particularly good terms with the King of the Ocean, ever since that squabble over the naming of what was now Athens.

Perhaps she should have brought a gift.

Finally the ocean began to boil at the far horizon. The frothing churn raced toward the shore where Athena stood, and an instant later a vast waterspout roared up to mate the sea with the infinite sky. Poised amid the mountainous column of water stood Poseidon, brawny arms crossed over his thick chest. His crown was crusted with barnacles, and his trident dripped blood and entrails.

"I bring the greetings of Olympus, Lord Poseidon," she said, bowing deeply.

"I have no time for you, Athena." The Lord of the Sea gestured curtly over his shoulder with the trident. "My business takes me far beyond the Pillars of Hercules."

Athena nodded sympathetically. "Atlantis again?"

"Those people are no *end* of trouble," Poseidon muttered.

"Your patience with them is admirable."

"Admirable perhaps, but irritation is a blade that whittles my patience dangerously thin. My brother asked that I hear your petition. Out of respect for him, I listen." The sea god leaned toward her. "Briefly."

Athena lifted an open hand. "Let there be no bad blood between us, my uncle. Our feud should be diminished by time, should it not? It was hardly so consequential that its wounds should be inflamed still to this day."

Poseidon reared up to an even greater height and poked his trident in her direction. "That city should be *mine*! I struck the rock on which the Acropolis sits and—"

"And a spring burst forth indeed, but of brine," Athena said sympathetically. "Am I to blame that the people of the city preferred my olive tree to your saltwater spring?"

The sea god said sullenly, "Athens is a *terrible* name for a city."

"Poseidia would be more melodious," she admitted. "If my beloved uncle might be appeased by some more *substantial* gesture, I hope to remind you that Athenians—thanks to my lord uncle's generous patronage—are the greatest sailors in all the known world. Their strength is in their navy, and they do honor to the Lord of the Ocean every day."

"Well . . ." Poseidon grumbled, the sound of waves crashing against an unprotected cliff. "I suppose that's true. Let us put our disagreements behind us, my niece. What business brings you this day to my endless shore?"

"My lord uncle, I have come to apologize for my brother's deadly insult to your sovereignty."

"What?" Poseidon's brows of sea foam drew together, and the ground beneath Athena's feet gave a warning rumble. "*Which* brother?"

"Ares, of course. What other god would so boldly dare to tempt your anger?"

"Besides yourself?"

"I know of late you have been preoccupied with Atlantis—which is the sole seemly explanation for allowing Ares's monsters to swarm your seas unchallenged."

"Swarm my—" His gaze went distant, and what his deific vision found caused him to gasp like a sounding whale. "A Hydra? In my Grave of Ships! The *impudence*—I have told Zeus, again and *again*, he is *far* too lenient with his children! Ares should have spent an entire age of the world beside Sisyphus! I am not so forgiving as my brother. I will crush him! Where is he? Where?"

"Far from your realm, my lord uncle—safe in a distant desert."

Poseidon roared, raised a fist, and all the world trembled. "Am I called Earthshaker for naught?"

"My lord uncle, please!" Athena cried. "Let not your wrath fall upon him directly! There is no shame in being bested by great Poseidon, ruler of two-thirds of all that is. No lesser god can hope to stand against any of the brother kings. If you truly want to punish Ares, you must smite his *pride*."

The tremors faded away. "There is truth in this," Poseidon admitted. "But how best to do so?"

"Show all the gods how even a mere mortal can best Ares's plans and defeat his will," Athena said with studied casualness.

"Yes, that is so," Poseidon said. "But what mortal? Hercules? Isn't he busy somewhere in Crete? Peirithous is in Hades, Theseus is old, and Perseus—who knows what he's been up to? I don't think he's reliable."

"There is another," Athena said, forcing herself to show no hint of emotion. "Has my lord uncle heard of one particular mortal, called by men the Ghost of Sparta? His name is Kratos."

Great Poseidon bent toward her, interested. "The Fist of Ares?"

"Fist of Ares no more—now the Ghost of Sparta serves *me.* Did you not attend the Challenge of War Gods?"

He nodded slowly, remembering. "Yes, yes, of course. It had slipped my mind—the fate of land-borne armies means little to the sea."

"Kratos had forsworn his service to Ares even before I won him and the rest of the armies of humanity in the challenge."

"Oh, yes, I remember, now that you mention it—something to do with that little village temple of yours that Kratos sacked, wasn't it?"

"Yes, Uncle. And for Kratos, a horror beyond imagining. It haunts him to this day."

"So this Kratos is the mortal you have in mind?"

"Your perception is justly legendary, my lord uncle. Ares hates Kratos with a passion even the gods can barely comprehend, and only a distant dream of vengeance upon the God of Slaughter keeps Kratos fighting on. There could be no greater shame for Ares than to be thwarted by Kratos."

"How can any mere mortal hope to overpower the legions of Ares?"

"As the Fates would have it," Athena said, a bit of a twinkle brightening the gray of her eyes, "I have an idea. . . ."

THREE

FOR HOURS, KRATOS FOUGHT through the Grave of Ships.

The Blades of Chaos flamed in constant motion, rising and falling, whipping to the extreme lengths of their unbreakable chains, slicing through the rotting flesh and brittle yellowed bone of undead legionnaires, shattering the scales of Hydra heads, puncturing eyeballs, severing tongues and ripping at throats. They slashed and hacked, stabbed and pierced, and through it all they burned with an unnatural flame, as though the hellish fires of the Hadean forge sprang from their edges to burn away the lives of all they touched.

Kratos burned with the same fire. Each slice of any creature's life that the Blades carved away flowed back up the chains to where they were fused with the bones of his wrists. The stolen lives charged his body and flooded his mind with inexhaustible fury. If he was not killing, it was only because he was sprinting toward more victims. He never stopped.

He never even slowed down.

The blades could not be broken; they could not be nicked or dulled. Even the black blood and putrefying flesh that should have clotted and crusted the blades and their chains simply vanished, consumed by unnatural fire. Kratos raced from ship to ship, balancing across floating beams above seas churning with the feeding frenzy of sharks below, who fought for scraps of his victims. The ships blurred together into an endless nightmare maze of decks and masts, of sails and cargo nets, and always there was the unending stream of mindless undead attacking with the same maniacal bloodlust, more harpies to swoop and dive and rake him with their shit-smeared talons.

He no longer knew if he was moving toward the merchantman he had followed into this watery hell or winding farther away. He didn't care. He didn't think about it or about anything at all. He threw himself into his work with the joyous abandon of a bacchant and lost himself in the purity of unchecked slaughter.

He killed. He was content.

He fought on until his path was once again blocked by another uprearing head of the Hydra. Each he faced was larger than the one before. When this great beast cracked its jaw wide to roar, Kratos might have been thrust into a tunnel with dark saliva-damp sides. All he could see was the huge mouth, gaping twice as wide as his body, and the yellowed razor-sharp teeth in front of him. He reached over his shoulders and gripped the handles of the Blades of Chaos.

The Hydra surged forward with a sinuous ripple of its seemingly endless neck. Kratos feinted, swung past the snapping teeth, and whipped the chains securing the Blades of Chaos around its thick neck. Muscles bulging with exertion, he tightened his grip, twisting the links ever tighter, strangling the creature with his chains. The monster roared in fury and whip-cracked its neck to shake him loose. The chains skidded, and the beast's scales scraped his arms into a bloody swamp.

Kratos kicked hard, twisted, and spun around, using his chains like a climber's belt to force his way back up the neck. But his next move came at just the wrong instant. As the monster spasmed again, the force of his own kick flipped Kratos away to swing free by the chains—and the Hydra snapped him from the air as a toad might snare an unwary fly.

The Hydra's jaws clamped down, teeth like swords chopping into Kratos's forearms. A different hero would have had both hands severed, but the chains fused to his bones could not be broken save by the God of War himself. Clenching its jaw tighter only chipped the monster's teeth—but the Hydra showed no signs of letting go.

As he struggled, Kratos realized this monster might send him into Lord Hades's embrace. Straining, he tried to pull his arms free of the Hydra's crushing jaws, then stopped and looked frantically below into the maelstrom of the sea. Sharks snapped at one another—and at Kratos's feet. The sharp pain of his greaves being bitten through by a huge shark forced him to fight on two fronts.

Deciding which was the more immediate threat caused a knot to form in his belly. Death beckoned from blood-crazed sharks *and* the Hydra.

Unable to free his arms, he lifted his legs away from the voracious sharks and tried to find leverage. Pain radiated the length of his arms, from where the Hydra's jaws clamped down with bone-cracking force all the way up to his shoulders. Grunting with effort, he yanked—and only drove the Hydra's teeth deeper into his forearms.

When the Hydra began to toss its head around, shaking Kratos like a rat caught in a hunting dog's jaws, Kratos saw his opportunity. A kick from Kratos could rock a warship away from its dock. He doubled up, bringing his knees under his pinioned arms. When his greaves and sandals began to tear at the Hydra's face, the creature could only growl in pain and rage.

Kratos kicked harder, faster. Desperation drove him now. His arms turned cold, numb, bloodless. Both feet worked as if he were pummeling the beast with his fists. A chance kick caught the Hydra's eye, causing the creature's growl to become a roar of pain that released Kratos's arms and sent him flipping upward, high into the air. As Kratos reached the top of his arc, the Hydra strained toward him, opening wide its maw to catch him like a casually tossed sweetmeat.

In a single instant, Kratos both feared and exulted.

As he fell, he returned the Blades of Chaos in one smooth motion to rest upon his back. He coiled himself into a tight ball and allowed the creature's mouth to slam shut around him—but before it could swallow, he planted his feet against the Hydra's lower jaw, braced his back against the slimy ridges of the vast hard palate above, and *shoved*.

The creature's jaw began to open. Kratos strained like Hercules lifting the sky from the shoulders of Atlas. The Hydra strove with all its monstrous power to bite down again, but when the Ghost of Sparta stood braced, no power on earth could crush him.

Once he had forced his legs to full extension, Kratos wedged his hands in above his shoulders and continued to force open the Hydra's mouth by strength of his mighty arms alone. A crack like the breaking of a main spar came from the hinge of the monster's jaw, but Kratos did not relent and could not be denied. Fear was gone, replaced with cold triumph. With one great surge, he blasted his arms up straight above his head, and now the sound was not so much a crack as a crushing, grinding roar and a wet, leathery *r-r-rip* as the Hydra's jaw shattered and its cheeks tore asunder.

The Hydra shuddered and released an ear-shattering bellow, and Kratos kicked himself free, leaping for the deck of the nearest ship. The endless neck and giant destroyed head slid back down into the Aegean's dark waters, which now churned and boiled even more, as the voracious sharks circling below got a taste of the Hydra's blood. The last Kratos saw, sharks were darting like crows into the Hydra's mouth, ripping out gory chucks of its flapping tongue. To them it mattered not if the flesh they dined on was human or monster. Ravenously, they tore at the Hydra's face, dragging it below the roiling surface.

Yet even that immense head was not enough for all the sharks. Hundreds—thousands!—circled endlessly, thrashing the sea with their tails as each hoped for its own meal.

Kratos would be happy to provide that for his unwitting allies. At his feet, his blood tinged the water that ran down his legs. Hooking a shark or two on the barbs of the Blades of Chaos would steal enough life to close these minor cuts. He seized the railing and pulled himself up the canted remnant of deck—but as he drew the blades, the circling sharks sped away. They had discovered a feast of their own.

Literally.

Everywhere he looked, sharks floated, their black eyes fixed and staring. Some were beginning to bloat and others had their entrails blown out, and even the sharks that swarmed these dead ones to strike their poisoned flesh soon were showing their own bellies to the sky.

Eating a Hydra was just as fatal as being eaten by one.

He took a moment to search the shattered hulk on which he stood, seeking a cask, a tub, anything that might have been watertight. Even an upturned bucket might have captured enough rainwater to slake his burning thirst, but there was not the tiniest drop to be found, either on the deck or in the one lower hold he could still reach. Then he saw the barrel near the rudder, water for the steersman. Kratos strode to it and thrust his head into the water to drink deeply.

He jerked back and spat, bile rising into his throat. Brackish water burned his mouth. He spat again, this time adding a curse.

"May the oceans turn to dust! It could taste no worse than this!"

But as these words left his lips, an eldritch light shimmered up from the invisible depths of the drowned hold in which he stood. Where before there had been only a stained and rotting bulkhead now stood an archway of alabaster and pearl, twice

Kratos's height and wider than he could span with his arms. That archway framed a vast face, bright as sun flash on a calm sea, the face of a man whose beard was sea foam and whose hair was braided with gleaming black kelp.

"Do you have so little regard for my domain, Kratos?" The tolerantly chiding voice boomed like a tidal surge blasting into a cave-pocked cliff. *"Ten years have you sailed my seas on your quests, without shipwreck or storm founder—is that not evidence of my regard for you?"*

"Lord Poseidon." Kratos's tone was respectful, but he did not bow his head. "How may I serve the King of the Ocean?"

"This Hydra that plagues my beautiful Aegean is a creature of your onetime master, Ares. Its existence is an insult. I would have you destroy it."

"I plan to."

"Know that thus far you have but scratched this monstrosity—its secondary heads, such as those you've destroyed, are without number. The Hydra barely notices their loss."

"Then how do I kill it?"

"You must destroy the master head—the one that holds the creature's brain. The master head is ten times the size of the others, and its might is near to limitless."

Kratos didn't care about its might. "How do I find it?"

"I will take you there. And to help you in your task, I will lend you a tiny fraction of my own power."

Kratos had a feeling that the sea god wouldn't look kindly upon refusal. "What sort of power?"

"You know how my anger causes the earth to shake, and my fury spawns sea storms no ship can survive. Step forward into the archway where you see the image of my face, and I will grant you power beyond any you've ever known—you will command a fragment of my rage."

Whatever Poseidon's Rage might be, it couldn't hurt any more than having the chains of the Blades of Chaos burned into his arms.

"All right," he said. "Let us kill this beast."

STEPPING INTO THE ARCHWAY brought a blinding flash and the sensation of his bones being on fire, burning him from the inside out. Stepping out through the far side dropped Kratos into dank gloom that smelled of sweat and urine. The slow roll of the floor told him he was still aboard a ship. As his eyes adjusted to the darkness, he could make out the shapes of what appeared to be cargo lashed into place on either side. From ahead, he heard a sobbing voice—a man, crying like a child, begging to be set free.

Kratos moved toward the mouth of the gangway in a battle-ready crouch. Screams came from above, and he suspected that the sea god had been as good as his word. Light gathered in an archway ahead, and as he approached it, he discovered that what had in the gloom appeared to be cargo was, in fact, people—people too sick or starved or thirsty to even move.

In the new light, Kratos saw the greenish gleam of bronze shackles on these people's ankles, and he revised his own revision. These people were cargo.

It was a slave ship.

Kratos nodded to himself; slaves meant there would definitely be fresh water nearby—slaves were too valuable to be allowed to die of thirst. Some of them managed to rouse themselves enough to beg him for mercy as he passed. Kratos ignored them. Near the archway, a slave was bound in some kind of punishment position—his wrists were shackled together and hung from a short chain affixed to the ceiling. The chain was just long enough that his toes brushed the deck as the ship rolled. He sobbed in a thready, broken voice, "Please . . . please don't leave me here . . . please . . ."

As Kratos moved toward him, the slave's sobbing turned to screams. "By all the gods, I beg you . . . please!"

Kratos came to a stop beside him. "If I help, will you keep quiet?"

"Oh, bless you—all the gods bless you for a good and

kind . . ." The slave's voice trailed away as he finally managed to focus his eyes on his presumed rescuer. "You!" His voice was choked with awe. "The Ghost of Sparta—I know who you are! I know what you did! I'd rather die right here than be saved by you!"

Kratos drew one of the Blades of Chaos and, with a businesslike flick of the wrist, slashed off the slave's head. "Your prayer is granted."

The slave had been so close to death already that the blade channeled only the faintest spark of life up the chains. Kratos glanced back into the slave hold, weighing the prospect of gaining more strength and healing himself by slaughtering them all—but they were so sickly that killing them would be more trouble than their lives were worth.

Kratos moved on. Beyond the slave hold stretched a broad companionway lined with doors. The screams from above were thinning already, and a chorus of thunderous roars that caused the whole ship to shiver warned him there was more than one Hydra head up there. Whoever was fighting them sounded as if they were losing. Kratos looked around for someone else to kill on his way up; he needed all the energy he could get.

The pair of doors near the end of the companionway were different from the others. Massively timbered and bound with black iron, they looked strong enough that even Kratos might have trouble breaking them down—and as he considered this, the blade chains began to warm, sparking with not-unpleasant stings. He drew one blade and pushed it toward the door before him. A brilliant shower of energy splashed over the door, and the blade never reached the timbers. The energy flickered longest around a deep slot in one timber—a lock. A magical lock.

Kratos nodded to himself. So: a pair of doors not only strong as a fortress but sealed with magical bindings and mystic locks and who knew what else. What sort of "treasures" might a slave ship's captain keep within such a vault? Something beyond tawdry gold must be secure behind this door. Whatever it was, it might prove useful.

THE MAIN DECK LOOKED like a slaughterhouse where the butchery was still going on. Everywhere Kratos turned, sailors struggled with undead legionnaires or tried to fend off Hydra heads with long spears. Every timber on the ship was slick with blood, smeared with rotting undead flesh, or both. This stench-filled abattoir of screams and panic and desperation took him back to his younger days, to the raids on which he'd led his Spartan companions, in the long-ago time before he'd sworn himself to the service of Ares.

Of course, there hadn't been quite so many undead soldiers back then. And the Hydra had been only a Spartan bedtime story—because even though Hercules was, through an accident of birth, merely Theban, he had also made himself a hero of Sparta by restoring its rightful king, Tyndareus.

Kratos moved out onto the deck, Blades of Chaos at the ready. The undead he simply ignored; the sailors would either handle them or provide enough diversion to keep them busy. Kratos had eyes only for the three heads of the Hydra that attacked this ship as a team.

The smaller heads to either side were still twice the size of any he had yet fought—and they were dwarfed by the inconceivable majesty of the master head. Rising on a sinuous neck higher than the ship's mainmast, the master head was large enough to swallow the ship whole in a single gulp, and its eyes burned with a lurid yellow inner light. The secondary heads weaved and struck like vipers, keeping the spear-armed sailors at bay.

"Er—you a god?" The voice came from behind him. "Y'look kinda like a god. We could use a god."

Kratos turned. Crouched behind a wheel coiled with anchor chain, a sailor peered at him through one good eye; his other was an empty socket bisected with a scar reminiscent of the one through Kratos's eyebrow. The sailor's remaining eye drifted about as though he couldn't decide where to look.

"Your captain," Kratos said. "Where is he?"

"Whatcha want with him anyways?"

"His surrender." Kratos cast a scornful eye about the carnage on deck. "This is my ship now. How do you call it?"

"The *Gods' Lament*," came the answer. "You think you can take her?"

"I already have," Kratos said. "It will be called *Vengeance*, and it is mine."

"May the gods smile on that—if they don't strike you down for hubris!"

Kratos squinted down at the sailor. Was the man mad? Who would dare to question the Ghost of Sparta to his face? Then he took in the sailor's filthy tunic and the empty purple-stained wineskin on the deck beside him and realized that the man was too drunk to actually see him.

"Your captain," Kratos repeated. "I won't ask you again."

The drunken sailor waved a trembling hand. "Over there. By the mast. The fella wi' the big key round his neck. Y'see 'im?"

"The one on his knees?"

"Uh-huh. On his knees. Tha's him."

Kratos's lip curled in scorn. "Begging for mercy?"

"Prrrrayin'," the sailor corrected him. "Prayin' to Poseidon . . . t' save the ship from the Hydra . . ."

"His prayer has been answered."

The sailor goggled up at him. "Y're gonna save us?"

"No, I am going to save the ship." As Kratos turned back to the fight, the vast master head dipped toward the base of the mainmast and snapped shut upon the kneeling captain. In an instant, the captain was gone—swallowed alive—and his key with him. The master head reared up, unleashing a roar of triumph that blasted the ship's sails to rags.

Kratos was undismayed. With a throat as long as the Hydra's, swallowing could take a considerable length of time.

The three heads were too close together for him to engage them individually. If he went straight for the master head, he'd have to defend himself against attacks from both secondary heads. Going after either of the secondary heads would expose his rear or flank to the titanic jaws of the master. If he couldn't take them one at a time, he'd kill them all at once.

He launched himself across the deck as if he'd been shot from a ballista.

The nearest head swept toward him as though to batter him right off the deck. Kratos overleaped the monster's neck, slashing down with one of the blades. It chopped into bone and wedged itself at the joining of the skull and one horn; the chain snapped tight as a towline and yanked Kratos sideways into a whirl. He let the head's swing wrap the chain all the way around its neck, leaving him standing on the top of its skull. Faster than thought, the other blade found his hand, then together they thrust deep into the head's eyes. Accurate slashes painted the blade with a gooey mass of vitreous humor and sent the head reeling blindly.

A looming shadow gathered inky darkness around him. The master head arrowed downward like a falcon the size of a house. Kratos stood and waited. The vast jaws of the master head gaped far too wide to pluck him off the secondary head with any sort of accuracy—especially since the secondary head was still whipping from side to side, faster and faster as it tried to shake Kratos off—and so the master head did exactly as Kratos had anticipated.

Those gargantuan jaws closed around the entire secondary head, and teeth like the ram spike of a war galley chopped into the armored scales of the neck, trying to bite off the secondary head and swallow it—and Kratos—whole.

But Kratos knew well how tough the scaly hide of the Hydra truly was. There was ample time for him to slip between the great teeth as the master head bit down and began to shake his head like a wolf worrying off the haunch of a deer. Kratos jammed one of the blades into the master's lower gums, then used the chain to swing himself under the creature's chin. There, he hacked into the scales with the second blade, while ripping the first one free. The master head roared at the sudden pain, releasing the half-chewed secondary head to collapse back into the sea.

Kratos went on hacking into its neck close under its chin, where the creature couldn't get at him. The remaining secondary head snaked over to strike like a viper at Kratos's back—but getting one of the Blades of Chaos up its nose made it rethink that strategy. With the jagged blade firmly lodged in the sinus cavity, pulling back made the creature unleash a screech of pain entirely unlike anything Kratos had ever heard. At this, the master head, instead of trying to bite Kratos in half, slammed its neck against the mainmast, crushing Kratos between its scales and the enormous spar.

Kratos's vision darkened. The master head held him there, leaning into him. The mainmast creaked alarmingly, as did Kratos's spine—but the mast gave way first, snapping off with a splintering roar.

The master head reared up again, and the secondary head tried desperately to pull away, but the blade up its nose was lodged like a fishhook—pulling away only seated it all the deeper. The other blade was similarly set in the master head's throat. Neither blade would rip free, and they could not be broken any more than the blade chains binding them to Kratos's arms could be broken by any earthly force. So when the master head pulled one way and the secondary head pulled another, there was only one thing linking them that could be broken.

Kratos.

He screamed in agony as he hung suspended between the two heads trying to rip him in half. Muscles bunched in his massive shoulders, but even his preternatural strength was no match for the titanic power of the Hydra. On another day, Kratos would have died there—but the Hydra was a creature of Ares. And the prospect of being killed by a minion of his enemy fueled Kratos's anger. More than anger. More than fury.

It filled him with the rage of a god.

And, just as when he'd entered the archway where he met Poseidon, he felt as if his bones were on fire, burning him from the inside out. Lightning blazed around him, causing the world to fade into a dim image of washed-out blue, and blasted along the chains to the blades. The flesh around the blade embedded in the master head's neck exploded like a sealed pot left on the fire too long, scattering immense gobbets of smoking remains.

The blade lodged in the secondary head's sinus cavity had an even more spectacular effect: When the inner membranes detonated, they blasted shards of bone out the Hydra's eye sockets, which popped the creature's sundered eyes from its face. Fragments penetrated whatever the secondary head used as a brain; the neck collapsed, and Kratos fell toward the deck far below.

As he fell, he reflected that the Rage of Poseidon had turned out to be more useful than he'd anticipated. He tumbled down beside the splintered wreck of the mainmast. The flick of one wrist sent a blade out to chop into the mast, catch, and let him reverse his direction in one long, smooth swing. The great beast saw him coming, and it arched its neck and opened wide a maw that could have bitten the ship in half.

Having determined to his own satisfaction that the giant master head was not filled with an equally giant brain, Kratos swiveled himself up to what was now the top of the mainmast— a porcupine slant of needle-sharp slivers—then swirled the blades around his head to capture the monster's attention.

He waited until the master head struck downward like a falling moon, engulfing him and several yards of mast. Even before it had been damaged, the wood of the mainmast had been in no way as tough as the Hydra's secondary necks. Kratos knew the Hydra could sever it in one swift chomp. So, once more inside the slime-dripping cave of the monster's mouth, Kratos released again the furnace of fury that always burned within him.

The master head convulsed as Poseidon's Rage blasted the rear of its mouth to bloody shreds. Kratos hurled a blade upward, toward the back of the Hydra's sinus cavities, then hauled himself up through an incalculable volume of salty slime until he reached the underside of the Hydra's brainpan. Before the creature even stopped thrashing about, Kratos had chopped his way inside its skull. Three or four deft strokes of the blades slashed the Hydra's brain into foul-smelling mush.

He swung back down into the Hydra's throat. It still twisted and spasmed a bit, as the rest of the Hydra's vast body gradually got the message that its brain was dead. Kratos picked his way down over the ridges of cartilage until the light from the beast's open mouth began to fade—and he heard a thin voice, sobbing faintly, "Please . . . please, someone . . . Poseidon, please . . ."

Kratos embedded one of the blades into a long, striated cord of muscle and used the chain to walk himself backward into the slippery gloom. There, just below the last of the light, Kratos made out a darker shape. He drew the other blade and spun it to ignite some of its fire, and in the light of the blade he saw the captain.

"Oh, bless you! Poseidon bless you and all your journeys," the captain gasped. "May all the gods of Olympus smile on you forever. . . ."

The captain clung desperately to one ring of cartilage. His feet dangled over what appeared to be a bottomless drop into the Hydra's stomach. And a thin leather thong around his neck held a key of gleaming gold.

Kratos let out a little more chain, stretching down with one enormous hand. Tears streamed from the captain's eyes. "Bless you," he kept saying. "Bless you for coming back for me!"

Kratos's hand closed on the leather thong. "I didn't come back for you," he said, and gave the thong a sharp yank that snapped it in two—and broke the captain's grip on the cartilage. His screams as he fell ended abruptly when he splashed into the Hydra's churning stomach.

When Kratos walked back out of the dead Hydra's mouth with the key in his hand, he could still hear the captain being digested. Kratos paused by the base of the mast on which the master head was impaled; a few strokes of the Blades of Chaos snapped the mainmast off at the root, and the great beast slid back over the rail and sank forever from the sight of men.

Kratos weighed the key in his hand. This had been a lot of work just to open a door. The fight had better be worth the reward.

FOUR

"**YOU GAVE KRATOS** a sliver of your own rage!" Ares's fist clutched the hilt of his sword. The muscles corded on his forearm as he fought to control his towering rage. "To help a mortal—against your own *family*?"

"If ever again you think to befoul my realm with any of your Typhon-spawned monsters, they will be destroyed." Poseidon's voice was as cold and dark as his seas' uttermost depths. "And you, nephew, are not immune from retribution. My brother forbids murder among the gods, yes—but do not tempt my anger, or you will *wish* I had killed you. Do you understand?"

Ares loosened his blade in his scabbard. "Words are no armor against the edge of a sword."

"Remember this, God of War: I am sovereign over the seas. Any who enter my domain must do honor to me. Even gods."

The two gods glowered at each other upon Egypt's Mediterranean shore. Invisible to mortal eyes, they both stood tall enough that they could have leaned upon the Lighthouse of Pharos as if it were a walking stick.

Ares finally broke the silent battle of wills. "We need not feud in this fashion."

"Your Hydra—"

"My Hydra, yes," Ares said. "But troubling your seas? I did not set the Hydra upon your realm."

Poseidon blinked. "Is this truth?"

"Tell me this, my lord uncle. Who brought you news of this Hydra? That scheming bitch Athena, I wager."

"Why . . . yes," Poseidon admitted. "But—"

"And did you know of its presence *before* she scuttled up to trick you into giving your power to her pet?"

"*Trick* me—"

"You know I no longer frequent Olympus, not as long as my father continues to indulge every petty fancy of my sister. Being so far away, I sometimes cannot counter her lies before they fall upon trusting ears." The God of War leaned close to his uncle, so close that the flames of his hair drew steam from the sea god's beard. "Ask yourself, my lord uncle, ask yourself only this. Why?"

The sea god did not respond, but a thoughtful cloud gathered upon his brow.

"Why would *I* offend your sovereignty? Why would *I* befoul your seas? What could I possibly hope to gain?"

"To kill this Kratos. That's what Athena said."

"And if I had commanded this Hydra to do so, why would I direct it to lurk at the Grave of Ships? Did I merely hope that Kratos might someday find his way there?" Ares snorted. "I hardly need summon a Hydra to dispose of Kratos. He is less than a worm. When I want Kratos dead, I will crush him as a mortal might snuff a burned-out taper. He still lives only because his suffering amuses me."

"But . . . if it was not *you* who inflicted the Hydra upon my kingdom . . ."

"I do not presume to accuse," Ares said. "But who has gained from this encounter? Who has made you turn your majestic face from me? Who has defrauded you of power simply to flatter some mortal maggot?"

Poseidon backed off a little and eyed his warlike nephew. "I cannot take back the rage given to Kratos."

"This I know too well," said the God of War. "A god with your sense of honor would never take what was given. But I am not asking this of you. I am here, my lord uncle, only out of respect for you. I know that you still have a certain . . . *affection* for the city of Athens."

"*That* place." The sea god snorted.

"Zeus forbids direct battle between gods—but as you so lately warned me, there are *other* forms of retribution. My armies march on Athens at this very hour."

"Why come to me?"

"As a courtesy, Uncle. I know that once you thought to have that city as your own. Should it be your will, I will leave Athens standing without so much as a scratch. If, indeed, you decide that all Athena has spoken is truth and all I have spoken is lies, I will not protest. I am not, as every Olympian knows, remotely so good a liar as my sister."

Poseidon took a breath, so deep that it changed the Mediterranean's currents as far north as Crete. Finally he said, "I do not know which of you is deceiving me—or if you both are. But . . . that *city* is no concern of mine. Burn it to the ground and salt the earth, for all I care." And with a gale's roar, he was gone.

Ares's cruel lips bent toward a smile behind his beard of flame. "I will, Uncle. I will do exactly that," said the God of War, and he rode the winds toward Athens.

IN HER CHAMBERS upon faraway Olympus, Athena dashed her hand into the scrying pool she'd been using to spy upon her brother. She slapped at the ambrosia-tinctured liquid as though she could reach through it and strike Ares and Poseidon both. And when she stopped and paused to listen, she could hear the faint cries of her worshippers, far below in Athens, supplicating for her mercy and support as Ares's monstrous legions drew in over the horizon and the God of War himself strode among them, ordering them to battle.

And with Ares upon the field, the Word of Zeus prevented her from meeting this peril personally.

Her lips thinned to a line as her anger rose. Poseidon had no cause to turn on her this way. At least her uncle did not actively support Ares. Perhaps . . .

Yes. She might still turn this to her advantage.

Without the interference of Poseidon, Kratos could sail to her beleaguered city in mere days. To again put Kratos in the position to frustrate Ares's plans seemed like an equitable solution — but the days his travel would require might well be days her city could not spare. How Ares would make her worshippers suffer!

Athena hurried from her chambers to the Hall of Eternity, down which she strode crisply until she reached the branch she sought. Along this corridor she walked more cautiously, treading softly as the marble gave way to finely trimmed grasses. Fawns nibbled at ivy at the edge of her vision, and soon she stepped out into an airy glade locked in perpetual summer. Athena stood perfectly still, waiting to be acknowledged.

Artemis did not like to be startled, and that bow of hers never missed.

Soon a rustling of leaves came from a myrtle bush nearby. The goddess Artemis stepped forth, suddenly visible as though she had materialized on the spot. With her bow slung over her shoulder and a quiver at her waist, she looked every bit the Huntress of the Gods.

Athena lowered her head formally. "Greetings, Artemis, my sister."

The huntress only looked her over curiously. She had never been much for formality. "I expected my twin."

"Is Apollo near? I would welcome his arrival. Matters are grave, and the wisdom of the God of Enlightenment would be welcome."

Artemis maintained that curiously expressionless stare, as though Athena might be a hart to which the goddess was judging the range. "Even my creatures know of our brother's war upon your city."

"Ares brings an army of underworld creatures to the fight. Undead legionnaires and archers take their toll, but the citizens of Athens can withstand their onslaught. The other creatures— the true monsters—are beyond mere mortals' power to defeat."

Artemis walked around a full circle, studying the other goddess from every direction. "In the hunt," she said slowly, "we know who is hunter and who is prey. In that simplicity lies truth. Between you and Ares, nothing is simple."

"I am not asking you to judge between my brother and myself. I am not asking you anything at all, my sister. I am here only to deliver melancholy news."

"Do you care for anything in that city beyond the name it bears?"

Athena's face went cold as stone. She had forgotten that Artemis's words could strike as sharply as her arrows. "Of course I care for my mortals," she said. "I must find what concerns you."

"Ares is no friend. His legions ravage my forests, but I cannot oppose him in the field. Zeus prohibits that." Artemis's hand clutched her bow, swung it to hand, nocked an arrow, and fired. The arrow sang through the air and embedded itself in the bole of a tree. "Would that I could aim my hunter's arrow at him!"

"Your forests," Athena said softly. "Your beasts—all are prey for our brother's legion."

"Your city dwellers," Artemis said, an edge in her voice. "Those in Athens scavenge my forests too."

"They husband the forests and beasts," Athena countered. "Ares *destroys*. His undead do not eat to survive or to worship us. They leave only destruction in their wake."

"An abomination," Artemis agreed.

"My city can celebrate the wilderness—if it survives," Athena said. "My worshippers admire and respect you. Only last year,"

Athena plowed on, "the prize at the Festival of Dionysus was taken by a play exalting *you*: *The Tragedy of Actaeon the Hunter.*"

"Tragedy?" Artemis said. "I seek to celebrate life."

Athena had always thought turning Actaeon into a stag and having him torn apart by his own hounds was a bit excessive for only a glimpse of the goddess as she bathed—but this private thought would *stay* private; Athena could see no profit in dredging that up. "It is a pity," Athena said carefully, "that my feud with Ares cannot be settled with, uh, a similarly elegant solution."

"And why bring this matter to me? Ares is as immune to my arrows as he is to your blade."

"Zeus would never permit even an arrow shot in anger," Athena agreed. "However, Ares's army marches through your sacred groves outside Athens. The foul creatures he commands lay waste to even the most inoffensive of your animals."

Athena held her hands in front of her, palms together. She parted them slightly and turned them upward as a vivid scene formed in the air between her and Artemis.

"Such slaughter . . ." A tear rolled down Artemis's cheek at the sight of the wanton destruction.

Athena parted her hands wider, and the floating scene grew in size. "The stream is befouled with blood—blood of *your* animals. Ares does not hunt, does not stalk for either food or pleasure. Death is only a passing satisfaction for him. There is no skill, no grace, only endless slaughter. This stream runs red with the blood of your fawns, elk, rabbits, even the birds of the air."

The scene expanded to encompass a large section of the woods a few miles from the Long Walls protecting Athens. The carcasses of mutilated deer and foxes stretched to the limit of the view. A Cyclops lumbered forward, swinging a heavy club carelessly. To the left and right, it smashed the skulls of the fallen animals, although they lay already dead. In the wake of the Cyclops came hundreds of cursed legionnaires, and behind them trooped undead archers.

"None shows respect for the wood or its inhabitants." Athena paused dramatically. "Its *former* inhabitants. They leave behind only death as they march to Athens, a city that honors you as it does me.

"There Ares's army will do the same to the mortals," Athena continued. "The coming fight will be between Ares's minions and mine—but you see the result of that conflict. I would preserve your woods and ensure their sanctity."

"Ares would never do so. He did not ask permission to cross my meadows and forests."

"He is focused only on killing," Athena said. "It matters naught to him what his army destroys." She let the scene expand once more to show other elements of Ares's army marching through other woods Artemis claimed as her sylvan domain. Only when she saw the expression change subtly on Artemis's face, going from despair to anger, did Athena continue. "Neither of us can fight Ares, by our father's decree. That does not stop our brother from destroying those who worship us."

"You swear an oath that my woods will be sacrosanct?"

"Turn your creatures of the forest against Ares's minions and my oath is made. I will see that all of Athens honors your bucolic temple," Athena said, passion tingeing her words. "We must not allow him to trample the shrine you hold most sacred: the woods filled with creatures of hoof and wing."

Artemis turned, drew another arrow from her quiver, and brought it to her string. She drew the bow back until it quivered with the strain. She loosed the arrow and it sang away, arching high into the air where it exploded with the fury of a new sun, rivaling anything her twin brother might place in the sky. The second sun rained down scintillant sparks.

Artemis said solemnly, "The army of Ares will find it impossible to pass through any forest where those under my protection roam." With that, the Goddess of the Hunt spun and disappeared into the forest. In seconds the leaves had stopped quivering from her passage. She had become one with her domain again.

Athena counted this a partial victory. She had gained a potent ally, but Athens—and, for that matter, Olympus itself—would never be safe while Ares lived. It was time to begin the next phase of her plan. Kratos must be trained. He must be tested. And most of all—

He must be properly *armed*.

FIVE

AS KRATOS TURNED the key he had struggled for so long to get, the mystical seal evaporated—and a soul-piercing scream came from the captain's cabin. He kicked open the door, expecting to find what commanded such potent protections. In this, he was not disappointed. Kratos found treasure beyond turquoise and gold.

The three girls were as lovely as any he had ever seen. Or perhaps they simply looked lovely by comparison to the blackened, rotting faces of the undead that ripped at them with taloned hands.

Kratos froze for an instant, paralyzed by incomprehension. How had the undead gotten *in* here? Through the locked door? The only answer that made sense was his own culpability. By opening the door he had released more than the locking spell. He had also released the undead magically sealed in this room to protect against intruders. The captain must have known how to prevent their release. Kratos had blundered in and put the women in jeopardy.

In an instant, his confusion whirled away like leaves before a gale. Such imponderables were the stuff of idle hours. Right now he was still in a fight, as two of the rotting legionnaires rushed him, swinging wickedly hooked swords. Kratos reached back over his shoulder, and the same motion that drew the Blades of Chaos also bisected each undead from crown to crotch. He moved into the room and with his next swing severed the legs of an undead strangling one of the slave girls. The creature fell, dragging the girl with it to the floor, and went on strangling her as though Kratos had not mutilated its legs.

Kratos hacked off its arms and crushed its skull—but the severed hands only tightened, throttling the life from the woman. Snarling, he bent to rip away the clenched talons, but the girl's head tilted at a crazy angle. Her neck had been snapped like a twig.

Another undead held a struggling woman in the air between itself and Kratos, making her a human shield.

"Steel works better," Kratos sneered as he jammed a blade straight through her torso, encountering only the slight resistance of internal organs, and then the tip crunched hard into the undead holding her. He twisted the blade and they both fell limp.

"Don't let it kill me. I beg you, don't—" The third woman died as the undead drove a bony hand against her chest, crushing her throbbing heart within her breast. Her pleas trailed to wet, gurgling gasps as she collapsed. Two quick steps brought Kratos within striking distance. Delivering a single accurate cut, he dispatched the undead with the beating heart still clutched in its hand. The undead fell and lay sprawled, the heart pulsating, slowing to a shiver, then finally stopping, as dead as the girl from which it had been ripped.

Kratos stepped back. The carnage seemed to reel around him. He reached out to brace himself against the bulkhead, and still he nearly fell. "Stop," he growled fiercely at himself; he had no more tolerance of his own weaknesses than he had of others. "These are not . . . are not . . ."

The women's deaths were no worse than he had seen thousands of times—no worse than he had *done* with his own hand, without the thinnest sliver of regret.

But the cabin faded as darkness settled around him and the visions began.

Blades slashing through necks, driving into exposed bellies. Screams of pain and the ghastly rattle of death. Heads exploding in a spray of blood. And the old woman waving her crooked hand, cackling like a damned thing.

"No," Kratos cried. "No!"

Limbs severed. Fields of corpses, crows pecking at eyes staring sightlessly at a leaden sky, maggots eating dead flesh. The blood pooling around bodies on the temple floor—blood pooling around bodies—blood . . .

And still the demented laughter and the wave of the crooked hand . . .

"*No!*" With an effort of will that left him gasping, Kratos wrenched open his eyes. He was *not* in the temple; he did *not* face the shrill cackle of the village oracle! He was here, at the far end of ten years, standing in the captain's quarters of a slave ship, and the slaughtered girls on the floor were *not . . . were not*—

"Athena!" Kratos spun about in a full circle, then fled from the cabin. "Athena!" He dashed to the hatchway leading to the deck. As he burst out onto the gore-soaked planking, he saw again the wooden statue of Athena that had graced his now-sunken ship. The statue stood at the prow of his new ship as she had on the old, impassive wooden eyes judging his every crime.

"Ten *years,* Athena! I have faithfully served the gods for *ten years!* When will you banish my nightmares? *When?* The visions haunt even my waking life!"

With a soft silvery shimmer like water in moonlight, the statue flickered to life. Those impassive wooden eyes now gleamed with the level gray stare of the goddess.

"*We require one final task of you, Kratos. Your greatest challenge awaits—in Athens, where even now my brother Ares lays siege.*"

Kratos stiffened as new visions assaulted his senses. He smelled fresh blood and raw meat, saw fire and destruction and fields piled with dead. He heard death cries, and he tasted the ash of burning corpses. Kratos forced his eyes shut, but he could not escape the vision. He shared every death with every murdered Athenian. He felt their shades—*his* shade—ripped screaming from his body, not by the clean stroke of sword or spear but by the gore-crusted talons of Ares's monstrous minions.

"*Athens is on the brink of destruction,*" said the goddess through her statue. "*It is the will of Ares that my great city should fall.*"

Kratos could only try to endure as ever darker, more gruesome visions assailed him.

"*Zeus has forbidden the gods to wage war on one another.*"

Kratos felt himself charred with imaginary flame, flesh boiled from his bones—what remained of him twisted into the air, riding a violent whirlwind until he witnessed the death of Athens as it might be seen by a soaring eagle. Then the vision released him, and he fell with shattering force back into his own body on the deck of the slave ship.

"*That is why it must be you, Kratos. Only a mortal trained by a god has a chance of defeating Ares.*"

"And if I am able to do this," Kratos said, once more standing firmly upright, as a man should, "if I can kill the god, then the visions . . . they will end?"

"*Complete this final task and the past that consumes you will be forgiven. Have faith, Kratos. The gods do not forget those who come to their aid.*"

The statue's eyes closed, and the shimmer of godhead faded.

Kratos stood motionless for a very long time, feeling a desperately unfamiliar sensation. He marveled at it, this feeling. He couldn't recall the last time he had felt anything like it.

He wondered if it might be hope.

———

LATER, KRATOS PACED the length of the deck, taking note of damage and how repairs should proceed. He had a cage filled with slaves in the hold. They would crew for him in exchange for their freedom. Since Athena had entrusted him with the quest to save Athens from Ares's army of Hades-spawned soldiers, he would have no further need of a ship once he arrived at the Harbor of Zea at Piraeus.

The locked captain's cabin where the three women had been killed hinted at how the former captain of this vessel had whiled away his hours, but Kratos would never again enter that compartment. Even if he had the slaves drag out the bodies and clean it from stem to stern, he would never step into that room again.

He dared not risk more visions.

But there was another room, also magically barred, lacking even a keyhole. The captain had kept concubines in his own cabin; what treasure would he have found precious enough to lock away even from himself? Kratos had little patience for idle speculation. The best way to discover the room's contents was to break the door and enter.

Edging past the door to the captain's cabin—he would not allow himself to so much as look at it—he stopped before the magical portal and began to examine it for any obvious way to open it. After all, if the room beyond held anything of real value, he might wish to be able to lock it away too. Finding no handle, lever, or keyhole, he tried simply to shove the door open. Corded muscle bunched in his massive shoulders, but he could not make the door so much as rattle. With a snarl he lost what little patience he'd had. He drew the Blades of Chaos and hacked at the door. Golden force flared, and the blades did not even touch the wood.

Fury rose within him, and outward from his bones surged the Rage of Poseidon. Power made him feel invincible, and the lightning of his fury burned the golden force away—and the door opened at a simple push.

Kratos stared in amazement.

In the middle of the room stood a half-naked woman whose beauty transcended anything in Kratos's experience. She had her hands on cocked hips and had hair of flaming red more radiant than the sunrise, but this was not what Kratos noted. She was naked to the waist, a skirt swirling about the rest of her trim body. Her bare breasts were firm and high, capped by pink nubs that pointed at him in wanton invitation.

"Were you a slave on this ship?"

"Is the captain dead? I hope so," the young woman said, leaning toward him with a beckoning finger. "I like *your* looks better."

Kratos heard ominous creaking in the hull and looked around to be certain the vessel was not breaking apart. When he turned back, he blinked in surprise. The woman still stood in front of him, hands on her hips, hair wild and red and lustrous. But she was no longer naked to the waist. Rather, she wore a tunic—and had no skirt. She was naked from the waist down, when only an instant before . . .

"Is that why you were imprisoned with a magical lock? You're a witch?"

"That's not a nice thing to say. We aren't witches!"

"We?" Kratos blinked. There were two women, identical in beauty, but one was naked above the waist and the other below. "What are you?"

"Twins," they answered as one.

"The captain was a cruel master. He gave us only one set of clothes," said the twin with the tunic.

The twin with the skirt showed a bit of a pout. "We shared the best we could. Do we not please you?"

"No, I—"

"No?" they cried in unison. "Then we'll take off these offending rags!"

And they did.

Kratos was willing to admit that this improved the view. "I begin to understand why the captain kept you locked away. Identical down to the last mole and freckle."

"Not so," said the one on the left. "Lora's mole is on the inside of her left thigh. See?"

Kratos did.

"Zora and I are *completely* different," said the other.

"Do you do everything together?"

The twins exchanged a look, then moved forward with a single mind. Their answer became obvious as they stripped him of his clothing and led him to a wide, soft bed. The only complaint Kratos had was clumsily knocking over a wine bottle in the midst of their doubled passion.

Afterward, he awoke with a woman on his left and another on the right—he had lost track of which was Lora and which was Zora, but he knew better than to check their defining marks. That would only spark demands for more lovemaking, and he had a crew abovedecks to command. Athena's demand must be met, and soon, from the vision of her city being laid to waste. "I want more wine," he said, reaching over one redhead to get his hand around the bottle on the deck.

"We are your willing slaves, Captain Kratos," one of them said.

The other added, "So long as you can keep us satisfied."

"The captain had concubines in this cabin—" Kratos began.

"Oh, yes, he kept girls of his own," a twin said, a little sadly. "He never touched us."

"Never?"

The other sighed. "He wasn't man enough. After two or three of the crew died, he locked us away."

"They . . . *died*?" Kratos couldn't quite make sense of this. "So the captain locked you up? They died doing . . . what?"

"Us," one said brightly.

The other contributed a perky nod. "He wanted to keep his crew safe. From us. We have been *very* lonely."

Kratos said slowly, "I see."

"And we're *so* happy to have met you . . . and that you didn't die. Really."

"Likewise," Kratos said. He reflected that this trip to Athens might be more interesting than he had anticipated.

The twin on his left stroked the bulge of muscle at his shoulder. "Are you a—"

"—king, Master Kratos?" finished the twin on his right side.

"I am only a soldier," he said.

"A *great* soldier," said one.

"A *champion*," agreed the other.

"I have been given a quest by the gods."

"That sounds—"

"—dangerous," the twins said.

"We sail for Athens. There I will set you free."

"We don't *want* to be free. We want to be your slaves."

"Forever," said the other. "Or at least until you die. You're *very* strong, master."

"And so *large*."

Kratos found himself without anything to say.

"We never wanted to go to—"

"—Attica. It's a terrible, cold place, or so—"

"—we've heard."

Kratos cursed the gods in his heart. If only he could be like other men and lose himself entirely in pleasures of the flesh. But even Lora and Zora could never drive away the nightmares and hold his madness at bay.

All he now lived for was Athena's pledge to erase his visions and to quell the ghastly memories that plagued his every living hour. Removing the visions of death and horror, guilt and abject pain, was a reward far beyond anything Lora and Zora could offer, no matter how skillful they might be.

"This vessel must get free of the Grave of Ships," he said, swinging his legs around and getting out of bed. The wine under his feet had turned as sticky as blood. He started to wipe it off, but the twins scampered lithely from the bed.

"Allow us to do that, Master Kratos." They cleaned his feet lovingly, but he had no time for this. Ares's Hydra was dead, but what other abominations might the God of War send to destroy him? Kratos did not want to find out, not trapped among the hulks of so many dead and discarded vessels.

"You can come on deck," Kratos told the twins, "but dress completely."

"There is nothing for us to wear in this cabin," they said in unison.

"Find something," he said curtly. He hesitated to have them search the captain's cabin. The three women left there must have had clothing aplenty, but stripping it from their corpses was not something he anticipated would be greeted well by the twins.

"We will be there soon," they said.

Kratos made for the deck. He was far from Athens, and once he arrived, he had a god to slay. Simply getting this slave ship free from the other hulks would be a daunting task.

On deck, the brisk wind and hint of rain warned of an impending storm. Trapped among the other ships as they were, the storm would toss them about and crack the hull like a walnut shell. He went below, to the slave hold, and peered at the miserable wretches. They whined and begged until he would just as soon have opened the scuttle cocks and let them swim away. Perhaps freedom would remind them what it was to be a man.

"I will free you. And you will work," he said. "Work harder than you ever have. We sail for Athens."

"Free us!"

"I have no need of slaves. I need a crew. Have any of you worked rigging before?" He saw a hand tentatively raised. "You are my first officer. The rest of you will listen and learn from him. His word is as mine. Go against either of us and I will feed your entrails to the sharks. Obey and you will be free once we reach Piraeus."

There was some muttering among the caged slaves, but the one he had designated as his first officer rose to the challenge and spoke for the rest. "We will be free?"

"On my life, you will," Kratos promised.

"Then let us out. The way this ship is wallowing about, a storm is rising."

"What's your name, First Officer?"

"Coeus."

"Get them on deck and at their stations, Coeus. You were right about a storm brewing."

With cuffs and kicks to the hind side, Kratos helped along the slaves who were strangely reluctant to leave their cage. When the last had made his way to the deck, the wind whipped along fiercely and sent tiny bullets of raindrops hammering into them.

"To the rigging. Get the sails lowered. There's no other way out of this damnable watery graveyard," Kratos bellowed. "We must run ahead of the storm or we are lost."

He saw that Coeus knew the rudiments of unfurling the sails and lashing them securely for running, but trying to teach each of the crew aloft was impossible in the wind. One screamed and tumbled from the cross spar. Kratos watched the man vanish beneath the waves. He never surfaced.

Kratos felt the ship lurch, as a horse reluctant to race might give a false start. Coeus did what he could. Kratos had to find a steersman to tend the flopping rudder. He grabbed a slave by the arm and dragged him along up to the poop deck and the tiller.

"Take this. Move it left or right as I command." The slave did as he was told, clinging to the beam as if his life depended on it. Which it did.

Once the man wrapped his arms around the tiller and began experimenting with the yield and resistance, Kratos went forward again. He stopped beside Athena's statue. It remained dead, inert, unmoving, and unseeing.

"We are on our way," he said softly into the teeth of the wind. Then he strained to lift the sea anchor that fixed them in place. His back ached with the strain, and veins stood out like cords of rope on his arms as he drew the heavy anchor up bit by bit. Once the huge iron hook had cleared the sea, the ship surged, free and floating.

"To the left, hard to the left!" His bellowed command was

swallowed by the rising wind, but the novice steersman saw him
gesturing and leaned into the tiller. Experiencing more resistance than he'd expected, the steersman redoubled his effort.
And again.

Kratos let out a howl when the ship hove to and filled its sails
with the heavy wind. Timbers creaked and the ship's keel rever-
berated as it struck underwater debris. Once, a huge wave rose
before Kratos and broke over his head. He lost his balance and
was washed along the deck until a strong hand grabbed him. He
looked up to see Coeus grinning like a fool.

"Watch yer step, Cap'n," the first mate said. Then he shouted
to those in the rigging above to lash down the sails more firmly.

Kratos got to his feet, thanking Athena for sending him one
tried-and-true seaman to assist him. A huge gust of wind seemed
to lift the ship from the water and sent it skimming the surface
at the speed of thought. The prow touched every lifting wave
and skipped forward, hardly descending into the deep troughs of
the waves.

"Ware the sails," Kratos yelled. His words were gobbled by the
hungry wind. The corners of the canvas sails began to shred
from the constant whipping. "Lash them down!"

"We need more men aloft," Coeus shouted almost in his ear.
"We're lost if we don't furl the sails. The wind's too high."

"Leave the sails as they be," Kratos shouted back. The ship
crashed into one piece of wreckage after another in the Grave of
Ships.

"The mast will break. The storm will destroy us!"

"Full sail and ahead," Kratos ordered. Coeus began to argue,
but Kratos cut him off. The steersman valiantly clung to the
tiller, but it kicked back too strongly for one man to restrain.
Kratos pushed past Coeus and rushed to aid the steersman. As
he crossed the quarterdeck, he grabbed a slave and dragged him
along.

"No, don't, let me be. We're going to die. We cannot survive
the storm. Poseidon will see us all in his watery graveyard!"

"Help the steersman keep the rudder straight ahead."

"We're going to die!" The slave fell to his knees. "By the gods, save us. I beseech you, gods of Olympus. Save us!"

"Help or get out of the way!" Kratos batted the man aside. The slave's arms rose above his head, then the gusty wind captured his body and, like a gull, he became airborne. Kratos took no notice. The man had had his chance.

"You going to heave me overboard, Cap'n? Don't think I got the strength left to fight the tiller." The steersman sagged under the strain of holding the ship on a steady course in the fierce gale.

"Only if you fail."

The tiller bucked like a thing alive, lifting the man off his feet. He clung fiercely to it, struggling for purchase. Kratos lent his strength to the task. The pair of them forced the rudder straight. Timbers creaked, and for a time Kratos thought the ship would tear itself apart.

When Zeus began sending his bolts dancing across the sky, Kratos saw gauzy lights of many colors sizzling on the spars, working up and down the mast and across the canvas, and he knew he had been given a reprieve. Athena protected him and the ship against the worst of the weather. The small globes of burning fire that did not sear were her message to him.

After what seemed to stretch to an eternity, the ship cleared the last of the hulks in the Grave of Ships and skated across open sea.

The wind remained steady, but the rain died away. Arms aching, back feeling as if it had been broken, Kratos sank to the deck.

"The sun, Captain Kratos, the sun's shining!"

"Praise Apollo," Kratos said. "Praise Athena." He felt that at least three of the gods dwelling on Mount Olympus favored him now. Poseidon had thanked him and given him special powers—and had not claimed the ship and crew for his own watery realm. For the first time since boarding this ship, Kratos knew that he would once more step onto solid land. When he did so next, it would be in service to the goddess Athena.

"Steady course," Kratos ordered.

"Even if I have to lash myself to the rudder, a straight course it'll be, Capt'n," the steersman declared. "I have a yearning for the countryside once more. The sooner we put into harbor, the sooner I can roll in the tall grass."

Kratos left the man and once more descended to Lora and Zora's cabin. He went into the cabin and closed the door behind him.

"Master," they both cried.

He was tired to the point of exhaustion, but he could only gape at the pair.

"You disobeyed me," he said. "You did not find suitable clothing." Both wore only tunics and no skirts or pants.

"We must make amends then, master," they said. "Will you punish us? Please?"

Though he did not find much rest in the bed he shared with the twins, the journey to the Harbor of Zea proved pleasant; their tender ministrations helped keep his nightmares at bay. But a full day before the great city topped the horizon, a vast column of black and swirling smoke warned him of the danger ahead.

Athens was in flames.

SIX

KRATOS STOOD in the tall tower that commanded the walls above Piraeus. From here he could see the great Long Walls that connected the port to the city of Athens, more than three miles inland. Though, as a Spartan, he considered Athenians to be weak, cowardly, and generally worthless, this day he had to give them a certain grudging respect. With only citizen soldiers to hold them, these twinned great walls still stood mostly intact. An impressive achievement, that, even against a conventional army.

Against Ares's hordes of harpies, undead legionnaires, Cyclopes, and who knew what other monstrosities scraped from the underside of Hades, the Athenians' ability to so far hold the walls was astonishing—something Kratos would not have believed if he had not seen it with his own eyes.

"It is said that the God of War, Ares himself, takes the field against us," said the exhausted, hollow-eyed captain of the tower guard. "Ghost of Sparta, is it so?"

Kratos ignored him. The last thing he needed was to give these pathetic part-time soldiers an excuse to run away. His mind was on something else that he would not have believed unless he had seen it with his own eyes; he turned to cast his gaze seaward, in hopes of catching a last glimpse of the sails of his onetime ship vanishing over the horizon.

Coeus and many of the others had proven their worth to him. Having them beside him, for only a brief instant, would not change the outcome of this battle, but it would afford the ship's new captain and crew the chance to die nobly in battle. Sailing off as they did only postponed their deaths.

Unless Ares was stopped at the walls of Athens.

And as Kratos had slipped away from the ship in the dark predawn hours, the statue of Athena at the prow spoke to him once more—to remind him that the death of Ares would earn him forgiveness for his crimes. As if he needed reminding. Athena also spoke to him of her oracle in Athens; the Oracle would tell him how to defeat the God of War.

He brought his attention once more to the battle for Athens. Ares's legions were arrayed mainly against the city itself—and not uniformly either. For some reason Kratos could not fathom, the creatures seemed to avoid the groves and grottoes that dotted the countryside around the city. Kratos shook his head, uncomprehending—putting those groves to the torch would have made more sense—but the God of War had never been known for his keen tactical mind.

Unlike Athena, who was legendary for the subtlety of her battle plans, Ares preferred to simply drive his armies forward in great waves, a rising tide of death, until they finally smashed through his enemies' defenses and slaughtered every living creature in their path.

Kratos knew this too well. For many years, he had been the one pushing the armies onward in great bloody battering rams of human flesh. For many years, he had laughed like a blood-drunk monster as his men put whole nations to the torch. And he would have been doing it still, were it not for that one little village . . . that one humble shrine to Athena . . . and those who sheltered within it.

Kratos shook himself free of the memories. Like quicksand, the madness that lurked always beneath the surface of his mind threatened to suck him down and drown him in an unrelenting nightmare.

His assessment of the tactical situation was unsentimental. Only a trickle of carts still crept up the wide road between the Long Walls. From what he'd seen in Piraeus, most of the draft animals had been already slaughtered for meat. No ships entered the harbor with fresh supplies; out past the breakwater, dozens of burning hulks sent the smoke of dead sailors toward the skies and formed a persuasive warning against daring the waters within. From the red-lit pall of smoke roiling upward from the city, Kratos guessed that Ares's creatures had found a way to hurl Greek fire over the walls—or, perhaps, simply had their harpies carry the smoldering pots and cast them to the ground from above.

Once Ares's legions breached the Long Walls, any hope of reinforcement or resupply would be lost—and, worse, those legions would have a wide paved road upon which to march against the weakest point in the defenses of the city in the hills above.

His army would march quickly and slaughter all as it went. Athens would fall, without doubt. To Kratos's practiced eye, it looked as if the city might not stand until morning.

"Athena has not abandoned us." The captain sounded as if he was trying to convince himself. "The gray-eyed goddess will break these armies—she would never allow her city to fall!"

"Hold fast to whatever courage you have," Kratos said darkly. "Athena has heard your prayer."

"She—" The captain sounded breathless with sudden hope. "What help? When will her aid arrive?"

"Today this Spartan is your Athena-sent ally," Kratos said, and vaulted through the tower's window, landing cat-footed on the wall below. Another leap took him to the road.

He fell into the ground-devouring stride he had used in the field so many times to move his soldiers into position. The Long Walls cast a cool shadow across the road. From atop them, archers fired endless volleys of arrows. Kratos had no need to see their targets; he heard them. Growls, snorts, animal noises—screeches and roars that could come from no human throat.

Kratos ran on. He saw no reason to waste time fighting for these walls, when any fool could see they'd not stand another day.

An Athenian archer, falling from one wall, crashed to the roadway a few yards ahead of Kratos. The man had a great spear sticking all the way through him, and his face had been ripped away by harpy claws, but as he hit the roadway with crushing force, he still held his bow high, protecting his weapon with the last of his strength. Kratos approved of this—the man was nearly as disciplined as a Spartan. Well, a very young Spartan. One not yet fully trained. Nonetheless, Kratos went to him, knelt, and heard the gurgle of the Athenian's last words.

"Take my bow. Defend the city!" was all the archer grated out before his spirit left to meet Charon on the bank of the Styx.

Kratos pried the bow loose from the corpse's clutches and dislodged the quiver with a dozen arrows still in it. While he preferred the Blades of Chaos or his own bare fists, Kratos was a master of all weapons. He tested the draw on the bow and let the string twang without sending an arrow on its way. The archer had been a strong man, and this weapon might prove useful.

As though summoned by his thought, shrill cries of panic came from the civilians who drove the carts ahead. Panic became agony as a whole section of the wall bowed inward, raining loose stones and falling archers. In an instant, a dozen feet of the wall had collapsed.

Without conscious thought, Kratos nocked an arrow and let it fly. His shaft flew straight to the undead legionnaire forcing its way through the breach in the wall. The arrow pinned the legionnaire's head to the part of the wall still standing. Two more undead legionnaires outfitted in bronze armor forced their way past, only to meet the same fate with an arrow apiece. The arrows didn't destroy the creatures, but pinning them to the wall like a rabbit on a spit held them in place so that even Athenians could dismember them.

"Flee," he growled at the screaming civilians. "You're in my way."

Without hesitation Kratos stepped into the breach, firing as he went. Six more arrows flew straight and true, pinning legionnaires to one another, but the undead behind them simply clawed them to pieces and kept coming. Three more arrows dispatched another five or six of them. As two more crowded through, brandishing swords, he reached for another arrow, only to find the quiver empty.

He cast the bow aside; without arrows, it was as useless as a eunuch.

The two rotting monstrosities crowding in upon him did not deserve the honor of destruction by the Blades of Chaos. Kratos simply stepped forward to meet them and drove his fists into and through their putrefying chests. His hands closed around their spines, and he shook them as though shaking filth from his hands, ripping their backbones free. As these two legionnaires collapsed, Kratos whipped their spines like flails, dispatching their fellows one after another. The archers to either side of the breach joined in, raining shaft after shaft into the monsters below.

The chains on Kratos's forearms heated up as creatures crushed in upon him. He drew the Blades of Chaos and swung them in front of his body to protect against spear thrusts. The chains burned like fire in his bones.

The blades sliced through undead flesh and littered the rubble of the wall with dismembered monsters. His twin swords flashed in fiery wheels around him, driving Ares's creatures back out through the breach—but the undead legionnaires had drawn back only to allow a Cyclops to advance.

The one-eyed monster lumbered up, three times Kratos's height and more than ten times his weight. The creature came swinging an iron-studded club so large that an ordinary man might be felled by the wind of a near miss.

The Cyclops rushed forward, eager to slay or die in the attempt. It wielded the massive club as if it were only a willow wand. Raising it high above its head in a double-handed grip, the Cyclops slammed the club straight down at the top of Kratos's head, as though trying to drive the Spartan into the ground like a fence post.

Kratos intercepted the blow with the Blades of Chaos crossed overhead. The impact drove Kratos to his knees. Briefly. An instant later, he powered himself back to his feet and sliced the blades together like pruning shears around the weapon's haft.

The end of the club exploded away like a rock from a sling.

The Cyclops let out a roar of pure disbelief. Kratos dug his toes into the scree of broken wall around him, found purchase, and hurled himself at the monster. He drove hard, ducked beneath the Cyclops's clumsy attempt to grapple, then stabbed upward with both blades, carving into its bulging belly.

The Cyclops screamed. Horribly.

Kratos twisted the blades and sliced them back within the wounds. When he finally pulled them free, they drew out entrails with them. Ducking another wild grab, Kratos dived forward to roll between the monster's legs. Behind the Cyclops, he spun and stared up the broad, hairy back. He jumped, grabbing hold of the Cyclops's leather harness straps for support and digging his toes into the creature's flesh for traction. The Cyclops screeched and thrashed about, trying to dislodge Kratos from its vulnerable back. The Ghost of Sparta kept climbing, even when the Cyclops began spinning about. Reaching the monster's neck, Kratos grabbed hold of greasy hair and reached about to repeatedly smash the hilt of a blade into the Cyclops's face. When he hit the lone orb, the Cyclops went berserk.

Kratos succeeded in grabbing the nose and finding the bulging, damaged eye. He plucked it out, viscous fluid squirting through his fingers. The Cyclops had been frantic before. Now it threw its arms high in the air, tipped its head to the sky, and roared in rage at the gods. This was Kratos's only chance to make a clean kill. As the Cyclops tilted back, Kratos struck. Feet on the creature's shoulders, he lifted the Blades of Chaos high over his head and drove the twin swords directly downward into the gaping eye socket.

Little by little, the Cyclops's powerful struggles weakened until it dropped to its knees, blood spurting from its sundered eye cavity. The Cyclops fell facedown on the ground. Only when he was sure the monster was dead did Kratos jump away from the broad back and shake blood free from his blades.

Above him on the wall, the Athenian soldiers stood stock-still, staring in openmouthed disbelief. Then one soldier let out a wild cheer. It was picked up by the others along the length of the Long Walls. "Death to the monsters!"

A full company of undead legionnaires scrambled toward Kratos, but a feathered shower of deadly shafts chopped them to bits. Again a cheer rose along the wall.

Kratos had begun edging for the hole in the wall when he saw what now moved to face him—wraiths, emaciated monsters whose bony arms ended in wickedly sharp blades. From the waist down, their bodies were nothing more than swirling black smoke. They floated toward him with deceptive ease, then surged forward to attack. Barely did Kratos have time to unleash the Blades of Chaos to defend himself. The wraiths coordinated their attack perfectly, circling him and attacking first from the left, then the right.

Arrows from above did nothing to drive back these creatures. Shafts passed completely, harmlessly, through them, as though their bodies were no more than smoke.

With a blinding flourish of his Hades-forged weapons, Kratos lopped off one bladed hand, but the other wraiths pressed in around him. He defended himself ably as he backed into the breach; the best way to face these creatures was one at a time.

"By the gods, we will stop them!" A squad of swordsmen rushed to Kratos's assistance, banging their weapons against bronze shields. Their courage far outstripped their skill, but they could take some pressure off him, even against the wraiths.

"Close the gap," Kratos shouted, engaging a bladed hand before deftly cutting it from the skeletal wrist. "You cannot defend this breach for long." And wraiths were starting to hack away at the ragged edges of the wall to make a larger hole. If it got much larger, the Athenians couldn't hold it at all—and Kratos didn't want to have to guard his own back as he ran for the city.

"I don't recognize you," said a young soldier, coming up behind. "Why aren't you in armor?"

"Send for engineers, fool!" Kratos snarled. "If the monsters take this breach, Athens's belly lies exposed!"

The young warrior began barking orders, and the other Athenians seemed relieved to have someone tell them what to do. The soldiers nearest forced their way into the breach, making a wall of their shields and their own bodies to keep back the Hades-spawned hordes. Others dragged heavy timbers, rubble, and anything at all they could use as a barricade to pile at the hole, but to Kratos it was clear this was futile. The pressure against a handful of men was too great, and no permanent repair could be made with wraiths and legionnaires constantly hacking to enlarge the gap.

The last of the Athenians at the breach fell to undead archers. A half dozen burst through, unleashing fire arrows wildly in all directions; each one that struck true exploded in a burst of flame and took an Athenian life. Kratos unleashed the Blades of Chaos once more and took out two of the skeletal creatures before they could create more havoc along the aerial walkways. The rest of the undead archers concentrated their fire on the fresh soldiers racing to plug the hole. They were devastatingly effective. By the time Kratos had killed the archers at the gap, the wraiths beyond had widened the hole enough for another Cyclops to barrel through.

Kratos plunged forward to meet the monster's charge. Using his preternatural strength, he lifted the Cyclops from its feet and drove it back through the breach, into the wraiths and undead legionnaires outside. The Cyclops cleared its way with a few swings of its immense club, knocking undead to pieces and sending wraiths flipping through the air, then strode forward to again vie with Kratos. New legionnaires pushed forward to continue chipping away at the wall, widening the breach with each blow.

Kratos judged his distance, then launched a long thrust with both blades. He slashed the Cyclops's throat on either side, then pulled back hard, hooking the curves of the blades behind the creature's neck. As the blades ripped free, the Cyclops's head flipped from its shoulders, bounced on the ground, and rolled past Kratos's feet. A fountain of blood shot skyward from the creature's neck, and Kratos lifted his face to the scarlet shower as though it were cool spring rain. He plucked the unseeing eye out and held it high over his head, then heaved it in defiance at Ares's advancing minions.

"More!" he shouted at the horde outside. "Come on! Come and die!"

One hard kick toppled the swaying bulk of the dead monster across the breach, creating a barricade over which the attacking creatures had to scramble. The archers on the wall above took a terrible toll as feathered shafts pinned legionnaires to the fallen Cyclops and to one another.

Before, his victory had been cheered. Now there was no time. A pair of Cyclopes moved up to the breach and began tossing aside undead legionnaires from the growing pile, clearing the way for more monsters, while wraiths floated overhead, their ghastly blades carving nearby archers into bloody chunks of meat.

Kratos again made a grim assessment of the odds. He did not know how Athena hoped he might save her city, but he was reasonably sure she did not intend he should give his life over one small gap more than a mile from the city proper.

He sheathed the Blades of Chaos and stared at his hands. Power welled up within as he unleashed his anger, and Kratos felt himself become the conduit for godlike power once more. The Rage of Poseidon was with him still.

Pushing through the struggling fighters, he climbed atop the dead Cyclops and looked at the hundreds and thousands of

Ares's killers readying themselves to pour through the ever-widening hole in the wall. Kratos held out his hands, as if to push them all away. He staggered as the power built within him. Lifting his hands, elbows locked, he closed his eyes and concentrated on what he wanted most.

Annihilating energy erupted around him, plowing a fifty-foot furrow deeper than a moat in front of him. Kratos spread his hands outward, and the furrow became a crater. He directed the Rage of Poseidon downward, outward, then downward a final time before he sank to his knees in exhaustion from the effort.

The corpse of the Cyclops was gone, burned so thoroughly there was not even smoke—as were the other Cyclopes, all the nearby wraiths, several hundred undead legionnaires, some few yards of the Long Walls and a number of the Athenian archers.

Between him and the remainder of Ares's army gaped a pit a hundred feet deep and almost as wide. To reach the gap now, the horde outside faced a long descent and a perilous scramble up a steep slope slippery with ash, fully exposed to archers above.

The monsters seemed undeterred; they were already sliding down the far rim of the pit. Even if they had to fill the entire crater with their own bodies, soon these misbegotten creatures would flood through the wall in their thousands upon thousands. Nothing could stop them.

Kratos drew the Blades of Chaos and settled into himself, grimly waiting at the breach.

This was going to be a long fight.

SEVEN

UNDEAD LEGIONNAIRES TRAMPED ALONG a game trail in the still forest, weapons clanging against their sides with every step. Some carried scythes and others swung spiked clubs as they made their way to support the rear echelons of the force attacking the breach in the Long Wall. The leader slowed and then raised a bony limb to halt his patrol.

Bushes rustled. The legionnaires turned toward the sound and drew weapons, but from behind them a large gray wolf leaped, snarling at the leader as it knocked the legionnaire to the ground. Strong jaws closed on a bony neck and crushed it, ripping away the undead head. As the wolf turned to do the same to the next, its savage growls called the rest of the pack to come loping out of the forest in their ambush. The creatures from Hades tried to defend themselves, but these wolves fought with a cunning and ferocity that would astonish any huntsman. Some of the skeletal beings could only jerk and twitch as their legs were gnawed off. Others threw knives and axes and even swords at the wolves, but the sleek gray killers slipped aside, then returned to match their jaws against the bony talons of the disarmed undead. Shortly, "disarmed" was no longer a figure of speech.

Quiet descended on the forest once again as the wolf pack melted away, prowling their territory in search of new victims, and two goddesses materialized at the scene of the slaughter.

Athena said, "Your creatures fight well."

Artemis squinted skyward, measuring the soar of eagles and the slow wheel of vultures. "The birds speak to me of new incursions," she said. "Our brother is slow to learn."

"So let us offer further lessons without delay," Athena said. "Though all the wolves in the world would not be enough to destroy his army, we can at least keep him from your groves."

The huntress favored her with a piercing stare. "We?"

Before Athena could respond, Artemis vanished. Athena sighed and with a brief gesture followed her to a large glade filling with Ares's soldiers. The monsters milled about in considerable disarray. The creatures who held the place of officers bellowed and screeched, trying to organize them into something resembling battle order. As they began their march across the glade, Artemis pointed to the tree line not fifty feet from their flank.

"There."

An enormous bull elk broke from the underbrush, lowered its antlers, and charged square into the ranks of the skeletal archers. Its rack speared four of them, and a toss of its head sent fragments of undead flying. The elk bellowed and turned to attack again, but the remaining archers now had arrows to their strings. A dozen bows thrummed as one, and the flaming arrows detonated deep within the chest of the mighty beast. It staggered, fell to its knees, and died.

Before it could even hit the ground, wolf packs broke from cover on all sides, striking deep into the archers' formation as they struggled to draw new shafts. Fangs ripped rotting flesh, and jaws crushed exposed bones. But a monstrous crashing and splintering of trees heralded the arrival of a new threat.

"Cyclopes—too many of them," Athena said, a cautionary

hand upon her sister's arm. "They are dangerous even to my Kratos. Your wolves cannot stand against them."

"They don't have to."

Some ten of the great Cyclopes came forward, their mighty war clubs shattering whole trees. The largest of them took the lead, thundering toward the wolves—but before it had crossed even half the distance, it stiffened, its eye rolled up, and it pitched suddenly onto its face.

"Fur and antler are far from my subjects' deadliest weapons," Artemis said with dark satisfaction. "Vipers can bring down even the Cyclopes."

"So I see."

As the other great brutes hesitated, unsure of their path now that their leader lay dead, the sky filled with an eagle's angry screech. Dropping like arrows from the heavens, the great golden raptors plunged toward Cyclopean eyes, slashing with extended talons. A few tosses of the beak ripped away gobbets of bloody flesh from the surrounding faces; then the birds took wing again.

"Now we drive them," Artemis said. She pointed to the spot in the forest where a trio of huge bears lumbered forth. As the wolves kept away the legionnaires and other undead, the bears attacked the remaining Cyclopes with gore-caked claws.

Ares's army began to dissolve as fear seized the creatures. Packs of wolves, charging bucks, the bears and eagles and snakes all combined to herd the monsters toward the Long Walls.

"Artemis, my sister," said Athena, "you are as good as your word. My Athenians should now be able to—"

"Shhh." Artemis tensed. With a gesture she summoned her bow; another gesture produced a golden shaft, nocked and ready to draw. "Hide."

Athena frowned. "Hide from what?"

Within an instant, the heavens were ripped asunder and Ares stepped through, so huge the flames of his hair might set the clouds afire.

Athena reflected that her sister's instincts were as accurate as her arrows and decided to take Artemis's advice. A graceful swipe of her hand drew mist around her . . . and when the mist evaporated, she was nowhere to be seen.

Ares didn't even notice. He scowled down upon the panicking mob his army had become. "*What is wrong with you?*"

The god's voice shook the very earth. He reached down and, in one titanic hand, swept up bears and elk and wolves alike. "*Animals? Mere* animals *drive you like* cattle? *Let me show you how to deal with animals!*"

His fist closed and began to clench.

Artemis said, "Don't."

Ares flinched as if he'd been stung, but only for an instant. Then his natural belligerence flared once more. "*Who dares give orders to the God of War?*"

Artemis stepped out of the tree cover, still only human size, her bow bent and her bowstring against her cheek as she sighted along her arrow. "Very gently, my brother. Very gently return my creatures to the ground."

Ares snorted down from a dozen times her height. "*Why should I?*"

"My grip is not as sure as it once was," Artemis said calmly. "I would hate to have to explain to our father how my fingers slipped when my arrow was aimed in the direction of your face."

"*You wouldn't dare. The Word of Zeus forbids—*"

"Killing," Artemis finished for him. "From this angle, an arrow in your eye would do little more than inconvenience you. I shouldn't imagine you'll be half blind for more than a decade or two."

"*You would aid that treacherous bitch Athena against me?*"

"I would," Artemis said, without the faintest flicker of an eyelid, "defend my realm and its creatures. Set those down, and be on your way."

"*You won't attack me. You can't. Not while I threaten only mortals.*" His fist tightened until gore ran from between his fingers. "*I can crush every one of these woodland beasts, and you can't give me so much as an itch.*"

"You turn your hand against my creatures." Artemis lowered the aim of her bow. "Witness how I turn my hand against yours."

She released her arrow, which shot from her bow more swiftly than lightning—and before it could strike, another arrow appeared and was released. So many arrows flew so swiftly that the glade seemed filled with a golden haze that buzzed and snarled like a nest of angry hornets.

After that single instant, Artemis lowered her bow and looked up at Ares. "So?"

The God of War looked down upon his army. Every once-living creature of his in that glade lay dead; every undead creature was mutilated beyond recognition. The wolves and bears and elk stood untouched. For a long moment, the only sound was the mocking cry of a distant eagle.

At length, Ares said, *"Perhaps I have been hasty."*

"Perhaps."

"And if my legions and I leave your woodlands in peace?"

"Then my creatures and I have no reason to attack yours."

"Done, then."

"Yes," said the Huntress of the Gods. "Done."

Athena, lurking invisibly just within the tree line, shook her head with a disappointed sigh. She hated it when her family members forged a peace, even if Ares and Artemis would violate it at the merest provocation. Still, her mission to Artemis was far from a total loss. This forest skirmish should have taken enough pressure off the Long Wall that Kratos could move on into the city. Slaying monsters was all well and good—not to mention moderately entertaining—but it didn't actually *get* him anywhere.

Athena took a deep breath, savoring the pine and earth scents. She closed her eyes and let herself go into a light trance, enabling her foresight to fill her mind with glimpses of the future. She gasped and her eyes flew open at what she foresaw. Coldness settled, and she realized that even had Artemis and the powerful Lord of the Ocean, Poseidon, joined her in opposing the God of War, they would have failed.

Ares had become too powerful—and increasingly insane. The very pillars of Olympus would be turned to rubble by his actions. And there was nothing she could do, because Zeus would never rescind his decree against one god killing another. She saw that while she and the rest of Olympus, including the Skyfather himself, were so bound, Ares would not obey.

Ambition and insanity made for a deadly mixture. If she could not kill Ares, Kratos must. But how? How could any mortal kill a god? Kratos had to reach the Oracle. It was the only way the answer would be revealed, for the Oracle's power was such that she could give Kratos knowledge hidden even from the gods themselves. Athena hoped that this would be enough—it *had* to be.

This accomplished, she turned about and with a breath of will sent herself once more to Olympus, passing through her own chambers to step forth into the Hall of Eternity. It was necessary that Kratos receive another gift of power if he was to get to the Oracle.

Mere paces along the hall brought her to an archway hung with scented diaphanous veils. She pushed through into a sybarite's delight of erotic architecture and seductive decoration. No matter the direction, mirrors of bronze, brass, and silver reflected images even more flattering than her favorite mirror in her own chamber. A pool of lilac-scented water extending along a low bed provided a different degree of reflection.

"Welcome, Athena," came the soft, sensual greeting, as gentle and inviting as a lover's caress.

"Lady Aphrodite." Athena bowed deeply in the direction of the tapestry to her right, which depicted humans and gods copulating in half a hundred ways; this was the best bet for where the Goddess of Love might be hiding. They had a tense relationship, the Goddess of Sex and the virgin warrior, complicated by the somewhat uncertain nature of their familial connection.

Aphrodite had been born from the genitals of Ouranos, when his son Cronos—Zeus's father—had ripped them from the elder god's crotch and thrown them in the Mediterranean. The drops of blood had become the Furies—which to Athena had always made considerable sense—and the organ itself had been reborn as the infinitely desirable goddess. Being born from the sea foam, Aphrodite in one sense could be considered not to be part of the family at all, except by marriage—as she was wed to Athena's brother Hephaestus. The goddess might be considered only Athena's sister-in-law.

However, she had also been born as the result of an act by Cronos, which in a sense made her a sister of Zeus, Poseidon, and Hades. Which meant that she would be due considerably greater deference.

Finally, she had actually been incarnated from the penis of Ouranos, Zeus's grandfather, which made her Zeus's aunt.

Aphrodite herself refused to clarify the complicated genealogy. For her part, Athena avoided the lust goddess whenever possible. Athena's guile was markedly different from Aphrodite's.

The Tapestry of Infinite Coitus stirred and Aphrodite emerged from behind it, warming the room with her beauty. Indeed, all Olympus took on a softer, more sultry glow. "From your tone," said Aphrodite, "I sense this is not a casual call, nor do you visit on business of my particular realm."

Athena nodded. "I bring sad news."

"Does this please you so that you cannot send Hermes?" Aphrodite lowered herself onto the seductively padded couch and lay along it languidly. "Hermes was . . . recently here . . . and he mentioned nothing."

"Perhaps other concerns distracted him," Athena said, knowing full well what Aphrodite and the Messenger of the Gods had been up to. The Messenger of the Gods was a frequent visitor to Aphrodite's chambers, and it was known he brought the goddess more than news.

"Are you suggesting that mere pleasures of the flesh might distract him from his duties?"

"I suggest nothing," Athena said innocently. "This young couple, whom you have lately had so much pleasure instructing—"

"In Mycenae?"

Athena thought, *Why not?* She'd had no one specifically in mind but knew Aphrodite's attentions might be lavished on thousands of such lovers at any given time. "There is a rumor they might have offended Medusa with their amorous activities," she said, thinking, *A rumor I have just invented, but a rumor nonetheless.* "It is possible she has vowed to turn to stone not only them but *all* your disciples—and perhaps your Olympian self."

"Medusa is hardly a threat." Aphrodite waved a dismissive hand. "She's just a vicious old hag."

"Not a hag but a Gorgon," Athena corrected. "She may be intending to destroy all who would devote themselves to your . . . pleasurable ways."

"You are still *angry* at her," Aphrodite said teasingly. "Still haven't forgiven her for her rendezvous with Poseidon in your temple over by Carthage?"

"My uncle's trysts are of no concern to me."

"Concern? No. But surprise, yes." Aphrodite gave Athena a decidedly naughty smirk. "Oh, if you only knew how many times—and *places*—he and I have—"

"Medusa is the issue," Athena said, with a slicing gesture, as though her hand might be a sword that could sever that line of conversation. "She may be a terrible danger to your worshippers."

"Why would she bother? She and her sisters are limited in their release."

"Limited to the blind, yes. Otherwise, they would turn their lovers into stone with a careless glance. But anger builds over the centuries. It has reached the point of consuming Medusa as she makes you the focus of her ire."

"I will speak with her. We can—"

"Wait, Aphrodite. There is more. She would harm you. Her rage is that great. You have lost many followers recently." Once more Athena made a calculated guess. In Athens she had lost hundreds of worshippers in only a day. War always caused upheaval and death. Aphrodite would be similarly encumbered

with her followers' deaths, even if they came at Ares's bidding
rather than Medusa's.

"She cannot. Zeus would punish her severely if she tried."

"You would be in no position to enjoy her penalty if you were
forever consigned to the underworld."

Aphrodite paced as she thought. Athena paid her little attention, being engrossed in her own image within image stretching
to infinity in the mirrors. Aphrodite with a lover would be excit-
ing. Athena had taken no lover, but the sight of herself alone
was enough to suggest what gratification might be gained in a
room such as this.

"I cannot kill Medusa, nor can you. Zeus forbids such squab-
bles."

Athena almost laughed. Aphrodite called the offer to kill another god a mere "squabble."

"That is so, but nothing says a mortal cannot kill a Gorgon."

"It's never been done."

"That does not mean it cannot be done, using the right instrument of destruction."

Aphrodite shook her head and said, "No, no, this isn't right.
To be the force behind Medusa's death is wrong. We can work
out our differences, whatever she might think them to be."

"Medusa is jealous of your beauty," Athena said. "She yearns
for a lover—any lover—as skillful as one you might accept into
your bed for one night only." Athena lowered her voice to a con-
spiratorial whisper. "She thinks you have stolen Hermes from
her."

Aphrodite laughed harshly.

"Hermes sleeps where he pleases." A small smile flicked on
her face. "He is always welcome in these chambers, but I cannot
imagine him bedding Medusa, even blindfolded."

"Beauty inspires Hermes. Ugliness certainly offends him.
Medusa blames you for his natural inclinations."

"How can she demand that he go against his nature?"
Aphrodite said. "That would introduce evil into the world,
where there should be only love."

"Such is her jealousy, such is her wickedness." Athena saw that Aphrodite stood a little straighter as resolve hardened the goddess's heart.

"I cannot bear the thought of Hermes being in danger from a Gorgon."

"And I cannot endure for a moment longer the knowledge that Medusa plots against you, dear Aphrodite. Let me tell you what we can do. . . ."

Athena left Aphrodite soon after, sure that Kratos's character would be tempered even more and his skills sharpened to perfection before the final battle with Ares—if he could reach the Oracle and discover the method to kill a god.

EIGHT

KRATOS CLIMBED ATOP a pile of dead bodies to look over the repair work being completed on the wall. The engineers had placed sturdy cross members against the wall, then had driven posts deep into the ground to hold them in place. It was crude but provided a barrier to keep Ares's minions from flooding into the roadway. As long as he didn't have to worry about those skeletal archers coming up behind him, Kratos could safely head for the city again. Without a word to the defenders nearby, Kratos sprang down the roadway and ran for the city.

Night fell upon Athens. The vast columns of smoke now swirled and spun, lit only by the fires below, and through the haze Kratos would occasionally glimpse Ares himself, large as a mountain, towering over the Acropolis. It was from the god's own hand that the Greek fire flew, great flaming gobbets that he cast at random around the city.

The roadway began to fill with refugees, civilians clutching whatever was most precious to them, fleeing the city while they still could to allow the soldiers the best chance to fortify and de-fend it. Every few hundred yards, the crowds became thick enough to impede his progress—but the impediment was momentary, because Kratos simply cut his way through with the Blades of Chaos. Bloody refugee body parts flew to either side of the Spartan as he ran, and any Athenians who witnessed such a slaughter wisely pressed out of Kratos's way.

Kratos spared not an instant's thought for these unfortunates. He wasn't here to save the civilians—and the Blades of Chaos could drink innocent lives as easily as those of opponents. The surge in his strength from each murder let him run ever faster, until he might have been wearing the winged sandals of Hermes himself.

The heavy black smoke took on a more noxious odor as he neared the ruined gate of the city. The memory of burning corpses could never be erased from his brain. After so many battles, digging graves had been impossible; there were always more dead than there were shovels and men to use them. Kratos had ordered the bodies stacked and set ablaze. The funeral pyre for one had become the pyre of hundreds, and so it was for many years.

The gates of the city lay in shattered ruin. Some few civilians picked their way through the rubble, but more Arean fire rained down upon them; their screams were brief, and soon they became extensions of the pyre. Only the guardhouse remained intact, though it seemed abandoned. As Kratos passed, however, a voice cried from the shadowed window, "You there! Halt!"

The voice was thin and wheezy, and when Kratos turned to look, he found one bent and wizened man, barely strong enough to stand upright in his armor. "State your . . . State . . . Uh, what are you doing here?"

"I seek Athena's oracle, old man. "

The ancient guardsman peered at him myopically. "The Oracle? What for?"

"Where is she?" Kratos asked with as much patience as he could muster.

"She's got a room in the Parthenon, on the east side of the Acropolis, but . . ." The old man shook his head woefully. "That area's on fire. Whole place is on fire. Oracle might be dead. No one has seen her since the fighting began. Once she told me my own future, d'you know that? Now, this was a long time ago. I had to sacrifice—"

Kratos successfully stifled a sudden urge to lop off the old fool's head. He growled, "How do I get to the Acropolis?"

"Well . . . you can't go through here."

"What?"

"I got my orders from the commander of the watch, just before the gate was knocked down by one of them fireballs. Nobody enters through this gate, what's left of it, that is." The old man held a dagger in one quivering hand. "Besides, what d'you want to go in there for? The place is lousy with undead, there's Cyclopes and worse—and I even seen a Minotaur too!"

Kratos shook his head, thinking of the fight down at the Long Wall. More wasted effort. Ares's army was already inside the city.

He left the old man babbling to himself and sprinted into dark streets illuminated only by distant unchecked fires.

RUNNING THROUGH THE DARKENING CITY, Kratos cursed himself for a fool, even as the Blades of Chaos sang their crimson song through countless bodies of Ares's minions. Undead legionnaires flew to pieces so quickly that none broke Kratos's stride. Skeletal archers fired flaming shafts as he passed, but none even grazed him. He nimbly sidestepped raging Cyclopes and dissipated ghostly wraiths with hardly more than a gesture.

And all for nothing. Just as the slaughter he had meted out at the Long Wall's breach had been for nothing.

Ares's army had attacked the wall in the first place not to gain access to the city but because that was where the soldiers were. Ares's legions lived only to kill. If Athenian soldiers had made a stand down at Piraeus, that's where those abominations would have attacked. They never needed to cross the walls at all. As

Kratos ran, more foes sprang from the earth itself, as though some impossible netherworld had opened the gates of reality to spew its spawn onto Athenian streets.

Kratos cursed himself for fighting them as if they were human.

He no longer paused to slay them. Why bother? Athens and its people could not be protected by the destruction of Ares's army—the god's army could not be destroyed. Like dragon's teeth, each beast Kratos might slay could be recreated on any spot, at any instant. Killing them did nothing but feed power to the blades—power that he didn't need. To Hades with fighting. He would seek the Oracle, learn her secret, and then be on his way.

As he should have done from the beginning.

From around a corner ahead, he heard snorts and growls and the voices of men shrieking like little children. Soon two Athenian soldiers came in view, running full tilt, their weapons and shields forgotten. They screamed to Kratos that he must *run, they're right behind us*! A heartbeat later, Kratos discovered what they were fleeing: a towering creature with the head and hooves of a great bull and the body of a man.

The Minotaur—the Cretan monster supposedly slain by Theseus. Kratos snorted. Why should he be surprised to find the creature alive?

Theseus had been Athenian.

The Minotaur wielded an enormous labris—the double-faced ax of Crete, its blade alone the size of a man and twice as heavy. The great beast raised the labris high overhead and, with a mighty heave, hurled it spinning through the thickening gloom.

One of the soldiers, looking fearfully over his shoulder, saw the blade coming and ducked aside. The other never looked back. The first he learned of the flying ax was when it lopped his head off in one clean slice and whirled on without even slowing. It sang through the air, spinning straight at Kratos's face.

Kratos judged the distance and the spin, then took one step

forward so that the haft of the swirling ax, instead of the gore-smeared blade, smacked his palm. It struck with enough force to kill an ordinary man. Kratos didn't even blink.

"*Run!*" the remaining soldier screamed as he sprinted past. "*You have to run!*"

"Spartans," Kratos replied with scalding contempt, "run *toward* the enemy."

The Minotaur gave a snort, lowered his wide-spreading horns, and charged.

Kratos hefted the labris. "You'll be wanting this back," he said, and hurled it at the charging monster, who pulled up short, snarling, and attempted to duplicate Kratos's feat. The Minotaur discovered this was trickier than it had looked.

The Minotaur misjudged the ax's spin by half a step: The blade sheared through its hand, through its nose and on through its brainpan, before whirling on to vanish in the smoky gloom.

The half-headless corpse stood swaying. Kratos lifted the severed head of the Athenian soldier and hurled it like a rock. The head struck the monster's chest and knocked the great beast flat.

Kratos sneered down at the dead soldier. As he passed the corpse of the Minotaur, he shook his head and snorted with contempt.

Theseus. Some hero. Only Athenians would make a hero of a man for slaying such a paltry little beast. Good thing Kratos wasn't here to save the people; he couldn't stand to look at them.

Before he reached the corner, however, he discovered that he had made a mistake. It had not been *the* Minotaur; it had been only *a* Minotaur. The truth of this was revealed to him by the appearance of three more of the towering man–bulls, thundering toward him with axes raised.

Kratos grimly drew the Blades of Chaos without slackening his pace. Another senseless delay. He'd make better time off the streets.

The three Minotaurs spread out to bar his path, but a headlong sprint faster than the gallop of a racing horse gave Kratos the momentum he needed. A dozen strides short of the monsters, Kratos hurled one Blade of Chaos high, where it whipped over the lip of the nearest balcony. The chain snapped tight and yanked him into the air, over the heads of the astonished Minotaurs. He flipped the other blade at a higher balcony and in this fashion swung himself all the way up to the rooftops.

From here, he could clearly see the Parthenon and beyond it the sky-spanning figure of the God of War, who still hurled handfuls of fiery slag into the city below.

Even that momentary pause was enough for Ares's minions to locate him again. Flocks of harpies swooped toward his rooftop, wraiths floated through nearby walls, and the building trembled as Minotaurs and Cyclopes scaled its walls.

"Ares!" Kratos roared his challenge, brandishing the undying fire of the Blades of Chaos.

The mountain of war god swiveled eyes like bloody full moons in his direction. Behind his beard of flames, Ares's lip curled in a cruel smile as he raised a burning hand high enough to scorch the clouds. He hurled a ball of fire larger than the entire building on which Kratos stood. As the blazing missile seemed to expand with alarming speed, Kratos had an instant to wonder if perhaps overweening pride had made him hasty in attracting the war god's attention.

He gave a mighty leap out from among the crowd of his enemies, reached a wall of a taller building nearby, and kicked off again, hurtling high over a broad plaza. He struck a great broken pillar and clung to it for an instant, glancing back at the rooftop from whence he'd come. What he saw gave him pause.

The whole building was a mass of flame; harpies screeched, Cyclopes howled, and Minotaurs bellowed as they burned. Then it was his turn to cry out as a gobbet of the gelatinous fire ran the length of his back. His grip slackened, and he slipped down and then tumbled to the street in agony. Twisting from side to side, trying to roll as if mere flames devoured his flesh, did no good.

More flame roared toward him, and the plaza below filled with monsters. With supreme effort, teeth clenched against the never-ending burning on his back, Kratos hurled himself on-ward. Toward the Parthenon. Toward the Temple of Athena. Pain could never slow the Ghost of Sparta. He stumbled on, toward the Oracle—and the secret of killing a god.

KRATOS RAN WHEN HE COULD, the pain abating some-what in his back, and killed when he had to; he stumbled through the streets, over the rooftops, and even waded the labyrinthine sewers connecting endless catacombs. Although the sewage burned worse than he thought he could endure without dying, by the time Kratos emerged, Ares's touch on his back had diminished. The skin felt taut-crisp. But he could still move, still fight when he had to. Finally, after what felt like days, he reached the broad avenue leading up the Acropolis to the Parthenon—and there he faced a new challenge.

The roadway was patrolled by Centaurs. Wild and untam-able, these gigantic man–horse monstrosities had a reputation for fierceness in battle that Kratos already knew was well founded. He had faced these creatures before and always found them formidable opponents.

But they never lived long. None who faced the Ghost of Sparta ever did.

The one nearest spotted him through the smoke. Bellowing its war cry, it reared and spun to face him, then without hesita-tion it charged.

Kratos widened his stance and waited.

Hooves pounding, the Centaur raced directly for him. Kratos realized he could not outrun the creature, not with the skin on his back cracking and giving new torment with every move-ment. He judged the distance and then dodged at the last possi-ble instant. Like all four-legged animals, shifting to the side during attack was impossible, once committed. Kratos let the man–horse race past. Unlike other four-legged animals, how-ever, the Centaur possessed the ability to swing its upper body about.

And this one did. Spear stabbing, it almost impaled Kratos. Only a quick parry with his blade prevented a vicious stab wound to Kratos's side.

The man–horse tried to dig in its hind hooves to stop so it could rear and twist about, but Centaurs could not turn to face the opposite direction of attack quickly. Kratos used this to his advantage. He attacked while the Centaur's weight pinned its rear hooves to the ground. If it had tried to kick him like a mule, Kratos's attack would have failed.

He arched up over the man–horse's back, Blades of Chaos swinging in wide circles of death. Either of the swords would have killed the Centaur. His right blade burrowed deep into the neck, while his left raked along the man–horse's side and streamed sundered guts out onto the city square.

Kratos lost his balance, slipped in the Centaur's blood, and fell heavily atop the corpse. For long minutes he could only lie in the puddle. He forced himself to his feet and stretched after recovering a bit of his usual power, though his movement was restricted by the skin taut as a drum's head on his back. He surveyed the area. It was as he feared: Ares had infiltrated many of his army into the city. Two more Centaurs galloped to attack him.

One Centaur held a huge spear tucked like a lance under its corded arm; the other swung an iron weight at the end of a long chain. As they bore down on him, Kratos dropped low. The chain and ball swung harmlessly over his head, but the spear stung his forearm—only the chain embedded in flesh and bonded to bone saved him from losing the hand. But even the powerful impact of the slash did not slow his counterstrike. If he had been whole, if his muscles and powerful back had responded as they should, his aim would have been perfect. Instead, he missed and the Centaur flashed past, unscathed by his blades. Kneeling like a penitent, he whipped the Blades of Chaos out to his sides, backhanded, and sheared through the nearside front leg of each Centaur. The beasts fell forward and skidded along, leaving bloody smears on the pavement. Kratos stood and, with one more flick of the blades, slashed their heads from their bodies.

He shook the gore from his blades as he looked about for new enemies—new victims—but found only flames and carnage. Fires sprouted like unholy weeds, devouring the city.

He started back up the road to the Parthenon, each step stronger than the one before. The Blades of Chaos, in taking life, nourished him and allowed regeneration. Stiffness remained in his back as a reminder of the foolhardiness of taunting a god. Kratos used his blades at times as walking sticks to help him up the increasingly steep road. The soldier had said Athena's oracle was in a temple near the majestic structure, which now stood blackened with soot and lit by the burning city below.

Kratos heard a rising-whistle sound he knew too well. In an eyeblink, he had thrown himself into a headlong dive that cleared a low wall one instant before another of the god's fireballs splashed liquid flame throughout the neighborhood. A wave of fire broke over him, and he ran deeper into the courtyard, seeking cover under the tiled eaves. One touch of such anguish was all he could endure. He found a half-full fountain choked with weeds. He leaped into it and rolled in the damply rotting muck. The stagnant water smelled of dead fish, but it smothered the last of the burning gel that had clung to his skin.

"By the gods," he said, gritting his teeth as a final wave of pain passed through him. Then he stood and knew he could fight on. For honor, for Athena—and because it was all he knew.

Returning to the paved street revealed only new obstacles. Fireball after fireball blasted all the roadways leading to the summit, making of them rivers of flame. As if he had divined Kratos's destination, Ares closed every path.

Kratos cursed and threw himself once more into a sprint. He moved to circle the Acropolis—there must be some gap in the war god's ring of fire.

His new energy took him into a quieter section of Athens, one that so far had escaped the worst of the destruction. People peered fearfully from windows as he passed, but no one lay dead in the street, though this was merely temporary; on the far side of the neighborhood, he met an undead patrol.

The skeletal horrors stalked the roadways, swinging scythes that looked as though they could slice through the columns of the Parthenon itself. And these particular creatures, Kratos noted, wore armor—armor that was blackened with soot but showed no other evidence of fire. Armor that could protect the undead from Ares's fires was exactly what he needed.

He fell in behind the well-armored skeletons and increased his speed, closing quickly. Some unholy instinct must have warned the creatures of his swift approach. They spun about, the long, wickedly sharp blades of their death scythes angled to taste Spartan blood. He blocked the swing of the nearest with his left blade. Sparks and flame exploded like the green pine in a campfire. He swung around to the creature's flank, keeping it—and its armor—between him and its companions.

Legionnaires crowded around him, hacking again and again; Kratos was too busy blocking to counter—especially because he didn't want to damage their armor, which was after all the only reason they were worth fighting.

The clash of weapons sent showers of flame in all directions. The house at Kratos's back caught fire. He ignored this; he saw an opening for attack. In one motion he released the Blades of Chaos and leaped forward to seize the haft of the nearest undead's scythe. Flames from the burning house began to blister his exposed, tortured back.

He *needed* that armor.

Instead of wresting the weapon from the creature's grasp, Kratos used his leverage to swing the undead bodily into the attacks from the others. Death scythes bit deeply through the creature's torso, and in the instant their weapons were hung up by their comrade's body, Kratos reached back and drew the Blades of Chaos once more. One lethal flourish, and undead heads fell like catapult stones. The bodies continued to jerk and wave their weapons convulsively, but the loss of their heads left them blind: easy prey.

Kratos dissected them with brisk efficiency, hacking off the arms and legs, leaving only the torsos. These undead, though, were no Spartans—it would take at least three of their corselets to make one sized for Kratos's massive chest. Kicking away severed parts, he picked out the least-damaged corselet, unfastened it, and then strapped it across his back; another, only slightly more ripped, he belted over his front. The coverage was imperfect, but then, he wasn't going to use it to defend himself against Ares's monstrous legions, only against the killing heat of the war god's fire.

A shrug of his shoulders settled the armor in the best fit he could achieve, but before he could once more search for a way to the summit, he saw another undead enter a house.

He'd fastened the armor barely in time when two more legionnaires attacked—and these held out magic shields. Kratos let out a cry of rage as he retaliated. The Blades of Chaos bounced off the shield of the lead undead and caused Kratos to stagger back. This instant of unbalance provided the opening for both legionnaires. Holding their gold-glowing shields high, they charged.

Kratos fought for his life. More than providing protection from his Blades of Chaos, those shields drained his strength. Every blow he landed sapped his power. Kratos retreated until his back pressed into a ragged stone wall. The two legionnaires parted slightly to come at him from different angles. With a loud scream of rage, Kratos launched himself directly forward, between the shields. Somersaulting, he came to his feet and reversed positions. He now had the undead backed against the wall.

He still faced swords wielded from behind shields impervious—detrimental!—to his own magic blades. Kratos dropped his Blades of Chaos and allowed them to snake behind his back as he dived low. The undead he targeted lowered the magic-blazing shield, but Kratos had anticipated this and twisted at the last possible instant. The shield exploded with eye-dazzling fury as it crashed into the ground. Kratos strained, his fingers wrapping around the undead's ankle.

Against the wall, the legionnaire could not retreat. Kratos squeezed as hard as he could and crushed the undead's leg. It stabbed at him with its spear. Kratos ignored the pain as the spear tip penetrated his arm, but the point did not sink deeply. The chains from the Blades of Chaos protected him from real damage.

Kratos grunted, lifted, and upended the undead before its companion could rush him from behind. A stomp to the head ended the threat from the fallen legionnaire. Kratos ducked as the other thrust at him. The spear dug into the stone wall, giving Kratos yet another opportunity. Getting past the enervating magic shield was impossible, so he caught the one dropped by his first foe. He spun it like a discus into the legionnaire struggling to pull its spear from the wall.

The magical edge severed the undead's legs and brought it crashing down to join its companion. Kratos's fist repeatedly smashed into the back of its head until it was reduced to dust.

Kratos kicked the magic shields aside. He started to continue on his way when screams from inside a building drew him to peer through the open door. A man and woman clung to each other as an undead legionnaire drew twin knives and clacked them together, as though savoring their terror.

Using the pommel of his sword, Kratos rapped sharply on the door frame. The undead glanced over its shoulder, then back at the man and woman. When it turned its face once more toward the Ghost of Sparta, it discovered only the edges of the Blades of Chaos in the final instant before being cut in two from collarbone to crotch.

Kratos stepped back and let the pieces fall. The legs kicked at him feebly. He ignored them.

"We are truly blessed by the gods!" said the man. "You have saved us!"

"You're not saved. I have only delayed your death a moment

or two." Kratos turned to go. "Your energy would be better spent in running away."

"We were paying tribute to Aphrodite," the woman offered, showing him a small carved wood box in her palms. It was filled with vials of fragrant oils.

"You should be on the walls defending your city."

"There is always time for tribute," she said, looking at her man, who was obviously an artisan and not a soldier.

"Maybe for you," he growled, and strode away toward the street.

Before his sandal could touch the paving stones, Athens vanished before his eyes. The world shimmered about him, and he felt as if he might be soaring into the sky.

Brightness blossomed into blinding empyreal glory . . . and out from that Olympian splendor appeared a woman of such full-bodied perfection that the sight of her hit him harder than any foe ever had.

Kratos had to clear his throat twice before he could speak. "Lady Aphrodite."

"Greetings, Spartan. I wish to bestow upon you my thanks for the rescue of my disciples."

"Goddess," Kratos managed to choke out, bowing his head, "it is an honor to serve you." He coughed and cleared his throat again. "However you might desire."

"Kratos." Aphrodite spoke his name as softly as a lover's caress. "Zora and Lora have spoken of your talents."

"Zora and Lora?" Kratos blinked. "The *twins*—they *speak* to you?"

"Not as often as they should," the Goddess of Love purred. "But then, every parent has a similar complaint, I suppose."

"You're their *mother*?" This explained so many different things at once about the twins that Kratos found himself with no idea what to say next.

One slender finger from that slim hand traced the curve of his lips to silence any comment. "Athena asked me to contribute a gift of my own, to aid you in your quest."

"The only gift I need is freedom to complete my task."

Her laugh was like the chime of silver bells. "What you *need*, Spartan, is to be grateful for whatever a god chooses to bestow." She caressed his cheek gently. The fingers turned cold as they stroked. "You will perform a task for me as well."

"I am already engaged—"

"You will slay the Queen of the Gorgons."

Kratos frowned. "But why her? Why now?"

"You are so adorable," the goddess purred, "that I won't have you eviscerated for daring to question me—this time. You must kill Medusa and bring me her head. The gift I will bestow on you is the power of the Gorgons: to turn men to stone!"

The goddess gestured and, with a wave, wiped away tranquil Olympus.

KRATOS TRIED TO SPEAK but had no breath, tried to see but had no light. He tried to move and did not know if the wild, whirling chaos he experienced was all around him or inside his head. Or both.

He crouched in a cold, dark place and heard the soft hissing of snakes.

He stood. The sooner he satisfied Aphrodite's thirst for Gorgon blood, the sooner he could return to Athens and find the Oracle.

The gloom around him hid the slithering serpents. He took a few blind steps to one side, sloshing through ankle-deep water. His hand found a slimy rock wall. Pressing his ear against the wall, he waited through many slow, measured breaths in an attempt to detect any vibrations. Nothing.

He sighed. What had he expected? That Aphrodite would just point and make Medusa appear in front of him?

As his eyes adjusted to the murkiness, he began to make out his surroundings. The goddess had transported him to the juncture of three low-roofed tunnels hewn from living rock. No light shone down any of the tunnels; the light by which he now saw was the product of faintly luminescent moss clinging to crevices in the rock.

The tunnel straight ahead proved to be a dead end. Kratos shoved hard against the wall blocking his progress. His anger mounted. More wasted time.

The Oracle was in danger of death or worse if Ares captured her. Kratos didn't care if the Oracle lived or died, so long as he learned her secret.

Kratos recalled campfire discussions among his officers before battle; some impious types had been speculating that the gods needed human worship the way a tree needs the sun. Could a god exist without worshippers? The way things were going in Athens, Kratos guessed he just might find out.

Would Athena's power decline? Would she simply disappear? Zeus might prohibit one god from killing another, but Ares might have found a way to sneak around the ban.

In the past, Ares had always chosen brute force over subtlety, but perhaps he had learned his lesson. While the siege of Athens had the trappings of Ares's old rage, he might have a different strategy in mind. Kill Athenians and Athena lost followers. Kill enough and her worshippers might abandon her for other gods—and who better to worship than the God of War, who had defeated their goddess?

Shows of strength in this uncertain world brought people to Ares's temples. Kratos had, once upon a time, been the author of many of those shows and had himself been the earthly symbol of Ares's might. Kratos's officers had believed that a god without worshippers simply faded away like mist in the morning sun. If such a fate befell Athena, Kratos's only chance for vengeance upon his former master would evaporate with her.

And the nightmares would continue unabated, rending sanity.

A few more blows upon the wall proved that it would withstand even his prodigious strength. Kratos turned and retraced his path. The water ahead began to ripple ominously before he reached the juncture where Aphrodite had deposited him.

Kratos had to bend almost double to slide the Blades of Chaos off his back and bring them down in front of him. Barely in time.

Up from the dark waters struck a serpent whose head was larger than Kratos's fist. Its fangs flashed as it struck. The venom dripping from their needle tips smoked in the gloom and caused the water where it fell to boil. Kratos blocked the strike with one blade while he struck back with the other. The snake's head and a span of its neck flipped through the air. Its body thrashed wildly as it died, but the head continued to snap at him, its black eyes glaring with malice. Kratos pressed both blade tips into the head and waited for the viciousness to fade and die. Eventually, it did.

He looked up in time to see more ripples approaching: snakes swimming just under the murky surface, too many for him to avoid. One caught him, its fangs driving hard into his greaves, chewing as though it thought to drive its fangs through the heavy bronze. Kratos didn't wait to find out if it was right. The pommel of a blade crushed a fragile skull. The fangs and jaw-bone remained clamped on his greave. The water ahead boiled as more snakes swarmed toward him, too many to count. Kratos slashed repeatedly down into the water in front of him, a blinding flourish that turned the blades into a shield of death. He drove grimly forward until he reached the juncture again. The water churned crimson with the snakes' blood. And then the water calmed.

The dripping of moisture off the walls was all he could hear.

Kratos looked into the water and saw movement, but not of snakes. He lifted his foot and brought it down, thinking to crush any creature just below the surface. He felt his foot slide into the outline of a boot cut into the stone. Curious, he scooted his other sandaled foot about and found a corresponding indentation. For a moment he stood with both feet in the underwater impressions. As he started to step forward, he felt a tiny vibration that built and passed upward until it shook the chains embedded in his wrists.

Kratos saw the phosphorescent moss writhing on the walls. He lifted one foot from its indentation and the moss stopped glowing. Replacing his foot caused the moss to glow once more.

Curious, he reached out to touch the moss. Like a snake, it writhed sinuously away from his fingers. He growled deep in his throat. It was the only sound save the slow drip of moisture.

Stabbing out with his finger, he forced the animated moss to go around his digit. It spun about, encircling the spot on the stone wall where he pressed, as if the moss showed him an exit from an otherwise featureless tunnel. Leaning slightly, he applied pressure. Nothing happened.

He stepped from the outlines under his feet, and the moss ceased glowing. Kratos stomped to the end of the tunnel and found only another blank wall. Extensive investigation proved to him that there was no exit from the subterranean tunnels— none that he could find. He reached for both of the Blades of Chaos, then stopped.

"Two hands. There might be something in using two hands." He returned to the indentations, slipped his feet into them, and moved his finger around on the right wall until the moss once more circled one specific spot. He pressed. Nothing.

Reaching to the other wall and repeating the movement produced another curlicue of green-glowing moss. This time, he moved his finger about and found a spot much higher on that wall before the moss stopped writhing and presented him with a specific spot.

Kratos pressed outward, fingers probing each of the marked spots.

"Mighty Zeus," he whispered. His eyes went wide when a portion of the ceiling began to descend. Rather than jump back to defend himself, he stood his ground until the trapdoor had opened and lowered, giving him a ladder leading upward. Moving his fingers from the spots and stepping quickly, he reached the ladder just as it began to retreat aloft. Hanging on, he let the closing trapdoor carry him upward into a room whose floor was a foot above a sluggishly flowing stream. A channel of tightly

placed stones held the stream in place. He shook himself dry.
The snake with its fangs buried in his greaves came free when
he scraped down his shin armor with the edge of his blade. He
had not even realized it still clung to him with such tenacity.

These poisonous water snakes were nothing compared with
the prey he sought. Not only must he face a monster who would
turn him to stone if he so much as glanced at her face, he had to
find one Gorgon in particular. Queen Medusa ruled her sisters,
but unless she wore a crown or carried a scepter, Kratos had no
simple way of picking her out from the rest.

Sandals scraped against stone as someone approached along
the dry tunnel ahead. He raised the blades, but some primitive
instinct warned him not to fight. Wit, for once, might bring victory, just as he had discovered the secret way into this lair. Kratos
backed off and tucked himself from ankle to neck into a shallow
stony niche lined with empty shelves. Other such niches pocked
the chamber's walls, but most of those had shelves stocked with
objects. It seemed a fair guess that whoever came would fetch
the items in storage and thus not even bother to look at a niche
they knew to be empty.

And if he was wrong, he still had the blades. They would find
this particular cabinet fully stocked with swift and bloody death.

Two men entered. One, a crookback, led the other, an old
man who wore a filthy rag tied across his eyes. They began se-
lecting items from nooks and crannies. The crookback laded the
blind man with two boxes for every one of his own.

"My back is breaking from the load," the crookback com-
plained. "Carry another for me, will you?"

"I can hardly stand, Jurr, but go and pile it on. We daren't
make two trips. We cannot be late or Queen Medusa will punish us both."

"Again," Jurr said. "Once a day is more than I can bear. My
back festers from the beatings she gives me." He stacked several
more heavy boxes onto the other's considerable load while keeping only a pair of light ones for himself.

Kratos watched as they left, the blind man crushed by his load while the crookback showed a sprightlier stride. Kratos cared nothing for this. Clearly there were two sorts of people in this underground maze: those who did all the work, and those who could see. Being one of the latter made Kratos disinclined to disrupt the arrangement.

The only sound Kratos made when he followed was the faint squish of water squeezing from his sandals. As he went, he scratched trail markers in the luminescent moss. If he succeeded, he might have to find his own way out of here. Maybe Aphrodite would just snatch him back to Athens, but maybe he was required to return to where she had deposited him originally. He had never lost by preparing against betrayal.

Especially by gods.

"BRING MY MEAL, you disgusting vermin!"

This was a new voice, coming from a chamber ahead, where a lamp held back the gloom. Kratos stopped and pressed himself into the shadows outside the archway. Though the voice had been low and rough, like rocks being shaken in a brass jug, he caught some hint of inflection that told him the speaker might be female.

If he was right, a careless glance would doom him to an eternity as a stone statue, taunted by Gorgons in this twilight perdition.

The sighted man, Jurr, replied, "At once, Lady Medusa. I have brought the supplies."

"You?" the blind man began. "*I* brought the—"

"Shh."

"Shut your vile human mouths and get to *work*! My sisters and I grow hungrier by the moment. And *angrier*." Her voice took on a dangerous edge. "It puts me in the mood for punishment."

"Ohhh," the blind man whined under his breath. "Oh, Zeus strike me dead before she touches me once more!"

"At least you can't *see*, you lucky bastard," Jurr snarled back just as softly. "Those mirrors, those accursed mirrors in her bedroom! Every way she turns, she can see her hideous self."

Clanking of pots and the sounds of a fire being stoked lured Kratos into a quick look. He flicked a glance swifter than a blink, but he took in the entire kitchen. The blind man decanted some kind of jugged meat into a bathtub-size cauldron, while Jurr built the cooking fire beneath it. It looked as if the Queen of the Gorgons favored spring lamb. . . .

No, those weren't lambs, Kratos realized, as a cold knot formed in his belly.

They were human infants.

Kratos balled his fists, wanting to strike out at such horrific fare. Children. Human children like his own daughter, his dear daughter, who—

He stepped out but forced himself back into hiding until the proper moment. His rage mounted at the cannibalistic meal, feeding his need to destroy the Gorgons. Taking Medusa's head had been decreed by Aphrodite—he would take grim pleasure in it, command from a goddess or not!

Shortly, the blind man loaded a huge trencher full of steaming baby stew and shuffled off toward a darkened archway across the small kitchen. Jurr watched him go, then cat-footed over to the vast kettle, snatched a ladle, and dipped a scoop, holding it up to his nose to capture the aroma. "That old blind bastard is finally learning to cook," Jurr muttered, bringing the ladle to his lips. But before he could taste the baby stew, an enormous hand seized the back of his neck and yanked him into the air.

He dropped the ladle into the tureen and tried to yell, but the hand around his neck crushed his voice down to a squeak. He struggled, kicking his legs and clawing at the hand, but the ash-white skin seemed harder than bronze. He found himself, a moment later, turned so that he was face-to-face with the Ghost of Sparta.

His eyes went wider and rounder, and a strangled croak worked its way up between Kratos's fingers.

"Medusa," Kratos whispered. "Where? Just point. Point and I'll let you go."

Through frantic waving of his hands, Jurr managed to indicate that the bedchamber of the Queen of the Gorgons was the first door to the right along the darkened hall. Kratos nodded.

One quick squeeze crushed Jurr's voice box, so that he couldn't scream and so that Kratos wouldn't have to listen to any pathetic begging. Kratos lifted this baby chef above the bath-size cauldron of boiling stew and then, true to his word, let him go.

Kratos knew that he was most in danger in the first instant of entering the Gorgon queen's chamber. If he mistook the real Medusa for one of the reflections and found himself looking upon her face, he wouldn't get a second chance.

Fortune favors the bold, he thought, and charged.

With a pantherish leap, Kratos sprang through the opposite archway, reaching the door to Medusa's chamber only an instant behind the blind man. The blind man balanced the trencher unsteadily on one hand while he opened the door with the other. Hearing Kratos behind him, the blind man half turned. "Jurr—" was all he had time to say before Kratos snatched the trencher and, with a mighty kick, sent the blind man flying into the middle of the chamber beyond.

Kratos took care to look only at the ceiling. Jurr had not lied—he had not even come close to telling the full story. Mirrors paneled the walls. Even more mirrors stretched from side to side along the ceiling. The mirrors there showed the blind man plowing straight into the hideous monster. Before either of them had a chance to react, the snakes that were Medusa's hair instantly unbraided themselves and struck at the blind man as one, latching on to his entire body and chewing on him as the water snake had chewed on Kratos's greave. The snakes writhed as the blind man went into convulsions and they clamped him to Medusa's face. Gut churning at the reflected sight, Kratos decided he didn't need the rest of his plan.

Three quick steps sent him past the dying man and the Gorgon, who shrieked in rage as she tried to claw the hapless slave from her face. Just as she finally succeeded in pushing him away, her head lifted and, in the mirrored wall, she saw her death standing at her back. Kratos sprang into the air, striking downward with both feet and driving the monster face-first to the chamber floor. At the same instant, the Blades of Chaos flashed in a converging slash that sheared through both collarbones and the back of her upper ribs.

Kratos released the blades and reached down into the wound with both hands. Driving his fingers into the slimy mess of Gorgon tissue, he caught hold of her spine and with one mighty wrench ripped her head from her body. Her head snakes struck at his arm, but weakly; their venom had been expended on the blind man.

He paused for a moment, regarding the reflection of her deadly gaze in the mirror: those fearsome eyes, the tusklike fangs, hair of living snakes.

KRATOS ARCHED HIS BACK as the feeling of sudden upward movement seized him once more. From the dim, moss-lit subterranean chambers he was transported to a place of dazzling, brilliant white.

"You have done well, my Spartan."

I'm not your Spartan, he thought, but he said only, "Lady Aphrodite?"

He used his free hand to shade his eyes against the glare and then could barely make out the diaphanous house silks that clung invitingly to the goddess's body. She took the severed head from his hands, holding it by its now-dead hair snakes.

"Lady Aphrodite, are you finished with me?"

"Oh, yes—one last thing now that I have made certain you have completed your mission for me. Here," she said, holding out Medusa's severed head, its face carefully turned away. "Take it by the snakes. That's right. Careful you don't look into its eyes yourself. Now, sling it back over your shoulder as if you were putting away one of those impressively large swords you wear on your back."

Kratos did so and felt the snakes evaporate from his grasp. "What happened? Where did it go?"

"It will be there when you want it. Just reach back for it, and it will be in your hand, turned the right way and ready to petrify."

"How does *that* work?"

"It's magic. One more thing you should know: Being dead diminishes Medusa's power."

"People won't turn to stone?"

"Oh, they will. They just won't *stay* that way for very long."

Kratos stared directly at Aphrodite, waiting for the full explanation.

"Ten seconds from a full blast from the eyes. And whatever you do, don't *lose* it." Aphrodite spread her hands and regarded him closely. "Athena wants it when you're done. She has some use for it. Something about a shield . . . maybe a cloak? Well, no matter. You have destroyed the Queen of the Gorgons, and now her power is yours!"

In an instant she towered above him like a mountain, as though her hair might brush the moon, and her voice rang like a great bronze bell. *"Freeze and destroy them all with Medusa's Gaze!"* the goddess thundered. *"Go with the gods, Kratos. Go forth in the name of Olympus!"*

Before he could draw breath to reply, he was in Athens once more. Ares still towered above the Acropolis, casting house-size gobbets of Greek fire on every side.

When Kratos recovered his bearings, he found himself once more in the quieter neighborhood from which the goddess had taken him. He was still on the far side of the Acropolis from Athena's temple—and from her oracle.

He put his head down and ran. Ran like the lion in pursuit of a lamb, swift as a falcon, tireless as the wind. He had to run. So much time had been wasted, and for what? A power he didn't need. A power that had nothing to do with finding the Oracle, nor with defeating the God of War. If Aphrodite had *really* wanted to help him, she would have set him down at the door of Athena's temple and put the Oracle in his lap.

Gods and their games. He was sick of all of them. Once he killed Ares, he would be done with them and their insane demands.

And the nightmares would be banished from his sleep, from his every waking instant. Forever.

NINE

SMOKE ROLLED DOWN from the heights of the Acropolis, a black greasy pall that smothered the Parthenon on the mountainside and came near to strangling Kratos. The tough armor he'd taken from the undead legionnaires shielded him from the killing heat of the flames and protected his Ares-burned back, but it couldn't help him breathe. Choking, gasping for air, he had to turn back and seek a clearer way toward the summit.

None of the war god's fireballs had yet touched this particular neighborhood, but the area had not escaped the attentions of Ares's legions. There were bands of roving monsters of all descriptions: combinations of Minotaurs and Centaurs for cavalry, Cyclopes for heavy infantry, skeleton archers, legionnaires, harpies, wraiths . . . and what was *that*?

The creatures looked like hideous women with a single long snake's tail instead of legs. Writhing serpents crowned their heads, and crackling green beams of power poured out from their eyes. . . .

It seemed that the death of their queen had brought the rest of the Gorgons into the fight.

But . . . all of Greece knew there had been only three Gorgons: Stheno, Euryale, and of course the recently deceased Medusa. Yet Kratos saw a dozen of the repulsive creatures, and he had no doubt that others were spreading through the city at that very instant. Killing them would feed his anger and give him momentary distraction from the ever-present nightmare fluttering at the edge of his mind, but that would be only a waste of time that he and the Oracle could not spare. A permanent solution to his visions awaited. He hunted for a clear path to Athena's oracle.

Kratos ducked into an alley and scrambled up a rain barrel, from which he could swing himself onto a balcony and clamber up another story or two to the roof.

Athens burned.

Save only the neighborhood around him, the entire city was in flames. Now and then he caught sight of the Long Walls through the smoke. The flash of firelight off brandished weapons told him that soldiers still wasted their lives in a futile attempt to hold a wall that no longer defended the city. Everybody had to die somewhere; if defending their useless wall gave them the illusion of dying for a noble cause, who was he to gainsay their futile heroism? Men had died under his slashing blades for less.

Kratos progressed slowly across the rooftop, scouting for a path to follow uphill. He moved with caution, to avoid attracting the attention of the harpies that swooped hither and thither through the smoke. The old man at the gates had said the Oracle's chamber was on the east side of the Parthenon. Across the face of the Acropolis, he could pick out faint brown tendrils that might be footpaths, but the billowing smoke clouded them and hid other avenues entirely.

When he moved to the edge of the roof to get a better view, an arrow sang past his ear. Kratos fell flat and let more arrows sail over him. He chanced a quick look over the edge of the roof and located a handful of undead archers who'd taken a nearby balcony for their vantage point. Kratos saw a man venture into the street, only to take an arrow through the belly, and when the arrow detonated, the blast of flame splattered the man's guts across the front of his own house. The archers held fire only when they could find no further targets.

Kratos ducked when a new ball of Greek fire exploded a quarter mile away, roughly where he thought the road leading to the summit of the Acropolis might turn upward. A grim picture painted itself within his mind.

Athena's worshippers would naturally run for the Parthenon when they found their city under attack by the God of War. Ares had sown fire across the whole city, sparing only this quarter, through which ran the road up the Acropolis—which would naturally draw those worshippers like flies to turds. Then the god had his monsters patrolling the streets, preventing further movement.

Kratos understood: The God of War was deliberately funneling the most pious and devoted of Athena's flock into one small area of the city—making it look as if this was the safest area, as well as the only route to the temple of their goddess. Instead of fleeing into the countryside, where tracking them down and slaughtering them would be a daunting task even for Ares's minions, they were packing themselves into the illusory safety of this single neighborhood.

Concentrating where they could most easily be destroyed. All at once. No fuss. No mess. No chasing people through the forest or rooting them out of mountain caves. The citizens of Athens had made of themselves nothing more than cattle rushing to the slaughterhouse floor. It was brutal, and he knew it would be very effective.

He'd done this sort of thing himself.

Kratos grabbed his temples to keep his head from exploding as an image burned hotter than the sun through his brain.

No! It couldn't be . . . The dead, those he had slaughtered in Athena's temple . . . Guilty! He had killed—

Gasping, Kratos forced the horrible vision away. It seized him more powerfully each time, but giving in to the horror wasn't going to make reaching the Parthenon any easier. He could conquer his own nightmares—for a short while—but it seemed the monsters were gathering on the streets below to block his path. And he knew those undead archers hadn't forgotten he was up here. He had to move. Fast.

On the other hand, he saw no reason to surrender the high ground.

Three strides for momentum took him to the lip of the roof, and a mighty leap sent him hurtling over the street to the opposite roof. The skeleton archers below were so startled, none of them got off a shot. As he sprinted along, he heard the commanding bellow of a Minotaur, and he knew he'd been seen by the forces below.

His next jump drew a scatter of fire arrows, though none came close—and he could see undead legionnaires mounted on the backs of Centaurs racing parallel to his path on the streets below. Another rooftop and another leap, and harpies began to swoop and dive at him. He dodged and ducked across roof after roof without slowing, using the blades as grapnels to swing himself over gaps too wide to bridge, and whirling them about his head as he ran to keep the harpies at bay.

He sprinted from roof to roof, running faster than the harpies could pursue—but the shouts and bellows of the monsters below came even faster. Not even Kratos could outrun the speed of sound. More of Ares's creatures streamed toward him, and he leaped from the last house of the neighborhood and dived once again into the fires and smoke of the rest of the city.

One Minotaur had the bright idea of calling for all Cyclopes, Centaurs, and other Minotaurs to forget about trying to catch the racing Spartan; instead, they should batter the walls of the burning buildings, weakening every structure in Kratos's path.

Battling the strangling smoke and roasting flames, Kratos jumped to a rooftop which collapsed under his weight. A frantic scrabble at the structure beneath the splintered roof tiles and a swift overhead whip of a Blade of Chaos, which embedded it in a more-solid rooftop ahead, gained him enough purchase to keep aloft. A quick glance below at the countless enemies of all descriptions crowding there told him in no uncertain terms the outcome of an unlucky fall.

Grimly, he ran on, knowing that each rooftop would prove more fragile than the last—and even if he could stay up there all the way to the foot of the Acropolis, he would then have to descend to the streets and either deal with his pursuers or be slaughtered along with all these useless Athenians.

Better a nameless death being swallowed by the Hydra in the Grave of Ships than having his corpse burned in the same fires as those of his people's most bitter enemy.

Along the base of the sheer cliffs below the Acropolis, Kratos raced parallel to the rock, making for the roadway. These buildings were sturdier, as they had the support of the rock wall at their back, and keeping close to the cliff face as he rounded the curve let him gain ground on his pursuers.

There! A gap in the greasy smoke showed him the broad flagstones of the roadway just ahead. With redoubled energy, Kratos hurled himself toward it—but only three houses short of the open ground he craved, roof tiles crumbled and the fire-weakened walls of the building collapsed around him. Worse, his charred, blistered back betrayed him. His usual strength had faded, and twisting about sent knives of pain into his shoulders, which prevented him from saving himself from the fall.

By the time he found his feet and shook himself free of the rubble, they were on him.

Undead legionnaires rushed him, swords drawn. The Blades of Chaos found first his hands, then their necks. More pressed in behind, and Kratos leaned in to them. He drove his way forward as though they were only earth, he was a miner, and the blades were his picks and shovels. Contemptuously, he stepped over their halved bodies.

Kratos found more legionnaires in the broad courtyard. These took a little more effort to dispatch, but he did so, regretting every second he wasted in mindless slaughter.

He made for the street, only to encounter more monsters at the gate. Three Cyclopes growled and swung their prodigious war clubs; any impact would have spattered his brains all over the street, but that wasn't what worried Kratos. Even when they missed him, those clubs knocked huge holes in the walls. The already-fragile structures shuddered with every blow. On the rooftops above the courtyard, skeletal archers clattered into place, beginning a rain of flaming arrows to cut off any hope of retreat.

One brief glance over his shoulder was enough to escalate his sense of peril: Now coming up to support the Cyclopes were six Minotaurs, spreading to fill all gaps.

They came for him. All at once.

Pinned between the archers and the combination force of Minotaurs and Cyclopes, he saw no way out.

But he wasn't ready to die. Not yet.

"Come on, then!" he roared. "Come and die!"

Kratos blocked an ax blow from one Minotaur and lunged, catching a Cyclops behind the hamstring. A slash hobbled the monster, but as he limped back, the other two crowded close to join the battle.

Kratos slipped out from under another earthshaking club blow from a Cyclops and began a steady parry. The Minotaurs had ditched their axes in favor of long spears, with which they could strike at him without getting in the way of the Cyclopes; one slip would leave him as full of holes as a cheese grater. They coordinated their attacks like a well-trained, experienced unit.

He was only one mortal against myriad creatures dragged from Hades, but it was he who attacked. "Out of my way or die where you stand!" he thundered, and then undertook to make his boast into a simple statement of fact.

Kratos slipped between the Cyclopes and struck a mighty double-bladed blow into the chest of the nearest Minotaur. New strength and power flowed up the chains into his body as the blades drank the man–bull's life. He whirled to hamstring another Cyclops, but the enormous monster was faster than it looked. The one-eyed creature swept its vast club into a rising parry and cleared the blades from between them, then dropped its club and wrapped its arms around Kratos's chest. The Cyclops squeezed until the Spartan's ribs began to crack and clouds of blackness washed through Kratos's vision.

The Cyclops roared its triumph—until its lone eye focused on the Spartan's face.

Kratos was smiling.

The blades came down at the joining of the Cyclops's neck and shoulders, carving a gore-splashing V downward until they met at the creature's monstrous heart. Kratos released the blades to seize the Cyclops's head—which still blinked its eye in astonishment—and then hurled it, along with much of the creature's spine, into the path of the jabbing spears of the Minotaurs.

As the rest of the Cyclops's body shuddered and collapsed, Kratos kicked off it into a small gap between the corpse and the stone wall.

His victory was short-lived. His battle with the Cyclops, quick as it had been, had allowed the Minotaurs to surround him. Kratos spun in a full circle and saw a dozen of the bullheaded monsters advancing. Even the Blades of Chaos would not slay so many. If he engaged one or two, that many more would attack from behind. He crouched behind the Cyclops's massive body, using it as a battlement, while he reached back over his shoulder—and his hand filled with twisting serpents. The Minotaurs rushed him from every direction. He swung the deathly head of Medusa out before him.

Emerald energy crackled out from the Gorgon's dead eyes, and each foe it touched instantly stiffened into cold gray limestone. One Minotaur, caught in mid-thrust, toppled sideways, knocking another to the street—where it shattered like a dropped clay pot.

Kratos sprang to action. Ten seconds was all he had.

The blades flashed out, and where they struck, the statues shattered. Kratos leaped up to the shoulders of the one remaining Cyclops and kicked himself up and out again, toppling the frozen creature, whose weight crushed its hamstrung brother and the last two Minotaurs.

And as Medusa's fell power abated, chunks and shards of petrified monster turned back into meat and bone and blood, a sprawl of carnage that filled the street.

"Lady Aphrodite," Kratos murmured, "I should never have doubted."

A whisper, hardly more than a zephyr in the tumult, came beguilingly to his ear: *"Perhaps someday I'll let you apologize. Personally."*

He released Medusa's head back over his shoulder, sheathed the blades, and ran as though all the forces of Hades snapped at his heels.

Which they did.

Dodging, he went uphill, although he found no easy path toward the Parthenon. It seemed that all the mountain burned. The acres atop the Acropolis flamed with the fury of a new sun.

"Helios . . ." Kratos wondered aloud. "Have you joined my enemies?"

Athena had enlisted the aid of powerful allies, but Ares might have Olympian aid as well. The political intrigues of Mount Olympus were mysterious and deadly for any mortals caught up in them. He wasn't too concerned. He had sworn ten years ago that whatever dared to stand between him and his vengeance would be destroyed, whether it be man, beast, or god.

Anyone who wanted to live had better stay out of his way.

He started up a narrow street that looked promising, but then mist swirled out of nowhere in front of him. He swatted at it with his right-hand blade, but the mist formed a thicker cloud just beyond his reach. Kratos settled the blades into a fighting grip. Whatever new threat this might prove to be, he would destroy it as he had all others. When the mist flowed and took the shape of a thin column, he swung as hard as he could.

The blade passed through the mist, leaving not so much as a swirl to mark its passage.

He was debating whether he should use the Rage of Poseidon or if Medusa's Gaze might give this mist enough form for him to strike. Before he had decided, the mist solidified into a tall, beautiful woman wearing little more than thin streamers of cloud for a skirt and a top wrapped around her bodice but once. The material was as transparent as the mist, but even as he watched, she became more substantial.

Some sort of succubus? A Siren? It didn't matter—she looked solid enough now. He slashed into the woman with a strike that would cut a mortal in half.

She did not appear to notice. *"Do not fear, Kratos. I am the Oracle of Athens, here to help you defeat Ares. Revealed in my divinations are secrets unknown even to the gods. Find my temple to the east and I will show you how to murder a god."*

"Oracle! Wait!" Kratos dropped the blades and stared through the once again empty space. He looked up the hill toward where the Oracle had pointed. A misty gesture, vagrant air currents—how could he know?

The path narrowed quickly, but he kept climbing. When he reached a spot halfway up, he looked back over Athens and shook his head in dismay. The fighting was nearly over. Ares roared with evil mirth, bellowing flame like a volcano, as his army flowed like the sea through the streets of Athens.

"God of War," Kratos said through his teeth, "I have not forgotten you. For what you did that night, this city will be your grave!"

An earthquake shook the city center. Kratos had to stop and widen his stance in order to keep his feet. Smoke from the burning buildings cleared for a moment to give him a direct view of Ares himself.

The huge god stepped over the Long Wall and strode up the causeway, stepping on Athenians too slow to escape his advance. The war god roared, shaking the heavens and the earth. He reached down, caught a soldier, and flicked him away as he might an annoying bug. The screams were thin and high and then died along with the man when he crashed into the roof of a temple devoted to Zeus. Then Ares began stamping on any who caught his eye, his fury palpable.

Ares rampaged through the city, crushing buildings and kicking away people in the square. The city was entirely at the mercy of the God of War, and mercy was in short supply. Ares had no more mercy than he did compassion or self-restraint. It was a bad night to be Athenian.

Kratos was a Spartan. Was there ever a *good* night to be Athenian?

He turned his back on Ares and followed the roadway upward onto the Acropolis. Another earthquake took him off his feet, forcing him to roll clear as a stone wall collapsed beside him. Kratos climbed back to his feet to look into the city.

Ares had drawn a sword the size of ten warships and raised it high above his head. The God of War brought it crashing down again with such force that houses for blocks around crumbled as the shock wave spread throughout the city. Ares delivered another blow, but this time Kratos was braced for it. He turned back to his path and set out toward the Parthenon.

"They come, they're coming!" A woman on the roof of a nearby temple shrieked the warning, then scrambled down a rickety ladder to the sacristy's front door. An undead archer fired from among Kratos's pursuers. The shaft pinned the woman to the wood frame, which caught fire as the arrow exploded.

Kratos ducked and shifted aside when he heard a furious flapping of wings that he knew all too well, but he was not this harpy's target. The foul beast swooped down to pluck at a woman running with a child in her arms. The harpy grabbed the child and carried it aloft. The woman screamed and threw rocks, but the harpy soared upward to hundreds of feet. Then it let the child drop.

"Noooo!" Kratos raged. He took a step and reached out, as if he could keep the child safe. He couldn't. A vision of his beloved daughter filled his eyes—and then blood replaced the vision. Again.

The woman frantically tried to catch her infant, racing toward it with arms outstretched, only to see her child's brains dashed out on the rubble of another temple. The harpy swooped low again, this time clawing at the woman. She fought off the flying monster but tripped on a broken flagstone.

Kratos raced forward and then leaped with all his prodigious strength. His fingers slipped away from the harpy's wing but caught a taloned foot. The harpy screeched in rage and fought to break free. Rage at the child's death lent Kratos the raw determination to clutch down hard enough to drag the harpy from the sky. The hideous creature crashed to the ground, only feet from where the child had perished.

A twist, a turn, and Kratos worked up to where he could smash his fist into the harpy's face. He continued to pummel the monster until only pulp remained. Panting, he held the scrawny neck in his grip, then cast the corpse away so its foul blood would not mingle with that of the fallen child.

"Help me, help me!" the bereft woman called to Kratos. "A trapdoor inside. Safety. Sanctuary is yours if you will help me!" The harpies had seen the fate of their companion and converged, thinking the woman was the easiest victim to slay.

Kratos let his revulsion for what crimes the harpies committed decide the matter for him. Swinging the Blades of Chaos, he charged. The first stroke took off a pinion. The second severed a clawed foot. A double swipe of his blades removed one harpy's head from its birdlike sloping shoulders. "Go," he said to the woman. "Find your refuge."

The woman did not plead with him to join her. Another harpy screeched as it swooped like a falcon. Kratos sprang into the air, hurling himself and his blades at the creature, but he was just too far away to reach it.

The woman took the full strike on her back.

Vicious claws opened bloody gashes, and then the harpy beat downward with its wings and plucked the woman's spine from her body. What remained fell lifeless to the ground.

Kratos ran, jumped onto an overturned crate, and launched himself through the air in a burst of furious attack. One blade sheared through the harpy's face, from her mouth to her ear.

The second blade sliced through her breastbone almost without resistance, opening its monstrous heart to spew black blood across the streets below. Man and harpy fell heavily to the ground. Kratos rolled free, jerked the chains around his forearms, and brought the Blades of Chaos whistling back to hand.

"There! There he is! Kill him! Kill him for Lord Ares!"

Charging toward him were a dozen Minotaurs, followed by six Cyclopes and half a hundred undead legionnaires—and behind them were still more. They choked the road; he could never fight his way clear.

It appeared his quest was about to end in a sudden and bloody failure.

He drew his blades. He was Spartan.

Just because he could not win was no reason to quit.

TEN

ATHENA STARED DOWN into the broad scrying pool below the throne of Zeus. A few ripples crossed it, but these came from the gusts swirling through Olympus. With a gesture, Athena stilled the waters so that they became clear as the sky. She bent forward to get a better view as Kratos unleashed Medusa's Gaze.

"Your mortal fights well."

Athena looked up. Her father had willed himself once more onto his throne, where he now leaned forward, peering intently into the pool. Could it be that Zeus showed the faintest hint of satisfaction?

Even Athena could not read the face of the Lord of Olympus for certain, but she dared hope.

She moved to one side, the better to keep one eye on the pool while she tried to fully decipher his expression. "I did not realize you were following the battle."

"Slaughter," Zeus said, "is mightily diverting. It has been many years since we've had such fine wanton destruction."

"Ares brings it to my beloved city," Athena said, a catch in her voice. "But Kratos's savagery comes from Ares. He is what my brother has made of him."

"He may be a bit more than that," the Lord of Olympus murmured. "You know, the sack of Athens is shaping up to be an epic poem—you should ask Apollo to compose an ode, perhaps. Commemorate the occasion. Doesn't have to be anything so elaborate as Homer's tale of Troy—after all, Troy stood against all of Greece for ten years. Athens hasn't lasted ten days. Nonetheless, many of your soldiers are managing to die heroically. And then there's your Kratos."

The Skyfather pointed to the scrying pool, which reflected Kratos's battle against a flight of harpies. "His furious quest for vengeance—one tiny mortal against the God of War? Very nice. Really. I couldn't have done it better myself."

"High praise, my lord father—perhaps the highest I have ever received." She didn't let it go to her head, because Zeus, premier among the other Olympians, was a deep planner. Athena wondered at his interest now and if he worked his own subtle plans.

Whatever the machinations, her Kratos played a prominent role.

"I am gratified you are taking such an interest in the struggle, Father. Would it be too bold for me to ask if your interest arises from the struggle itself?"

"My dear daughter, this is not about you. It had better not be. This is only your mortal against Ares's mob of horrors raked from the dregs of Hades. That Kratos has survived so far makes this a bit more interesting than certain gods had been expecting."

"Do you favor Kratos?"

Zeus turned pensive, running fingers through the wisps of his cloud beard. Athena tried to read the thoughts behind his eyes and could not. She caught her breath when her father spoke, his words slow and obviously carefully chosen.

"My son shows increasing disrespect, and that distresses me. He kills your worshippers in Athens, but that is to be expected."

Athena started to point out that Ares also singled out Zeus's worshippers, destroying the Skyfather's temples and corrupting

sacrifices to win his favor, but she saw that he already understood this.

"Ares's hubris grows with every victory. Do what you can to
support Kratos if your mortal can bring about a greater humility
by thwarting Ares."

"My brother cannot be stopped in this fashion," Athena said,
immediately regretting her words. Her passion betrayed her true
intentions. "Not directly. Everyone on Olympus knows my support for the valiant when they face impossible odds. Seldom do
they win—poor old Leonidas at Thermopylae, betrayed at the
last—but when they triumph . . . Well, even the Lord of Olympus knows how to honor a hero.

"So, would you see Kratos win? What are you suggesting?"

"I suggest nothing," Athena said. "I suggest nothing more
than that Kratos can use divine help in his struggle."

"I will not openly oppose Ares, no matter how impudent he
has become." Zeus stroked his beard more fiercely now, lightning bolts dancing through the clouds and leaping from finger
to finger. Athena tried to read her father's mood and could not.
But she hoped when he spoke next.

"It has always been worrisome to me that the oracles know
what I, Lord of Olympus, cannot see with all my powers."

"Perhaps it is for the best," Athena said.

"Best for whom, dear daughter, best for whom?" Zeus turned
his attention back to the scrying pool and the vast destruction
Ares delivered to the city and people of Athens. The Skyfather
leaned still farther forward. "We're just getting to the good part."

Athena caught her breath as Ares appeared on the battlefield
and began to crush Athenians under his sandal. Zeus gestured,
and the view dissolved to a vision of Kratos sprinting up the long
roadway toward the top of the Acropolis, just as a mortal woman
failed to save her infant from a harpy—and another harpy
snatched up the woman and savaged her with its talons.

"That woman is one of your worshippers!" Athena pointed at
the bleeding woman. "Do you see?"

Zeus frowned. "Indeed. In fact, she's a priestess—that little building of hers is an inn, consecrated to me in my Zeus Philoxenos role."

"He thinks to destroy *my* worshippers," she said. "Are you certain this priestess of yours was an accident? Perhaps he has aspirations for a higher throne."

"Please, dear child." Zeus thrust out his finger and touched the woman just as the harpy ripped out her spine. The ruler of the gods sighed and drew back his finger, now dotted with a single drop of water from the viewing pool. He turned and flicked the water droplet high into the air. It caught a ray of sunlight, turned into a rainbow, then vanished.

"There," he said, looking satisfied. "She will be well judged by Aeacus at the gates of the underworld."

"Why do you intercede in this way for a simple mortal worshipper, when you won't allow me to intercede for my thousands?"

Zeus's eyes flashed. "Because I can."

He held her gaze until she had to look away. Then he became once more caught up by the vision reflected in the pool. "Look—there, do you see him? He's killed the harpy, but now a whole company has him cornered! Perfect!"

"It is?"

"Tell me, how many monsters has Kratos destroyed today?"

Athena frowned. "Almost four hundred. Why?"

"Only *four* hundred?" Zeus looked exasperated. "What is his problem? He will never reach your oracle this way."

She had faith in Kratos's prowess. She would have even more if Zeus did not actively oppose him.

ELEVEN

MONSTERS CAME AT HIM from all directions.

A Minotaur let out a loud roar and charged ahead of its broth-ers, swinging a ball and chain over its head. Behind it trotted eleven more and six lumbering Cyclopes—and behind them, half a hundred undead heavy infantry.

A quick slash of the Blades of Chaos severed the chain of the Minotaur's weapon, sending the weight at the end flying. Kratos cast a quick glance in the direction the weight had flown, hop-ing it might take out another of Ares's army—it caught the near-est Cyclops full in the eye.

Then the Minotaur was upon him, but Kratos had judged his range to a nicety. He spun the blades in an intersecting flourish. One slashed through the Minotaur's throat, while the other carved out the creature's liver. The monster's legs buckled, and it pitched forward onto its face in a last flurry of legs and horns and the spew of blood. Kratos drove both blades down into its skull and, with a wrench of his mighty shoulders, shattered the creature's skull and painted its comrades with its brains.

Cyclopes pressed in upon him, ponderous clubs upraised. Kratos dove forward and rolled between the bowed legs of the one who'd been blinded by the flying chain weight. Clubs thundered to the ground on all sides, making the very earth tremble. One landed on the blind Cyclops's left foot, crushing its bones with a spray of blood. The wounded monster howled and lifted its foot, holding it with one hand, while its other hand remained clapped to its bleeding eye. The creature hopped about, howling in agony, and Kratos—never slow to press an advantage—kept rolling and diving around the creature's leg, drawing more club blows that only made the Cyclops's howl ramp up in volume. Finally the monster lashed out with its free hand and somehow seized one of the others' clubs, then began to lay about itself with prodigious energy, actually managing to land a number of powerful whacks on its companions.

Kratos gauged his distance and attacked. One thrust went upward into the creature's heart. The razored edge of his other blade cut just behind the Cyclops's knee—and caused it to topple onto Kratos. As quick as he was, Kratos found himself unable to get out from under the massive body that struck him and pinned him to the ground.

All around he heard Ares's creatures going wild. Helpless under the quivering, dying mass of the Cyclops, he fought to escape. Then he fought for breath. The Cyclops crushed the wind from his lungs. Try as he might, he could not breathe.

Kratos heaved, but the beast's bulk was like sand on the beach. It flowed and filled in any space around him. His lungs began to burn. Venting a huge roar, he tried to shove the Cyclops off him—and failed.

Rage engulfed Kratos as surely as the Cyclopean flesh. He bit down on the hairy belly smothering him and twisted, ripping away the flesh and opening the stomach cavity. A torrent of fluids doubly threatened to suffocate him; the air in his lungs was being used up fast. He bit again, rending intestines and stomach and moving upward like some vile maggot in the Cyclops's guts. He spat and strained, arching his back. His head and shoulders entered the creature's body cavity. Head spinning as the world went black, he heaved again and banged against a mighty rib.

Turning to the side, he made one last mighty snap. His teeth closed on sinewy muscle before he sank back, almost dead.

He sputtered and gasped as fetid air reached his nostrils. He spat out the gore in his mouth and gasped in huge drafts. The sky showed through the hole his teeth had ripped in the Cyclops.

Kratos shifted from side to side, got his shoulders around, and finally freed one arm that had been pinned under the Cyclops's bulk. Once he reached up and grabbed the rib, he was able to pull—hard. Half the creature's body ripped free. Coated with gore and digestive fluids, Kratos struggled upward and finally tumbled from the Cyclops's side to lie panting on the ground.

IT WAS TOO MUCH to expect that he would not be noticed by Ares's marauding horde. He got to his feet and faced a half dozen Minotaurs. Still weak and shaking from his excursion through the Cyclops's gut, knowing his physical prowess was inadequate for this fight, Kratos reached back over his shoulder with his left hand. In desperation, he again found the serpent hair of Medusa's head materializing in his grasp. He brought the Gorgon's head whipping forward, its eyes ablaze with emerald fire. The Minotaurs averted their eyes.

Kratos sprang straight up to kick the nearest Minotaur behind the ear, which knocked its head forward with such force that one of its horns gored the monster next to him. Kratos left them to sort that out for themselves. He landed in a roll that brought him to a crouch by another's ankle. He grabbed the beast's hoof with both hands and yanked it from its feet. If he had been able to recover his full strength, he could have broken its legs. Instead, the Minotaur slammed to earth with a painful-sounding thump—but a little bit of pain was a great deal less than Kratos had intended.

He stood and dragged the Minotaur with him, getting it in a headlock. Putting his entire body into the move, Kratos twisted so hard he broke the creature's neck. The other Minotaurs began to regroup, sure now that Kratos could not use his magic against them successfully. They looked sideways at him, ready to avert their heads if he produced Medusa's head once more. For Kratos, that was magic better forgotten in favor of the sword.

He reached for the Blades of Chaos as the Minotaurs backed away.

"Cowards," he snarled. Then he realized the battle was joined by undead infantry with javelins.

Needle-pointed steel rained around him. His only escape lay within the building and the trapdoor that the unfortunate woman had been shouting about.

Dripping blood, he backed into the archway of the inn the woman had indicated. To retreat burned him like white-hot iron—but this was not retreat. He was *pressing on* to complete his mission, to find the Oracle and learn her secret. He kicked the door shut with his heel as he entered, then barred it. Instantly the door began to splinter under repeated blows of the Minotaurs' enormous axes, and a javelin whistled through a window to embed in a table a few feet away.

The stone-and-mortar hearth still crackled with cheery flame. If the javelin-impaled table and the sounds from outside could have been ignored, this would have been a pleasant spot to while away an hour or two. A quick scan around the room showed Kratos that this had indeed been some sort of inn, confirmed by multiple representations of Zeus shown with wide and welcoming arms on the walls. There was even a statue of the King of Olympus set behind an altar beyond the hearth. This statue, like the frescoes around the room, had arms widespread in welcome. The woman had spoken of a trapdoor, though none was evident, nor were there rugs or floor tiles that might conceal such an exit.

Kratos squinted at the hearth. This building had been sanctified to Zeus Philoxenos, the grantor of hospitality; could another part of the structure have been similarly sanctified to Zeus Katachthonios, Zeus the kindly protector underground?

Kratos released the Blades of Chaos and bent to examine the hearth. As was common in hostelries, the hearth had been constructed in a ring of stone and mortar in the middle of the room, set upon a slab of limestone thick enough to keep the heat from the hearth from endangering the wood-plank floor. Neither the hearth nor the slab beneath it showed any sign of being willing to move—whether to slide aside, or lift, or fall—despite Kratos's best efforts.

The chopping and hammering of axes against the heavy door suddenly doubled in speed and impact. The orange glow from fires outside began to glimmer through splintery holes, and Kratos knew he had only seconds to either uncover the trapdoor, or prepare to make a stand.

Kratos looked again about the room, muttering through his teeth, "Zeus . . . Zeus . . . show me your wisdom!"

"*I am with you, Kratos.*"

Kratos's head jerked up and he spun around. Had that been a voice in his ears or only in his mind? He did not take time to ask or investigate further, for he now noticed a detail of the huge statue that previously had escaped his hasty scan.

Chains dangled from the statue's wrists—chains very much like Kratos's own. Now Kratos saw the smoothly finished cracks where wide and welcoming arms joined the god's mighty shoulders, as though these shoulders might have joints not unlike those of a man.

Kratos leaped to the top of the altar and sprang again. He caught one chain and swung across the statue's front to grab the other, then bunched the knotted muscles of his arms and his back to pull both chains simultaneously. He understood then why the woman had not taken her infant down through the trapdoor. These arms could not have been moved without three or four men using the chains to pull each one.

Three or four men—or one Ghost of Sparta.

The arms swiveled down so that the welcoming hands came together, palms up, fingers pointing at the hearth behind

Kratos—the hearth that now had lifted straight up from the floor. Supported by heavy vertical timbers, it revealed a dark opening below.

From the continuing tension on the chains he held, Kratos knew the hearth door would slam shut as soon as he let go, but Kratos had outsmarted similar devices in the past. He braced his feet against the thighs of the marble Zeus and strained outward with all his might. In the instant that he released the chains, he drove out into a hurtling dive as the hearth slab crashed down like a boulder from a cliff. He went headfirst into the hole, the falling slab barely clipping the heels of his sandals.

He landed hard on damp stone in the blackness and cast a wary glance at the slab above. Not the faintest glimmer of light showed through any crack. Unless the Minotaurs were a great deal smarter than he gave them credit for, or more driven to find him than was likely, they'd never figure out how he had escaped.

But that didn't mean he had time to waste congratulating himself. The Oracle still waited.

Kratos stood, then fell to his knees as dizziness assailed him. His lungs burned anew, and his blistered back again delivered constant pain. He needed time to heal, to mend his wounds and—

There would be no time to pause. Above, he heard the chipping of axes against Zeus's statue. The Minotaurs might be unable to open the way into the underground passage, but they had somehow figured out where he had gone and worked to follow as best they could by destroying the statue.

Kratos brushed his hand over his face, then laughed harshly. The Minotaurs did not need to be smart to follow him. All they needed to do was follow the trail of the Cyclops's blood he'd left behind. He was still covered in gore. His footsteps had led the Minotaurs to the statue of Zeus. His bloody handprints on the chains showed what he had done to escape. They would be after him in scant minutes.

He tried to stand, but his legs failed him. He sat again, still panting from exertion—from exhaustion.

Welling up from deep within the hard core that was his heart came resolve. He was Spartan. Ares had used him.

Kratos screamed as the visions rushed back to him. *The temple. The old woman and those within . . . the woman and child within . . . and he had—*

With a mighty surge, Kratos got to his feet, using the wall as support. He closed his eyes and turned slowly in the darkness until he felt a faint puff of air against his face. Without opening his eyes, he walked hesitantly into that air current. Only after he had gone several dozen paces without bumping into a wall did he bother to open his eyes. Vision now dark-adapted, he quickly spotted a tiny glow at the far end of a narrow, low tunnel.

He walked steadily toward the light, wary of a trap along the way. If he had been the builder of this escape tunnel, he would have dug a pit to cause the unwary intruder to break a leg. If the builder had been more ambitious, there might be trip wires, swinging hammers, or other perils that the innkeepers and guests would know to avoid, leaving unpleasant surprises for any pursuers. The light grew brighter, bigger, more inviting, and he'd encountered no traps. He walked faster.

He was almost running when someone called his name.

"Kratos."

He thought that Ares had found the tunnel and had come for him in person. Swords held in a shaky grip, he turned the tips toward a tiny glowing spot in the darkness.

"Show yourself. We can have it out here and now." His muscles quivered from fatigue, but if he finally faced his ultimate enemy, he would die like a Spartan.

The sudden burst of light forced him to throw up an arm to shield his eyes. Squinting, he saw a massively muscled man step forward out of a shimmer in the air like a sun dog in the brilliant blue of a summer sky. The gray-shot curls of storm clouds that served him for hair and beard would have instantly told Kratos who this was, even if Kratos hadn't leaped off a statue of him only moments before.

"My Lord Zeus!" Kratos bowed. "I am surprised. I had thought you might be Ares."

"That particular son of mine is still on the other side of Athens, enjoying his rampage," Zeus said.

Kratos couldn't tell from Zeus's tone whether the Skyfather approved or disapproved of Ares's onslaught. He decided not to ask. "How may I serve the King of the Gods?"

"Kratos, you grow stronger as your journey continues. But if you are to succeed in your quest, you will need my aid."

"What is your will, Lord Zeus?"

"I bring you the power of the greatest of all the gods, the Father of Olympus. I give you the power of Zeus!" The King of Olympus reached out and said, *"Give me your hands, son."*

Kratos let the Blades of Chaos slip back into their sheaths. The brilliance pouring into the tunnel at once warmed him and threatened to burn the flesh off his bones. Kratos lifted his arms to the ruler of the gods.

"Take my weapon, Kratos," cried Zeus. *"Take my power and destroy your enemies!"*

The tunnel roof opened and revealed bright blue sky dotted with clouds. A lightning bolt seared down a jagged path and exploded against Kratos's outstretched hands. He recoiled—it felt as if he'd plunged his hands into a cauldron of molten iron.

He pulled back his hands and stared in astonishment at his unburned skin—astonishment arising mostly from the burned-meat smoke that rose from them. Now seared into the palm of his right hand was a tiny jagged white scar that blazed with the light of the sun.

"Your *thunderbolt?*" He looked up, but the portal where the god had emerged had already closed. Above there was no longer blue sky and billowing white clouds. All he saw was dirt with roots growing down through it. He had not left the escape tunnel.

But the scar on his right palm proved almost too brilliant for him to examine.

Kratos reached back over his right shoulder, as though draw-

ing back his arm to throw a javelin. He grunted in surprise when
a solid bolt of lightning manifested in his hand. He hurled it forward, and it lanced along the tunnel quicker than he'd thought.
The detonation caused the far end of the tunnel to begin col-
lapsing, opening a sliver of night sky above the Acropolis. Kratos
set out toward it, but again he heard a voice—with his ears or
with his mind, he could not say.

"*Go back and fight!*"

Kratos stopped, still weak from his earlier conflict. "But the
Oracle—"

"*Destroy another three hundred monsters and she'll be there
when you arrive.*"

Kratos was sick of sneaking around underground, feeling like
a mewling babe and almost too weak to stand. Once more he
reached back, and again when he threw his hand forward, a
blast of lightning flashed the length of the tunnel. This one destroyed the timbers that supported the hearth slab, and the
whole thing dropped and shattered, scattering the tunnel's floor
with burning embers.

He nodded to himself. Using the thunderbolt buoyed his
spirits—and erased some of the weakness in his muscles. Being
so near a godlike power rejuvenated him. Time to go back and
see exactly how well this thunderbolt worked against a real
enemy.

TWELVE

SLAUGHTERING THE MINIONS OF ARES outside the inn proved to be more fun than Kratos had anticipated. When Zeus gave him the power of the thunderbolt, apparently he'd also refilled that general magical reservoir; Poseidon's Rage crackled more deadly than ever before, and Medusa's Gaze turned monsters to stone by the dozen, and Zeus's Thunderbolt shattered a mob of petrified monsters in a very satisfactory fashion.

Best of all, the flood of potent magic through his palm when he used the thunderbolt healed his wounds. Stretching and turning failed to cause the slightest discomfort on his back, where the touch of Ares's fire had so sorely injured him. After a few throws of the thunderbolt, Ares's minions had fled, giving Kratos a chance to bathe in a fountain and clean some of the Cyclops's gore from his body.

When he'd finished his ablutions, he felt certain he could take on and triumph over the worst that Ares had to offer.

He found a particular sequence to be most effective: He'd leap into the midst of a crowd of monsters and call on Poseidon's Rage, then whip out the Gorgon's head and turn them all to stone, because they would be too stunned from Poseidon's Rage to avert their eyes. Then he would hurtle into the midst of another squad of the undead legionnaires, fire a thunderbolt back at where he'd come from, and, while the petrified monsters were raining down in pieces, he would once again fire Poseidon's Rage against the fresh meat around him.

He became adept enough with Medusa's Gaze to petrify swooping harpies as they passed, turning them into the equivalent of sharp-edged catapult stones that could mow down a half dozen undead at one blow. And he found that the bronze armor of the undead legionnaires had an interesting property when struck with Zeus's Thunderbolt: If other similarly clad undead were near enough, the thunderbolt would arc from monster to monster, popping them off in a pleasingly swift succession like chestnuts tossed into a bonfire.

Kratos stood appreciating his handiwork when the clack of hooves against the cobblestones alerted him to approaching Centaurs. He turned, thinking he would face only one. A herd of the half-horse, half-man creatures trotted into the plaza and quickly arrayed themselves against him.

Somehow, one had managed to come up behind when his attention was diverted by the main herd. Powerful hands lifted him off the ground and held him high. He saw the sky and struggled to draw a weapon—any weapon. In a flash, Kratos realized he was unable to fight like this. He kicked his feet up high and rolled backward, breaking the Centaur's grip.

The man–horse cried out in rage as Kratos landed on the creature's rump, legs dangling down on either side of the equine body.

"You are the one Lord Ares seeks!" The Centaur swung half about and tried to land a fist on the side of Kratos's head. The Spartan ducked easily, shrugged his shoulders, and brought forth a loop of the chain fused to the bone of his forearms. He didn't draw the Blades of Chaos—he snapped the chain holding the pommel to his flesh about in an iron garrote.

Kratos rocked back, strangling the Centaur. The creature

tried in vain to pry loose the chain wrapped about its throat. It went to its haunches and reared, hoping to throw off Kratos. The Ghost of Sparta clung to the chain as if it were a bridle and reins rather than a strangling weapon.

He scooted forward, came closer to the man part of the monster, and kicked hard so his heels drove into the Centaur's belly. As the creature galloped forward, Kratos guided it to the spot among the others in the herd that he desired most.

At the last possible instant, he released the chain and raised his right hand. The star brand burned furiously, then released Zeus's Thunderbolt. Kratos aimed not at the Centaurs' bodies but at the ground where they stood. Suddenly molten ground beneath their hooves caused them to rear and crash into one another. Not satisfied, Kratos loosed another thunderbolt, this time directed at their horseshoes. As with the bronze armor worn by the undead legionnaires, the metallic horseshoes sparked and blazed, burning upward until not a Centaur in the herd commanded a full four legs. Several had lost all four legs up to the fetlocks; none was able to fight.

Kratos kicked free of the Centaur he rode, but before he could draw the Blades of Chaos to dispatch it, the creature raced away, leaving behind only a high-pitched keening of stark fear.

Kratos realized, as much as he appreciated the stark power of Zeus's gift, he had to press on to find the Oracle. He lost track of how many monsters he had destroyed; when finally no more came to assault him, the roadway was paved with corpses three deep in all directions. He didn't bother to count. Despite Zeus's assurance, he felt time pressing down upon him. Kratos ran up the incline of the roadway, falling into an easy lope. As he ran, his mind cast forth, considering different courses of action, but most of all his mind always returned to the Oracle and her mysterious secret of how a mortal might murder a god.

He was so lost in thought that, as he rounded a turn in the path, he ran smack into an undead legionnaire. They collided, Kratos rebounded, and the armored skeleton warrior crashed to the ground. The clatter of its bones against its sword and shield when it fell echoed through the Acropolis. Kratos recovered more swiftly than the skeleton warrior, drew the Blades of Chaos, and scissored off the undead's skull.

Kratos laughed. None stood against the Ghost of Sparta. And when he saw a dozen legionnaires coming down the path to investigate the noise, he laughed even more. These undead legionnaires were well armored and impressively weaponed. Hollow, disturbingly evil eye sockets glared like embers in a darkened room, through bronze helmets decorated with black feathers. They carried bucklers studded with brass nails. A few swung scythes, but most were armed with swords, and they marched in a tight, disciplined formation, with more pressing in at their backs.

And a single thunderbolt blew them all to pieces.

The ravening blast radiated outward, zigzagging on its way like lightning from Mount Olympus itself. The leading trio of legionnaires exploded. As did the next rank and the next and the next.

Kratos gingerly stepped over the smoldering bones and burned parts blasted from the legionnaires' bodies. Beside the path lay a bronze helmet, the black feathers smoking, as was the skull strapped inside. Melted swords and sundered helmets lay scattered along the path.

Kratos stared in wonder at the white scar on his palm. Then he hurriedly turned the palm away. Should he accidentally trigger a thunderbolt while he stared at his own hand, his death might be both swift and humiliating.

Once more he fell into the distance-devouring lope that was his habitual pace up the increasingly steep path. In places, pilgrims had painstakingly carved steps from the rock for the weaker supplicants. As if in a dream, he no longer climbed the Acropolis of Athens toward the Parthenon but instead some winding mountain path thousands of feet in the air. It became more difficult to breathe, and his legs—those tireless legs that tramped fifty miles in a day—began to ache from exertion.

He came to a bridge spanning a deep gorge ahead of him.

Along the bridge marched fifty or more Athenians, all bearing large wicker offering baskets and going to Athena's temple. He understood now how the Oracle's temple had withstood the assaults of the God of War—it wasn't in the Parthenon at all but was at the summit of some magically concealed path, which could be seen and trodden only by the faithful!

As he hurried toward the bridge, a shrill whistling filled the air. He looked up and saw a fireball descending from the heavens, and it occurred to him that even if he could not see the path or the temple, Ares could apparently still see him.

The Spartan dove and rolled aside. The clinging, burning fire never touched him this time—but it splashed across the bridge. Dozens of supplicants screamed. Some leaped from the bridge to plummet hundreds of feet to the rocks below, blazing like small suns as they tumbled downward. Those on the bridge struck directly by the Greek fire were now encased in charcoal shrouds that had once been their skin. He heard soul-curdling screams from them. Hideously burned, trapped in their sooty sheaths, each second of life was an eternity of agony.

But someone took pity on them—Athena, or perhaps Zeus himself—for with a grinding, squealing shriek of bronze on stone, the bridge dropped, and the burning Athenians were granted death upon the rocks far below.

Kratos rushed around a final turn in the path and stared across the chasm. From his glimpse before, he thought Ares's fireballs had destroyed the bridge; instead, more than half the bridge survived—but it was tilting upward into the air, away from Kratos, cranked by an enormous winch on the far side of the chasm. A short, powerful man struggled with the handle to lock it in place.

"Stop!" Kratos shouted. "Lower the bridge! I must reach the temple!"

"Go away!" the bridgekeeper shouted back. "The monsters prowl everywhere. Whole companies mount the path behind you. If you love the goddess, you'll help me destroy the bridge!"

"I *serve* Athena! She has tasked me with finding her oracle!

Lower the bridge!" Kratos took a step forward, to the very brink of the chasm.

"Even if I do, a third of it has been destroyed! How will you cross the gap? If you can fly, what do you need the bridge for?"

"Lower the bridge," Kratos growled. "I won't ask again."

"I will die for the goddess!"

"Fine." Kratos reached back over his right shoulder, filling his hand with solid lightning.

The bridgekeeper squinted across the chasm. "Hey, now—hey," he said uncertainly. "What's that in your hand?"

"See for yourself."

The thunderbolt shot from his hand and blasted to flinders the platform where the man stood. The bridgekeeper's scream echoed through the gorge even after his broken body splattered across the rocks below.

Argument with the bridgekeeper at an end, Kratos was still left the problem of crossing the chasm. Kratos scowled at the winch. He could certainly use a tame harpy right about now. Or even an owl. If Athena *really* wanted him to reach her oracle, she could at least share a couple of her sacred birds.

Neither friendly harpies nor Olympian owls made any sudden appearance. Kratos reached back for another thunderbolt.

He let fly at the winch, blasting it to scrap. The huge chains shrieked as the drawbridge swung down. The crash as it fell back into place finally erased the echoes of the bridgekeeper's death.

Kratos paused to judge the remaining gap. Twenty-five or thirty feet, no more, but a misjudgment of distance spelled his death on the rocks below.

He took a couple of steps for momentum and hurled himself into the air. As he sailed toward the wreckage at the near end of the bridge, another whistle from the sky rose to a scream. He caught the end of the bridge, fingers clutching at splinters of wood and stone, and swung himself into a rising backflip that carried him to the somewhat more solid structure a bit farther in. He looked up toward the rising scream and saw another ball of Greek fire hurtling from the sky, directly at him. Even if he survived the fire, it would certainly destroy the bridge; Kratos had no desire to follow the bridgekeeper down and add his body to the gory pile below.

Acting rather than consciously deciding, he loosed another thunderbolt from his hand, slicing the night to meet the fireball. The detonation splattered the fireball in all directions. Kratos spun to avert his face as bits of the tarry fire rained down on him. The last things he needed on his face were more scars. Some caught on the flooring of the bridge and sizzled to life upon the new fuel of the bridge's span.

He leaped for the other side, sprinting to outrace the sizzling flame, but before he could reach the safety of the rocky outcropping, he felt the structure shift under his weight, shudder—then collapse. Kratos scrambled up the burning planks as though they were a ladder, barely reaching the rocky path before the bridge came apart and tumbled into the chasm.

Kratos stared back across the rocky gap for one brief moment. At least the bridgekeeper should be smiling up from Hades. No monster would cross that chasm unless it could fly. He turned and moved on.

The steep path became stairs that led straight to the top of the mountain. At the summit towered a vast many-tiered structure, three or four times the size of the Parthenon below and ten times its height, all of elegantly constructed marble leafed in the purest gold.

As he climbed the stairs, sounds of battle came from above. He straightened and drew his blades. Slow passage through the air caused the Blades of Chaos to hiss and trail sparks. Kratos took the steps into the temple swiftly and silently, moving as stealthily as he could until he found the source of the clank of sword on sword.

A large devotional area in the center of the temple was spattered with fresh blood. Two soldiers staggered from behind the statue of Athena that towered over the far side of the chamber, trying desperately to hold off the attacks of five or six undead heavy infantry.

Kratos nodded to himself. Of course—as soon as the God of War had located the temple, his foul Hades spawn had begun to appear. Even here, within the holiest sanctum of the goddess.

He cat-footed across the open area and cut the legs of four undead from under them before the creatures knew he was there. A few quick slices settled the others. One soldier was down, bleeding out the last of his life on the goddess's pristine floor. The other Athenian cast one grim nod of thanks toward Kratos, then let out a war cry and charged back behind Athena's statue.

His head rolled out an instant later.

Kratos—reluctantly—admitted to himself that maybe not *all* Athenians were cowards.

The monster that had just sent the valiant soldier to Hades rounded the statue and came at him. Another undead legionnaire, but this one towered taller than a Minotaur, was clad in impenetrable armor, and both its arms terminated in death scythes instead of hands.

The banefires within its empty eye sockets fixed on Kratos as if issuing a silent challenge to combat. The hideous monster attacked with a speed that caught Kratos by surprise.

Barely turning aside the wickedly sharp blade, Kratos gave ground and got to the center of the temple where he could fight unhindered. The legionnaire rushed him and lost a leg. As it fell past, Kratos delivered a second cut that took off both the legionnaire's hands. The death scythes clattered across the floor. Kratos looked at the struggling monster, then swung his sword a final time. The head rolled after the scythes.

For all its fierce aspect, the legionnaire had proven to be no great opponent.

"Aid me!" came a new shout from behind the statue. "To my side, if you love Athena!"

A third Athenian soldier fought a pair of legionnaires by himself, fighting on though weakened from a dozen cuts, some deep and at least one likely mortal.

Kratos added his strong arm to the fight. Brave Athenians were rare enough that he felt he should contribute to this one's survival. He pressed the legionnaires back and saw why the Athenian soldiers had been engaged behind the statue: There a hidden door had been broken to shards, opening a narrow corridor that led, Kratos surmised, to the Oracle's quarters.

These legionnaires were no more challenge than had been their larger brother. Kratos wove a curtain of death about them, pressing in for the kill—and the world exploded around him.

A fireball burst on the temple roof and burned through, laying it open to the sky above. A great gobbet of the Greek fire fell fully upon the Athenian and killed him instantly. The undead this brave spirit had dueled also returned to Hades in a flash of eye-searing combustion. Even the legionnaire Kratos fought perished, as a fist-sized glob of fire splashed upon his helm and burned down until nothing remained above the bony shoulders but a puddle of molten bronze.

The armor Kratos had looted from his victims also blazed with dozens of droplets of fire. A quick flourish of the Blades of Chaos sliced away his improvised bindings, and the armor dropped to the floor, where it was swiftly consumed.

Kratos never even looked back.

He stepped over the Athenian's smoldering corpse and entered the narrow corridor.

"I am Kratos of Sparta," he called. "The goddess commands me to speak with her oracle."

The ghostly woman who had come to him in Athens now appeared in the flesh, and her beauty stole away his voice. The translucent strips of green silk she wore as a skirt beguiled, moving to hide and then reveal her legs and thighs and hips. Wrapped around her bodice, the diaphanous cloth clung with static fierceness to every delicate curve.

"You *came*," the Oracle breathed. Her voice soothed and aroused simultaneously. "I had begun to doubt you ever would."

"The temple is not safe," he said. "Ares's dark spawn hunt within."

The Oracle closed her eyes, then her heavy breasts lifted and fell with a deep, melancholy sigh. "My other defenders have perished. May their souls find nothing but joy as they join their beloveds upon the Elysian Fields."

The Spartan thought this unlikely but held his tongue.

"Only you remain, Kratos." Her eyes, like pools of moonlight, opened and fixed upon Kratos, and for a moment the Spartan could not remember even the battle around him. "You are all I have left."

He shook himself back to the present. "And I am all you need. Hurry."

He looked around the small room where the Oracle lived: only a bed and a few personal items. She led an unsophisticated, innocent existence, free of vanity or guile.

But the chamber itself was a tactical nightmare. If Ares's minions came upon them in this room, the low ceiling and closed-in walls would hinder the use of the Blades of Chaos, and to unleash any of the gods' powerful magic in such an area might well be suicidal. Worse, the corridor leading to the temple was the only exit from the room. Sufficient force at the entry would catch them like flies in a bottle.

"We must speak together, you and I," the Oracle said, indicating a three-legged stool beside her bed. "Sit and I will tell you what you need to know."

"Why did not Athena tell me everything I need to know to kill Ares?"

The Oracle made a dismissive motion to silence him and said, "I will reveal what I have *seen*. Sometimes my vision is precise. Other times, it is as if I am looking through a veil. Or perhaps it is better described as a shroud." A distant expression changed her from anxious to ethereal. Kratos saw the power of her talent—or was it a curse?

"Revealed to me are secrets hidden to the gods," the Oracle said. "For as far reaching as their wisdom is, there are some things to which even they are not privy."

Kratos felt exposed under her unwavering gaze, which focused not upon him but seemingly on something beyond— something through him.

"The visions fill my every waking moment, my every dreaming instant, telling me what you must do." Her voice dropped to hardly more than a whisper. "I know how to kill a god."

ALL-TOO-FAMILIAR SCREECHING that echoed among the temple's columns brought Kratos around, his blades ready for action. "This room is a trap. Ares wants you dead. Move and I'll keep you alive."

He raced back to the temple and skidded around Athena's statue. Other than the corpses and blood splattered on the floor, the room stretched empty and quiet. He looked up to the sundered ceiling and found a reeking swarm of harpies.

He headed out to more-open ground, where he could meet them with all his force. A harpy screeched and hurtled down at him like an attacking eagle. He stabbed upward and drove the point of his sword into the hideous monster's breast. Blood exploded and blasted into his eyes, but he still dismembered the monster with but a flick of his wrist. He slashed at the air as he blinked hard to clear his eyes.

More screeching harpies swarmed around him. His blades met monstrous flesh more than once, but their talons tore at his skin from all sides.

When he finally wiped the harpy gore from his eyes, he saw injured harpies scuttling along the temple floor. Ichor continued to stream from their wounds as they used their leathery wings to drag themselves along. When one saw him watching, she screeched at him again and they all clacked jagged teeth in a fierce challenge.

Kratos took one last swipe across his eyes, then moved in for the kill.

"*Kratos!*"

Terror in the Oracle's voice brought Kratos whirling back toward the statue of Athena. Two harpies held the Oracle in their filthy talons. He leaped for them, blades at the ready. He had seen too well how swiftly even a single harpy could slaughter a mortal—the haunting memory of the child being dashed against Athenian cobblestones caused bile to rise—but they seemed to have some other plan for their captive.

They beat at the air with their wings, wrenching the woman from the ground. Powerful claws sank into the Oracle's shoulders. The harpies screeched with evil glee and took wing, the Oracle dangling from their punishing talons.

"*Kratos!*" she called, her voice going faint from despair. "Kratos, *save* me!"

Kratos leaped with all his might, but another harpy had timed his spring and slammed down onto his back like a falcon taking a rabbit. He spun with a snarl, and a single cut with the Blades of Chaos took one wing and the top of its head. Not yet understanding it had been mortally wounded, the screeching monster raked at him furiously with her claws. A second flurry from the blades sent those claws to the temple floor, lacking the arms to which they had been attached.

But even that single second of distraction had proven too costly.

Before he could gather himself to spring again, the harpies carrying the Oracle flapped powerfully and disappeared through the hole blasted in the temple roof, and all their sisters followed. Kratos watched helplessly as the creatures and their prey disappeared into the murky clouds of night.

Alone in the temple, Kratos turned to the blank-faced statue of Athena and spread his hands.

He did not pray to the gods, he cursed them. Then he formed a plan to rescue the Oracle.

THIRTEEN

INSPIRATION FROM THE GODDESS did not appear to be forthcoming. Kratos would have to come up with a plan of his own. As usual.

He peered through the smoldering gap in the temple ceiling, trying to catch sight of the harpies and the Oracle. No luck.

He ran outside and circled the temple, thinking furiously. How could he rescue the holy woman if he did find her aloft? Zeus's Thunderbolt would fry the Oracle along with the harpies. Medusa's Gaze might work, but using it would involve being in a position to catch the Oracle as she fell. The probability that she might be falling attached to a pair of solid stone harpies—or that she might be turned to stone herself—did not increase the plan's attraction. To use Poseidon's Rage, he'd have to practically catch the fleeing she-raptors with his own hands—and if he got his hands on them, he'd hardly need magic to do what needed to be done.

A *bow*, he thought, wistfully remembering the fine strong bow he'd been given by the dying Athenian at the gap in the Long Wall. *A bow and two arrows.*

Two would be all he'd need, to injure, to weaken, to shoot from the sky.

Desperately searching the sky, he was slow to register a scraping sound at the side of the temple. Kratos rounded the side of the building and saw a freshly dug grave. He drew back as a flurry of dirt sailed from the hole. He advanced cautiously, unsure what was happening. When a hand appeared over the rocky edge, Kratos spun and drew the Blades of Chaos, instantly ready for a fight. Grunting, mumbling to himself, an elderly man in ragged, filthy clothing dragged his withered carcass up to the grave's edge. He blinked at Kratos with age-dimmed eyes, then tossed a shovel onto the ground near the pile of dirt and placed his hands flat, trying to pull himself out. He failed.

"You gonna help an old man or just stand there gawking?"

Kratos could only stare. How could any mortal—let alone an ancient man—have dug a grave in such rocky ground?

"Come on," the old man snapped. "What, the Ghost of Sparta is afraid of *me*? Can't you see I'm older than the dust from a Titan's beard?"

Kratos released the blades and took the man's hand. The old fellow seemed not to weigh anything at all. "You know me?"

"Of course I do. You have the blades, the skin as pale as the moon! You are the one, indeed. Perhaps Athens will survive, at that!" The gravedigger laughed. "But be careful. Don't want you dying before I'm done with this grave."

"A grave, in the middle of a battle? Who will occupy it, old man?"

"You will, my son!" The gravedigger looked Kratos over, from his sandals to the top of his shaved head. "Oh, I've got a lot of digging to do, indeed. All will be revealed in good time. And when all appears to be lost, Kratos, I will be there to help."

"The Oracle," Kratos said. "Have you seen her? She was taken by harpies."

"Oh, sure enough, I saw her." The gravedigger picked up his shovel and stabbed its blade into the earth beside the grave with surprising energy. "Many a thing I could tell you 'bout *her*, if I had half a mind," he said.

If the desiccated old coot *did* have half a mind, this conversation would already be over. "All I need to know is where they're taking her."

The ancient gravedigger turned toward the Ghost of Sparta, and all suggestion of senility drained from his voice. His eyes burned with the fires of Athens below.

"Well, where d'you *think* harpies'd be takin' her?" the old man said scornfully. "Don't you know the first thing about harpies?"

"I know how to kill them."

"That's the *last* thing about harpies, boy! First thing is, they like to eat where they kill. Second thing is . . . they roost up high!"

The ancient gravedigger threw back his head, laughing while Kratos stared, anger growing. Then the old man fell silent, turned, and looked upward to the sundered temple roof. Kratos heard the screech of a harpy and the scream of a woman in pain. . . .

Blades found his hands, and Kratos charged back in to the temple. His sandal slipped on a pool of blood and he skidded across the floor, one knee sliding through gore on the cold marble. High above the temple floor, only a level or two below the topmost reach of the temple, the harpies appeared to be having some kind of disagreement—as though one of them wanted to carry the Oracle off to some secure dining area, where they could enjoy themselves without the fear of being rudely interrupted by the Blades of Chaos, while the other seemed to have decided to forgo the formalities and just eat the Oracle here.

The Oracle fought back with all her human strength and will, hammering at the monsters with her fists and prying at the powerful talons sunk into her shoulders. As the harpies fought back and forth, the Oracle's blood trailed down her breasts and flanks and dripped from the ends of her toes. Her struggles began to weaken.

Kratos dropped the blades and let them return to their

sheaths on his back. His only weapon effective at this range was the thunderbolt, which would fry all three of them when it hit . . . unless he missed. It seemed unlikely. On the other hand, it might be worth his trouble to just go ahead and miss after all — but in a useful fashion.

Again he gathered solid lightning in his right hand, and he cast the bolt a span or two high, close enough that it startled both harpies, then struck the balcony just above them. The thunderbolt blasted out huge chunks of white marble that slammed down into the harpies, who seemingly decided that this particular meal was turning out to be more dangerous than they'd anticipated. They stifled their squabble, let go of the Oracle, and beat their wings as hard as they could, angling for cover. A swift appraisal of the rate of the Oracle's fall told Kratos he had time for one last shot—and lightning from below blew both harpies into smoking gobbets of flesh.

Kratos sprinted toward the spot where the Oracle would strike the temple floor, trusting to save her. But she didn't land.

"Help me!" The Oracle hung from a hawser dangling from a crane affixed to the temple's roof. Ares's barrage of Greek fire, or perhaps Kratos's own lightning, had broken something loose; the Oracle clung for her life hundreds of feet above the temple courtyard. Worse, the hawser swung erratically and threatened to send her over the side of the mountain—down past that sheer cliff. Kratos knew, if she fell that way, all his strength would count for nothing.

He scanned the temple courtyard for any way to get close to her. He saw a structure of rickety timbers that might allow him to cross an upper tier.

"Kratos, save me! You must hurry!" she screamed from high above. This rescue needed to be accomplished now.

He reversed the Blades of Chaos to an underhand, dagger-style grip, then leaped as high as his mighty thighs could propel him up the legs of the marble statue. The same qualities of workability that made marble the choice for statues now made it the choice for a ladder.

With strike after strike, the Blades of Chaos chopped into the marble, driving deep enough that Kratos could use them as pitons to haul himself ever higher. When he withdrew the blades to chop again, the chipped-out gaps left by the blades made admirable footholds. In this fashion, he scaled the vast statue, reaching the goddess's serving tray in only seconds.

"Kratos! I can't hold on!"

"You won't have to," Kratos said, as he took three steps for momentum, then hurled himself through the air from the very edge of the tray.

He stretched out, and out, and at the last instant the hawser swung back toward him. He struck the Oracle with his shoulder as though tackling an opponent in a pankraton free-for-all. This broke her grip on the hawser and let them fall free. . . .

With one arm around the Oracle's slim waist, he grabbed at another rope with his free hand. His fingers touched the rough rope, closed—and for a moment he thought they were safe. Then the rope began playing out over a pulley above.

Kratos grunted, twisted, and snapped the rope hard, sending a shock upward that dislodged the rope from the pulley. The fall stopped suddenly as the rope fouled on a hook, and Kratos and the Oracle swung back and forth like a pendulum. Loosening his grip, Kratos slid down the static rope to stand on the temple floor once more. He released the Oracle, who looked at him intently.

"Kratos! As Athena herself has foretold. But you are late—perhaps too late to save Athens." She moved closer until her face was only inches from his. She reached up and took his head in her hands, one palm pressed warmly into each of his temples. Kratos tried to pull away, but her grip was surprisingly strong—and his strength surprisingly lacking.

"Or is it *Athens* you have come to save . . . ?"

Kratos cried out, "No! I—" He jerked to free himself, screwing shut his eyes and trying to step backward—but it was too late. Her power spread irresistibly through his mind.

Needles danced across his brain, pricking ever faster and

causing discomfort that built into abject pain. His head felt as if it would explode at any instant—and when he opened his eyes he was elsewhere.

HE SAT ASTRIDE A HORSE, a sword gripped in his hand and held high over his head, exhorting his troops upon the bloody field of battle against the barbarians.

"Rally to me, men of Sparta! Though we are only fifty, we will fight like a thousand! Kill them! Kill them all! No quarter! No prisoners! No mercy!" His breath gusted like fire from his nostrils and his heart hammered like Hephaestus's forge. The stench of blood and death filled him to bursting. A thousand deaths this day would belong to him and him alone! He led the charge ...

... at the head of a thousand Spartans as they rushed into battle on his command. He was a hero now, a legend. Spartans vied among themselves for the honor of serving the legendary Kratos. As his victories mounted, their numbers swelled. He carried two swords into battle. When the first dulled from hacking through the bone and flesh of his enemies, he discarded it in favor of the second, which served him through another dozen or hundred opponents until it, too, dulled. Then he gathered weapons dropped by the dead or fleeing enemy so that the carnage would never slow, let alone stop. His valiant soldiers looked to him for guidance—the kind of guidance a legendary commander could offer. He gave them the lessons he himself had learned.

He showed them how to kill. "No quarter! No prisoners! No mercy!"

The warring became nothing more than a stage on which Kratos played. He killed for the God of War, he killed for the glory of Sparta, he killed for the sheer joy of watching men die under his sword. All feared him, ally and enemy alike ...

... except one.

His calm and patient wife, who seemed the only mortal with the courage to stand against his fury. "How much is enough, Kratos? When will it end?"

"When the glory of Sparta is known throughout the world!"

She made a gesture, as if shooing away an annoying insect. "The glory of Sparta," she said with scalding mockery. "What does that even mean? Do you know, or are you just mouthing the excuses you tell yourself to justify your bloodlust?" She gathered their daughter against her skirts, and the flash of anger vanished, replaced by a resigned melancholy. "You do not fight for Sparta. These things, you do only for yourself."

Before Kratos could respond, he saw his wife change, grow older, and . . . her eyes began to shed bloody tears, tears that caught fire as they ran down her cheeks. Where they fell, a wall of fire sprang up between Kratos and his wife—exactly like the flames kindled by his own men to drive the enemy before them and to hear the lamentations of their women. The flames blinded him and seared his flesh.

But his wife! She was on the other side . . . the other side of—

ATHENA'S ORACLE pulled her hands off his temples and looked at him, her face bloodless. "By the gods! Why would Athena send one such as you?"

Kratos took her by the throat with one mighty hand. "Stay out of my head!"

For an instant, a need to snap that pretty neck shook him like an unfurled banner. His head rang with memories of war trumpets and the screams of terror and despair. He cast her aside, and she fell to the temple floor.

She sat and rocked back on her hands, staring up at him. Then she stood and faced the Ghost of Sparta, unafraid. "Choose your enemies wisely, Kratos."

She turned from him and walked toward a section of temple wall where he made out the faint outline of a door. The wall beside it was marked with an insignia, where the Oracle stopped. "Your brute strength alone will not be enough to destroy Ares."

She leaned against the insignia, causing the wall to fade away and the door to open. "Only one item in the world will allow you to defeat a god."

Kratos squinted at the bright light pouring through the portal; it intensified until he had to use one enormous arm to shield his eyes. Heat boiled toward him as if he stood near an open furnace. What lay beyond confused him. This door should lead out onto the rocky night-shrouded cliffs surrounding the temple. . . .

But through the portal, as his eyes began to adjust, he saw noontide and swirling sands.

If the Oracle found this in any way unusual or disturbing, she gave no sign. "Pandora's Box lies far beyond the walls of Athens, hidden by the gods across the desert to the east," she said with calm assurance. "Only with its power can you defeat Ares."

She stepped aside and turned her unreadable eyes on him once more. Kratos feared no man, no god, but he shied away from Athena's oracle. She had entered the hidden realm in his mind and witnessed his shame.

"Be warned, Kratos. Many have gone in search of Pandora's Box. None has returned." She pointed to the portal. "Go through the Gates to the Desert, Kratos. There begins the path to Pandora's Box. It is the only way you will defeat Ares and save Athens. The *only* way, Kratos. The only way." Her voice faded to a whisper, hardly audible over the whistling desert wind.

Kratos ran forth from the temple, skirting the ramparts of the sacred mountain for a few minutes. Then before him loomed a crumbling gate, attended only by a vast statue of a hoplite. He pressed on through the gate without pausing. A strong wind whipped up a storm that cut at his face like tiny razors—and when he turned back for a last look at Athens, the city was gone. There was nothing to be seen in any direction save an eternity of sand.

He was alone, more alone than he had ever been in his life.

FOURTEEN

"SO LITTLE LEFT. Would you care to wager on how long before your city will be rebuilt in honor of Ares?" Hermes fluttered above the reflecting pool, breeze from his winged sandals rippling the water and blurring the view of Athens's destruction. He bent down and poked a finger into the liquid and disturbed the image just under the surface. A heretofore undamaged building fell into rubble at his touch.

"Stop that," Athena said sharply.

"Why? I would say Ares is the clear victor here," the Messenger of the Gods said, smiling broadly. "Do you think that building would have survived his assault? He has left you nothing, and now he reduces that nothing to . . . even less."

Zeus appeared, thunder rolling from his sudden entrance. Hands tucked into his toga, he frowned at Hermes, appearing wroth. "He's done better than I expected. Ares usually blunders about like a Minotaur in a potter's shop."

"*Better* than you expected?" Athena said pointedly. "Have you chosen to support my brother?"

"No," Zeus said, looking angrier yet. "He destroys too many

of my shrines. It is almost as if he picks them out, but I must be wrong. It is your worshippers he kills, Athena."

Athena could only glower.

"Ah, Lord and Father," said Hermes cheerfully. "You have won handsomely in this business so far, haven't you?"

Athena looked sharply at Hermes.

"What do you mean by that?" Zeus's voice thundered and lightning sizzled his beard.

"Is Kratos not your creature?" Hermes asked, fluttering up and away, seeming a little frightened. He looked to Athena for support, but she had none to give. She worried that Hermes understood Kratos's true quest into the Desert of Lost Souls and would tell Ares, simply to relieve himself of boredom by stirring more trouble.

"He is Athena's pet, not mine," Zeus said.

"Yes, of course. I was wrong to assume you were aiding him, though someone in Athens uses a thunderbolt similar to your own against Ares's creatures."

"Do you know that or is it only another of your whispered calumnies to set one god against another?" Athena asked.

"You accuse me—me!—of inciting civil war in Olympus. Never!" Hermes turned his attention back to Zeus. "I am your loyal subject and son, Skyfather! I seek to harm no one but only to keep all informed."

"And amused," Zeus said. "You would go to any length to avoid boredom."

Hermes nodded, smiled, then caught himself. He fluttered higher so he could bow deeply while hovering above the scrying pool. More somber, he bowed his head and swept his arm through the air as he said, "My loyalty is without bounds, my king. You need only command me."

"Very well," Zeus said, grating his teeth. "Go to Ares and tell him I order him to cease his destruction of my temples and supplicants."

"Ares?" Hermes looked so distraught that Athena fought to

keep from laughing. Then she realized the gravity of the situation. Ares would never accede to Zeus's wishes and, if anything, would redouble his effort to snuff out not only her followers but the Skyfather's as well.

"My father, there is no need for Hermes to interrupt Ares. The God of War is only pursuing his true nature." Athena's gray eyes met the storm-filled ones of Zeus. She did not flinch. If Zeus sent this message, Hermes would become curious and would undoubtedly discover that Kratos sought Pandora's Box. She knew the Messenger of the Gods well. He would never be able to restrain himself from slyly hinting to Ares that he knew something the God of War did not—and Ares would take only moments to learn all that she wanted kept secret from him.

Pandora's Box, Athena thought in wonder. *Kratos must find it before Ares realizes there is danger in the quest.*

Zeus's words startled Athena and relieved Hermes.

"You need not deliver the message to Ares," Zeus said.

"How may I be of aid in other ways, my father?" Hermes almost babbled in his respite from delivering such a challenge. The Messenger of the Gods usually enjoyed such discord, being above the content of the news. With Ares willing to slay anyone, though, even the messenger would be at risk, in violation of Zeus's decree against one god killing another.

"Father," Athena said, choosing her words carefully, "the mortals bear the brunt of my brother's rage. If Hermes were to warn our priests and priestesses, telling them the best avenues of escape, they could save themselves."

"Well, get to work on it, then," Zeus said. "I would see this conflict at an end." Zeus grumbled some more, stroking his beard, then looked hard at Athena. "You are not goading your brother into destroying my shrines as a way to humiliate me, are you, Daughter?"

"Father, no! I would never add to the destruction in my city!"

"Even to save your pet mortal?"

"Kratos is nothing to me," Athena said, forcing herself to remain as calm as possible. If she dared not provoke Ares into hunting Kratos, neither did she want Zeus spying on him. She had no idea how the King of the Gods would respond to a mortal killing not only a god but Ares, his son.

"Be gone," Zeus said in a booming voice to Hermes.

Hermes took a single pass around the chamber for airspeed, then his winged sandals carried him high into the clouds around Olympus.

"Thought he'd never leave," Zeus said, lowering himself gratefully onto his throne. When he regarded the Goddess of Wisdom, the noble gravity of authority shadowed his eyes. "I wouldn't say this in front of Hermes—you know how he gossips—but I am growing concerned for you, Athena. Ares has delivered a surprisingly thorough destruction. Within a week or two, you may not have any worshippers left."

"It's been difficult," she admitted. "He's won the battle—but I always knew he would. I can still win the war." She watched her father for any hint that he would aid her.

"Can you?" Zeus asked, a bit sadly. "I have great faith in your powers, my daughter—but so far you haven't even hit back."

If she admitted to doing nothing, Zeus would become suspicious, since this would be unlike her. His concern for her rang true and brought her to an audacious confession. She had worried that her father would hinder Kratos when he found that there was a way for a mortal to destroy a god. But perhaps he would remain neutral, if not aid her valiant hero. It was a risk, but one she had to take to prevent unwanted interference.

"That's about to change." Athena squinted at the Chariot of Helios where it hung in Olympus's everlasting summer noon. "If everything has gone as planned, my oracle in Athens has just now opened the portal to the Desert of Lost Souls and sent Kratos through."

"What does Kratos seek?"

Athena again paused, wary of her father's power and his possible opposition. Then certainty settled upon her like a cloak. She told him of the object of Kratos's search, revealed through the divination of the Oracle.

Zeus sat up straighter. His voice caught. "The *box* . . ."

"Yes, Father," she said with grim satisfaction. "Pandora's Box."

FIFTEEN

LOST IN THE BLINDING SAND, Kratos had no idea where to go.

His eyes watered so hard that he might have been swimming in the sea, were it not for the grit in his mouth and the way the dust filled his nose. Kratos put his head down and slogged forward. He was keenly aware that there were an infinite number of wrong directions, and only one right one. He hoped.

He could not know if there even *was* a right direction to walk.

The Oracle had summoned the visions that haunted his nightmares. The revulsion at what she had seen in his head had been writ plain upon her lovely face. He found it all too easy to imagine that she might have decided a man as corrupt and evil as he knew himself to be was best taken forever from the company of humankind. She might have sent him to this terrible desert to die.

Worse, she might have sent him to this terrible desert to *not* die.

He had heard tales of the punishments of the Titans in Tartarus. This endless desert, endless slash of sand, endless heat, and endless thirst seemed all too similar to such tales.

He cursed the gods as he trudged along, then added their oracles. If there had chanced to be a rift in the sandstorm through which he could glimpse the sun, he might have gauged the passage of time. Or, at least, he might have discovered whether time did indeed pass in this awful waste or if this had become his eternal fate. As it was, all he knew was growing heat and the ever-present wind laden with blinding sand.

Above the howl of the wind came a shrill keening. He reached for the blades but did not draw. Slowly turning, he aimed himself toward the sound and advanced warily. Ares could lay a hundred traps in such a storm. Worse, Kratos knew he might be lured away from his true destination. The only hope he had was to get a fix on the sound and find what it might be. The sound was the first hint he'd had of anything other than his own sorry soul trudging through the storm.

A bright light flashed once, twice, then shone to rival the sun. His stride lengthened. Whatever lay ahead had to be better than stumbling blindly through the desert. As he neared, he saw that the twin beacons were eyes in a statue of Athena.

"Athena," he said angrily, staring into the goddess's gray eyes. He felt abandoned, and she was only the most recent of the Olympian pantheon to use and then discard him. "Why have you brought me here?"

The statue spoke. *"Kratos, the journey forward is perilous but one you must complete if you are to have any hope of saving Athens."*

"The Oracle spoke of Pandora's Box. Can it be real?"

"The box exists. It is the most powerful weapon a mortal can wield."

"Can I defeat Ares with it?"

"With the box, many things become possible. And so it is hidden well, far across the Desert of Lost Souls."

For a brief instant the clouds of roiling sand cleared, and Kratos saw to the horizon. As quickly as the window opened, it closed.

"*There is safe passage through deadly sand, but only those who hear the Sirens' song will discover it, for only the Sirens can guide you to Cronos, the Titan. Zeus has commanded him to wander the desert endlessly with the Temple of Pandora chained to his back, until the swirling sands rip the very flesh from his bones.*"

"How do I find him?"

"*Stay true to the song of the Siren, Kratos. Your journey begins here. Pray it leads you back to Athens—with Pandora's Box. Remember this: Seek the summit for only death awaits you below. There is no escape without the box.*"

"How do I resist the Sirens' song?" he asked. Athena's statue did not answer. He moved closer and saw the eyes were featureless orbs of marble. The spirit of the goddess had left—and had left him. He held down his rising wrath. *Hints, nothing but hints!*

HE GRITTED HIS TEETH and trudged on. It was not given to mortals to understand the whys and wherefores of the gods. That was what his mother used to tell him, back before he turned seven and was taken from her to begin his training. He had always assumed that it meant nothing more or less than "Hush and do as you're told."

As he set forth, he saw that the statue had changed. Now the right arm was raised, pointing into the desert. As he turned to follow that direction, he heard the faint keening once more. He stood a little straighter against the wind. Now he knew that sound to be the song of the desert Sirens.

Athena had set him on his path but, as usual, had not even hinted at how he might overcome the Sirens. He assumed she trusted him to figure it out for himself—or, if his cleverness was unequal to the challenge, he could always rely on his native savagery and the Blades of Chaos.

Odysseus had stopped up the ears of his crew with beeswax, while he remained chained to the mast of his ship. Kratos had nothing that would block the insistent, seductive sound. Even at this distance, he felt his heart quickening and his body responding to their call. If he succumbed, he would be their dinner.

As he walked along, Kratos clapped his hands over his ears, hoping to muffle their insidious song. That failed. He found himself walking faster, hunting through the sandstorm for the creatures, *wanting* them as he had never wanted another before.

The heavy flapping of wings caused him to look upward. Through the dust clouds he saw a harpy struggling to carry a dangling body in its claws. The monster veered and disappeared in the storm, but Kratos knew it took the body to the Sirens.

Once, on a battlefield outside Sparta, he had come across two Sirens and had ordered his men to fill them full of arrows. The Sirens had been dining on the dead of both sides, greedily gobbling up human flesh and smearing the blood all over themselves. Their death cries had cost him three expert archers. As the Sirens had died, they screeched at such a pitch that the men's heads exploded. Kratos had ordered the Sirens' carcasses to be carved into pieces so small that even crows would ignore them and then be flung to the four winds, so that the monsters' shades would wander forever restless upon the earth.

He pressed his palms harder against his ears. The Sirens' song grew ever more enticing. The wind slackened, and their evil song lifted and filled him with irresistible lust. Soon he stared across a sandy dune marked with wavy ripples from the wind. Beyond lay the ruins of an ancient temple—perhaps where the Sirens made their home.

And then he saw them: four tall, spectral creatures floating about the plaza before the ruined temple.

The Sirens' seductive sound turned Kratos weak. Sheer sexual allure pulled him forward like a shade in Hades shuffling toward Charon's boat. Every move he made was slow, unsteady, and increasingly uncoordinated. One of the Sirens had seen him now. Drawn by his mortal blood, she turned toward him, and her part in their song rose.

Kratos tried to draw his swords but found he could not. The

Blades of Chaos were never meant for creatures so lovely. The
Siren who'd seen him slithered down the slope, her face unbear-
ably beautiful as she smiled. The sharp yellow teeth that
rimmed her gaping maw didn't bother him in the slightest.
Lovely, she was so lovely, and she became more so as she
neared.

"Come to me, lover. I want you as much as you want me."
Her voice carried the Siren's song. Kratos knew the song for
what it was—knew it sang the melody of his doom—but still he
could not resist. With a mighty exertion of will, he forced one
hand back to his shoulder, fingers brushing the hilt of one
blade.

The Siren didn't flinch. She knew well the power of her vile
song. "There is no need, lover. Come to me and love me. I love
you. I want to feel you in my embrace."

His resistance faded as he went to the most beautiful woman
in the world. His arms wrapped around her as he pulled her
close. Kratos jerked as he felt a bite.

"A love bite, my dearest," came her cooing words. "You like it.
You want me to give you more, many more!"

He felt blood running down his chest from the neck wound,
but he knew she loved him—and he desired her above all others.

*Even above Aphrodite's twin daughters. Even more than Lora
and—*

He pulled back, struggling in the warm embrace of a woman
he treasured.

"No," he said. "I can't . . ." His ears filled with song, shrill at
first and then so melodious that he wept. His lover sang for him.
She sang a haunting song of love and desire. For him and him
alone.

"Another love peck," she said.

Again he recoiled as blood spewed from the other side of his
neck.

*Blood, blood spilled in battle, not in a lover's tryst—*He straightened his arms and shoved hard. The Siren let out a screech of

pure rage, momentarily breaking the spell. Kratos saw the Siren for what she was, and then she sang to him. Sang a melody so lovely and beguiling he knew she wanted him above all others in the world.

But she is not my wife . . . my wife and daughter . . . Those memories hammered at Kratos's mind even as he felt more love bites. The pain offset the pleasure. He had known pain, so much pain, and he concentrated on it. And his wife. And his daughter lying dead at his feet—

Again he pushed away, but this time he heard other voices.

"Share! You are greedy!"

"Hungry! We're all hungry. You must give him to us!"

The voices turned strident, and the lovely, loving melody faded in his ears.

My wife! My daughter!

Kratos lifted his hand and felt energy flow. The Thunderbolt of Zeus built . . . but against his lover, his lovely, caring lover. He couldn't. Not this way . . .

The cacophony of demands to dine on his flesh grew as the Siren's song diminished. Kratos reached down deep within, the visions—the nightmares—powering his determination. The thunderbolt erupted from his palm. A force greater than anything he had ever felt lifted him from his feet and threw him high into the air, spinning, turning, and tumbling. He crashed into the sand, dazed. When he looked up, he saw Sirens scattered about, lifeless.

He shook himself and stood, aware that he had destroyed only a few of the creatures with the power of Zeus. Three other Sirens rushed toward him. Kratos had never seen creatures so lovely or loving—but he did not fall under their spell. Within a moment he understood why.

The Sirens had begun to fight over him. His hand went to his neck and found fresh bite marks, all bleeding freely. His nightmarish vision had allowed him to break their spell to fight, and when he had blown them apart with Zeus's lightning, the thunder had partially deafened him. He might not have the beeswax that Odysseus carried, but he had a makeshift method of temporarily blocking the Sirens' call. His hearing was already returning, though—had he waited too long?

He raised his right hand again, but his body betrayed him. His hand trembled, rebellious flesh refusing to grasp the lightning. The Sirens soothed and cajoled him to relax, not to use his weapon. They loved him. He wanted them more than he'd ever wanted anything.

A final twist of his will curled his fingers into the proper form, but his weakened arm could no longer hold his hand upraised. It fell to his side, and the thunderbolt in his grip blasted the sand in front of him to glass. The thunderclap and shock wave staggered him. Two steps back, three. He launched another thunderbolt. Again came the blast—but this time he could barely hear it.

"Well, all right, then," he did not hear himself say. He set out toward the desert monsters at a walk—with purpose but without haste. The Sirens drifted back from him, exchanging glances that seemed to cry, "How can this mortal resist our power?" Suddenly the Sirens were uncertain that Kratos was human at all. They howled at him, pitching their voices in various harmonics—one chord could set a man afire, another could blind him, still a third could cause his skull to explode like a chestnut in a bonfire.

Kratos kept walking. He didn't even bother to draw the blades.

The Sirens spread out as though to encircle him. But Kratos had dealt with Sirens before—and these Sirens, to their misfortune, had never dealt with Kratos.

They had never seen Kratos move faster than a walk, and they had no idea just how swiftly those powerful legs could drive his massive body. He allowed them to close in around him until he judged they were near enough, then, in a blindingly swift uncoiling of his mighty thighs, he sprang at one of the Sirens the way a tiger pounces on a goat.

With one great hand, he seized the Siren's long, flowing hair, while with the other he punched her in the chest so hard that her sternum and clavicles shattered and ripped the upper part of her spine out her back.

He wrenched off her head and swung it by its hair like a flail. The nearer of the remaining two took her sister's head square in the face, hard enough to shatter every monstrous bone in her skull and drop her dead on the sand. The last Siren turned to flee, but Kratos whipped the remains of the first Siren's head around his own and hurled it like a throwing hammer. The severed head struck the fleeing Siren between the shoulder blades, hard enough to shatter her spine. Splinters of bone shredded her lungs, which put a stop to her hideous keening cry.

Kratos stood over the dying Siren for a moment, with nothing resembling pity on his face. He crushed her head with a stomp of his sandal.

He hurried up the steps into the razed structure. Oddly, though the place appeared to be a ruin, the stairways and corridors were all lined with burning lamps, so he had not the slightest difficulty seeing his way. He followed the light . . .

. . . and eventually burst out into daylight again, on a balcony of dizzying height, looking upon the endless sandstorm raging across the Desert of Lost Souls. Kratos paused to examine crude reliefs carved on the walls to either side. One depicted gods appearing before Pathos Verdes III, commanding him to build a mighty temple to house the greatest weapon on earth or Olympus. The other showed the temple being chained to the back of Cronos—a disrespectful way for Zeus to treat his own father, even if Cronos had tried to eat Zeus as soon as the future king was born. Chained to the stone at the far lip of the balcony stood a horn larger than Kratos's whole body. Curious carvings raked backward along the length of the horn; precious jewels rimmed its far end. Heavy chains fastened the horn into place at the edge of the balcony. Kratos went to the smaller end of the great horn, put his lips to it, and blew.

A mighty blast roared from the horn's opposite end, harrowing apart the swirling desert sands before Kratos and somehow holding them at bay to open a path before him. Far in the distance along this path, he glimpsed another structure, a grander and more curious one. As he squinted at it, trying to make out details, that mighty temple began to move toward him. Kratos sucked in his breath as he saw Cronos arch and cause the Temple of Pandora chained to his back to shake and rumble. Then the Titan, on hands and knees, turned and passed close to the edge of the balcony where Kratos watched.

Kratos had no time to think. He reacted. A heavy chain dangling from the Titan's side swept past. With a powerful leap, Kratos launched himself into the air. His fingers closed about the chain, and then he was whipped about as Cronos changed direction and plunged back into the depths of the sea of sand.

SIXTEEN

HANDS BLOODIED AND ACHING, Kratos finally reached the top of the Titan's mountainous side. For three long days he had climbed—and for the whole of the most recent day he had no longer been scaling Cronos's hide but instead chipping his way up the mountain chained to Cronos's back. He had lashed himself to the Titan's side and slept fitfully several times, but on the long, long rock climb he had pushed upward without true rest. Worse was the lack of food and water as he worked ever higher on the vast Titan. When he had begun, Kratos thought the Titan moved slowly, but the higher he climbed on the side, the more he realized that Cronos sped along. Even though he crawled on hands and knees, each motion was so huge that the wind of his passage had very nearly stripped Kratos from his side more than once.

Kratos's blasts on the horn had summoned from the depths of the Desert of Lost Souls this great mountain of a Titan, his immortal face worn by time and sand into smooth curves of eternal sadness.

A mountain nearly as tall again rested on the mighty Cronos's back. At its uppermost lip, Kratos crawled up and over, to find himself face-to-face with an enormous vulture, who was happily ripping an eye from the corpse of a dead soldier.

Kratos frowned. What was that soldier doing here?

Kratos stood to get an idea of the landscape. The mountain's height would have let him see leagues away, if not for the permanent swirl of sandstorm in the Desert of Lost Souls. But he was more interested in what lay near at hand.

Not far away rose huge but plain sandstone blocks and a crude bronze-and-wooden gate at the front of the magnificent temple. The walls could be solid gold and the plaza paved with diamonds for all Kratos cared. Kratos was indifferent to wealth. He would secure what the temple had been constructed to defend and be on his way.

Kratos reacted instinctively when a harpy described a long, sweeping arc through the skies overhead. He drew the Blades of Chaos and set himself to fight—but the winged creature completed its curve toward the temple.

He jogged forward.

Kratos watched warily as harpies flocked around the Temple of Pandora like bats around a bell tower. Below them, on some sort of broad stone deck, an immense bonfire burned, and the smoke that twisted upward from it was greasy and black. A shift in the wind brought it to Kratos's nose, and he knew the smell.

The fuel for this fire was human corpses.

Scaling the last few feet proved too much for him. He had to spend considerable time searching before he found some stone blocks that could be fashioned into a crude stair. After scrambling up to a level place, Kratos discovered that what burned here was not a funeral pyre but instead was contained within a huge fire bowl of bronze and stone, whose rim was twice Kratos's height.

As Kratos approached, the harsh screech of a harpy drew his eyes skyward, in time to see the hideous she-creature open her talons and let drop another corpse—another soldier, it seemed.

Bronze armor glinted briefly in the afternoon sun, then clashed like cymbals when its bearer hit the bowl.

"That'll be you one day. And sooner rather than later would be my bet."

Kratos spun and the blades found his hands. Limping toward him, using a long staff as a crutch, came some sort of undead too decrepit to even wield a sword or scythe. Its head was mostly exposed skull, one arm ended in a splintery stub of bone, and its right leg was gone below the knee. The one side of its rib cage that was exposed to Kratos's sight did seem to house internal organs—leathery lungs and a black heart, which pulsed as slowly as the creature stepped. The staff on which it supported itself was fire-blackened and charred at one end.

Kratos scowled at him. He didn't know how to deal with an undead that wasn't trying to kill him, let alone one that could actually speak. "What are you?"

"Once I was a soldier. Now . . ." It jerked its head toward the fire bowl. "I look after this."

From above came fierce flapping as a harpy circled and released another body to impact in the huge bowl.

The eye within the skull socket seemed to flicker like the flames in the bowl above. "Everybody around here ends up in the fire. Except for me."

"Everybody?" Kratos asked with a frown. "There are others?"

"Still alive? Probably not. But you never know."

"I have come a considerable distance—"

"And you're no closer to your goal. Not really. Zeus hid Pandora's Box in this wretched temple so no mortal could ever claim its power. And yet, year after year, I open the gate for more and more seekers—and shove more and more bodies into the fire."

With another screech, a new harpy appeared. The winged monster dropped a fresh-looking body that missed the center of the bowl, ending up draped over the rim. Rather than descend to rectify its mistake, it merely shrieked in annoyance before flapping hard and flying off. It caught an updraft from the sun-heated stone of the mountain and circled skyward before disappearing above the summit of the temple.

The firekeeper spat a black gob, then said, "Here, give me a hand with this."

It led Kratos over to the bowl and handed the Spartan its staff, leaning his nub of arm bone against the searing bowl for balance. "Poke that bugger in for me, will you?"

Kratos used the staff to shove the corpse into the bowl, reflecting that at least he'd figured out why the staff was charred at one end. "You said *you* open the gate."

"It opens at my command."

"Then do it."

"In my own time, Spartan. You think you can conquer the Temple of the Gods? It's never been done, you know. Sooner or later, the harpies will bring what's left of you back for me to burn. If I were you, I'd leave now."

"I will leave," Kratos said, "when I have the box."

"And luck to you on that." The decrepit undead chuckled. "You want water? Food? Armor? There's not much, but take what you will."

"Why?"

"Why give you supplies?" One bony shoulder lifted in a shrug. "Why not? It's not like I have any use for them myself." With the nub of arm bone, it pointed toward its guts — or, rather, to the ragged gap where his stomach, liver and bowels ought to be. "Bloody vultures got my innards decades ago."

"Where's the food?"

"Over there," the decrepit creature said. "I rob the bodies."

"Of what? *For* what?"

"Whatever they've got. For fun, mostly. It's the only interesting part of my job. Never quite know what you'll find."

Kratos hefted a half-empty water skin. The water inside smelled like goat. "Drink up," the creature said. "And here's some decent meat. Hardly any maggots at all. I got it off a body

only a day back. Or was it two? Five? You lose track of the days
out here. One's pretty much like the next, and both today and
tomorrow are like all the ones before."

Kratos drank of the water and ate what he could. The worms
tasted better than the meat they infested. He licked what little
grease there was off his fingers and wished for more. He drank
the last of the water in the skin. The undead seemed not to
mind. Why should he? Then he donned bronze armor from the
pile.

When Kratos had finished, he frowned at his host.

"I can see your curiosity, eh? You want to know my story.
Questions, questions. It's always the same," the firekeeper said.
"Madmen seeking power, and fools seeking glory. I know. Too
well I know. As you can see by what's left of me"—it indicated
it's maimed form—"I was no luckier than the rest of them. Un-
luckier, really. At least they got their burning and their souls released to the Lord of the Underworld. I got . . . this." It swung its
staff about, showing the area filled with the pilfered possessions
and the huge fire bowl.

"*You* attempted to conquer the temple?"

"That I did, and I'm sorry for it now. I was the first mortal to
enter the temple. And so I was the first to die. As punishment for
my presumption, Zeus doomed me to tend this corpse fire for all
eternity—or until Pandora's Box is taken. Which is close
enough to eternity, for no man will ever gain the box."

The creature nodded toward the towering gates and gave out
a whistling sigh. "The Architect—he who built this temple—
was a zealot. He lived only to serve the gods, and for that he got
the same reward we all do: an eternity of madness. The tale is
that he's still alive, still inside, still trying to appease the gods
who abandoned him centuries ago."

Kratos stepped closer and stared into the fire, where bodies
sizzled and popped.

"I see your question. How many bodies a day do I burn? Go
on. You can ask. I tried counting, for the first few years, that is. I

gave up after the tenth year. Five a day? A dozen? I know your questions, I do, since I've heard 'em all before. Did every one slay desert Sirens and sound the horn to get here? Did I?"

Kratos grunted, looked past the remnant of a man, and studied the gates for a way to open them. If he could not, he might scale the walls beside the bronze-and-wood gates. But he recognized the danger in that, with the harpies fluttering around above, eyeing him hungrily.

"You shouldn't think so much," the firekeeper said. "It'll only make you crazy—but then, you're here, so you must already be crazy." The way it laughed warned Kratos of something more. "You're right to question me. I know what happened to you because you *didn't* question the gods."

A fist of dread clenched in Kratos's guts. He fixed his gaze on the firekeeper.

"I know you are the Ghost of Sparta." The empty eye socket glimmered as though the undead stared at him intently. "I know why your skin is white as ash."

Kratos lurched forward and seized the firekeeper by the throat. "Your job is difficult for a creature missing a hand and a foot. Imagine how difficult it will be when you're missing your head."

"You'll have no luck entering the temple if that gate stays closed." Kratos's grip didn't impede the creature's mocking speech. "Think it over, Ghost of Sparta. Can you risk mindlessly serving your lust for blood? After what happened *last* time?"

With a wordless snarl of frustration, Kratos cast the firekeeper to the ground. Chuckling, the creature rose and hopped over to grab a skull from the ground. With speed and accuracy astonishing for such a broken creature, the firekeeper hurled the skull at an outcropping above. It shattered against the stone, its impact disturbing a pair of harpies. They fluttered down toward some sort of mechanism at the top of the massive gate. Kratos could not see what they did, but soon the gate began to lift slowly, as one harpy on each side flapped frantically to lift with all her might. The gates ratcheted upward and locked in place. "See you soon, Ghost of Sparta!" the fire-keeper cried. "I'll see you again when the harpies drop you in my bowl!"

Kratos strode through the gate without a backward glance.

SEVENTEEN

THE BOOK LAY OPEN before a massive door like the eye of a god, its upper arch decorated with arcane symbols. The book itself seemed to be only a statue, a replica, carved from stone to look like a book on a pedestal—no real book could have survived exposure to the Desert of Lost Souls, open for a thousand years.

Its nature was irrelevant. All the import was conveyed by the words graven into its stone pages.

THIS TEMPLE WAS CONSTRUCTED IN THE HONOR OF AND AT THE COMMAND OF THE MIGHTY LORD ZEUS.
    ONLY THE BRAVEST HERO SHALL SOLVE ITS PUZZLES AND SURVIVE ITS DANGERS. ONE MAN WILL RECEIVE ULTIMATE POWER.
    ALL OTHERS SHALL MEET THEIR DOOM.
                          —PATHOS VERDES III
                    CHIEF ARCHITECT AND
                LOYAL SUBJECT OF THE GODS

Kratos scowled as he read the graven words. The Architect had actually *designed* the Temple of Pandora, deliberately, to be solved by "the bravest hero"? Kratos snorted in disgust. He was no hero, having committed the bloody murders he had, but he would not meet his doom here. His hatred for Ares—and the promise of the gods to erase his nightmares—would carry him to victory. Kratos spun about when the great temple doors slammed behind him. There was no going back, even if he had wanted to.

He looked around and saw that the only way forward was through a portal carved with more of the curious symbols. At cardinal points around the circular doorway were large gemstones, dull and lifeless in spite of the sunlight slanting down from behind him. Kratos placed a hand on one huge stone that might have been a diamond. He felt it quiver and drew back his hand.

Spinning, drawing the Blades of Chaos, he faced a ten-foot-tall heavily armored undead. Kratos crossed his blades above his head to fend off a powerful downward strike by the undead's massive sword. The blow was so hard that it drove Kratos to his knees.

Rather than force his way back to his feet, Kratos suddenly released the pressure on his blades and rolled forward between the undead's legs. As he whirled under, he knocked it down by grabbing its skeletal ankles. The undead soldier toppled forward, giving Kratos the opening he needed. He came to his feet and slashed with all his strength. Two things happened, one expected and the other surprising. The undead's head exploded from its neck, as he'd intended.

The diamond Kratos had touched on the doorway began to glow. He stepped over his fallen adversary and pressed his callused hand to the now-illuminated, flame-hot diamond. He reached up and brushed his hand over the next jewel, still coldly inert.

He quickly found himself engaged with a Cyclops that materialized behind him. The fight was fierce, but Kratos dispatched the one-eyed horror with a feint to the leg that caused the Cyclops to bend low. The blade in Kratos's left hand speared deep through the single orb, causing eye goo and brains to gush out.

The stone in the door now glowed a bright ruby red.

"So," Kratos said, smiling grimly. "This is the key to your doorway, Architect. Blood!" He quickly touched the remaining two gems, producing two fighters. Knowing the secret of the portal allowed him to waste no effort sending the monsters to Hades where they belonged.

The two remaining gems—one peridot, gleaming greenish-yellow, and the other a blazing sapphire blue—sent lightning arcing around the circular portal. Slowly, the doorway into the Temple of Pandora opened to him.

Kratos entered a long, curving corridor lined with doors on both sides.

Here, too, wall-mounted braziers burned with cheery flame. They could be magical—apparently everything here was, to some degree or other—but they certainly wouldn't have been the work of the Architect; there was absolutely no reason to illuminate the interior if one wanted to keep intruders out. Everything would be doubly challenging in the kind of inky blackness the stone-shrouded interior would otherwise be—and anyone attempting to reach Pandora's Box would have to do it before his lamp oil ran out.

Then Kratos laughed harshly. The Architect undoubtedly thought the sight of the monsters awaiting anyone who had come into this maze would unnerve them, add to their fear, make their deaths all the more certain, as terror froze their arms and loosened their bowels. The Temple of Pandora was not only about keeping out those who sought the box. It would be designed to inspire gut-churning fear in those who dared come this far. More than once, Ares had told Kratos that the purpose of war was not to kill your enemy but to kill him after breaking his spirit.

He looked to either side, calculating the curve. If this corridor formed a ring, it would be very large. His first order of business was to investigate the lay of the land, because apparently any part of this structure could, without warning, become a battlefield. He trotted around the circle . . . and when he returned to his starting point, he discovered that the great circular door through which he had entered had closed, sealed to his best effort to open it again.

Kratos ignored this. Retreat was not in his fiber. Win or die. The way it always had been.

He found an open archway as he continued around the ring—one that hadn't been open a moment ago, when he'd first passed. The view along the hallway open before him looked promising—every few yards, giant spiked walls slammed against one another with enough force to shake the stone floor on which he stood. Reasoning that the Architect had gone to so much trouble to discourage intruders along this particular path made it a likely place to start his quest.

Timing a succession of dashes took him through the corridor without so much as a scratch. Kratos stopped to look back. He had passed the first test within Pandora's temple. How many more to come? Many.

He stepped into a wide area, the walls carved with the mysterious symbols he had seen outside. Kratos ignored them, because he faced a chamber full of monsters. Reaching back, he drew the Blades of Chaos and, with a toss, sent them to the limits of their chains. A quick spin sent the fierce-edged weapons in a sweeping circle of destruction around him, catching two of the undead legionnaires unaware. He cut off their legs and toppled them to the floor so they could not continue the fight. The others rushing forward were not as easily vanquished.

Kratos drew in his weapons and began the methodical destruction of his enemies. His skill, his experience, and the towering anger he felt toward Ares powered his thrusts, enhanced his slashes, and brought him to the far side of the chamber with only a few scrapes. He faced an archway that appeared harmless, but he approached warily, then stepped away, blades in hand, when a low-pitched humming filled the room.

He looked around the room and noticed a circular portal that had begun to glow with pure white light. The archway at the side of the chamber was now filled with the image, traced in living fire, of the face of a goddess—not as voluptuous as Aphrodite nor so severe as Athena, this goddess had a curious innocence to her, a sort of eternal golden adolescence.

This could be only one goddess. Kratos inclined his head out of true respect. "Lady Artemis."

"*Kratos, the gods demand more of you!*"

Kratos just nodded. The gods always demanded more.

"*Much depends on your skill,*" said the Huntress of Olympus. "*You have learned to use the Blades of Chaos well, but they alone will not carry you to the end of your task. I offer you the very blade I used to slay a Titan. Take this gift and use it to complete your quest.*"

Kratos reached out and the sword appeared in his hands. It was a huge, unwieldy weapon, longer than Kratos was tall, and not shaped like any honest Spartan sword. Its broadly curved blade was wider than the span of his hand, jutting out beyond the haft, more like the *khopesh* favored by the heathen Egyptians.

"Thank you, Lady Artemis."

"*Go with the gods, Kratos,*" the image of Artemis said. "*Go forth in the name of Olympus!*" With that, the huntress vanished, leaving only the open archway leading deeper into the temple.

Artemis's blade cool in his hand, he approached the archway. Some glyphs were letters he could read, but most were strange, alien, and beyond his ability to decipher. If only he could read them, he might get some hint as to the challenges he faced before reaching them! He peered into the room beyond the arch and saw no one. It was nothing more than a foyer, such as he had seen leading to many a king's audience chamber. The trappings were richly appointed, but he had claimed more-elegant furniture, statues, and tapestries as the spoils of war for the glory of Sparta.

A staircase provided the only way forward. As Kratos climbed, he noticed that the walls narrowed until, at the top of the stairs, his broad shoulders brushed the rough stone. The narrowing continued down a corridor until he came out on a platform, high above a room filled with rotating gears and distant screams of agony. The dim light afforded him a good look only at the gigantic creature blocking his way to a catwalk across the room.

The giant roared its wordless challenge and charged. A heavy sledge that replaced its left hand smashed down hard, shaking the catwalk and threatening its structure. The Blades of Chaos came easily to Kratos's hands, but he found that his opponent was as wily as it was strong. His usual attacks—weaken the creature, then ram his blade down its throat—were not going to work. The giant agilely avoided even his quickest thrust and slash and forced Kratos to dance back to avoid the heavy hammer blows. Any hit with that crashing hammer would mean death, but, worse, the creature seemed inclined to destroy the catwalk and prevent Kratos's crossing.

"By the gods, you are different," Kratos said. He thought a spark of intelligence showed in the eyes buried under bony brows. Great intelligence. Then it attacked, using its right hand to strike at Kratos's eyes as diversion for the sweeping attack from the hammer. A simple move to the side allowed the fist to pass by harmlessly, but this was not the creature's intent—it delivered a more subtle attack. The haft of the hammer blocked Kratos's weapons, allowing it to step closer still.

It tried to grapple with Kratos but succeeded only in a potent head butt. A fraction of an inch closer and it would have caught his eye. Responding the only way he could, Kratos hammered at the monster's powerful sloping shoulders with both pommels of his blades. The creature danced away more lightly than any spawn of Hades Kratos had ever faced.

They circled, each studying the other for weaknesses and how best to attack. The blood trickled down Kratos's cheek as a reminder that this monster considered its assault carefully and was a skilled opponent. But it had never faced the Ghost of Sparta before.

Kratos roared and rushed forward, pressing the giant back a step, then changed the direction of his attack, dropping flat to the platform and kicking out. One bronze greave smashed into the creature's knee, unbalancing it. Kratos worked his other foot behind the leg and swept around hard, further staggering it. Not content with this, Kratos spun about so his feet tangled his foe's legs—and then it was time to end the battle.

Off-balance and facing away from Kratos, the creature tottered on the edge of the platform. Swinging a blade out on the end of its chain, Kratos felt the Hades-forged weapon crash into the exposed back and send the giant forward—into space. It roared all the way to the distant floor, where its cries ended suddenly with a huge crash.

Kratos looked over the edge of the platform and felt no victory. The hammer-swinging giant had been a worthy opponent but nothing more. It had been only an impediment to finding Pandora's Box. Kratos looked across the narrow catwalk and then began to walk on it. The walk was hardly wider than his sandals, and the drop to the floor where the monster's body lay had to be a hundred feet, but he never faltered. Confident strides took him to an island in the middle of the room, where a lever had been locked into place. Studying the area, Kratos saw that his only hope for getting to another entryway in the chamber wall some fifty feet under him was to reach a cable strung from one side to the other. A jump might allow him to grab the cable as he fell, but if his hands slipped or he misjudged his trajectory off this isle of safety, his fate would be sealed. There was nothing below the cable for him to seize if he missed it.

Another path suggested itself to him. He followed the mechanism controlled by the lever and saw how it dropped a huge weight to the floor below. That descent would unwind a chain and give him a safer way down to the cable, although it would be at the far end of that stretched line, requiring him to work his way hand over hand to the portal. He never hesitated. He took off the securing line on the lever and yanked hard, setting the massive gears and pulleys into motion. The huge weight lowered from above.

As the weight passed, Kratos jumped and grabbed the chain holding it. For a moment he swayed, because his added mass disturbed the mechanism as it unwound the chain and lowered the iron block. But he found himself ready when the weight flashed past the cable. He gathered his legs under him and made a powerful leap, hands outstretched. Success! He gripped the heavy cable and caused only a slight sagging from his added weight.

Kratos began working hand over hand toward the far side of the chamber. He kept his goal in sight to avoid looking downward at the gears clacking and clashing underneath. A slip and he would be ground up and sent to Hades in tiny pieces. Working swiftly, he'd reached the midpoint along the cable when he felt it sag more than it had only seconds before. Like some arboreal creature in its element, he reversed his direction and looked behind along the length of cable he had already traversed.

One hand left the cable as he reached for the Blades of Chaos. Following him along the aerial pathway were two grasping, chittering monsters with saliva-dripping fangs and an ability to swing and move that he could never match. Kratos considered severing the cable, which would send the far half crashing into the distant wall while the half he clung to would swing forward so he could climb to the portal when he hit the wall.

Such was not to be. The monsters swarmed forward, climbing over each other in their haste to kill him. Taloned fingers swiped at him, forcing him to recoil. Bringing up his feet to kick out held them at bay for only an instant. As he swung back down, they came at him. His grip on the cable firm, he dared to swing his blade. It struck at an awkward angle and did little damage to the first creature—long, deep scratches appeared on his sword arm as talons raked him. Worse than the pain that threatened to cause him to abandon the use of his sword was the second creature's attack, swarming over the first along the cable.

It went not for his sword arm but for the hand holding the

cable. It snapped savage fangs and caught a finger, almost severing the digit from his hand. Kratos roared in anger and let the
bloodlust he had known for ten full years rise to take control. He
caught the second creature between his thighs, twisted, and
pulled it away from its hold on the cable. He swung away and
simply released his vise grip, sending the creature plunging to
the distant floor. But it never struck. Its body was tossed high on
a spinning gearwheel, then caught and minced in the ponderous mechanism that seemed to have no purpose other than to
grind out death.

The creature's companion made the fatal mistake of watching the death below. With one hand on the cable, Kratos released his hold on his blade and grabbed. His fingers closed
around an exposed neck. Tendons stood out on his forearms as
he squeezed the life from the creature, but he did not stop when
all movement ceased. His blood from the deep scratches ran
down his hand and onto the flesh of the dead monster, tainting
it. Only when Kratos was satisfied that he had marked the creature forever in Hades with his blood did he send it tumbling
after the other to be dismembered in the gears below.

Kratos swung back and gripped the cable, only to have his fingers slip and almost cause him to crash to his death. The blood
from the cuts and scratches had turned his fingers slippery. His
strength remained, but the cable might as well have been oiled
for all the traction he now had on it. His right hand came free,
leaving him dangling precariously. Even as he wiped off his
hand, he knew this would not work; more blood oozed from his
wounds to again slicken it.

Kratos doubled up and swung his heels over the top of the
cable, locking them to give more support. He had no way of
stanching the blood leaking out of his bone-white flesh, but
keeping his ankles locked above the cable prevented him from
following his enemies to the floor beneath. Dangling upside
down, he pulled himself along the cable as quickly as he could,
finally reaching the end of the line. A quick twist allowed him to
clutch an outcropping under the portal.

He wiped his hands, one at a time, to clean them of blood, and then pulled himself up to the ledge. Standing, he faced a short corridor. Stride long, Kratos went to see if he had finally reached Pandora's Box. In only a few minutes he realized that he hadn't.

EIGHTEEN

"I KNOW THAT SWORD," Zeus murmured as he looked into the scrying pool. "That blade is one of the most powerful weapons in all creation. How did you trick Artemis into giving it to Kratos?"

"Trick her, Father? I?" Athena shook her head. "She and Ares have reached a kind of truce—but she has seen his vicious rampage of insanity firsthand. She did not relinquish the sword lightly. I believe that she wishes to show her support by helping Kratos through the temple."

"I've seen my son's bloodlust as well," Zeus muttered darkly. "He has burned most of Athens to the ground. Only a few buildings remain around the main square, and only the temples atop the Acropolis stand. Even your Parthenon has been blackened with soot from the fires and is falling into disrepair."

"Most of your shrines are gone. He kills your worshippers just as he singles out mine for his brutal murders."

"War is always messy," Zeus said. "Ares has again refused to attend me and explain why he attacks my followers so aggressively, though. It is one thing to burn Athens to the ground, another to flaunt it in such a fashion that it offends me. Unless,"

Zeus said, turning thoughtful, "his passion for war has turned into a cancer burning away at his brain."

"He wants it for his own." With her usual focus and determination, Athena steered the conversation back onto her course. "And Kratos, Father? Will he receive your favor?"

Zeus was uncharacteristically slow in responding. He did not look at her directly but studied her reflection in the scrying pool. "I am curious, beloved daughter. I have watched you go to considerable lengths to support and protect your pet Spartan."

"He is the last hope of Athens."

"Really? And yet, when you intercede with me—with the other gods as well—you never seek help for your worshippers. Or your city, only your priests. You say that Kratos is their hope—as you seem to be his—but wouldn't your powers of persuasion and manipulation be better spent entreating direct aid? Hephaestus, for example, might have extinguished all those fires with a single wave of his hand. Apollo might have healed your wounded. I myself—"

"Yes, Father, I know. You have the right of it. As always, you see more deeply than any other."

Athena took a deep breath and decided—in this extremity—that her cause would now, finally, be best served by the straight truth. "My Lord Father, Ares's true target is not me, nor is it my city."

Zeus looked at her, his thoughts veiled behind an expressionless face.

"Father, his target is your throne!"

"So your goal all along—the final truth of your endgame—has been solely to protect *me*?"

"Forgive my presumption," Athena said. "I only feared that you might allow your well-known fondness for your children to cloud your judgment of Ares."

"Or, perhaps, that my well-known fondness for my children might also cloud my judgment of you." Zeus still showed no emotion, but Athena had heard just a hint of concern at the way Ares destroyed the shrines to Zeus throughout Athens. "You seek only to save me from myself? Because I have forgotten the lessons of my own life?"

"All Olympus would welcome Ares's death."

"Would they? Or do they huddle to one side, hoping to gather whatever scraps of power remain after an Olympian patricide?"

"You condemned your own father to crawl on hands and knees through the Desert of Lost Souls for all time, rather than kill him, after you won the Titanomachy," Athena said. "Because you know too well the consequences of family slaying family, you have decreed such will never come to pass between Olympians. But Ares may have in mind a fate similar to that of Cronos for you, Father. An eternity of torment, bound by unbreakable chains—and that is only if he can overcome his own madness enough to show self-restraint."

"And how long have you known Ares's ambition? How long have you been planning your brother's death using Kratos as your instrument of destruction?"

Again, Athena told the simple truth. "Since the day that my brother tricked Kratos and drove him into my village temple in his blood frenzy. It was then I knew that Ares's insanity had no limits, that his overweening ambition knew no bounds. What do you think he was planning for Kratos? Why give his mortal subject near-Olympian strength and toughness? Why would he affix the Blades of Chaos to Kratos's wrists? *Chaos*—the primordial realm, conquered and brought to order by your grandfather Ouranos?"

She drew herself up to her full height and turned to her father. "Kratos was always meant to be the weapon that killed a god. This truth names the coldest dread my heart has ever known: The god that was to be Kratos's victim was *you*, Father. Ares was grooming Kratos for the same task I am, and for the same reason: to slay a god but to avoid Gaia's immortal curse on any who shed their family's blood. Father, you *must* help Kratos! He is not the true hope of Athens—he is the hope of Olympus itself! My lord father, I have seen this future in my darkest nightmares. If Kratos falls, so falls Olympus."

Breathless and nearly in tears, the goddess of foresight and clever stratagems had left to her only truth and love. "Father, *please*."

"My edict stands. One god may not kill another."

Athena had nothing to say.

"Kratos may reach the Arena of Remembrance and face his final challenge. But that will not be the end."

Zeus looked grim, his beard crashing with lightning amid the thunderheads. "That, my beloved daughter, will be the beginning. Until then he has much to conquer, not the least challenge being his own nature. If he does—*if* he does—then I might find him worthy."

"Worthy of what, my father?"

Zeus did not answer.

NINETEEN

THE TUNNEL THROUGH the living rock wound about with sudden right-angle turns and eventually opened onto the face of a cliff. Kratos looked up and saw the overhang was such that he had to find ledges and handholds to cross an expanse of rock before going upward.

A quick glance convinced him that nothing but death awaited him below. He wiped his hands against his thighs once more to remove the last vestige of blood. The wounds he sustained had now clotted over—and more. The deaths of his opponents had renewed his own energy and accelerated healing once again. Since that day when Ares had answered his prayer before the barbarian king, it had been thus. Wounds healed quickly, but the aftermath always wore on him, because, while his body was whole, his spirit never was.

"SHOW NO MERCY!" he ordered his warriors as they entered the vile village. A shrine devoted to Athena stood at the far end— a shrine that mocked Lord Ares and angered Kratos. Whatever angered the God of War angered his servant.

Kratos was the first to light a torch and throw it onto a thatched roof. The flames burned brightly in the night but were a guttering candle flame to the anger and bloodlust that boiled within him. The entire village was an affront.

"Kill them all!" he shouted, then set to using the Blades of Chaos to show his men the proper way of slaying. From one end of the village to the other, he killed without hesitation. The blades swung in a pattern, a deadly arc, that ended the lives of those trying to fight him with scythes and forge hammers—and those who did nothing but beg for his mercy.

Kratos knew no mercy. And he would show no mercy to the old woman hobbling from the shrine. He shoved her aside. Those within would die by his sword.

"Beware, Kratos," she called in her cracked, ancient voice. "The dangers in the temple are greater than you know!"

He laughed harshly. He was Kratos and feared no one, no thing, especially not the feeble thrusts and blows from the acolytes within. His mighty Blades of Chaos began swinging, slicing, slashing, and killing, until he saw nothing but a red veil of their spilled blood.

And then there were two more bodies on the floor at his feet, fresh victims of his bloodlust. Kratos stared at them and screamed.

Ares's callous voice filled the temple. "You're becoming all I hoped you'd be, Spartan. . . ."

ANGER FILLED HIM ANEW at how Ares had used him so vilely. Kratos took a deep breath and forced back the dark tide threatening to drown him. The visions would be his legacy forever, unless he did as Athena had commanded. The gods would erase his nightmares—his memory—and again he could live in peace with himself. All he needed to do was cross the sheer face of the rocky cliff.

He stepped out, shoved a sandaled foot into a small crevice, and reached widely for a handhold he spotted barely within reach. His fingertips clamped on the narrow outjut of stone, allowing him to move his other foot and continue across the cliff face. Many times he had scaled mountains to outflank an enemy, so this was not a new challenge for him.

"By the gods, no!" The words escaped his lips when he saw a bulge of stone ahead begin to swell and take shape. The stone exploded outward as a man-sized, scorpion-tailed creature flowed from the very rock to block his way.

Drawing the Blades of Chaos required stability he did not have. He jumped, caught at new hand- and footholds, and grabbed for the scorpion thing. Its tail whipped about, but Kratos had a firm grip on its throat and turned its body so that the deadly tail flicked past him harmlessly. He grunted, focusing all his strength on crushing the monster's armored windpipe. Chitin cracked; the scorpion thing thrashed about wildly, its tail even more menacing now. Kratos jerked away as the tail sang through the air, aimed for his eyes. A droplet of poison that had beaded on the tip of the stinger splashed his forehead and burned like fire. His grip on the creature weakened as the poison trickled down into his eyebrow, searing the hair and threatening to run into his eye.

Kratos swiped his arm against the poison drop to prevent it from blinding him—but his arm was coated with gore. Blood got into his eye and turned him blind. As he had experienced in battle, the blood dropped a Stygian dark veil across his vision. He blinked furiously to clear it. Blood in his eye was better than permanently blinding poison—but the distinction quickly vanished when he heard talons scraping on rock below him.

The scorpion monster had fallen a few feet when he released it but was now returning to kill him. And he could not see it.

He squeezed his eyes shut so hard they turned painful. Then he remembered the two bodies in Athena's shrine. Anger and tears exploded within, and his vision was crystalline again. The rock scorpion was only a few feet away and approaching, its tail with the poison-laden stinger readied for a killing blow. Kratos made a wild grab, caught the creature by the neck again, and wrenched hard. The tail drove around in an arc over the creature's head—into the rock, missing Kratos by inches.

With another loud shout to focus his strength and rage, Kratos brought his fingers together, completely smashing the rock-dwelling monster's throat. He held it suspended now, away from the rock, and did not have to see clearly to finish it off. It twitched feebly, then all life fled. He dropped it, watching the body rebound repeatedly from the rock face before disappearing far below.

Kratos wiped the gore from his hand and continued traversing the cliff, blinking hard and recovering his vision. He had gone only a few yards, not even reaching the spot where he might scale the cliff and go straight to the top, when new scraping sounds alerted him to other scorpion things popping from the very rock.

"Athena, you ask much of me," he said, trying to speed along the path he had scouted across the stone face. Kratos had barely reached the point where he might climb directly upward when two more of the monsters overtook him, scuttling across the vertical rock as if it were level ground.

Kratos found a ledge and positioned both feet on it. Still hanging on to a secure handhold, he wrenched a rock free with his right hand and flung it with all his might. The missile sailed true. The nearest scorpion reacted instinctively and lashed out with its curved, deadly tail. This was all the opening Kratos needed to hurl a second rock, which accurately struck the creature in the middle of its head. The tail flew to fend off this new attack—and the scorpion monster stung itself.

Not waiting for the dying creature to fall from the cliff, Kratos threw a third stone, dislodging it. Now he faced only the one. This monster arched its back and showered stony splinters in all directions. Kratos protected his face against the calcified needles and futilely sought another rock. None was to be had. He looked up, charted his way to the top of the cliff, and started climbing, the scorpion directly under him and scuttling along faster than he could hope to scale such featureless rock.

Just feet from the top of the cliff, Kratos released his grip and fell. He crashed into the scorpion at a spot where all eight of the monster's legs were occupied with simply hanging on. With a twist, Kratos came about and caught the stinger as it arched out and upward to slice and poison him. A tiny drop of yellowish venom dripped from the tail. His weight was being supported entirely by the huge scorpion, and his drop onto its head had stunned the creature so much that its legs came free one by one.

Kratos held on to the thrashing tail until he was certain the scorpion thing could not maintain its grip an instant longer. With a vicious twist, he wrenched at the tail and dislodged the monster. At the same instant, he kicked hard against the face of the cliff and sought a handhold.

The scorpion thing followed its companions to the distant ground—and Kratos hung by the fingertips of one hand on a small, dusty ledge. Bit by bit his fingers slid off. He looked down, not to see where he would fall but to find footholds. Unable to locate any, he kicked as powerfully as he could. Pain lanced up his leg, but his toes chipped away enough of a hold for him to support his weight. His fingers fell away from the ledge, but his feet supported him as he sagged down.

He stood in his hard-won footholds, then made his way across and upward to reach the top of the cliff. Once there, Kratos dropped to his knees and gave a silent prayer to the gods, though what aid he had received from them was a mystery. He had survived through his own effort and would continue to do so.

From ahead, through an open portal in the side of the mountain, came crashing sounds—machines running, a rumbling noise that he could not identify. Drawing the Blades of Chaos, he approached the portal and advanced down its tunnel. He stopped beside a conveyor belt that disappeared under a rocky ledge. Kratos swung his blades against the stone, but even the potent magic locked in their metal could not dislodge a pebble.

He turned and looked against the direction of the rapidly running conveyor belt and saw what had produced the crashing noise. Huge blocks studded with long spikes collided repeatedly.

The only way to advance was to run against the direction of the conveyor belt and past the rhythmically opening and closing jaws. Kratos returned the blades to their resting spots on his back, gauged the action of the deadly jaws, and jumped onto the conveyor belt.

He misjudged the speed and was carried along with it to smash into the rock wall. He screamed in pain and recoiled. While the face of the wall appeared to be ordinary stone, the merest touch drove lances of white-hot pain into his body. Kratos began running, until he canceled the speed of the belt under him and remained in place. Then he exerted more effort and gained against the conveyor belt, coming to the first set of jaws smashing together. Beyond lay several more sets. Once committed to this venture, he had no choice but to plunge ahead, never faltering. The slightest mistake would bring him between those spiked panels, impaling him. If he sank back to the conveyor belt, he would be swept into the wall and receive torture that burned at the very core of his being.

With such incentive, he put on a burst of speed and successfully raced past the first set of jaws. The Scylla and Charybdis of his passage forced him to concentrate fully on avoiding the crushing jaws and sharp teeth. Only once as he raced forward, checked speed to run in place, and then burst ahead as the jaws opened did he receive any injury. The final gateway did not operate on a pattern but was inspired by Chaos.

Kratos turned as a slender knife drove through his biceps, holding him in place. Realizing the danger of being restrained, he jerked savagely and left behind a gobbet of bloody muscle so he could race along the conveyor belt toward a stone ledge where he could step off safely. Rather than diminished sounds of machinery, Kratos heard more ahead, along a tunnel opening into a room that convinced him the Architect had been driven mad by the gods.

Deep double grooves formed a field of squares. Rolling end-lessly in those grooves were double-bladed wheels, their edges gleaming knives so sharp that Kratos had to squint as they raced by. To one side of the room, an iron gate blocked the way out, but he saw the key to opening it. A lever protruded from the center of one square. Throw it and the gate would rise. But to get to it would require even more timing and daring than avoiding the slamming jaws along the conveyor belt. The knife wheels never stopped, never rested, would slice him to ribbons if he committed a single misstep.

With a powerful jump, he vaulted over one wheel and landed safely in the middle of a square. He stood erect as knife wheels raced past him on one side and behind. Kratos judged the periodicity of the wheel in front of him and stepped out just as it passed, achieving a square closer to the lever. Only then did he notice that the frantic pace of the deadly wheels had increased. The closer he got to the lever, the faster they rolled.

He reached for the Blades of Chaos to destroy any of the wheels in his path, then stopped. Would the Architect guard against such mechanical intrusions? The metal of the wheels carried a silvery sheen unlike anything Kratos had ever seen before. Although the Blades of Chaos were magically forged, and Ares had never warned him how they might be broken, Kratos obeyed his gut instinct that the blades were the wrong weapon to use against the knife wheels. Other weapons were his to command, but he wanted to slay Ares with the Blades of Chaos. Since the God of War had fused them to Kratos's forearms and he had used them for ten long years to murder in Ares's name, it was only fitting that the Ghost of Sparta drive the tips through the god's body and watch him die from his own gifted weapons.

Kratos abandoned the hilts of the blades and plunged forward, depending on coordination and innate skill to dodge the rolling death wheels.

He stumbled onto the square holding the lever, regained his balance, and pulled with all his might. The response was all he had hoped for. The metal gate on the far side of the room clattered and clanked open. Kratos took a few seconds to gather his wits and had started to jump past the knife wheels to exit this chamber when he saw the gate slowly descending.

"You are diabolical," Kratos said, offering a half dozen inventive curses on the Architect's head. The lever, once thrown, allowed the gate to remain open only a short while. Twice more Kratos threw the lever and counted off the time to determine how quickly he had to cover half the room crisscrossed by wheeling death scythes. It wasn't long.

But it would be long enough.

Kratos braced himself, threw the lever, and then jumped to the adjoining square. Gathering speed, he hopped to the next and the next, then realized time was dwindling and he still had two more squares to traverse. He put on a burst of speed that allowed one knife wheel to rake along his chest, opening a shallow wound under his ribs. Spinning about and using the impact to add to his speed, he vaulted high over the last wheel denying him exit, somersaulted, and went under the falling gate with only inches—and seconds—to spare.

Kratos lay on his back, staring up at the low ceiling of the corridor as he regained his strength. With the clanking and clashing of metal against stone at his back, he wended his way through a tunnel until he came out in front of a huge circular doorway. Pressing his eye against the crack in the middle of the stone, he saw an altar outside in the bright desert sun. Even with his most powerful effort, he could not pry open the door from this small crack. He had been given the tantalizing look at where he had to go but not how to open the door.

Kratos turned and stared down the length of an immense room.

He ran into the chamber and looked up, knowing he had seen this before. High above he saw the ledges and walkways where he espied a statue of Atlas holding the world balanced on his mighty shoulders. All his travails had brought Kratos to the floor of what could only be described as a shrine to the Titan. Running forward to a point under a walkway hardly twenty feet over his head, Kratos took in the details and what had to be done.

Atlas was crushed by the weight of the world. The burden had to be relieved. Kratos went to a crank mounted before the mighty statue and hesitantly pushed against it. The crank moved only a small distance before resistance increased to the point where Kratos had to either stop or commit greater effort. Looking away from the statue to the walkway he had passed under revealed a second lever. Mind racing with possibilities, Kratos came to a swift decision and applied himself to turning the crank.

Bit by bit it moved. With more effort, he swung it around in a complete circle. With still more exertion, muscles straining and sweat pouring from him as the resistance increased, he brought the crank around a second time. The statue now half-stood with the world on its shoulders. Knowing that he had successfully figured out what had to be done next, Kratos bent his back, got his powerful legs under him, and began moving the crank at a steady rate around and around. With every circuit the world lifted a little higher on Atlas's shoulders, until the statue was no longer bent double.

In spite of Kratos's best effort to turn the crank more, he now met total resistance. He stepped away, looked back at the bridge across the vast shrine and the lever there. Legs pumping, this time speeding him up steps and around to come out onto the walkway, Kratos was on a level with Atlas's eyes. Though the orbs were chiseled from cold stone, he thought the son of Iapetus and brother of Prometheus and Epimetheus stared at him with relief.

He applied pressure to the lever on the walkway. This required little effort compared with hoisting the world above Atlas. Kratos recoiled when he saw the statue stand a little taller, then heave the huge globe toward him. With nowhere to run, Kratos awaited death.

Instead, the globe of the world bounced twice, then rolled under the walkway. He whirled about and watched as the stone smashed into the portal he had been unable to open. The size of the globe matched the perimeter of the doorway exactly.

Kratos stared out at the altar, where a sarcophagus of beaten gold shone brightly in the hot sun. He jumped down from the walkway and went to see what new trap the Architect had placed in his path.

TWENTY

HEAT BLASTED KRATOS as he stepped out into the desert sun. Slowly, he turned his face upward and basked in the light, relishing it after being trapped inside the darkened maze. He sucked in a deep breath and felt the air sear his lungs. The wounds in his side were almost healed, and he swung his arms about, feeling the power flow once more through his muscles. Along with this, the poison that had threatened his vision was purged from his system. The blinding was a memory he cared not to revisit—but it was one of the few memories he could be free of.

He had no time to linger, because memory of what Ares was doing to Athens goaded him as much as his hatred for the God of War. Athena had warned that time was critical, and lazing about like a lizard on a hot rock accomplished nothing.

He ran along a paved pathway to the base of the altar where the large sarcophagus gleamed in the sunlight. Kratos squinted against the brilliant reflection as he stepped to the edge of the bier, then pulled himself up so he could look down at the lid. Someone of great importance had been interred within such a gaudy coffin. His fingers curled around the edge, and he applied

his prodigious power to rip away the covering, exposing a desiccated body within.

"This is all?" He looked upward to the heavens, arms outstretched. "This is all you have sent me?" Kratos bent, grabbed
the head of the skeleton, and jerked hard. The head came away
easily, leaving behind a cloud of dust from its ruined spinal
cord. He cocked his arm back and flung the skull high, as if he
could assail Olympus itself with this relic to show his disdain.

The skull arrowed upward, then came back down, retracing
the trajectory to land in Kratos's outstretched hands. Again he
threw it, this time outward. It tumbled whitely in the sun and
then described a circular path to return. Kratos started to heave
it aloft once more, then common sense took over and replaced
his blood rage. If the skull proved this difficult to get rid of, perhaps he ought to keep it.

He dropped down beside the bier and ran his fingers over the
glyphs etched into the golden sides. Little by little, the words became clear. Kratos rocked back and stared at the skull he held in
the palm of his hand.

"The son of the Architect? Your father placed your miserable
body inside this fine coffin? To what—" He spun at the grating
sound as stone dragged over stone and a huge cavity opened at
the base of the altar.

Kratos threw back his head and roared in defiance, then
jumped. He cleared the edge of the pit and fell for what seemed
an eternity. But he didn't fall all the way to Hades, impacting
hard on the bottom of the pit. In a crouch, he looked around
and saw only one possible corridor to follow. Lifting the skull, he
stared into the empty eye sockets.

"Have you seen this before? Did your father betray you as
Ares did me?" Kratos expected no answer and got none. He ran
down the decrepit corridor, alert for an enemy attack. When he
reached the end, a huge door emblazoned with a skull insignia
blocked his way, and Kratos pressed against the door, trying to
force it.

When it didn't budge, he got his fingers under the edge and

tried to lift, until his back felt as if it would snap. Panting harshly, Kratos knew force would not triumph. But how could he defeat this door?

He stepped back two paces to get a better look at the pattern on the door. After several minutes of study, he let the anger always smoldering within him come rushing out. Two quick motions drew the Blades of Chaos so he could charge forward and bring the swords to bear against the heavy door. Striking repeatedly produced no results, though the air filled with the acrid stench of burned metal after a dozen hard strikes. Kratos growled, redoubled his effort, and finally stepped away, the rage not fading but a semblance of rationality sneaking in.

"The skull," he said. "The door has a skull pattern etched into it." He lifted the skull of the Architect's son and positioned it so the design matched the outline on the door. Walking forward, he saw that a small depression in the center of the pattern matched the skull in his hand perfectly. He shoved it forward. For a moment he thought nothing happened; then he felt the skull being pulled from his grasp and dragged into the door itself, until only an outline remained.

Kratos reached down and unleashed his rage once more. This time the door lifted, slowly, one inch at a time. When he got the bottom even with his chest, he ducked, somersaulted, and came to his feet on the other side. As the heavy door crashed back into place, Kratos cried out in mindless fury. Keeping the darkness of his visions at bay had been easy enough as he dealt with the minions of Hades he had bested in the temple, but now the nightmarish reality swirled about him like a shroud swaddling the dead.

Fighting to hold the memories at bay, he stumbled blindly down the corridor as if he could outrun them, heading on and not caring where he blundered as long as the nightmares did not seize control of his mind. Blocking his way was the sprawled body of a warrior clad in Athenian-style armor, a sword still clutched in his lifeless hand. The only marks of the battle he had fought were the black reeking smears of undead blood that painted him from head to toe. Kratos stepped over the body and found scattered bones farther along the tunnel, which sloped gradually upward to an arched portal.

He looked through the doorway onto a hellish scene: a vast chamber lit by the fires of bodies of dead men. The stink of this black smoke was worse than the undead blood. At the center of the red-lit chamber, lent a gruesome illusion of life by the dancing flames, rose a huge pyramid of skulls.

A thousand skulls.

He knew the number because he had raised such pyramids himself in the past, when he served the god who was now his enemy. Pyramids like this one had been raised with the heads of the barbarian horde after Ares had answered Kratos's prayer.

Try as he might, he found it impossible now to hold back the visions. Memories roared into him as the ocean floods through a shattered dike. The room, the temple, the quest for Pandora's Box—all were ripped away from his mind, and the visions that seized him were of years ago, the good years, when he had been the youngest captain of Sparta, leading his ever-burgeoning corps to victory after victory. . . .

THE BATTLEFIELD WAS SILENT, and it was the silence of death. He could hear only the crows and the vultures in the distance, cawing out to announce their bellies were full with the flesh of fallen soldiers. No other sound. Not even a moan of a wounded but still living man.

He heard no survivors because he had ordered it so. He had ordered complete death.

No quarter. No prisoners. No mercy.

His men had driven hard through the weaker army, and when their commander had tried to surrender, Kratos had slaughtered the envoys where they stood. Any soldier too wounded to leave the field had his throat slit by camp followers for the bounty, an ear taken as a trophy. Kratos paid his camp followers according to how many they slew.

Blood saturated the ground; walking among the piles of corpses was very much like slogging through mud after a heavy rain. Except this was blood. Gallons of blood. Blood from ten thousand slashes, stabs and slit throats.

HE FELT A MOMENT'S DIZZINESS—and the next he knew, he was mounted on horseback, waving his blood-soaked sword.

"CHARGE!" The command ripped from his throat and set his army in motion. Kratos bent low and swept his sword along as he rode. Warrior after warrior died as he rushed past. The bodies piled up. He laughed aloud as the Spartans rushed to . . .

. . . defeat.

Kratos lay on his back, staring up into a sky the color of an ugly bruise. Heavy clouds boiled above the battlefield, and the barbarians killed without quarter. All around, Kratos heard his finest soldiers dying as the barbarians slaughtered them. He tried to sit up but could not—one of his arms was pinned to the earth by a barbarian spear. He reached over and yanked the weapon from his arm.

Towering over him was the barbarian king, a vast spiked war mallet dripping with Spartan gore clutched in a brawny hand. His grin was scarlet with the blood he had chewed from Spartan necks. He strode forward, lifting the unstoppable mallet to crush the life from Sparta's greatest general. . . .

AND IN HIS NIGHTMARE, Kratos could not stop himself from yelling the same words he had screamed on that black day more than ten years ago.

"Ares! God of War!" The words echoed in his ears and his memory at once. "Destroy my enemies, and my life is yours!"

––––––

THE BARBARIAN KING LIFTED his war hammer but hesitated when a flash of lightning illuminated the carnage. The king looked over his shoulder . . . and then above . . . and then he screamed in terror.

The clouds were pulled apart by Olympian hands, and down from the rent in the sky climbed a man larger than a mountain, with hair and beard of living flame. At the first touch of the god's hand, the eyes of the barbarian king's nearby soldiers burst open like drawn boils, black blood spurting from mouths and ears as lifeless bodies crumpled to the ground. Then the eyes of the men farther from him did the same, and then those beyond, until—as Kratos had demanded—all the enemies of Sparta lay dead, all save one.

Kratos screamed as the Blades of Chaos wrapped around his forearms and the chains burned through flesh to fuse with bone. He lifted the blades forged in the lowest level of Hades and stared at the scintillant swords. Without hesitation, he rushed forward, swinging the Blades of Chaos in front of him. When the barbarian king's neck settled into the V formed by the blades, Kratos drew back hard. A scream of victory ripped from his lips as the barbarian king's head leaped from his shoulders to go rolling across the battlefield.

Ares's shadow fell across his newest protégé. . . .

KRATOS STAGGERED to find himself in the Temple of Pandora once more, his hands filled with the Blade of Artemis.

He mopped sweat from his forehead with a trembling hand.

He was grateful the visions had stopped when they did; who knew what *other* memory might take hold of him? That was a question he could not bear to answer.

"Athena, you promised to erase the memories and end these visions," he muttered under his breath. "You cannot fail me."

Fires burned, and the stench of flesh roasting gave him another moment's pause. This, too, was familiar from his years in the service of the God of War, though it mercifully triggered no new flashback. Kratos slipped to the side in a crouch, keeping the great blue-gleaming blade low but ready.

Snuffling and gobbling sounds came from nearby—grunts and lip smacks, like a glutton at a feast. He cat-footed around the mound of severed heads, leaning to catch a glimpse of the feaster.

A Cyclops hunkered down, chomping at what could only be the haunch of a human. The broken yellowed teeth crushed the femur, allowing the Cyclops to noisily suck out the marrow. When it finished, it casually tossed aside the broken bone and hunted for another meaty haunch. As it ripped the second leg from the corpse, some feral instinct warned the creature of Kratos's approach. It lifted its head, blinking its one great eye; its mouth hung slack, shreds of human flesh dangling from its carious teeth.

Kratos brought up the Blade of Artemis and kept coming. This Cyclops was merely a beast—it was not like its brothers of old, who had been great artisans and stoneworkers. This one looked too stupid to know what a pyramid was, let alone to build one. The monster could not be alone. "Where are your partners in this grisly feast?"

By way of answer, the Cyclops sprang to its feet and snatched up an iron rod longer than Kratos was tall. The bar hissed through the air and struck Kratos's sword just above the hand guard.

Kratos turned the blade to meet the Cyclops's weapon with its edge—and a hand span of iron sheared away from the bar and skittered off along the floor.

The monster's eye bugged out, and it turned to flee. To Kratos, a retreating enemy was only one he hadn't killed yet. He leaped after it, swinging the Blade of Artemis overhand to catch the beast on the back of its right shoulder and slice clean through without resistance. The creature's huge meaty arm and gnarly knuckled hand fell to the ground.

Before the Cyclops understood how badly it had been hurt, Kratos spared it the shock. His next swing sent the blue-shining sword directly to where neck met shoulder. Muscle and bone gave way to the magical blade. When the razor edge severed the beast's spine, its legs could no longer carry it away, and the creature pitched face-first to the floor, with a resounding thump.

As Kratos reached the doorway leading into another room twice the size of the one where the Cyclops had feasted, a wave of heat threatened to singe his beard; it seemed most of the next room was given over to a huge fire pit, not unlike the one outside the temple's gate. Suspended over it by a long chain was a cage, and within the cage lay a body. Slowly, the chain lengthened, lowering the cage into the fiery pit.

Kratos stepped forward, then froze as he felt a thin wire pressing into his leg. He used the flat of the sword blade to trace the path of the wire. It led to a simple stone buttress supporting one smooth wall. Rather than stepping back and releasing what little tension he already applied to the wire with his leg, Kratos carefully drove the Blade of Artemis down into the stone, to keep the wire from slackening.

With the flat of the blade holding the wire taut and the sword itself secure in the floor, Kratos stepped back. Then he went to examine the buttress. The barely visible wire ran through a small hole at the base of the column. On the far side, the stone had been hollowed out where the wire wrapped around a clay jug stoppered with a cork.

If he had moved forward another inch, the wire would have pulled over the jug and caused the cork to pop out, spilling the contents. Kratos decided it was worth seeing what this trap would have done. He stepped back to the doorway and jerked the trip wire. The cork popped free, releasing a thick black stream from the mouth. He shook his head, chuckling. What a sorry trap! Even if the black treacle were a deadly poison, anyone triggering the trap would be long past.

But his laughter faded as the black treacle smoked and burned through the stone beneath. An instant later, the entire wall tipped and slammed to the stone with killing force—and the floor next to it, where a nimble man could have leaped to escape the falling wall, sank away into great pools of the burning black substance. A substance that destroyed stone in seconds—what would it have done to mere mortal flesh?

Kratos decided he could live with not knowing.

And now smoke or gas of some kind, released by the liquid as it burned through the stone, curled up from the bubbling black surface. A stray wisp trailed upward over his hand—and where the gas touched, his skin blackened, and blistered, and began to burn, and Kratos decided he could also live without knowing what this stuff would do to him if he breathed it. The section of floor on which he stood shifted and began to sink, as black oil boiled up through its joints.

Three or four yards to the side of the door in the new room stood another buttress, this one also supporting one of those ever-burning braziers. Kratos hurled one of the Blades of Chaos out to the full length of its chain and yanked back on it to make the blade chain wrap the brazier. Then he leaped through the door with all his force, using his anchored chain as a pivot point to whip his body out and over the black liquid in a tight arc that would have sent him safely to the stone beyond—except that the convenient brazier proved to be just a little bit too convenient. When his full weight hit the brazier, the device pulled out from the buttress on about a foot of rod, which ran back into the wall and triggered another dozen yards of floor to sink into the deadly fluid.

A desperate cast of his other blade slammed the edge deep into the stone of the ceiling, at a sharp-enough angle to support him for an instant or two. A superhuman yank on the chain of the other blade ripped the whole brazier right off the wall and allowed Kratos to swing himself away from the viscous death below—right into the vast fire pit that dominated the center of the room.

Every Spartan boy underwent a ritual of fire-walking at the age of ten, to be certain that the future warrior could master his fear instead of allowing fear to master him. Another man's instinct would have been to spring back out the way he had come—but that way held only black slimy death and skin-charring gas. Kratos took a step for momentum, then sprang straight upward for the hanging cage. Its iron was hot enough to blister his fingers, but his impact set the thing swinging enough that he could launch himself beyond the fire pit.

He paused for a moment while he tried to catch his breath, just barely in the clear, and looked back from where he had come. His lungs burned from the deadly vapors. He jerked around when the withered man inside the cage rose from the floor where he had been curled and gripped the bars to stare at Kratos.

"There's more, you know. The wall, the oil—that's only the start." The voice was cracked with age and raspy enough that Kratos could believe the ancient man who now approached might have breathed some of that gas from time to time. "You'd be well advised to retreat. You would have been the one in this cage if I hadn't been caught here first."

Kratos grabbed the bars and drew himself up to his full height, towering over the frail ancient inside the cage. "I wouldn't have been trapped like a rat."

"No? Then maybe you should charge right on. There must be more traps to catch the impulsive." The man's hair was singed, and his clothing was as black as the soot from cremated corpses. He nodded at the flames in the pit below them. "You'll be back soon enough, in any case."

"You've studied this trap. Tell me of it." Kratos looked down into the fire and at strange spiral tubes that disappeared into the pit walls. They performed some service, but what he could not tell—and lacking that knowledge could be deadly.

"Since I've been here so long, I've had time to study and think. The heat boils water, and the Architect uses the steam to power great engines, like those Hero of Alexandria built."

"An aeolipile? What does it power?" Kratos asked.

"The Antikythera that controls the entire Temple of Pandora."

"I have heard of the steam device but not this Antikythera. If the fires died, would it stop functioning?"

"There must be many fire pits like this," the parboiled remnant of a human being said. Kratos knew he lied. "Ceasing steam generation here would mean nothing once you reached the guts of the temple."

"Where do I go in?"

"There, if you're brave enough!" The man pointed to a huge locked door embossed with the sigil of Zeus. Kratos thought the man told the truth, but there had to be more. "Now that I've aided you, free me from this cage."

After only brief consideration, Kratos knew what had to be done. He began swinging the cage in ever broader arcs so he could reach the edge of the pit.

"Thank the gods! I will be forever grateful to you."

"Be content knowing your sacrifice serves the gods' purpose," Kratos said. His toes found purchase at the side of the pit, and he was again on firm footing, next to a lever controlling the position of the cage. He pushed the long wooden arm on the device around so the cage dangled over the middle of the fiery pit once more.

"No, you can't do this. All I want's to live."

"The gods require a living sacrifice," Kratos said. From what he could discern, only this tribute to the gods would open the way to the next portion of the temple for him.

"Please, no! *Please!*"

Kratos pulled the lever. Below, burners ignited and sent up waves of rippling heat. The man screamed as Kratos lowered the cage into the consuming fire.

"Accept my sacrifice, Lord Zeus," Kratos intoned, "and watch over me as I go on."

He ignored the screams of agony from the pit and went to the doorway leading away from this abattoir. Pandora's Box was nearly in his grasp.

He tasted Ares's blood already.

TWENTY-ONE

"HE SACRIFICED to win your favor, my lord father," Athena said. "Will you answer his prayer?"

"Kratos is impudent." Zeus ran his fingers through his beard of clouds and turned from Athena to stare into the scrying pool. "He does not pay proper obeisance to me."

Athena noted that this was not actually an answer. "Impudent he may be," Athena said carefully, "but his impudence pleases you. I can tell."

"Your impudence, Daughter, is not pleasing," Zeus said gruffly.

Athena saw the way he stared into the pool. She tried not to cry out in joy. Kratos had surpassed her expectations, reaching this point in Pandora's temple far sooner than she had anticipated. So much danger lay ahead, but he fought well. Better still, he was taming his bloodlust and thinking now. The Architect had designed his traps to swallow the bold and thoughtless, but Kratos won despite them, sometimes with great difficulty, and still he pressed on toward Pandora's Box.

"I have considered this. The sacrifice is pleasing, after Ares has killed so many of my worshippers." Zeus scowled as he pondered this. "Kratos is showing his true mettle."

"So the caged man was an adherent of Ares?"

Zeus said nothing, but Athena read her father well. Ares had sent a mortal into the temple to claim Pandora's Box. Her brother's ambitions were far greater than she had ever considered. He wanted to destroy Athens, yes, but this was added proof of how his arrogance soared to the very edge of Olympus itself. The box gave great power to a god—but only Athena's oracle had seen that it also contained the way to killing a god. Ares must not learn this secret until it would be too late for him to stop Kratos. Athena worried that, for all his speed and cunning, Kratos might be moving too slowly through the temple.

"Your mortal fights well. Look. See that?" Zeus beckoned her to his side. Together they watched as Kratos picked his way through a succession of fiendishly inventive death traps. "He does have talent," Zeus mused. "It's a pity about the madness, isn't it? Those awful visions—it's astonishing he's borne them for so long."

"He hopes for release, Father. We talked about this before, do you recall? You yourself have decreed that if he succeeds, his sins will be forgiven. And forgiveness will banish the nightmares, will it not?"

Zeus waved a hand vaguely, now caught up in watching Kratos slice through another company of undead, Gorgons, and Minotaurs, first with the huge Hades-forged blades and then with the sword given him by Artemis.

"This is the most diversion I've had in eons."

"Father, Kratos's nightmares. Will they—"

"Look, look there, Daughter." Zeus pointed into the scrying pool again, and Athena knew she would get no answer for Kratos.

For *her* Kratos, as she now thought of him. She became as engrossed in the unfolding battle as was her father, and Athena fell silent.

TWENTY-TWO

KRATOS STEPPED THROUGH A DOORWAY that slammed shut behind him. He had grown used to such imprisoning behavior in the Temple of Pandora. The Architect was cunning in his design, but now Kratos felt rising anger. Cheated! He had come full circle and was again in the ring corridor circling the central core. All his effort had been for naught. Raging, he slammed his fist hard against the inner wall, then stepped back as a panel slid away, allowing him entry into another annular corridor. But this one showed a more extreme curve, telling him he was now nearer the center. His anger faded as Kratos realized he was closer to completing his quest. There was no other explanation. He stepped through the door, which closed immediately behind him.

Other than the more extreme curvature, this corridor might have been the twin to the outer ring. He began hunting for different ways inward to locate Pandora's Box. He was close. He felt it. Then he *felt* something more: The floor vibrated.

Turning, he saw that a huge roller stretching from one side of the corridor to the other had begun to spin, sluggishly at first and then with increasing speed. He quickly judged that the weight—the stark power—of the roller exceeded his ability to stop it.

Kratos ran in the direction away from the roller, following the curving corridor. Ladders on either wall beckoned, but a quick glance at them convinced him they were traps. Their rungs would allow a man to climb only so high before they gave way and dropped him to the floor in front of the roller to be crushed.

He realized the ring around which he ran had to provide an escape. The Architect's stone-graven promise outside the temple would not be a lie—why bother? Kratos ran past stairs cut into the wall, leading upward. He jumped onto the bottom step as the roller rushed by, scraping skin from his arm. He looked up the steps but did not ascend. Rather, he waited, counting slowly. It was a full minute before the roller ground past again.

Jumping back into the corridor and following the roller gave him no way out. If he flagged for even a step, the roller would continue on its inexorable path and eventually lap him to crush him from behind. Kratos ran up the stone steps to the top of the ring wall. In the center was a large pool of water, but his attention focused on a different course of escape. On the far side of the corridor stretched a walkway disappearing into the heart of the temple.

Reaching it would be difficult, because he judged that the ladder from the corridor floor up to the walkway was as treacherous a trap as the other wooden ladders. The roller whirred past. A smile curled his lips. Kratos braced himself, waited for the roller to come by again, and jumped atop it.

The spinning stone beneath his sandals forced him to adjust his gait to match its speed as it rolled about the annular corridor. As it traversed the full circumference of the ring, Kratos edged to the far side of the roller, and when the walkway came even he jumped. His powerful legs propelled him forward, and still he missed. Frantically reaching out, he caught the edge of the ladder—he had been correct in his earlier judgment. A trap. The ladder collapsed under his weight.

Reaching back, he caught at the hilt of a blade of Chaos and cast it outward so that its curved tip embedded in solid stone. He fell a few feet, dangling from the chain fused to his wrist. Kicking, he got his feet against the wall, leaned back, and began to walk up it. Then he saw the roller returning, faster now than before. With a mighty jerk, Kratos pulled himself up to the walkway just as the roller flashed past. He had escaped being crushed by a fraction of a second.

He ran along the walkway, taking the turn that went into a tunnel and up a long flight of steps. A puff of air warned Kratos he was going outside the temple. He slowed, then stopped, wondering if he had somehow missed the proper way through the temple, away from the concentric rings behind him. Then all chance of retreat vanished. From higher on the steps came an ear-splitting roar. Outlined against pale light stood a cursed legionnaire, its sword whistling through the air. To run from it was anathema to Kratos.

He charged up the steps, the Blades of Chaos weaving a terrible curtain of death in front of him. His blades crashed into the long sword carried by the undead legionnaire and rebounded. Kratos dodged to the side to prevent a lowered shoulder spike from puncturing his chest as the legionnaire turned.

It vented hideous screams as it renewed its attack. Kratos fought furiously, slowly pushing the creature into the daylight. A broad open area interrupted only by a huge box towering high over his head lay behind the cursed warrior. Kratos's heart almost skipped a beat. Could this be Pandora's Box? Redoubling his efforts, he forced the creature back, but the legionnaire was a doughty opponent, clever and quick and deadly—as Kratos found out when the legionnaire cut at his leg, caught a greave, and knocked him to the ground.

The blow embedded the jagged sword edge in the bronze greave, but it also gave Kratos the chance to kick, twist, and stomp down hard against the blade. He dislodged it from a fierce grip. Sword still stuck in his greave, Kratos spun about and got to his feet in time to use his blades against a furious onslaught of bony fists and armored elbows. The spike at either elbow could have disemboweled him, but a quick turn allowed it to slash past, leaving only a bloody gouge in his belly.

The legionnaire tried to unbalance Kratos to regain the sword still caught in his leg armor but never got the chance. Kratos abandoned his sword hilts in favor of using his fists to pummel the creature, driving it to its knees. This was all the opening he needed. Avoiding the shoulder spike, Kratos got behind the cursed legionnaire and gripped its chin and helmeted head. A powerful heave broke the undead's neck.

Kratos reached down and pried loose the creature's blade from where it had caught in his greave. He tossed it aside, but the heavy body armor looked better than the cobbled-together set he had worn and discarded in Athens. Kratos scraped away dried blood and scabs from his bare flesh, lingering only on the red tattoo that showed his rank as a Spartan leader. Darkness threatened him again. Kratos refused to permit the memories to flood back, though he had little control—only willpower now kept him from deep depression and frightening nightmares. He donned the fallen undead's sturdy bronze-plate armor and found that it came closer to fitting his powerful body than most that had not been specifically forged for him. Only then did he turn to examine the huge box, towering twice his height.

"By the gods, can it be?" Kratos placed his hand against the unadorned side, thinking such a potent artifact would radiate power. He felt nothing. Jumping, he caught the upper edge and pulled himself to the top. A simple hasp fell open and he looked into an empty box. Before he could curse the gods for their spitefulness in giving him hope and then dashing it, a flaming arrow bounced off his newly acquired bronze armor, staggering him. He fought to keep his balance, then saw ample reason to continue his fall. He dropped behind the box an instant before a dozen more flaming arrows filled the space where he had stood.

Tiny explosions kicked up rock wherever an arrow impacted the ground. Kratos looked at the dent in his new armor and saw that the arrow had detonated and almost penetrated.

The cursed legionnaire had been supported by a squad of cursed archers.

Kratos chanced a quick look around the side of the huge box and saw six archers on a ledge higher along the pathway leading around the mountain.

"Forward," he muttered. "By Zeus himself, never retreat!" Kratos got behind the box, dug his toes into the ground, and pushed with all his strength. The box gritted along a few inches, caught, then yielded to his constant pressure. It began to slide faster. He felt the impact of arrow after arrow against the far side of the box. Every hit caused a small explosion. To be open to this assault would have spelled his death for certain.

Kratos pushed faster, getting the box close to the ledge where the undead archers fired down on him. When he crashed into the bottom of the ledge, he found he had only a small space behind the box to safely stand. But standing was not what the Ghost of Sparta did. He drew the Blades of Chaos and cast out the one in his right hand, swinging it at the end of the length of chain binding it to his wrist.

The blade did not injure an archer but did cause it to turn slightly and release its arrow in front of the others. This forced them to fire off-target. All of them having to nock new arrows simultaneously gave Kratos an instant to attack. He did. Using his blades as climbing hooks, he scaled the side of the box and then jumped to the top of the ledge, where he played out the chains on his swords and spun in a furious circle. The vicious blades cut through unwary legs and arms. He drew back the blades and began a more directed attack.

Two of the cursed archers fell. A third. The remaining archers fired their deadly arrows at him from mere feet away. The first arrow crashed into his armor and detonated, blowing him off his feet. He landed hard and skidded away. Another archer fired and missed. From his position, Kratos could not cast his Blades of Chaos or hope to evade the arrows much longer.

He reached behind him and drew out Medusa's head. Radiance blasted from the Gorgon's eyes, transfixing the remaining archers and turning them momentarily to rigid stone. Kratos knew he had only seconds. He leaped to his feet, played out the chains, and spun in a furious circle. He felt his blades strike repeatedly as he whirled about; then he dropped to one knee, drew back the swords, and took in the battlefield in a single experienced glance. He had seen such carnage before, often—perhaps too often.

His enemies were scattered about, arms here and legs there. A severed head lay a few yards distant. Two of the cursed archers' bows had been cut into firewood. Only Kratos had survived.

The Ghost of Sparta ran up the road carved with cruel intent from the side of the mountain atop Cronos's back. The rocky path quickly turned again into a tunnel leading into the mountainside, and Kratos found his way inside blocked by a Minotaur warrior. The creature lifted the war hammer fastened where its left hand should have been and banged menacingly on the ground. The reverberations passed through the rock and up Kratos's legs, giving him a weak feeling in the knees.

"You will die if you try to stop me." Kratos spoke not to deter the Minotaur warrior—nothing short of death would do that. Rather, he listened to the echoes of his voice, gauging the size of the room behind the massive creature threatening to pound his head to pulp if he foolishly attempted to advance.

He widened his stance and waited for the inevitable. It came fast as the Minotaur warrior rushed him. Kratos ducked past, but the Minotaur was quicker than he had anticipated and spun behind him. With a powerful leap the creature went into the air, then aimed its hammer directly for his head as it plummeted.

Kratos somersaulted forward, the heavy sledgehammer barely missing his skull. He slashed as he went past but inflicted only minor wounds on the creature. He turned and faced it; as before, the Minotaur warrior proved more aggressive than the usual—and the ordinary man–bulls were tenacious fighters and strangers to fear in battle. Avoiding the hammer blow, Kratos hacked at any tiny target the Minotaur presented him. A wrist. The back of a knee. The man–bull's ribs. One blow from

Kratos's blade careened off one of the Minotaur's ebony-black horns and caused a quick head shake to throw off the effect of impact. No matter how Kratos fought, he was unable to land a death-giving blow.

Back and forth they shuffled, dodged, and leaped. Bit by bit he weakened the bull. He ducked another heavy hammer blow, thinking to slip past the creature's guard and drive a blade into its gut. Instead, Kratos caught a horn in his upper arm. Blood spurted and his right hand went numb. The Blades of Chaos slid from his grip, leaving him helpless.

Thinking this was its chance to end the fight, the Minotaur charged, head lowered. The man–bull learned that Kratos might not wield the swords forged in Hades, but he was not un-armed. Kratos avoided the assault, stepped inside, and wrapped his left arm around the bull's neck. The Minotaur reared, tossed its head, and tried to throw him to the side. Grimly, Kratos held on, his hand finding a wicked horn. He threw his right arm over the Minotaur's sloping shoulder, got leverage, and jerked power-fully. His first effort only enraged the creature.

Far from being injured, it even tried to crush him with its hammer. The effort only made the Minotaur damage itself as it tried to strike him. Kratos used the war-hammer blow against the Minotaur's own shoulder to get a better grip. By now both of his hands were functional. With his right arm around the heavily muscled bull throat, he grabbed a horn again and arched his back in extreme effort.

"By the gods, die, die, *die!*" Kratos went spinning through the air and crashed into a far wall. He came to his feet, dazed but ready to continue the fight. There was no need. He had broken the man–bull's neck with his bare hands. The immense crea-ture lay on the floor, bleating piteously and kicking out its last moments before finally succumbing to death.

Gasping for breath, Kratos stepped over the corpse and en-tered the chamber. He looked about but saw only one way out other than the portal where he had entered. A circular door marked with Poseidon's trident mocked him. Kratos pushed against the door. It didn't budge. He tried to roll it to one side. No movement. Then he slid his fingers under the stone door and lifted. Inch by inch the door rose until Kratos held it open up to his waist. With a grunt to coordinate his strength, he heaved and the door flew upward. Kratos rolled forward and came to his feet just as the door slammed back into place. There was no way to open it from this side, since the door had dropped into a protective slot, allowing no grip to be gained.

He didn't care. His way lay forward.

Running down the narrow tunnel carved deep into the mountainside, he quickly saw that the only light came from the braziers in the chamber at the far end.

As he entered the vast room, the glow instantly blossomed into a blinding glare, brighter than the Chariot of Helios at midday. Kratos shielded his eyes with one enormous arm until the brilliance faded enough that he could bear to look upon it. Immediately ahead was a huge door with the sigil of Poseidon on it. In front of the crest gleamed a shaft thrust into stone.

"The trident of Poseidon," Kratos said, looking about as he advanced. His caution saved his life as red beams swept across the room, driving him away from the trident. Somersaulting, he came to his feet and faced a wraith.

He reached back for the Blades of Chaos but instead drew the weapon he had been gifted by Artemis, turning its broad blade sideways to reflect the red beams. Everything touched by the reflected wraith light sizzled. His flesh would boil from his bones if he remained in that gaze for more than an instant.

He attacked with a battle cry intended to freeze the blood of any enemy.

The wraith twisted about, the filmy black mist comprising the lower part of its body trailing behind as it moved. Kratos swung the Blade of Artemis for the spot where the wraith would be, not where it was. The creature emitted an earsplitting shriek of pure pain as the goddess's sword slashed through the inky mist that passed for legs.

Deep within the wraith's eyes flickered the dread crimson

light again. Kratos spun about, holding the Blade of Artemis out as far as possible. The unwieldy thick blade thinned and snaked out while remaining metal-hard. The edge drove deep into the wraith's arm, causing the creature to emit an even higher-pitched ululation of pure agony. Yanking the sword free of wraith flesh, Kratos spun it around beneath his adversary once more. The wraith tumbled in midair and tried to ball up and avoid his final thrust.

The Blade of Artemis cut the wraith in half. Before the pieces could float to the floor, Kratos swung again and halved those pieces. Then the swirl of mist *popped* into nonexistence. Kratos looked at the blue-glowing sword he held and knew this to be a potent weapon against both substantial and ethereal enemies. It would serve him well in any battle with Ares.

He cast a quick look around for other opposition but saw nothing. He went to examine the trident thrust into the floor. The shiny metal of the shaft caused him to squint. Reaching out, he touched it, expecting some defense to repel him. His hand rested on cool metal. Grasping, he tugged to pull it free. Strength that had lifted immense stone doors failed to draw the trident from the rock.

After placing his feet to either side and pulling with all his might did not bring forth the trident, Kratos released it and continued to explore. The altar to Poseidon consisted of more than the huge sigil and the embedded trident. To the right stood a stone platform. Kratos judged its size and walked the perimeter of the room, finding a box hidden behind a column that would fit the outline of the stone platform perfectly.

Kratos went to the far side of the box, bent down, and pushed. The box slid easily across the floor, faster and faster toward the stone platform by the altar. With a final shove, he sent the box skittering onto the stone platform. Once on the platform, a brilliant yellow light bathed the box for a moment, then its weight caused the floor to sink beneath it.

Kratos went to the trident and grasped it again. He pulled slowly, and this time it slid from the stone, as if it were nothing more than a knife thrust into a wheel of cheese. Kratos triumphantly held the trident aloft and stared at it for a moment, then slid it behind his back, where it magically reposed with the other gifts he had received from the gods. He lifted his right hand and looked at the white scar. Zeus had blessed him. His eyes rose to the shrine to Poseidon, but Kratos had no feeling that drawing the trident from the stone had been another gift from the God of the Ocean.

"Thank you, Lord Zeus," he said. In a softer voice yet, he added, "Thank you, Lady Athena." But he wondered if thanks were truly in order. So much lay ahead of him. He stretched aching muscles, tensed them all, and then relaxed to prepare himself for the next challenge, whatever it might be.

He went to the circular stone wheel holding Poseidon's sigil and pressed his hands against it. No amount of effort budged it. He swung the Blades of Chaos, but they bounced harmlessly off it, sending fat blue sparks dancing into the chamber around him. Just as he began to wonder if the gods favored him in the least, he reached back and drew forth the trident. At eye level he saw three small holes. Leaning forward, he shoved the trident prongs deep into the exactly spaced holes.

The huge portal opened easily. He withdrew the trident, and the portal immediately began to close. He ducked under the ponderous weight and ran forward to the rim of a circular pool behind the door. Nowhere else in the tiny room did he see an exit, and without returning to be certain, Kratos knew the door would not open from this side. Every way in Pandora's temple became only one way: forward.

This time it had to be down into the crystalline water of the pool. He knelt first and washed off the blood he had accumulated from his many fights, grimly pleased that much of it was not his own. He stretched and flexed again to judge his full fighting capability. Many were the times he had gone into battle in worse condition. But one thing worried him as he thrust his head beneath the surface of the water, striving to find the bottom of the well. No man could hold his breath long enough to reach the seemingly limitless bottom. All he could do was explore to the limits of his lung capacity, then assess his situation.

He sucked in a huge draft of air, then plunged into the bracingly cold water. Downward he swam, powerful strokes carrying him deeper and deeper. A faint light glowed all around, permitting him to see that the sides of the well were etched with the curious arcane symbols he had seen throughout his journey thus far. Again he wondered whether, if he could decipher them, he could find an easier way through the traps to the chamber holding Pandora's Box.

He swam deeper still until he found a huge tunnel curving away from his position at the bottom of the well. His lungs were beginning to burn a little. He let out a few bubbles that built at his nostrils, burst forth, and raced toward the distant surface. Kratos tried to estimate his chances of going on with his lungs increasingly on fire from lack of air. This was a decision to be made while gratefully breathing the air above. He turned and began to rise, only to see iron bars moving from the sides of the well, crossing its diameter entirely. He kicked powerfully, trying to get past the bars before they trapped him underwater.

He failed. By the time he reached the bars, they had secured themselves on both sides of the well, leaving only small squares of opening between them. He strained, reached high. His hand broke through the surface of the water—but this did him no good. He breathed through his nose, not his fingertips! Straining, he applied his shoulder to the bars, but they refused to yield. Kratos moved to grasp the rim of the well to give him more leverage. Again he failed. The iron bars were impervious to his strength.

His lungs felt like bladders ready to burst now. He let out more bubbles and watched as they mockingly burst just above his head. The bars had been cruelly placed to allow a swimmer the promise of safety—and then deny it by mere inches.

Reaching behind him for the Blades of Chaos caused him to spin about in the water. More bubbles released from his lungs,

doing nothing to ease the building pressure he felt. His vision
dimmed, and a roar of the ocean sounded now in his ears.

The roar of the ocean. The God of the Sea. Poseidon.

Poseidon's trident!

Close to succumbing and sucking water into his lungs, Kratos
fumbled about over his shoulder until his fingers felt the cool
haft of the trident. He drew it, thinking to use it against the iron
bars. His breath exploded from his lungs, and death rushed inward in the form of water intended to drown him.

He felt the liquid assault of the clear water through his
lungs—and the discomfort he had felt vanished. His eyesight returned, possibly sharper than before and unblurred by the re-
fracting water. He felt his lungs moving rhythmically, taking in
and expelling water as if he were a fish. Or the God of the Sea
himself.

The trident had allowed him to become a denizen of the underwater kingdom. He shoved and pushed and tried to move the
bars from their position, to no avail. As it had been with other
portals, once closed he could never return, but with Poseidon's
trident in hand, he knew how to proceed. Spinning in the water
so he headed downward, Kratos kicked powerfully and swam
back to the bottom, then followed the curving flooded tunnel as
easily as if his sandals worked against solid ground.

Strong strokes carried him along until he came to another
well. He paused at the bottom, looking upward. A quick scissors
kick sent him rocketing upward. He exploded from the water
and landed on a tiled floor surrounding the well. Getting to his
feet, he worried that he would suffocate in the air now that his
lungs had become adapted to breathing water. As he slid the trident behind him, he coughed, brought up a gobbet of water,
and then drew a regular breath again.

"Is that what it's like to be a god?" Kratos wondered aloud. He
was not sure he wanted to use the trident again, but he knew he
had no choice if that was necessary to attain his goal. This chamber was small, hardly more than an anteroom. He made his way

to the far side of the chamber, where a narrow crevice opened to a long slide downward. Kratos heard strange, almost chirping noises mixed with gurgling echo up from the water below. A quick test of the sloping floor confirmed his suspicion. If he stepped onto this incline, the slimy surface would make return to this chamber impossible. This was no different from any other passage inside the temple.

But the sounds? They both drew him and repelled him. No Siren sound, these. Something else awaited him.

Kratos stepped forward and his feet shot from under him. He landed hard, then straightened his body as he plummeted downward feetfirst. He hit the water and was completely engulfed once more.

The hunting cry of the naiads filled his ears. Then they attacked.

TWENTY-THREE

THEY WERE AS TRANSPARENT as jellyfish and moved with the same easy sinuous grace through the water. Kratos gripped the trident and prepared himself for the naiads to attack. Every undulation carried the inner-glowing creatures in a wide circle about him, just beyond his reach. One swam gracefully nearer and beckoned to him. Kratos started to stab out with the trident but held back, not sure what the naiad's threat might be, since it did not seem to be armed. Still, like a jellyfish, it might have stingers that delivered painful, if not instantly fatal, poison.

Their song filled his ears. He could not help comparing it to the song of the desert Siren and noticing how different it sounded. The naiad closest swam a little closer, a long-fingered hand reaching to him. All his training, the years as Ares's killer, the years of service he had given to the gods, everything in his being bespoke death and blood. A simple thrust with the trident would end this lovely creature's life.

Kratos lowered the trident and held out a hand to the naiad, which drifted nearby. In spite of the slender, almost formless streamlined body perfectly adapted to an underwater existence, he saw faint, seductive curves that suggested the naiad was female. He lowered the trident still more and reached out. Their fingers brushed. Kratos jerked back as if stabbed, but there was no pain—only pain in his mind and memory. The touch had been feathery and beguiling, not in the least hurtful.

The naiad held out her arms. Pushing aside his innate distrust, Kratos stripped away his heavy bronze-plate armor and took the elegant creature in his arms so their bodies pressed together intimately. He kissed her, and deep within his mind he heard, *You are come at last. Free us from this watery prison and let us swim free in the oceans once again.*

"How?"

Remove Pandora's Box from the temple and we will be free. We will swim the seas once more and honor you as our savior if you do this.

Kratos laughed. The sound of laughter underwater came strange and oddly musical to his ears. It pleased the naiad, who smiled and fitted her body closer still against his.

They kissed again, and within his mind he heard, *Press the lever, mount the stairs, but not to the top. Jump into the water to your left and you will be able to free us.*

"What more?" Kratos kissed the naiad again and felt both a carnal stimulation and a curious peace settle upon him. He could remain forever in this underwater world with them—with her.

To the center of the Rings of Pandora, swim once more and enter Hades. The naiad shivered in his embrace as she communicated these words to him, then she gave a flip of her tail and jetted away. No matter how the trident aided him underwater, no matter how strong he was, Kratos knew he could never overtake the rapidly disappearing naiad. He lacked the grace—and this was not his world.

Remaining here with the naiad was not his quest.

"What's your name? Tell me your name!" His words burbled and bubbled, but no answer floated back on the current to him. Again, he found himself alone. Alone.

With powerful kicks that now seemed puny compared to the naiad's, he swam along until he located the mouth of a well above. He broke through the surface and saw an immense statue honoring Poseidon's wife high above, but more than this, the lever on a pedestal at the other side of the room drew his attention. The naiad had told him of stairs, but he saw none. The lever might provide the answer to this lack. He went to it, applied a considerable amount of pressure, and marveled at how different it felt to work in air again, rather than fighting against or using the eternal resistance of water all around his body. The lever snapped over, and a deafening rattling sound filled the immense chamber. Steps of the finest jade rose from the middle of the room and led up directly to the statue, the shrine to Amphitrite.

Kratos vaulted over the pool and ran up the steps, then slowed and glanced to the left of the stairs, into the water. The naiad had told him to jump into the pool at this point. Kratos licked his lips, tasted salt and the memory of the naiad's lips. It had been so long, so very long, since he had trusted anyone. Why should he believe an undersea creature who might be ordered to lead him to his ruination?

He dived and cleanly cut the water to the left, not bothering to use the trident. Several quick strokes took him to the side of the pool and a cage there. Without hesitation he swam into it, only to have it clatter and clank around him and begin an upward climb that quickly brought him above water once again. The room looked familiar, and as he stared through an open portal, the heavy stone roller in the circular corridor rumbled past. The naiad had said to return to the Rings of Pandora. That could only mean the annular corridor. Kratos offered a quiet thanks to the naiad.

Kratos was immediately trapped once again in front of the roller, which spun about and threatened to crush the life from his bones. He ran lightly ahead of it, found the steps upward, and this time when he came to the top looked not across the cor-

ridor but down into the watery core. Before he had seen no bottom to this well, and that had prompted him to go in the opposite direction, but now he possessed Poseidon's trident.

And he had been told by the naiad to dive. Taking the trident
in hand, he submerged himself in the water and let the strong
current sweep him ever downward to reach a door marked with
a skull. Pounding fiercely on it produced no result. Kratos
pushed away and swam some distance into a crossing channel,
hunting for a different path forward. He soon found himself at
the bottom of a new well. The light above flickered and danced
as if the fires of Hades burned there.

Again the naiad had given him the truth. Now Kratos added
one more reason for securing Pandora's Box to stopping the destruction of Athens and killing the God of War. He would free
the naiad and all her sisters so they could swim unfettered in the
seas again after a millennium of imprisonment.

He kicked twice and shot out of the pool, caught himself on
the edge, and turned to the opening through which came the
heat and intense light of lava dripping from stone spouts high
above into troughs. Kratos went to the portal and quickly as-
sessed everything in the immense room. The ceiling arched
more than a hundred feet above, with the lava drains pouring
out their heated, noxious molten rock to splatter twenty feet over
his head. At his far left towered a statue honoring Lord Hades,
but to the right he saw a more curious device: A ballista had
been mounted under a catwalk. Kratos found a ladder,
mounted, and walked to a firing lever. On impulse, he threw the
lever, felt the catwalk quake beneath his feet, and then a huge
fireball exploded outward to crash into the center of the statue.

Kratos grabbed for his weapons when he saw a brightly lit
spinning circle appear on the floor at the base of the statue. The
glyphs that had vexed him since entering Pandora's temple
pulsed with blue light—and moving out into the vast arena between the catwalk and the spinning circle came four Centaurs,
each armed with a spear.

The Blades of Chaos were comfortable in his hands, but he instinctively knew a more potent weapon would be required. The Blade of Artemis whispered out and blazed in his grip. With a long jump, he landed in a crouch near the Centaurs. Kratos reacted instantly to their attack, swinging the Blade of Artemis and cutting the legs of the leading Centaur from under it. A swift circular motion lopped off the Centaur's head—and caused a blazing blue flame to erupt at one of the cardinal points in the circular pattern on the floor.

He somersaulted, rolled to the side, and still barely managed to evade another of the Hades-spawned creatures. He came to his feet, swinging the weapon Artemis had granted him with powerful slashes that kept the remaining three Centaurs at bay. But this was not the way of the Ghost of Sparta. To defend was to die. He attacked. With a mad cry, Kratos rushed forth, every cut of the blade exact and dangerous. He brought down another man–horse, jumped atop its fallen body, and rammed the sword blade down its throat. A new, different speck of light blazed on the circular pattern, the second antipodal to the first.

The two remaining Centaurs proved warier—or less confident—than their now-dead companions, but this caution did not save them from Kratos's swinging, thrusting, slashing blade of magical blue fire. When he had sent the two remaining Centaurs back to Hades and illuminated the final spots on the rotating ring on the floor, he heard a rumbling noise. Stone doors parted to reveal yet another corridor illuminated in the red-orange light of hell.

A sense of urgency drove him now. He ran to the doors and through them, not bothering to look behind as they crashed shut. The tunnel was narrow, and he quickly found yet more of the Architect's devices: Trapdoors in the floor began opening to show pits of sulfurous lava before snapping closed again. He jumped these traps, only to find himself almost impaled by darts exploding from the walls.

Kratos laughed without humor. He had endured far worse to

reach this point. He would not be denied Pandora's Box. He would kill the God of War and forever have his nightmares erased by the gods.

He ran along the winding corridors, slaying wraiths and cursed legionnaires, hardly slowing in his headlong rush. In his gut he knew his mission was almost over. Only one more room, one more adversary to kill—and Pandora's Box would be his prize.

The corridor opened onto a catwalk halfway up the distance to the vaulted ceiling, allowing him to peer back at where he had fired the ballista into the statue's chest. But Kratos looked straight down and saw rising from the lava pit, a head—a horned head. Next came shoulders and crossed arms forged from a dull black metal. He held the Blades of Chaos in his grip, but Kratos released them as the new statue of Lord Hades rose until a walkway jutting from around its neck came level with where he stood. Kratos gathered his strength and jumped as hard as he could—and barely caught the edge of the statue's shoulder. He kicked, then kicked harder and rocked up, rolling onto the walkway.

A handle protruded from the side of the neck. Like a sailor turning a windlass, Kratos put his back into it and pushed the spar about, turning the statue's head slowly. As it rotated, its mouth opened and a beam of eye-dazzling yellow light stabbed forth. Kratos saw that the beam hit the side of the huge room without effect. He pushed harder on the handle, turning the head about until the beam shone fully on the burned statue at the far end of the chamber.

The burned spot began glowing until it was orange-hot. Then red-hot. Kratos raised his arm to protect his eyes as it turned white-hot. Even at this distance, the heat proved enough to cause sweat to bead on his bare chest. With a puff of molten metal, the chest of the statue opened. He knew where his path lay.

Descending the side of the new statue, Kratos returned to the floor and immediately faced another of the Architect's diabolical traps. Rolling balls of molten rock spewed from the opening where he must go. The heat threatened to blister his bone-white skin, but Kratos never slowed. To do so would spell his death.

Feet pounding against the floor, he ran forward as hard as he could, dodging the spheres of death as they tumbled outward. Less than fifty feet into the tunnel, a door emblazoned with Lord Hades's smirking face had been set into the wall. Rolling, diving, he crossed the pathway intermittently filled with molten death and grabbed the bottom of the door. From his right came another rock—thundering directly for him.

With a convulsive yank, Kratos lifted the door and rolled under it a split second before the rock would have crushed and burned him.

The tunnel stretched before him. Stride sure, he set off. He returned to the floor of the huge chamber, where molten rock poured down the walls and lit it with an eerie glow more suited to the underworld than a temple. This aspect was fearsome, but he saw at the far end of the chamber guarding the way forward what had to be the most deadly creature he had ever faced. Armored like a soldier, the Minotaur towered thirty feet above him. Every snort produced thick pillars of roiling black smoke from its nostrils, and as it opened its mouth Kratos reacted instantly, spinning away from a gout of hellfire that singed his back and arms in spite of his quick reaction.

He somersaulted forward, drew the Blades of Chaos, and attacked.

For all its size, the armored creature, which looked more like a machine than a living—or undead—beast, moved slowly and gave Kratos many opportunities to hammer at it. Bit by bit he chipped away its armor, but he eventually saw that this would never be enough. The creature was too large, too powerful, and withstood the most savage blows he could deliver with his weapons. After having used the Blade of Artemis, Kratos knew that even this potent sword would not be enough.

He rolled, barely avoiding a huge armored fist that crushed the floor and left only stony shards behind. He slashed with his

swords but produced nothing but a nick. The immense Minotaur reared up, and dazzling light shot forth from the gorget
around its neck. Wherever those beams touched the stone walls,
huge holes appeared. The Minotaur swung its head about,
roared, and drove both fists downward in an attempt to smash
Kratos flat. He bounced one blade off an iron-clad wrist, then
rolled forward and cast forth the Blades of Chaos as if they were
climbing hooks. He fastened the curved tips into the Minotaur's
armor and yanked, hauling himself up onto the Minotaur's
metal-spined back. Swinging around, he tugged hard, feet
pressed into the creature's back in an attempt to weaken the
powerful neck muscles and bring up the head to expose the
throat.

The beast roared in defiance and again smashed its fists down
hard on the ground, sending Kratos flying through the air. He
landed flat on his back. Looking up, he saw the armored Minotaur's eyes blaze with infernal light. It opened its mouth and
spewed deadly fire. Kratos rolled onto his belly and drew himself
up barely in time to avoid the devastating breath. From this position, he launched himself again, blades swinging. He singled
out the left wrist and succeeded in cutting the straps holding
part of the gauntlet to the Minotaur's hand. It was so little, but it
was a start.

Kratos backed away, judged what had to be done, and then
did it. He attacked, bringing the creature to its full height; then
he somersaulted to the side of the chamber, found the way up to
the lower catwalk, and ran to the lever controlling the ballista.
The creature roared, and its eyes flashed fiery red as it retaliated.
When it opened its mouth to spew forth more flame, Kratos
shoved the lever down and sent a ballista bolt directly into the
monster's chest. It stood a little straighter, touched the spot
where Kratos had ripped away several armor plates, then
screeched in fury and came for him again.

Kratos vaulted off the catwalk, hit the stone floor hard, and
used some of his forward momentum to augment the power of
his slashing attack. This time he severed part of the Minotaur's

left wrist and was rewarded with a bellow that deafened him. He knew it could be hurt. That meant it could be killed. As he stepped up to take another cut, he grew careless—his minor victory had filled him with false confidence.

The Minotaur's armored right fist crashed into his blades, tangling their chains, and Kratos found himself lifted high off the floor. Dangling from the chains fused into his forearms, Kratos was powerless to attack—or escape. He stared into the Minotaur's burning eyes. The monstrous man–bull opened its mouth as if to bite him in two, but Kratos saw the fire within the creature's gut building. He was going to be roasted as he hung by the chains of his swords. A sharp jerk to the side set him spinning. He heaved and spun in the opposite direction and then bunched his powerful belly muscles and kicked hard. The toe of his boot found purchase against a protruding spike on the Minotaur's shoulder armor. He swung away as the hell creature's searing flame erupted from its mouth.

Kratos wrapped his legs around the armor spike, twisted as hard as he could, and wrenched himself upward and back. The chains snapped free and he slid down the Minotaur's spine, fighting to keep from impaling himself on the spikes mounted everywhere. Kratos caught one, stopped his slide, and immediately renewed his attack. Again the Blades of Chaos served as hooks, but this time he penetrated the armor and sank their punishing tips into man–bull flesh.

The Minotaur roared, reared, and tried to throw him off. Kratos hung on tenaciously, refusing to quit—to die. He got his feet under him and pulled as hard as he could on the chains until the blades ripped free, bringing with them gory hunks of the Minotaur's neck. From the way the creature's head drooped now, it was weakening. Grasping the hilts of his swords, Kratos jumped free, cutting at exposed man–bull at every possible opportunity. The left hand, where he had exposed flesh by cutting away armor, proved an exceptionally vulnerable area. He left deep, if not fatal, wounds all the way down the arm before he hit the stone floor once more.

The Minotaur roared in frustration at its wounds, at being unable to crush the Ghost of Sparta. It smashed its fists down in an attempt to turn him to bloody pulp, but again it missed by inches. Kratos waded in and severed an artery on the man–bull's left forearm. As the blood spurted forth, the creature roared, and light blazed from both neck and eyes. Kratos noted that whenever the deadly beams hit stone now, they caused less damage than before.

He rolled, avoided another furious fist blow, and ran up the steps once more to the catwalk. The Minotaur vented its rage, reared, and presented him with a perfect target. He yanked hard on the lever, firing the ballista. The huge wooden shaft sailed forth and hit the Minotaur in the face, pinning the monster to the door. It shuddered as death throes racked its monstrous body, its thunderous roaring slowly fading.

Kratos caught his breath, waiting for the door to open. It did not. The Minotaur hung suspended from the still-secured door.

Other than the hissing as lava waterfalled from the highest reaches of the chamber, there was only silence. A final convulsive spasm left the Minotaur a ghastly decoration mocking Kratos in its death.

His rage mounted. Looking around for another ballista bolt and not finding it only fed his anger. The Minotaur had died from the heavy shaft; Kratos had thought to send another through it to break down the door, but this was denied him. Pulling the Blades of Chaos out, he dropped from the catwalk and stormed forward, the deadly swords hissing through the air as he swung them. He would carve up the Minotaur and then hack his way through the door. He would not be denied!

As he approached, he saw a new danger. Blood dripped from the man–bull's sundered head. Every drop hissed and burned the stone floor. The pools of black blood spread, forcing him to vault over them. Then Kratos looked up and saw the horned head loll to the side as it pulled free of the impaling bolt. What had been a steady drip of blood now became a waterfall.

Kratos sprinted forward. Spartans never retreated! He winced as the acid blood spattered his back, his arms, his legs. Pain goaded him forward until he slammed into the door next to a huge bull leg. Panting, he looked up at the body, which was now slowly sliding down the door because the head had pulled free of the bolt. More Minotaur blood cascaded downward, but Kratos ignored it when he saw the condition of the door that had blocked his progress.

A crack in the door made its way downward from where the ballista bolt had slammed through the Minotaur. Hope flared. Kratos drove both blades into the thin fissure. His powerful shoulders screamed in exertion as he levered apart the crack. At first nothing happened. The blades did not budge and the crack did not widen. His entire world was reduced to the pressure he applied to the blades and the waterfall of poisonous blood from above.

Pain. Burning. His muscles at the breaking point. Then Kratos vented a victory cry. The crack exploded in all directions as a section of the door shattered like glass, giving him a crevice hardly the size of his massive body. He turned sideways, squeezed through, and fell to his knees on the far side of the door, only to roll forward as torrents of Minotaur blood gushed after him.

Kratos stood and ran down the new passageway, winding back and forth through the walls until he came to a sarcophagus matching the one he had found earlier. A stone book on a pedestal commemorated the death of the Architect's second son.

With a savage growl, Kratos jumped to the top of the coffin, shoved back the lid, and tore off the head of this mummified body. He held it high, but, unlike before, he did not think to throw it from him. He stared at it and knew what to do with it, where it fit, knew that it was the key to the Temple of Pandora.

Retracing his steps to the Rings of Pandora, he avoided the stone roller and once more stood on the rim of the water-filled core. Below he had found a door that blocked his way, a door with a skull etched into the stone. Kratos dived down, kicking powerfully through the water, and hung in front of the portal.

Pressing the skull into the outline on the door caused the water to drain all about him. The water level in the central pool descended rapidly, allowing him to pull open the door.

Behind the door was an elevator. He stepped in, and the cage dropped downward with a speed that took away his breath. The sudden stop drove Kratos to his knees, but when the door opened, he knew where he was.

He stepped out to claim Pandora's Box.

TWENTY-FOUR

KRATOS STOOD in a circular room with two arches exactly opposite each other that opened on corridors leading away. He rocked back, expecting creatures or fighters to pour through one or both of the archways. Back pressed against a blank wall, he waited for death to rush forth.

Nothing came.

He looked around, baffled. Had there been one other room in this entire infinite, ancient complex that did nothing at all? No monsters. No death traps. No impassable obstacles.

Two exits. That was all.

For the first time, he was starting to worry.

He walked to one archway and peered through. The floor turned in a downward spiral, cutting off his view of what lay more than a few feet away. He pressed his ear against the wall. Nothing. He spun about, sword leveled . . . but nothing was creeping up behind him.

The other archway differed from the first only in that the corridor spiraled upward instead of down.

A simple choice. A straightforward choice. Up or down. Athena had said that Pandora's Box rested at the summit and that downward lay only defeat and death. He supposed he'd gone a bit far to start doubting the goddess now. He moved carefully onto the upward spiral, stalking upward with blades in hand, ready for anything. Almost anything.

Anything except what he found.

The space he came upon was huge, open to a midnight sky and the cold shimmer of countless stars. There was light here, though: firelight. This firelight was the color of burning cities, and it shone from the hair and beard atop the mountainous figure of the armed and armored god before him.

A terrible icy shock raked his body and shook him like a dead leaf in a winter gale. His voice came out a whisper, a bare breath.

"Ares . . ."

Gods always hear their name when called, even if only in the dream of some creature on the far side of the world. Kratos's whisper brought the God of War wheeling about like a thunderstorm spinning into a tornado.

"Kratos . . ." Ares's voice grated like a landslide. "*I knew you were too stupid to run from me forever!*"

And, now that the end had come, Kratos discovered he was ready for this after all.

"Run? From *you*?" Kratos shouted at the top of his lungs, throwing wide his arms to flourish the Blades of Chaos. "You trained me too well—I learned too much to ever run!"

Ares drew his warship-size blade with a sound like the screams of murdered children. His flaming hair rained fire down upon Kratos as the god stepped forward. "*You talk like a man, but you shake like a woman. Did your wife shiver so?*"

All hope of restraint incinerated in the white fire of Kratos's rage. He hurled himself at the god with every shred of his superhuman strength, releasing the Blades of Chaos and drawing the sword given him by Artemis from behind his neck. As he fell, he drove the irresistible edge of the blade down like a spike through the foot of the god.

The blade of Artemis drove into Olympian flesh to its very hilt—and Ares laughed.

"*I thank you, Spartan. Sand fleas had given me a terrible itch.*"

"I'll give you more," Kratos snarled, as he rolled himself across the god's instep. He leaped headlong up toward Ares's knee, Artemis's sword raised to slice the hamstring—but the huge blade of the god flashed downward and slapped Kratos from the air as though the Spartan were no more than a wasp or a biting fly.

Kratos hurtled through the air until he crashed into a wall with stunning force. The rock at his back crumbled, and he slid down it to the ground, trying to shake the blurriness from his eyes and the ringing from his ears.

The god had bladed him. Slapped him with the flat of the blade, as a Spartan father disciplines a naughty child.

Ares didn't respect him enough to use the edge.

"*And why should I?*" said the god, as if he could hear Kratos's thoughts. "*You would be no more than picked bones and crow shit had I not saved you. Do you remember, Spartan? Do you remember falling to your knees with tears on your cheeks, as you begged me—begged like a whipped cur, like a* slave—*to save your worthless life? If one of your men had begged you thus, you would have killed him for dishonoring Sparta!*"

"You *should* have killed me," Kratos growled. "My weakness dishonored Sparta—and all the world would be better today if I *had* died on that field."

"*Your Spartan honor means nothing to me. You begged. I answered. I arose from my bed on Olympus and descended upon that field to dry your tears. To fight your battle for you. To win where you had lost. To triumph where you had failed.*"

The god lifted one house-size foot, as if to crush Kratos like an ant beneath his sandal. Kratos tried to dive out of the way, but the god was as fast as he was huge. The sandal pinned Kratos facedown to the ground. Kratos tasted dirt and blood, and in that second he saw himself again, battered to the bloody earth by the immense war mallet of the barbarian king. He heard his voice cry out to Ares and swear eternal servitude.

"Do you remember what you said to me that day? The price you set for your worthless survival? Say it now, Kratos. Say it."

The pressure of the vast sandal crushing his back increased. Kratos felt his ribs cracking, and he could no longer draw a breath.

And he heard in his memory the words he had spoken on that day.

My life is yours, Lord Ares. I swear it.

But here and now he could not make his lips form the words. He tried—he did try, telling himself that nine little words meant nothing, that to give the god his petty victory would mean Kratos might yet have another chance to recover Pandora's Box and face the blood-mad Olympian on equal terms—but the words would not come out.

He couldn't even truly *think* them.

The room and the crushing weight of the god all vanished behind the visions, the waking nightmares that had turned his life to an ocean of blood and suffering.

He had served Ares not only with his sword arm but with his whole heart, his mind, and every scrap of his gift for unstoppable brutality.

THE ARMY OF SPARTA became invincible. Opposing warriors quaked in fear to see Kratos's Spartans take the field; at the first javelin cast, they dropped their weapons and ran home to tremble behind their mothers' skirts. The Fist of Ares gave no quarter. Fleeing soldiers would be cut down, to a man. Parties suing for peace were brutally slaughtered. All the world trembled before the battle cry of the Spartans when Kratos stood at their head.

No quarter. No prisoners. No mercy.

Many were the princes who pled with Kratos to accept their surrender, to save a remnant of their army and their city, even if it meant slavery in a Spartan kitchen. He refused to hear such pleas.

Surrender was never granted. Victory or death in battle were the only acceptable outcomes—Kratos expected no less from his own soldiers.

Kratos told his soldiers that he killed because Ares commanded him—but in truth he killed for his own pleasure. He killed because slaughter was his gift. His passion. Because he loved nothing more than the smell of blood, the screams of the dying, the sight of an army of corpses rotting on the battlefield.

"**AND IF THAT WERE TRUE,**" rumbled the god who now held him pinned in the arena, "*you would still be the Fist of Ares on earth, and the world would still quake at the merest rumor of Sparta marching out to war. It was because you did not love me enough, Kratos. Because your heart still held close your—*"

"No . . ." *Kratos croaked out with the last of his voice.* "No . . ."

The visions took him wholly now: He saw himself on the very last night he had served the God of War.

"**THE VILLAGERS PRESUME** *to kneel first before Athena! Before Athena! This place is an affront to Ares! Burn it to the ground!*"

Kratos grabbed a torch and sent it spinning through the night to land atop a thatched roof. The tiny sparks became a fire and then the entire roof collapsed, devouring the hut in minutes.

With a battle cry, Kratos led his horde of savage murderers into the village. The few villagers coming out to defend their homes were armed with shovels and planting sticks, without hope of resistance against his battle-hardened warriors. Kratos strode through the mêlée, hacking and slashing, killing without effort, without even really noticing whom he might be slaying . . . until he came to the village temple.

The Temple of Athena. And the wizened, age-crabbed old witch of an oracle who thought to bar his passage . . .

A knot formed in his belly. The stench of burning meat combined with wood and thatch as house after house was reduced to cinders. The temple looked deserted. But some dark foreboding gave Kratos pause. . . .

But . . .

It was a shrine to Athena. Its existence was the reason for this massacre. How could he leave it standing?

"Everyone out!" he shouted, rapping hard on the thick wood door with the pommel of his sword. When no one answered, he stepped back and used the Blades of Chaos to reduce the door to splinters. A small, hunched-over Nubian woman shuffled out. She wore a shining green gown marked with the letter omega on the front.

"Sacrilege," she said, shaking her finger at him. "Beware of blaspheming 'gainst the goddess, Kratos! Do not enter this place!"

Kratos backhanded the old woman, knocking her to the ground. "Never presume to give a Spartan orders."

He kicked open the door and rushed into the temple. Two priests came toward him. The Blades of Chaos flashed and delivered fiery death to both men. Kratos roared in rage when other supplicants in the temple stirred. He rushed forward, not needing to even see his victims as he cut left, right, left, and then plunged ahead. There was no thought of restraint, no need for caution; there was only blood and death and triumph, Kratos in his element . . . and so he did not heed the last of his victims, and he did not hesitate to slaughter the last two supplicants in the village temple: a woman, and her young daughter . . .

THE TERRIBLE SHOCK of what he had done shattered the vision and brought him back to the temple arena where the god now crushed out his life. But at that instant, miraculously, the weight on his back vanished. Ares had lifted his foot away and once more returned to the center of the huge arena.

"Come on, you contemptible nothing, you insane murderer! You wanted to fight—let's fight!"

Kratos picked himself up from the floor and shook the fog out of his head. The foot that the god had lowered upon his back had been the same one he'd stabbed with Artemis's sword. He saw clearly the gouge left in the stone by the magical blade as it had spiked down through godly flesh. . . .

But that gouge in the floor was dry as the Desert of Lost Souls outside.

There was no blood.

Kratos looked at the wall behind him, at the smear of shadows he cast in the light of the ubiquitous braziers. He looked at the wall beyond Ares, where the god's gargantuan form cast no shadows at all.

Ares wasn't *Ares*. The god wasn't real.

"I am real enough to break you, Spartan. You want to kill me? Come on and try, you miserable mortal!"

Kratos's ribs still ached with the memory of the god's sandal crushing him to the floor; blood still trickled from a gash on his skull where his skin had split under the impact of the flat of Ares's blade. Though it seemed Kratos could not harm this Ares, the reverse clearly did not apply.

"Why do you wait? Do you realize now how hopeless it is to try to kill a god?"

Kratos did want to kill Ares. His lust for the god's blood burned like sun fire in his veins. But this was not Ares. No wonder the god seemed to be reading his mind—this phantasmal "god" was itself a product of his mind.

Like the barbarian king in his visions.

Like his nightmares of his wife and his daughter.

To destroy this phantom Ares, Kratos would have to be strong enough to prevail against his own mind—but if he had such strength, he would never have needed to take service under Athena in the first place. He would have been strong enough to conquer his nightmares—to banish the memories of his crime—on his own. But he didn't have that strength. He knew it. For ten years he'd labored to silence the voices in his head, to blind the eye of his memory. This phantasmal Ares was a foe he could never defeat until he conquered himself.

Kratos backed away.

TWENTY-FIVE

AS DAWN CARESSED the eastern desert with her rose-red fingers, Kratos stood on the roof of a huge building atop a mountain—the mountain that grew from the midst of the Temple of Pandora, which itself was built up from the mountain chained to the back of the laboring Titan who bore it on his eternal crawl through the Desert of Lost Souls.

And in the first gleam of Helios's chariot on the far horizon, three huge figures around him shone and shimmered: statues, hundreds of feet tall, of the Brother Kings. Zeus, Poseidon, and Hades stood facing one another, and the hands of all three were extended to support a disk the size of a marching field with a hole in the middle, like a wagon wheel of the same material as the statues themselves. This material—some mystical substance more transparent than glass—reflected the glints and highlights thrown off by the statues' curves. Below where the golden chariot had yet to touch, the Brother Kings were wholly invisible.

Kratos trotted toward them. Athena had said the box rested at the summit of the temple, and obviously nothing stood higher than these. But when he reached them, their bases on the dawn-shadowed roof were not only invisible, they were insubstantial—as though the statues did not exist except in the light of dawn.

Kratos scowled upward at the images of the gods. His opportunity to reach the treasure they supported would last only as long as the dawn itself.

Zeus stood to the east, and so more of his statue was exposed to the dawn light. Kratos sprang to the figure of the King of Olympus and leaped high to see if he could touch the statue where the dawn struck it. At the top of his leap, he felt a surface warm and solid but more slippery than oiled glass. He drew one of the blades and leaped again to strike the statue. The only effect his blade could produce was to make the immense statue ring like a great crystal bell. Not so much as a scratch marred the nearly invisible surface.

But instead of fading like a sounding bell, this ring deepened and broadened, becoming louder and louder until Kratos had to clap hands over his ears against the growing pain. Poseidon's statue was the next closest to the eastern edge of the roof. Kratos ran to it, steeling himself for the blast of sound he knew would come when he took his hands from his ears, then leaped into the dawn light and struck Poseidon, too, with a powerful blow from a Blade of Chaos.

The belling that rose was deeper, more resonant, and grew in power more swiftly than had the sound from Zeus. Farthest from the rise of dawn—*appropriately enough*, thought Kratos—stood Hades, King of the Underworld. And this note sparked by Kratos's blow was darker and deeper still. The volume of their conjoined chord rose until it seemed to Kratos that there was nothing in the world except sound.

Hands over his ears did him no further good. He staggered to the central point between the three statues and fell to his knees. As the rising sun finally struck the spot where he huddled, what had been featureless stone became a magically clear window. Directly below him, he saw the chamber of the Architect, with its throne, on which the armored figure sat as though oblivious to the universe-destroying sonic blast from above.

This disk felt to be the same sort of substance as the statues, which his best effort had not managed to even scratch. Now that he thought of it, though, he recalled a tale of the great brass gong of Rhodes; it was said to ring so powerfully that it shattered glass for a league or farther. Since it seemed as if much more of this noise would do the same to his skull, Kratos decided there could be no harm in trying. He reached down to the transparent disk and rapped it sharply, once, with his knuckle.

The disk instantly shattered with a sharp report, scattering shards so tiny as to become dancing motes of dust. The awful sound fell to instant silence. Kratos plummeted through the hole like a stone down a well.

A convulsive wrench of his body twisted him enough in the air that he could catch himself by straddling the Architect, one foot on either arm of the throne.

The throne began to rotate, with much grinding and clattering of gears. Kratos sprang from the arms to the dais on which the throne rested. The rotation stopped.

"So, Architect," Kratos said. "You foretold my death, yet here I am."

The Corinthian helmet turned just enough that Kratos could see cold green fire through the eye slits. *"No man has ever survived the Arena of Remembrance."*

"Until now."

"But Pandora's Box will never be yours."

The Architect raised an armored finger, and the lid of the box on his lap slid open. Kratos seized the Architect's wrist in a grip no mortal being could break. The armor was shockingly warm.

"No more tricks," Kratos said. "Tell me how to reach the box, and I will let you live."

"You will not, for I am not."

Kratos tightened his grip on the Architect's wrist until the armor buckled under his fingers. "You're alive enough to speak, so you're alive enough to suffer."

"Do as you will."

Kratos snarled and clenched his fist. The armor crumpled

like a dry leaf, but from his crushing grasp, no blood flowed—
only steam, hot enough to scald Kratos's hand. With a curse,
Kratos wrenched on the arm, and it tore away at the shoulder.
From the severed joint hissed another burst of steam, which
faded away as a metal plate within the armor slid into place over
the hole.

Kratos scowled down into the armor—empty of flesh or bone,
containing only brass tubing and gears of unfamiliar design.
"What manner of creature are you?"

"*I am,*" said the voice, which Kratos now noted seemed to
come from beneath the dais rather than from the helmet, "*what
remains of the Architect. I am his final device.*"

Kratos's eyes widened. "The Antikythera . . ."

"*I control the temple. I am the keeper of its final challenge.
Look into the box on my lap.*"

Kratos stepped closer and peered into the device filled with a
multitude of tiny rods—needles, Kratos realized—set on end
and packed together. Here and there some of these needles were
depressed to one height or another; the depressions were exactly
the diameter of the armored fingers in the empty gauntlet in
Kratos's hand. He guessed their height and conformation somehow controlled the various mechanisms throughout the temple.
There were also needles mounted horizontally on all four walls.

"*Press them. Anywhere.*"

Kratos considered this. There could easily be more going on
in this box than just the needles, and those were discolored at
their tips. Poison? What poison could still kill after a thousand
years?

If anyone would have known the answer to that question, it
would have been the Architect.

Instead of his own finger, Kratos used the armored finger of
the gauntlet he held. Instantly, the horizontal needles licked out
from the walls and stabbed the finger of the gauntlet. Rebound-
ing from the bronze, the needles returned to their places.

"*Had you pressed with your own finger, your hand would be
trapped—pinned in place by the needles, and you would be*"

dying, in tremendous pain, from the blood of the Lernaen Hydra that paints every tip."

"So? I must guess the shape that will reveal Pandora's Box?"

"No," the Architect—or, rather, the Antikythera—replied. *"I will tell you: It is the shape of a man's face, pressed into the needles."*

Kratos thought about the many statues and reliefs throughout the temple—surely the head of a man-sized statue . . .

"The face must be of flesh. The needles must drive fully in and remain in place," the emotionless voice said. *"To reach Pandora's Box, a man must die."*

Kratos thought of the man in the cage; for one brief moment, he regretted having killed the old fool.

"And this is your only chance. This conformation of the needles will work only for a tiny span after the window above is shattered. Once the Chariot of Helios rules the sky, the statues—and the box on the disk they bear—will vanish into the noonday light. Only you have reached this far. No one to follow will have a chance at all."

Kratos nodded. He appreciated the elegant intricacy of this final trap. He said, "But you always—that is, the Architect, your creator—leave one way through."

"Until now."

Kratos squinted up at the disk supported by the hands of the Brother Kings, far above in the shining sun. He now saw a speck upon it, and his heart swelled with rage. He had not come so far to be denied. Here, where he could *see* the box, he would not allow himself to fail.

"Athena herself has told me that there is no way out of this temple without Pandora's Box," he said. "So I will die here, in success, or die later for my failure."

"You are about to die."

"Since I am about to die, there is no further need for secrets, is there?" Kratos said. "Tell me why this temple was designed in this way—tell me why each trap, maze, and puzzle has a solution? Why design fantastical defenses around the most powerful weapon in creation—but *deliberately* design each of them with a *hole?*"

"*Because Zeus commanded it so.*"

"Zeus?" Kratos frowned. "But why?"

"*I am a loyal servant of the gods. I do not question. I obey.*"

The logic was obvious: Zeus commanded that every puzzle have an answer, every trap an escape, and the Architect was fanatically loyal. Which could only mean that this final deadly puzzle was no different from the others.

The Architect had placed his sons in coffins. At Zeus's bidding? Their heads had proven to be the key to gaining entry to progressively dangerous challenges. Twice this had happened. Twice. Would the Architect so misuse his children unless. . . .

"One last question."

"*Your time is growing short.*"

"I know," Kratos said, thinking, *So is yours.* "My final question: How can a mere device, a steam-powered *mechanism*, no matter how cleverly designed, understand and respond to whatever I say?"

Without waiting for a reply, Kratos sprang to the rear of the throne with pantherish agility and seized with both hands the Corinthian helmet that rested upon the armored shoulders. It seemed to be more firmly anchored than the arm had been. Kratos had to twist fiercely and wrench upward with all his strength to rip it free. Then he tucked the helmet under one arm and reached inside with his other hand, scooping out what he found as he would a snail from its shell.

It was a human head. Whatever hair once adorned it had centuries ago crumbled to dust, but this head clearly still held some semblance of life. Tears spurted from its rolling eyes, its mouth worked silently, and the voice from below the dais finally exhibited some emotion.

Terror.

"*Stop! What are you doing! You can't!*"

"I can." He thought he should really tell the ancient undead who tended the fires out front that he'd been right all along and that the insane Architect of the Temple of Pandora *did* still live, haunting his millennial masterpiece.

In his hands was the key to the final lock. Kratos saw no reason to hesitate.

"*No! No no no PLEASE —*"

Kratos jammed the undying head of the Architect face-first into the box. The pipe-and-reed voice below the dais screamed in panic and despair as the poisoned needles stabbed out from all four walls of the box and upward from below. They lodged in his face, in his neck, drove through his temples, and punctured his eyeballs as one might lance a boil. With his lips pinned to his teeth, even the Architect's artificial voice could only moan and whimper without words.

The walls of the chamber groaned as they came alive to lower themselves around Kratos. An instant later, he realized that it was the dais of the throne where he stood that was instead lifting, becoming a rising pillar of stone that went up, and up, fitting perfectly through the hole left in the ceiling by the shattered window. Outside it rose still more, and more, lifting Kratos and the throne hundreds of feet into the air, until finally it thrust him up through the hole in the center of the enormous disk . . . and stopped.

Kratos stood for a moment, feeling the eyes of the Brother Kings upon him. Only a pace or two in front of him stood a vast chest, as tall as Kratos and thrice as wide, constructed of impossibly lustrous metalwork that surrounded golden jewels larger than his head.

And so: There it was. Pandora's Box.

At last.

But Kratos felt no relief, no triumph, for this was not the end of his quest. It was only one more point along the way. The end of this story must lie in Athens.

He glanced upward and saw that the head of Zeus's statue had vanished down to his eyebrows, dematerializing in the rising sun of day. As he watched, the cirrus clouds of Zeus's eyebrows evaporated. And then so did the top of Poseidon's head.

He sprang from the throne, raced across the transparent disk toward the enormous box, and discovered a new problem when he tried to come to a stop—he couldn't. He slid right into the box with breathtaking impact, which also pushed the box a few paces farther from the throne pillar.

The mysterious substance was still more slippery than oiled glass.

Kratos looked around in desperation as he carefully circled to the far side of the box. Flames trapped within the sides blazed. The golden gems encrusting the top pulsed with energy. But none of this helped him. He'd never get enough purchase on this surface to push or pull something so massive. If only he had something to throw, perhaps he could knock it on its way . . . but what could he throw that would have enough heft to move the box?

It struck him then that the placement of the box on the disk would not have been an accident—it was almost halfway to the rim. And it rested exactly on the line between the throne pillar and the statue of Zeus, as though this final test had been designed specifically for him: Looking up at the vanishing statue of the Skyfather, Kratos realized that Zeus himself had given him the one and only possible way to move that enormous weight on this impossibly slick surface in so short a time.

He took a few careful paces toward the statue and inclined his head. "Lord Zeus. Did you foresee this moment? Is this why you granted me a fraction of your power?"

With no answer forthcoming, Kratos wheeled and reached back over his right shoulder to grasp the solid lightning of the thunderbolt. He took up a wide stance for balance and threw the thunderbolt at the disk just short of the box. The impressive detonation had exactly the effect Kratos had hoped for—the box slid a few feet toward the throne pillar. Six more thunderbolts pushed it to the very edge of the pillar itself. Kratos scrambled around to the firmer footing of the pillar and set his foot against the back of the Architect's throne.

"You love the gods so much," Kratos said as he kicked the

throne off the pillar and sent it spinning toward the statue of Hades, "stay with them forever."

He turned, took hold of a projecting piece of the box's metal-work, and dragged the vessel of Ares's destruction onto the pillar—which immediately began to descend.

On the long, long trip downward, Kratos could only stare at the box pensively. He had been told this thing was a weapon—the only weapon that would allow a mortal to slay a god—yet Zeus had commanded the Architect to design the temple so that a mortal might achieve ultimate success and claim its power. He remembered the words of Athena: *Zeus has forbidden the gods to wage war on one another.* Such a decree must be binding even upon Zeus himself.

Had Zeus ordered a single path be left open because, even a thousand years ago, he had foreseen that someday a god must be killed?

TWENTY-SIX

"YOU CHOSE WELL, my daughter," Zeus said, as together they watched the scrying pool display the slow descent of the Architect's throne pillar.

"Ares chose, I refined," Athena said, unwilling to take her eyes from the image of Kratos until the Spartan and Pandora's Box reached the entrance level of the temple. "My brother did not understand what he had in Kratos."

"And so he blunted his best weapon."

"A weapon that is now deadlier than Ares could ever have forged," Athena said. They watched the progress of her mortal as he looked around the temple atop the mountain behind Athens. "A question, my lord. Is this the result of *your* planning?"

He turned from her to point.

"Father . . ." she began again, but the King of Olympus simply nodded toward the scrying pool, where the throne pillar still descended on its steady pace through the innumerable floors of the temple.

"Your Spartan has nearly reached the temple's antechamber," he said. "Is there anything you want to tell him before he goes outside?"

"Why do you ask?"

"Once he brings the box out of the temple, events might begin to unfold swiftly."

Athena saw that the descending pillar had now reached the antechamber itself, extending downward through the ceiling until it broke through the floor below and continued to sink. The earthquakes this triggered began to shake the whole temple, as well as the mountains above and below it. Chunks of masonry burst outward from the mechanical stresses, and boulders began to rain down upon Cronos's head.

She willed herself from Olympus to the antechamber of the Temple of Pandora, where she stood, waiting invisibly, while the throne pillar ground its way down to reveal Kratos and Pandora's Box.

The Spartan appeared unusually pensive as he put his shoulder to the box and began to shove it toward the immense outer doors of the temple. At his touch, a great spray of crackling energy erupted from the giant gemstones.

Athena gathered the sizzling lightning into a semblance of her face. *"Kratos, your quest is at an end. You are the first mortal to ever reach Pandora's Box. There is still time to save Athens. You must bring the box back to my city and use it to kill Ares."*

Kratos lifted his eyes to meet hers, and she noted how meeting the challenges required to free Pandora's Box had changed him. Bloodlust had been tempered with thoughtfulness. Mercy was beyond his pale, but he had been forged into a more potent weapon, one that would surprise Ares. *"Return to Athens, Kratos,"* she said. *"Return and save my city."*

As she willed herself back to Olympus, Athena heard Kratos's grunt as he began pushing the ponderous box.

She rematerialized before the throne of Zeus.

Zeus, to her surprise, was still there, still watching the scrying pool. "He's opening the doors. Watch," he said, "here it comes."

"Father, I must transport Kratos and Pandora's Box back to—"

"Don't worry about it."

"But, Father, even to lower the box from Cronos's back—"

"I *said,*" Zeus snapped, "don't *worry* about it."

"With every passing second, more of my city burns!"

Zeus gestured down at the images in the reflecting pool. "Watch."

As Kratos pushed Pandora's Box out from the temple into the morning sun of the Desert of Lost Souls for the first time in a thousand years . . .

Zeus gestured, and the scene in the pool changed.

Athens lay in flames. Ares strode through the streets, stamping fleeing Athenians, laughing as his sword slashed whole neighborhoods to rubble and hammer blows squashed houses flat. His evil laughter echoed from the mountains to the harbor.

As the God of War lifted a fist to smash another building, he paused, fist upraised, and turned to the east as though an invisible hand had tapped him on the shoulder.

"So, little Spartan, you've recovered Zeus's precious box." The flames of Ares's hair blazed like the sun. His eyes burned with a fury not to be contained, and his entire body shook as anger fed his muscles. *"You will not live to see it opened!"*

Ares reached down to snap off one of the great marble columns of the Parthenon. The god hefted it as though the column were no more than a child's toy spear but one with a deadly, jagged point. He ran four ground-shaking steps and hurled his prodigious javelin, which streaked upward into the sky so fast it vanished with a thunderclap.

Ares turned back to his task of destruction, a sneer on his face. He did not even bother to watch his weapon strike.

"Good-bye, Spartan. You will rot in the depths of Hades for all eternity."

His laughter pealed over the ruins of Athens like the doom horn of Hades himself.

"Father, stop him—"

"Athena," Zeus interrupted sharply, *"your* plans are at an end. There is only one more thing for you to do until this is all over."

Athena lowered her head, worrying about Kratos's fate and that of her city. "And what is that, Father?"

"Watch."

TWENTY-SEVEN

KRATOS'S FEET KEPT SLIPPING. He moved closer to Pandora's Box, got his legs under him, and pushed harder. The monstrous box moved slowly. Weighing an imponderable amount, the box proved difficult to slide even across the polished floor of the antechamber. The earthquakes caused him to lose what little traction he found under his sandals. Even as he finally shoved the box through the titanic doors, more masonry tumbled and shattered around him.

With the box in the doorway, Kratos stopped to gather his strength for one last hard shove and found himself gazing up at the beauty of the desert sky: vivid cerulean, shading toward indigo in the west, studded with clouds that took on curious shapes that chilled his soul.

But there was more up there than clouds. Four specks drifted high in the sky, slipping in and out of feathery clouds only to reappear as dark, almost invisible dots warning of approaching danger. Harpies!

His attention returned to Pandora's Box. He had no idea how he'd lower it from Cronos's back, let alone drag it across the Desert of Lost Souls. He reached up and gripped the lid. No matter how hard he shoved, the lid refused to budge. Taking the entire box back to Athens would be easier if he possessed whatever power lay locked within. While it might not grant him the ability to move this massive box from Pandora's temple all the way to Athens, he guessed it would make the task easier.

He tried to slide the lid, lift it, swing it to the side, but whatever force locked this box was more than he could overcome. Perhaps it could only be opened after he took it to Athens, or the box might have to be placed in Athena's temple, where her oracle could use it to bestow the power upon him. Kratos wished he knew more, but he didn't have the time to waste in speculation.

He started pushing again. Getting out of Pandora's temple had to be his first goal. When finally he had shoved the box fully outside, the massive doors of the temple boomed shut behind him. He stopped to catch his breath and to choose a path. He squinted at the sky and the harpies on their way down.

And one of those low clouds suddenly developed a large hole in the middle, as if Zeus had shoved his finger through it. A ripple spread outward from the hole, like the ripples from a stone tossed in a still pool. Kratos's scowl deepened.

With only an instant's flash of white, his chest was struck by an invisible hammer, wielded by an invisible Titan. Nothing in all his decades of battle had ever hit him so hard. The impact blasted him backward off his feet and drove him flying into the vast stone door of the Temple of Pandora.

Pinned to the stone door, blinking his incomprehension at the immense white marble column sticking out of his chest, Kratos fought to breathe. The spear of marble had struck so fast, he never saw it until he was already hit. He looked down and knew he had only seconds of life remaining in his rapidly failing body. He could not speak, for his lungs had been punched from his chest along with his heart and liver, stomach and spleen. Weakly, he scrabbled at the column. He knew that only the last drops of blood in his brain gave him awareness in these final seconds. . . .

And even in death, the nightmares would not leave him.

He again saw his career, his life as a man and as a weapon in the hands of the war god. He saw his victories beyond number, murders beyond all imagination, but two murders he didn't have to imagine. He remembered them.

He saw them every night in his dreams.

He saw the ancient, wizened village oracle and again heard her words: *"Beware of blaspheming 'gainst the goddess, Kratos! Do not enter this place!"*

If only he'd had the wisdom to heed her words . . .

And the massacre in the village temple replayed in his mind once more as it had every night for ten long years: the murder of the priests, the slaughter of Athena's worshippers huddled there, and then the final two, a woman and a girl, only silhouettes against the fires he had set to burn the temple and every building in the village . . . those last two silhouettes, who didn't fall to their knees, didn't try to run away, didn't beg or plead for their lives . . .

Kratos again felt his blades sear through their flesh, and he knew when their souls fled, sent to Hades as he had done to so many others. He had killed too many for too long not to be an efficient soldier. Too efficient.

His final two victims had not fallen to their knees, had not tried to flee, did not beg or plead for their lives because Kratos's wife and his daughter could not believe that their husband and father would ever hurt them.

Kratos again felt himself fall to his knees, and then it was he who begged, who pleaded, who wished he could flee what he found there. Once more he was haunted by the sight of his beloved wife, his precious daughter, lying in pools of their own blood, slaughtered like lambs by his own hand.

"My wife . . my *child* . . . how?" The words had choked him—a final, fatal question that he asked of no one, because he was the only living creature within that burning temple. "They were left safe in *Sparta*. . . ."

The flames of the temple had answered him—in the voice of his master.

"You are becoming all I'd hoped you'd be, Kratos. Now, with your wife and child dead, nothing will hold you back. You will become even stronger. You will become DEATH ITSELF!"

On that night, Kratos realized his true enemy was the god he had served all too faithfully. Upon the cold bodies of the only two people on earth he had ever loved, Kratos swore a terrible oath. He would not rest until the God of War was destroyed.

The ancient village witch, Athena's oracle in that tiny village, had come upon him as he stood by the pyre on which he burned the bodies of his beloved wife and his precious daughter. For only a moment, her senile cackle had transformed into words clear and strong, in a voice from the gods themselves.

"From this night forward, the mark of your terrible deed will be visible to all. The ashes of your wife and child will remain fastened to your skin, never to be removed."

As the ashes had arisen from their resting place and painted themselves upon his skin forever, Kratos was able only to stand, to swallow his grief, and to accept the doom the gods had pronounced upon him. With that curse, all would know him for the beast he had become.

His skin white with the ash of his dead family, the Ghost of Sparta was born.

But he had never dreamed he would come so close—he had never dreamed he would die in the Desert of Lost Souls, Pandora's Box itself the last sight his failing eyes would ever behold. . . .

As the darkness of death closed down his vision, the four harpies flapped down from the sky, seized the box in their talons, and lifted away again.

West.

Toward Athens.

Knowing how completely he had failed, he could no longer hold on to life. With one last convulsive shudder, Kratos died.

But for the Ghost of Sparta, even death was not the end.

TWENTY-EIGHT

KRATOS FELL, AND FELL, and fell alongside hundreds of other men and women falling beside him. He plunged through the blood-hazed gloom of Hades, falling toward the shores of the river Styx.

He knew this place.

He had been here before.

But his previous sojourn had been as a living man, a mortal invader among the shades of the dead. Now he was a shade himself—and no shade, no matter the greatness of the hero it had been in life, ever escaped from the kingdom of Hades.

He checked himself over as he fell endlessly. His skin appeared as white as it had been in life, his tattoos as red. His flesh felt as solid as it ever had, his arms as strong. No mark remained of the giant weapon that had ripped him out of mortal life. He felt, surprisingly enough, thoroughly fine.

He thought of his wife and child already in the underworld ahead of him. His punishment might be to kill them over and over for all eternity, unable to stop himself, in the same way as fresh fruit and pure water were eternally just beyond the grasp of Tantalus.

The wind whipped at his face; resolve hardened in his chest. He was a warrior of Sparta. Until he found himself in Charon's boat, rowing across the river Styx, he was not dead. Not quite. What state he might actually inhabit was a question best left for a philosopher, since Kratos had never been interested in abstractions. He didn't mind dying. He only wanted to make sure that the weeping shade of Ares reached the Styx first.

He had fallen so far that now he began to see the landscape of the underworld. Though he was still too high to see the river, he began to pick out solid-seeming bone-white structures that stood or crossed or loomed in the blood-colored gloom below. Falling still more, he discovered that these structures were bone white for a very good reason.

They *were* bones.

Bones too large to belong to even gods. Kratos fell past a rib cage in which each rib was larger than the Hydra's master head. Below the ribs, he spied a spinal column in which each vertebra was the size of the Parthenon.

He tucked his arms tightly to his body and spread his legs just enough to tip him facedownward. As he fell, slight adjustments in the span of his legs, or the angle of one or both of his hands, kept him angling toward the great bony protuberances. He didn't worry about how hard he was going to land. He was already dead; how much harm could it do? He plummeted toward the spine at an astonishing speed. As he fell closer and closer, he could make out the tiny figures of other shades who'd had the same inspiration—they sat or lay or clung desperately to the bones, seeming to want only to delay their final plunge to the Styx.

His last few yards passed at blinding speed, and the impact came in a shattering white flash—with no pain at all, which was what he had expected. What he had *not* expected was that he would bounce.

He found himself tumbling again, flailing. He struck another vertebra but skidded over the edge before he could get a grip. Scrambling desperately now, he clutched at anything he passed, because he was about to go over the edge of the tailbone and he didn't see anything else between him and the sluggish black river that marked the border of Hades.

At the last instant, his hand caught something. He heard a scream of panic, and as he dangled by one hand above that all-too-final drop, he discovered that he had grabbed a bony, withered ankle.

"Let *go*, idiot!" the man he'd grabbed screamed. "I can't hold us both!"

"Just hang on," Kratos said through his teeth. "Hold tight and I'll get us out of this." Grimly, he pulled himself up to where he could get a grip on the man's knee with his other hand.

"My arms," moaned the man. "You're pulling my arms out of their sockets! Let go!"

Kratos counted himself lucky: The man was so withered that the Spartan could close his hand around the fellow's thigh.

The man tried to kick him off. "You won't drag me down to that cursed river!"

"There's a task left for me above," Kratos growled, "and I will see it completed."

"I don't care! Let *go*!"

The man screamed as Kratos hauled himself higher and drove his hand like a spear deeply into the man's side; he hooked his fingers over the man's hipbone and kept on climbing.

His next handhold was at the man's shoulder, then his other shoulder, and finally Kratos could grasp the same prominence that the other clung to. It was then a simple matter for Kratos to clamber up onto the vertebra. He turned back to the man he had used as a ladder.

It was the captain of the merchant ship from the Grave of Ships.

The captain recognized Kratos in the same instant. A look of pure horror twisted his face. "Oh, no. Not you again!"

Kratos stepped close to the edge and kicked the captain's hands off the bone.

The captain had a penetrating voice, and Kratos heard him

screaming curses as his shade cartwheeled downward to vanish in the blood mist above the Styx.

Kratos turned and scanned the skeletal landscape. He began to climb.

Scaling vertebra after vertebra, he toiled upward for an unknown span of time. The light here never changed, and Kratos never tired. He kept climbing.

When he reached the ribs, miles above where he had begun, he discovered a new feature of this peculiar realm: Undead. Skeletons. Legionnaires. But these were no naked shades; they were armored, armed with all manner of weapons, and thirsty for blood, as they had been in the world above.

They spread out to intercept his passage. As they moved into position, Kratos saw that they were not alone. Two Minotaurs bearing battle axes and a massive Centaur brandishing a sword as long as Kratos was tall stood with them. The Centaur looked familiar.

"I know you, Spartan!" the Centaur growled. "You sent me here only days ago, on a street in Athens."

"And it's so with all of you, isn't it? I killed you all."

The Centaur grinned hugely, opening his arms as if in welcome. "And all of us are here to return the favor!"

Kratos looked farther up and discovered he could chart his path by noting where creatures waited for him. Every bone that led upward was crowded with enemies who had died at his hands. He began to climb the bone up to the first group. The Centaur bellowed, whirling his enormous sword around his head.

HOURS—DAYS, MONTHS, DECADES—Kratos spent in battle. Still he never tired, and the light never changed, and he never ran out of enemies. He climbed and then he fought. He jumped, then found himself facing a column of immense height—studded with counterrotating segments of viciously sharp blades.

Kratos stepped back and tried to see the top of the column. It vanished into the blood-red mists above. The *swish swish* of the rotating blades cut through the air but could not drown out the cries of men and women falling to Lord Hades's embrace far below. Kratos had come a considerable distance to reach this point, and there was more to go if he wanted to kill a god.

Taking a deep breath, Kratos watched the blades whirling about and judged the "safe" rings—but he knew they could never be considered islands of refuge. The rings did not spin at uniform rates. Some above went faster, while those on either side rotated more slowly. Once he started the climb, there would be no turning back, no rest, not an instant of hesitation.

Two quick steps and a jump took him above the first ring of curved blades. Kratos almost found his escape from Lord Hades's grip at an end as the blade under his left foot cut off part of his sandal. He jerked upward and almost foolishly looked down.

No rest. No stopping.

The blades above came fast at eye level. Scrambling, finding purchase against the ever-moving rings, a toehold and a hard push upward barely allowed him to escape decapitation. He slowed, then shot upward, fingers finding the right gripping points to avoid the next ring of blades and the next and the next. Then he saw that the ring above rotated against the others and forced him to retreat. Kratos dropped down, but surged up when a break came in the deadly ring.

He found a rhythm to the climb, a certain logic to the seemingly random whirl of death around him. But a screech from behind warned him of a harpy coming at his back. Not daring to take his attention from the segmented tower of blades, he kept climbing.

Blood spattered his back and ran in thick rivers to drip down to the spot where he had begun the climb. The harpy had incautiously attacked him and ignored a set of blades coming from the opposite direction; it paid the price. A quick glance showed the headless body tumbling away in one direction. He never saw the head. He was too occupied with preventing such a fate from befalling him.

Twice, the flashing blades almost lopped off vital pieces of anatomy. One wound was minor, but a steady gush of blood came from a deep cut to his ribs just as he saw the top of the deadly column. Sanctuary in sight spurred him on, and wind whistling from the blades chilled his body as sweat evaporated from his exertions.

Close to the pinnacle, with only one ring of blades to pass, Kratos surged upward, let a sharp edge graze his leg, and then tumbled flat onto the top of the column. He immediately found himself faced with a tall legionnaire armored in flames. Kratos somersaulted, came to his feet, and brought the Blades of Chaos into his hands. The climb had set his pulse racing, and every sense was heightened. The legionnaire had no chance against his quick cuts and sudden leap high into the air. He hurtled downward, the blades preceding him. The legionnaire exploded in a ball of fire as the tip of one blade drove down hard onto the back of the undead's skull.

Kratos stood, staring at the pile of ash that marked the legionnaire's final resting place. He kicked the ash over the edge, sending it floating eventually to drift on the river Styx.

Looking around, he saw nowhere to go from the apex of the column. Kratos looked back down through the blur of spinning blades. If he had to retreat and find another way, he would. As he stepped to the edge to begin his descent, a new sound filled the air, drowning out the cries of those unfortunates falling to the underworld. He jumped back in time to avoid being crushed by a heavy block.

A grim smile curled Kratos's lips. Tied to the block was a rope that vanished upward. He might have to deal with harpies, but the spinning blades of the column beneath his feet were a danger past. Gathering his strength, he bent his legs and exploded upward, grasping the rope as far above as possible. Hand over hand, he continued his escape as he went through dozens—or thousands—of weapons looted from the corpses of his enemies.

Though a shade, he could be hurt by these enemies, he discovered, but victory healed his wounds.

The underworld behind him vanished as he clambered higher, finally seeing a ceiling above. Kratos wondered at what appeared to be roots dangling from the bottom. As he got closer, he saw that they were roots—roots of living plants from the world above. The living world above!

Kratos climbed faster and followed the rope into a hole that blocked all senses. His shoulders brushed dirt, and then the hole narrowed even more—but the rope still stretched taut above him. Ascending more slowly, he felt himself being crushed and smothered, and he knew the smell in his nostrils and the taste in his mouth.

Dirt. Clay.

Earth.

He spat out a mouthful of grit and sealed his lips. With an effort greater than he'd ever before believed he could summon, Kratos forced his hands and then his arms to move. He pressed his limbs outward, using his great strength to pack the smothering earth away from him, opening a little room to work. He began to move his legs as well, struggling to bend his knees or widen his stance. His heart hammered, and his lungs burned for air. . . .

He told himself repeatedly, *Shades don't need to breathe.*

Without pausing to marvel at this miracle or to ponder the question of its source, Kratos clawed his way upward, snarling and gasping and forcing his weakening limbs to move, to climb, to rip apart the dirt above him and break through to light and air. Just when his pounding heart seemed to be choking him to death, his hand broke through.

Fresh air gusted into his face. His fatigue vanished. Furiously, he attacked the imprisoning earth until he could see a night shrouded by clouds glowing blood-red with the light of fires below.

"Athens," he croaked. "I'm in Athens . . ."

He pulled himself up to the mouth of the hole he had dug and discovered there were still six more feet to go.

He stood in an open grave.

TWENTY-NINE

IN THE OPEN GRAVE, Kratos's skin prickled as though he had felt a sudden chill. He turned and looked up, and, yes, he was where he thought he was: the grave that had been dug beside the Temple of Athena.

Kratos vaulted from the grave and looked out over the burning city. In the distance he saw the immense shape of Ares striding through the city, stomping buildings at random.

"Ah, Kratos, right on time. I finished digging only a moment ago."

The unexpected voice startled Kratos into a whirl. He crouched, ready to fight for his newly regained life, but there was no danger here. Behind him stood only the old gravedigger.

Now, though, the gravedigger did not look so old or nearly so decrepit, and his voice had none of his formerly senile quaver. Intelligence burned brightly in his once-murky eyes.

"Who *are* you?"

"An interesting question, but one we don't have time to answer, my boy. You must hurry. Athens needs you."

"But . . . but . . ." Kratos gestured in helpless bafflement at the empty grave. "But how did you know . . . how *could* you know I would—"

"Athena isn't the only god keeping watch on you, Spartan. You have gone far to prove your worth, but your final task lies ahead of you."

Kratos turned as a thunderous roar erupted from the direction of Athens. Ares towered above, meting out destruction and laughing in triumph. Kratos felt his rage building. Without turning to the gravedigger, he asked, "Who are you?"

Kratos spoke to empty air. The gravedigger had disappeared like smoke in the wind. There came an answering whisper, a zephyr blowing in his ear. "*Complete your task, Kratos . . . and the gods will forgive your sins. . . .*"

The Spartan shook his head grimly. "How can I do this without Pandora's Box?" For all the weapons he still carried, Kratos knew that they would hardly even muss Ares's flame-laced hair.

He gazed across the burning ruin of Athens to where the God of War stood shouting his triumph to the heavens. Kratos steeled himself as he remembered an old maxim: *Spartans fight with the weapons they have, not the weapons they want.*

The hour of decision had finally come. Time to kill.

Time to die.

Kratos started walking. A strangled, gasping moan came to Kratos's ear as he headed for the chasm he had only barely crossed as the lone bridge was destroyed. It came from within the Temple of Athena. It sounded like a woman moaning in agony, gasping for a last few breaths.

Hearing this, Kratos found himself glad that at least his wife and daughter had not suffered. He had given them swift, almost painless deaths. Cleaner than the woman inside. *Probably the Oracle*, he thought, and then he stopped.

If it *was* the Oracle, he had one last question for her.

He trotted up the front steps of the temple. The whole floor was splotched with dried blood. He went to the immense statue of Athena and stood before it, gazing up into the blank marble eyes.

"No box. Only the weapons I had before," he said, spinning the Blades of Chaos around. "Any advice?"

The marble face of the statue remained stubbornly blank. Kratos turned away and went behind the altar, to the corridor that led to the Oracle's quarters. A dozen long strides took him to the empty room. Nothing in there but a few dead leaves.

Back in the temple, he looked around for the source of the soft moans. He turned slowly, listening hard. Above. Somewhere above.

The temple roof had been blasted to pieces. A quick sprint and he leaped onto the altar, springing again up the side of Athena's statue to the head, and then a prodigious leap propelled him to the edge of the sundered roof. He barely made it; his left hand latched on to a shard of a rafter and he hung there, dangling.

Again the visions captured his mind. His wife and daughter in his arms, cruelly slaughtered on the village temple's floor. The curse of the Oracle that remade him into the Ghost of Sparta. The swirl of his family's ashes clinging to his skin, forever staining both his flesh and his soul.

Kratos grunted and pulled himself up to the roof.

Sprawled a few steps away lay Athena's oracle, her contorted position warning that her back had been broken. Many times in battle, Kratos had seen warriors in similar positions. It took hours, sometimes days, for them to die.

He knelt beside the Oracle. She had seemed diminutive before. Now she was frail and old beyond her years. Her eyes flickered open when she felt his fingers on her cheek, and she squinted against the glare of the flames devouring distant Athens.

"You *have* returned," she said in a whisper. "You won the box—and lost it. My visions . . . I saw."

"Then you know what happened to me."

She closed her eyes. Her skin had gone waxy, transparent as parchment, revealing the tangle of veins just under the surface. Kratos pressed his fingers harder into her cheek. She stirred.

"Tell me what you foresee," he said. "Tell me how I kill the God of War."

The Oracle's lips twitched. Kratos bent closer to hear.

"The box . . ." The Oracle twitched spastically. She shook her head. "Why are you chosen by Athena? You are a terrible man. A monster . . ."

"A monster to kill a monster."

There came no reply; he spoke to a dead woman.

He stood and stared at her body, hardly more than a child's in size, no matter the powers she had possessed in life. Now her shade was consigned to Lord Hades's embrace.

He looked down upon the city, and then into the chasm. How would he get down from here?

He noticed that one building on fire near the base of the cliff was moving, as though it somehow walked through the city—but then the fire turned a face toward the sky, and Kratos realized what he had thought was a building was in fact the blaze of Ares's hair, seen from above. The god seemed to be contemplating the view.

In the blink of an eye, Ares was wiped from existence. Again, Kratos felt a chilly prickle spread over his skin. That had been too much like the phantasmal Ares in the Arena of Remembrance. If the real Ares was as invulnerable as the imitation . . .

He didn't let himself think about it.

Then the voice that haunted Kratos's every nightmare roared from right behind him.

"*Zeus! Do you see what your son can do?*"

Kratos whirled—and let his heart start beating again. Ares had no idea the Spartan was there. He'd only willed himself to the mountaintop because it held the most sacred Temple of Athena.

Ares boasted at the sky.

"*You cast your favor on Athena, but her city lies in ruins before me!*"

The echoes of that gargantuan voice brought down more masonry around the temple.

The god raised his fist, threatening the sky. *"And now even Pandora's Box is mine. Would you have me use it against Olympus itself?"*

Kratos, from his vantage point atop the temple roof, saw that the god was telling the truth. Though the massive box was dwarfed by the fist from which it dangled, there was no mistaking the eerie golden glow of its jewels. Pandora's Box twisted at the end of a long, slender chain, as though it were a locket, an amulet for the god to wear for luck.

Ares went on with his ranting, but Kratos no longer heard him. All his attention was now focused on that slender chain linking the box to the god's fist. He looked from that chain to the white scar on his palm, then back to the chain.

"Do not strike at the god, you say?" He showed his teeth to the night like a rabid wolf. "Fair enough."

He said softly, "Ares."

Hearing his name, the god turned to look back over his shoulder. He sniffed the air, as if to catch a pleasing savor.

"Kratos. Returned from the underworld." Ares did not sound surprised; he seemed pleased. He lifted his face to the skies again and threw wide his arms. *"Is this the best you can do, Father? You send a broken mortal to defeat me, the God of War?"*

Kratos didn't feel broken.

He raised his right hand, felt the power of Zeus's thunderbolt surging within him as he took one step forward, and unleashed war upon a god.

THIRTY

"WHO IS THE GRAVEDIGGER?"

Zeus appeared to be taken aback by Athena's sudden question. "Why, he . . . digs graves."

"That's not an answer."

"But it is. Just not the answer you're hoping for."

Athena hid the beginning of a smile. The Skyfather's words led her to an inescapable conclusion: Zeus himself had been the gravedigger, and he supported Kratos. She knew he could not openly favor the Spartan, because of his own edict. The other gods would protest. With so much turmoil in Olympus, thanks to Ares and his disobedience, Zeus walked carefully. He was King of the Gods but could never withstand open rebellion among all the other gods.

She exulted. Zeus aided Kratos in ways she did not know, but aid him he did. That increased Kratos's chance for success.

Zeus had bestowed the power of the thunderbolt on her Kratos surreptitiously.

Athena needed even more from Zeus. "Father, we *must* help Kratos more openly. He cannot hope to conquer Ares without our aid."

"No!" Instantly changeable, Zeus jerked to his feet and now towered over her so that her whole body was in his shadow. "You will *not* help Kratos, because Ares's blood will not stain *your* hands!"

Everything fell into place. The intricacy took her breath away. Zeus had maneuvered her so she would guide Kratos to where *he*, the Lord of Olympus, could bring about Ares's death.

"What more is there, Father? You said that Kratos had to prove himself to be worthy. Of what? What more than killing Ares do you plan for him?"

"You thought to use your mortal to accomplish your end, but I foresaw failure. Now there is a chance for Kratos to kill a god and . . . attain more."

"A chance," Athena said, "but not a certainty."

Zeus did not answer.

THIRTY-ONE

SWIFT AS THE THUNDERBOLT WAS, it seemed to Kratos to be creeping through the thickest sort of treacle. The interval between it leaving his hand and reaching its target stretched longer than Kratos's whole life.

He didn't wait to watch it hit. If it missed, he was dead anyway, and so he put himself where success would do him the most good. The instant his hands were free, he dove for the edge of the temple roof, caught an ornamental carving, and kicked off it again for the statue of Athena, heading for ground level. He was still in the air when the thunderbolt struck its target.

Ares, still shouting his defiance at Zeus, never saw it coming. His first hint was a stinging shock in his right hand—and then he felt no more the weight of Pandora's Box.

The thunderbolt had struck home and done its job, severing the chain that joined the box to the hand of the god.

"*What?*" Ares stared blankly at his fist as though it had somehow betrayed him. "*What have you done?*"

From Ares's upraised fist to the ground below was fully a hundred feet. Kratos judged where the box would land and made for it with all his speed. His guess was good. The box landed on a pile of rubble only steps in front of him, and he dashed to it before Ares understood what had happened.

Reaching up, Kratos gripped the lid and shoved as hard as he could. Unlike his attempt at Pandora's temple, the lid slid away without effort, almost as though the box *wanted* him to open it.

Among the ruins of the Temple of Athena, Kratos of Sparta had opened Pandora's Box for the first time since it was hidden in the temple atop Cronos's back a millennium ago.

Kratos scrambled up the rubble and stood on the rim of the box, staring into its warm sunny glow. Whatever was within shone too brightly for Kratos's eyes. He experienced a terrible instant of vertigo, as though he were about to plunge headlong into a hole deeper than the universe. But when that vertigo passed, his entire body warmed in the light—and the box seemed to shrink, dwindling to the size of a matron's jewel box.

Kratos cried out as power surged through his body, filled his soul . . . and more. His arms rose above his head, and tiny sparks danced between his spread fingers. Never had he imagined such power. Was this what it felt like to be a god?

Then Kratos looked at the God of War and discovered it was not the box that had shrunk.

He had grown.

Where before he had not stood as tall as Ares's anklebone, he now looked the god square in the eyes. And in those eyes he saw a flicker of fear.

Ares chased away his dismay with towering fury. His face twisted in a contemptuous sneer. *"You are still just a mortal, every bit as weak as the day you begged me to save your life."*

"I am not the man you took that day." Kratos straightened, and when he spoke, his voice, too, shook the mountain. *"Ten years I have waited. Tonight you die."*

Ares's sneer expanded into dark laughter. *"Athena has made you weak."*

Kratos dropped into his fighting crouch. *"Strong enough to kill you!"*

"*Never!*" The god spread wide his arms, as though welcoming the arrival of his favorite son. "*Give my regards to your family.*"

Instead of meeting Kratos hand to hand, the god tapped some dark and eldritch power that washed over Kratos, and into him, and seized his mind entirely. The temple, the mountain, Athens, and the god himself were all wiped from before Kratos's eyes, replaced by a village in flames.

He fell to his knees. He knew this terrible place. He suffered it nightly in his dreams, in the visions that racked his days and filled every instant of his life.

Mocking laughter rang in his ears. "*I taught you many ways to kill, Kratos. Flesh burns, bones break—but to shatter a man's spirit is to truly destroy him.*"

Snarling wordless rage and denial, Kratos shoved himself to his feet. He staggered through the flames in front of the village temple where he had killed his wife and daughter.

"*Do you recognize this place, Spartan? Perhaps you can undo your crime. If you beg me for mercy, I might let you stay your murders.*"

Kratos burst through the temple door. His wife, his daughter, alive and unhurt, stood before him like the answer to every prayer to every god of his life. He tried to speak, but no words could break through the grip of the emotion that held his throat closed. Every nightmare during this terrible decade of torment whirled around him, smeared into one another, and took physical form before his eyes.

"Kratos?" his wife said uncertainly, shading her eyes against the flames at his back. "What is happening? Where are we?"

"Daddy!" His daughter threw herself toward him, but her mother caught the little girl's arm and held her back.

The only time in his life Kratos had felt a blow so powerful and soul-killing was when Ares's javelin column had pinned him to the door of the Temple of Pandora. "By the gods, can this be *real*?"

"Kratos?" his wife said. "Have you come to take us home?"

The wall of the temple suddenly shimmered, rippling as if it was no longer wholly a material thing, and out through that shimmer stepped . . .

Kratos.

His younger self, the Kratos of a decade past, came striding into the temple to slay everything that moved.

HE PUT HIMSELF between his family and his younger self.

His younger self came at him with the efficient, straight-ahead style that had been his trademark. Every step was a strike. Every strike was a step. His younger self was faster and stronger than Kratos was now—but strength and speed were never the only elements of victory.

The air sizzled with the song of the Blades of Chaos. As they flashed around him, opening small cuts across his body, Kratos discovered he didn't like being on this side of the blades.

The next time Young Kratos hurled a blade outward to whip through the air, Old Kratos stepped inside the strike and caught the blade by the chain. Its heat seared his hands, but he didn't care. He was used to pain. To win back his family, he could endure anything.

He grabbed the blade's haft and yanked with all his might. His strength threw Young Kratos into the air, but his younger self was fully as agile as he'd ever been. Instead of tumbling helplessly, Young Kratos turned his flight into a pounce, the other blade raised for the kill.

Old Kratos guessed it must have come as a considerable shock to Young Kratos when his weapon arm was severed at the elbow, so that his hand, blade, and chain all fell harmlessly to the floor. Old Kratos mercifully spared him any additional shocks by slicing his skull into two pieces.

"Are you watching, Ares? You took them once. I will never lose them again!"

As if in reply, spots on the temple walls shimmered again. Three of them.

From each one, a young, strong, fresh Kratos stalked forward.

Kratos cursed Ares as he swung his Blades of Chaos at the trio of himself. "One at a time would have been too easy."

As the three advanced on his family, Kratos felt his uncontrollable bloodlust return, fed by the familiar Blades of Chaos in his grip.

Kratos waded into them without hesitation, engaging two at once. The third took advantage of this opportunity to flank Kratos and kill his family—but he discovered to his dismay that his attack had been anticipated. And countered. Blood showered from his severed neck, while his head bounced across the floor.

These duplicates were younger and stronger, but they fought with the same blood-crazed ferocity that had driven Kratos to the worst of his crimes. Old Kratos, whatever else he might be, fought to control this blood rage and was no longer a mindless killing machine. As his wife had wanted, he discarded the need only for spilled blood and substituted a fight for honor and family. Within ten seconds, both of the remaining duplicates lay dead before him.

Kratos stood over them, panting harshly, bleeding from dozens of cuts.

Waiting.

"Kratos, please, I don't know where we are!" cried his wife. "Take us *home*."

"Soon, I hope," Kratos said softly. "There is still work for me here."

This time, there were five.

They met the same fate as the others.

"You'll *never* get them, Ares. Send ten of me. Send a thousand. I'll kill them all. Not one of them will touch my family."

The flames of the burning temple spoke to him in the voice of Ares. *"You gave them up in your quest for ultimate power. There is a price to pay for everything you gain."*

"Not that price. Never."

"No price is too high for what I offered you, fool! You dared to reject a god!" The fire's voice softened to silken malice. *"Here is the cost of that foolish act."*

"I don't care." Kratos hefted the Blades of Chaos. "I'm ready."

"*Are you?*"

The Blades of Chaos came to life in his hands, moving with a will not his own. It was as though they had become hands that seized his wrists in unbreakable grips—and they began to drag him toward his family.

"No!" he howled. "Not again!"

He tried to drop the Blades of Chaos, to hurl them away, but they were welded to his hands. The chains in his forearms burned with a fury that blurred his vision with soul-tearing pain. For now the blades controlled him, not the other way around.

"Not again!"

The blades went up.

The blades came down.

And again, now, ten years on, Kratos stood over the bodies of his wife and child. Murdered by the God of War.

"*You should have joined me.*"

Kratos screamed then and fell to his knees. This scream was not one of terror or regret; it was not sorrow that unstrung his legs. It was rage.

The fires in his heart burned hotter than the Blades of Chaos ever could.

"*You should have been stronger.*"

Kratos could only howl with incoherent fury.

"*Now you will have no power. No magic. No weapon.*"

Invisible hands seized the blades and yanked them from his grip. They surged away from each other, cranking his arms wide, stretching them out as though he was being broken on a wheel, harder and harder, until his shoulders screamed in pain, as though his arms would rip from their sockets.

At the last, his flesh gave way before his joints did.

The chains ripped free, shredding his arms, leaving the blackened tatters trailing smoke.

"*All that is left for you is . . . death!*"

With that final word from the God of War, the burning temple disappeared around Kratos.

Kratos knelt on the night-shrouded rubble of the shattered Temple of Athena, atop her sacred mountain, above her ruined city. A single tear trailed down his cheek and fell to the scree of broken masonry. He brought up a hand, gazing upon the charred ruin of his forearm, and then turned it toward the temple itself, as though inspecting how it dwarfed the great statue of Athena.

When he looked up, his eyes were dry.

Ares faced him across the ruin. He leaned upon his red-hot great sword as one might on a walking stick.

"*No magic?*" The growl of god-sized Kratos boomed across the city, raising echoes from distant mountains. "*I have enough.*"

"*You are still only a mortal, worthless and weak,*" sneered Ares.

"*There's a dead woman on the floor of this temple. She said I'm a monster, and she was never wrong.*" Kratos stood. He shook the kinks out of his limbs, sending drops of his lifeblood flying in all directions. "*I am your monster, Ares, and I've come to kill you.*"

Ares unleashed a roar of laughter.

Then the fury of Ares erupted in a blast of flame and a thunderous shout like a million soldiers screaming their war cries in unison. He raised the great sword over his head. "*Fight!*" he roared. "*If you dare!*"

Ares came loping across the mountain summit, each step shaking the rock and breaking the temple to pieces. Kratos watched him like a stalking lion. And the real battle, finally, began.

ATHENA WATCHED THE FIGHT shown by the scrying pool before the throne of Olympus, Zeus at her side, her heart pounding until she could barely breathe. This was more than anxiety at having reached the climax of a decade-long plan. Astonishingly, she *worried* for Kratos!

Though she could hardly believe it, she somehow had come to *care* for this surly, murderous mortal. When Kratos met Ares's charge by casting a handful of masonry chunks like sand into Ares's eyes, she caught her breath. When Kratos slipped aside from Ares's blind sword blows and tackled the God of War to the ground, she gasped. Kratos next pried up from the bedrock of the mountain a boulder that must have weighed tons; now he was straining to bash Ares's Olympian brains into blood pudding, and Athena found herself on her feet with no memory of having stood.

"Now, *this* is a fight!" Zeus exclaimed. His eyes danced, and color was high on his cheeks. Tiny lightning flashes showed in his beard of clouds. "None of this modern leaping around, swords and shields all the time—this is the way it *used* to be."

The King of Olympus shifted to a more comfortable position on the rim of the scrying pool. "Kratos reflects well on your . . . judgment—and on all mortal kind. Can you imagine what must be going through Ares's head right now?"

Athena found her fists clenching and her shoulders twitching as though she could somehow *will* Kratos to win. When Ares kicked him off and made it back to his feet, she again could not breathe. The Spartan, though, without hesitation threw himself back into the fight.

"This Spartan boy means a lot to you, does he?"

She jerked at the question and then flushed with shame for being so transparent. "Of course," she said, forcing a veil of calm to cover her anxiety. "As you care for your eagles, Father. I hope for his health . . . and for his happiness."

"If he takes care of our Ares problem, at least he won't have to worry anymore about his curse of kin slaughter. If he defeats Ares, his crimes *will* be forgiven. I have decreed it so."

"It is all he still hopes for," Athena said. "With forgiveness, his madness—the visions, the nightmares—will finally end."

Zeus looked at her sidelong. "Who said anything about his nightmares?"

She stared at her father. A dull shock of dread coursed through her heart and spread outward to her limbs. "Father, the end to his nightmares—that's all he's been *working* for all these years!"

"And to avenge his family's death," Zeus pointed out. "Which he looks fair like to achieve, from how things are going."

"Revenge is only a part of it!" she insisted. "What good is *forgiveness*? He doesn't need his sins washed clean; he needs a decent night's sleep!"

"Perhaps," Zeus said. "But what he needs and what he deserves are not the same thing."

"Father, you can't dangle this hope in front of him to gain ten years of service and then just snatch it away!"

"I dangled, as you say, nothing at all. Whatever bargains have been struck between the two of you are none of my affair. There is more to this fight than you realize."

Athena could only sit and gape.

Zeus drew himself up, and all his cheerful mockery and petty gamesmanship fell away. The radiant majesty of kingship shone from his face like the sun itself. "There is no crime worse than to spill the blood of one's own family. I bear the curse of that crime myself. It is a crime that may be justified, perhaps since I acted to defend myself and to save all of you, and yet I am forever tainted with the curse of my crime. Kratos acted out of simple blood frenzy. That can never be changed."

"He's not *responsible* for this—"

"His guilt will be cleansed. But still, he *is* responsible. What has been done can never be undone. A deed so vile may be expiated, someday. Even forgiven. It can *never* be forgotten. He must find peace in his own way."

"But, Father—"

"Calm yourself, child. Do not fear for your Spartan. I will take care of Kratos for you." He nodded down at the scrying pool. "Look there: Ares may instead kill Kratos. Then we don't have a problem, do we?"

"You think *Ares* will win?"

"He does seem to have the upper hand at the moment. . . ."

KRATOS AND ARES WERE LOCKED TOGETHER, chest to chest, snarling and tearing at each other like maddened bears.

Kratos had kept the whole fight inside grappling range, so that Ares never got enough distance to use his weapon effectively. He kept one hand clenched on the god's sword wrist, and the other he forced up under the god's chin, driving back his head. The flames of the god's beard blistered Kratos's hand, but he had grown accustomed to such pain through all the years of wielding the Blades of Chaos.

Ares snarled obscenities through his locked teeth as he punched with his free hand again and again into Kratos's kidney. A spreading numbness there buckled the Spartan's knee. Feeling his joint give way, Kratos—as any Spartan would—used what he was given. If he couldn't stand on that leg, he could still slam it into Ares's groin. For every punch the god delivered, Ares took a knee shot to the testicles in return, until even through the firelight of his hair and beard, his face began to show the pain.

Kratos gave over the chin pressure in favor of slamming his elbow into the side of Ares's head, staggering the already weakened god. As Ares fell off balance, Kratos dived to his left, using his grip on the god's wrist to make Ares's sword hand take the full impact of both their weights as they fell sideways to the ground.

Ares's fist shattered the bedrock where it struck—and the rock did the same to Ares's knuckles.

Kratos got his knee between them then and kicked the god away from him, while twisting the sword from Ares's grasp. Ares scrambled drunkenly to his feet, cradling his broken hand. Kratos rolled up smoothly and slashed the air with a blurring flourish of Ares's sword.

Lips peeled back from the Spartan's teeth. *"How do you like your monster now?"*

Ares straightened and let his injured hand fall to his side. His feral predator's grin was a near-exact mirror of Kratos's face. *"You have no idea what a true monster is, little Spartan. You get one lesson."*

Ares hunched over, and his face blackened with strain. Bursting through the impenetrable armor on his back came jointed appendages, writhing like the legs of some nightmarish scorpion, armored in black shell, and ending in blades longer than the columns of the Parthenon. *"You won't live to need another."*

With a clatter of his bladed limbs, Ares sprang like a wolf spider, every blade angled to drink deep the Spartan's blood.

Kratos backpedaled. This was a foe he'd never imagined. Ares pressed the assault, stabbing his scorpion blades in concert, in a complex sequence impossible for Kratos to counter. The Spartan kept giving ground, parrying furiously, cutting at the limbs when he could, but their black shells were no less impenetrable than the god's mystic armor. But that mystic armor, Kratos noted, did not cover the war god's whole body. . . .

The next time Ares came for him, Kratos lunged and ran ten yards of red-hot great sword through the god's inner thigh.

On a mortal, that would have been a deathblow; cutting the large artery in the thigh would cause a man to bleed out in seconds. Gooey black ichor came oozing from the wound, but the only real effect it seemed to have was that Ares now used his blade limbs to lift his body from the ground. Just as they had served him for a sword arm, they now served him for legs.

He lunged at Kratos again and again. Kratos gave ground, trying to circle, seeking any opening in the limbs' baffling weave of death through which he might strike at the god's more-vulnerable flesh. He was tiring rapidly now. Without the Blades of Chaos to feed life energy into him, his wounds stayed open and poured his strength out on the courtyard's flagstones.

For one brief moment, he actually thought that he would lose . . . but in that instant, the faces of his wife and his daughter rose up within his mind and ignited a fury unlike any he had ever known. All his strength roared into him, and more. The next time Ares came for him, Kratos smashed aside one limb's stab with such force that its blade struck a neighboring limb—and cracked its armor.

Kratos blinked at the obsidian ichor that leaked from the crack. A *weakness?*

Ares drew back, his confidence shaken for a moment, but then he gathered himself for another assault.

Let's make it final, Kratos thought. He let his knees buckle, so that he swayed dizzily, and let the sword droop out of line. When the tip scraped on courtyard stone, his fingers opened nervelessly and the sword clanked to the ground. Seeing such weakness, Ares sprang into the air, leaping high so as to fall upon Kratos and impale him on two blades at once.

But as the war god leaped, Kratos's weakness vanished and he sprang up to meet Ares in the air. His hands closed around the joint of one blade limb, and he twisted and bent it with irresistible strength, jamming its needle point through Ares's cuirass into the god's chest. Ares spasmed, and they fell—and Kratos wrenched his weight to fall on top of the god, letting his weight drive the blade limb fully through Ares's chest and out the back.

With a roar that was more outrage than pain, Ares flung Kratos from him and spidered to his feet, staring down at the immense blade jammed through his chest with a kind of bafflement Kratos recalled all too well—it was exactly how he'd stared at the column with which Ares had speared him at the Temple of Pandora.

Ares fell to his knees.

Kratos rose and recovered the war god's sword.

Ares stared up at him, in his eyes only fear and pleading. "*Kratos . . . Kratos, remember . . . it was I who saved you at your hour of greatest need!*"

Kratos raised the sword.

"*That night . . . Kratos, please . . . that night I was trying only to make you a great warrior!*"

Kratos thrust Ares's own sword through the god's chest.

As he limped away from the god's corpse, it began to twinkle with myriad lights. The lights turned into dancing motes that pulled away from the body and then swirled upward to the heavens, until with a blinding flash and a clap of thunder like the end of the world, nothing of Ares remained.

Kratos was battered, and bleeding, and, once again, only a man. He stared in awe up at the vast blade that only moments before he had wielded so lightly. Now he wasn't half as tall as the blade's narrowest point was wide.

He limped back over the broken walls of the ruined temple to stand before the statue of the goddess.

"Athena," he said, "your city is saved. Ares is dead." He gazed up into the blank marble eyes. "I've done my part. Now do yours. Wipe away these nightmares forever."

The shimmering glow of immanent godhead played over the marble. The eyes came alight, and the lips moved as Athena spoke.

"You have done well, Kratos," the statue said. *"Though we mourn the death of our brother, the gods are indebted to you."*

Kratos stood a little straighter. A dark chill trickled into his veins.

"We promised your sins would be forgiven, and so they are. But we never promised to take away your nightmares. No man, no god, could ever forget the terrible deeds you have done."

"You can't—Athena, I've done *everything* you asked! You can't!"

"Farewell, Kratos. Your service to the gods is at an end. Go forth into your new life, and know that you have earned the gratitude of Olympus!"

The shimmer of the goddess faded. Kratos stood alone in the ruined temple above the shattered remnant of the city. He stood there for a long, long time.

Then he started walking.

EPILOGUE

AT THE BRINK of nameless cliffs he stands: a statue in travertine, pale as the clouds above. He can see no colors of life, not the scarlet slashes of his own tattoos, not the putrefying tatters of his wrists where chains were ripped from his flesh. His eyes are as black as the storm-churned Aegean below, set in a face white as the foam that boils among the jagged rocks.

Ashes, only ashes, despair, and the lash of winter rain: These are his wages for ten years' service to the gods. Ashes and rot and decay, a cold and lonely death.

His only dream now is of oblivion.

He has been called the Ghost of Sparta. He has been called the Fist of Ares and the Champion of Athena. He has been called a warrior. A murderer. A monster.

He is all of these things. And none of them.

His name is Kratos, and he knows who the real monsters are.

His arms hang, their vast cords of knotted muscle limp and useless now. His hands bear the hardened callus not only of sword and Spartan javelin but of the Blades of Chaos, the Trident of Poseidon, and even the legendary Thunderbolt of Zeus. These hands have taken more lives than Kratos has taken breaths, but they have no weapon now to hold. These hands will not even flex and curl into fists. All they can feel is the slow trickle of blood and pus that drips from his torn wrists.

His wrists and forearms are the true symbol of his service to the gods. The ragged strips of flesh flutter in the cruel wind, blackening with rot; even the bone itself bears the scars of the chains that once were fused there: the chains of the Blades of Chaos. Those chains are gone now, ripped from him by the very god who inflicted them upon him. Those chains not only joined him to the blades and the blades to him; those chains were the bonds shackling him to the service of the gods.

But that service is done. The chains are gone and the blades with them.

Now he has nothing. Is nothing. Whatever has not abandoned him, he has thrown away.

No friends—he is feared and hated throughout the known world, and no living creature looks upon him with love or even affection. No enemies—he has none left to kill. No family—

And that, even now, is a place in his heart where he dare not look.

And, finally, the last refuge of the lost and alone, the gods . . .

The gods have made a mockery of his life. They took him, molded him, transformed him into a man he can no longer bear to be. Now, at the end, he can no longer even rage.

"The gods of Olympus have abandoned me."

He steps to the final inches of the cliff, his sandals scraping gravel over the crumbling brink. A thousand feet below, dirty rags of cloud twist and braid a net of mist between him and the jagged rocks where the Aegean crashes upon them. A net? He shakes his head.

A net? Rather, a shroud.

He has done more than any mortal could. He has accomplished feats the gods themselves could not match. But nothing has erased his pain. The past he cannot flee brings him the agony and madness that are his only companions.

"Now there is no hope."

No hope in this world—but in the next, within the bounds of the mighty Styx that marks the borders of Hades, runs the river Lethe. A draft of that dark water, it is said, erases the memory of the existence a shade has left behind, leaving the spirit to wander forever, without name, without home . . .

Without past.

This dream drives him forward in one final, fatal step, which topples him into clouds that shred around him as he falls. The sea-chewed rocks below materialize, gaining solidity along with size, racing upward to crush his life.

The impact swallows all he is, all he was, all he has done, and all that's been done to him, in one shattering burst of night.

But even in this, he is doomed to disappointment.

HE DOES NOT SEE the figure at his side in the Aegean's dark waves; he does not feel the hands that lift him from the sea. He does not know that he is being carried far beyond anywhere mortals can ever go.

When next his eyes open, he stands before a mighty gate of gold and pearl set in a rampart built of cloud. And with him stands a woman of supernal loveliness, clad in glittering armor and bearing a shield on which is set the head of Medusa.

He has never seen her before. But he has known her for years, and she cannot be mistaken for any other.

"Athena."

Her flawless face turns toward him, and the serene majesty of her gaze takes his breath away. "You will not die this day, my Spartan," she says, and her voice is martial music of pipe and drums. "The gods cannot—I cannot—allow one who has performed such service to perish by his own hand."

He can only stare, struck dumb both by bitter injustice and incomprehensible grace.

"There is more at work here than you may ever know." She lifts a hand and the immense gate swings open before him, revealing stairs ascending into cloud. "But you have saved more than your own life today and worked a greater deed than taking your own revenge. Zeus has declared you worthy, and you will not deny him. There is now an empty throne in Olympus, my Kratos, and I have one last service to require of you. Take these stairs. They lead to that empty throne. To *your* throne."

"I don't understand . . ." Words fall thickly from his numb lips.

"It's possible you never will. I will tell you only this: You should not die by your own hand and stain Olympus with your blood. And so you are here. With us. Forever. It is Zeus's wish."

Kratos mounts the long, long stair. Now he can see at the top a throne of glistening jet: deadly gleaming black, befitting the god he is to become.

With each step, the sights and sounds of battle rush in upon him, from all across the world and throughout all eternity, for time and place are different for the gods. He fears for an instant—or for a millennium—that his nightmares return to rape his mind, but he does not recognize the soldiers he sees. They wear metal armor and march in phalanx; cavalry and chariots support their swordsmen, pike men, and archers. "Cross the Rubicon," a general bellows in a strange and foreign tongue, but Kratos understands.

At the next step, again he gasps. Curious armor here replaces the more-familiar design. Rushing past him are men with Asiatic eyes, shouting in a language he does not recognize, though again he understands—Sekigahara. "For the shogun!" The names spring up unbidden and mean nothing to him, but as foreign as their aspects and armor are, the carnage they wreak is all too familiar. Thousands lie dead on all sides, although he is still on the stairs to his throne.

At the next step he finds himself almost flinching, as a huge bird with stiff metal wings and a spinning wheel in front dives down on him. Sudetenland. Huge explosions rock him as the machine—not a bird but a flying machine, a Stuka, another unfamiliar word that he somehow understands—pulls out of a dive and roars away into the dirty gray sky.

And just above, a brilliant glare has him squinting and shading his eyes, but he knows somehow that this light cannot harm him. Nothing can harm him. The light comes from a vast cloud curling upward from a burning city, burgeoning as it lifts into an astonishing shape, like a blazing white mushroom larger than Athens itself.

He looks in another direction, and there before him unfold wooded hills where the rivers run red with blood. Antietam? What language might this be?

These people, these places, come to him with every step. Waterloo. Agincourt. Khyber Pass. Gallipoli. Xilang-fu. Roncesvalles. Stalingrad and the Bulge and Normandy. The chaos of war rages around him, an endless looping chain of stunning victories and horrific defeats.

When he reaches the throne, he pauses for a moment and looks back down from whence he came. Spread before him is all of Greece, all the Mediterranean, Africa, Europe, Asia, and the strange lands on the far side of the world. Anywhere that battles rage—anywhere war will *ever* be fought—this is his kingdom. But among it all, his kingdom, the quarter that means most to him, will be the scene of battles that will tear the world asunder.

For Olympus, too, is of his kingdom, whenever he might choose to make it so.

Kratos, once of Sparta, lowers himself upon his throne, and dark designs unfurl behind his brows. They want a God of War? He will show them war the likes of which they've never conjured in their worst nightmares.

Kratos of Olympus, God of War, gazes down upon his realm, and his fury burns.

ABOUT THE AUTHORS

MATTHEW STOVER is the *New York Times* best-selling author of the *Star Wars* novels *Revenge of the Sith*, *Shatterpoint*, and *The New Jedi Order: Traitor*, as well as *Caine Black Knife*, *The Blade of Tyshalle*, and *Heroes Die*. He is an expert in several martial arts. Stover lives outside Chicago.

ROBERT E. VARDEMAN is the author of more than one hundred novels, in the fields of fantasy, science fiction, mystery, high-tech thrillers, and westerns (under the pen name Karl Lassiter). Among these titles are tie-in novels for four other RPGs. He holds a bachelor's degree in physics and a master's degree in materials science, and he worked in solid-state research before becoming a writer. In addition to being a past vice president of SFWA, he is a member of the International Association of Media Tie-in Writers. For more information see his website, www.CenotaphRoad.com.